One Summer in Provence

Also by Carol Drinkwater

Novels

The Haunted School

An Abundance of Rain

Akin to Love

Mapping the Heart

Because You're Mine

The Only Girl in the World

The Forgotten Summer

The Lost Girl

The House on the Edge of the Cliff

An Act of Love

For Children

Molly

Molly On the Run

Non-Fiction

The Olive Farm

The Olive Season

A Celebration of Olives

The Olive Harvest

The Illustrated Olive Farm

The Olive Route

The Olive Tree

Return to the Olive Farm

One Summer in Provence

Carol Drinkwater

CORVUS

Published in paperback in Great Britain in 2025 by Corvus,
an imprint of Atlantic Books Ltd

10 9 8 7 6 5 4 3 2 1

A CIP catalogue record for this book is available from the British Library.

Paperback ISBN: 978 1 80546 276 7
E-book ISBN: 978 1 80546 278 1

Printed and bound by CPI (UK) Ltd, Croydon CR0 4YY

Corvus
An imprint of Atlantic Books Ltd
Ormond House
26–27 Boswell Street
London
WC1N 3JZ

www.atlantic-books.co.uk

Product safety EU representative: Authorised Rep Compliance Ltd., Ground Floor,
71 Lower Baggot Street, Dublin, D02 P593, Ireland. www.arccompliance.com

TO GISÈLE PELICOT

We have two lives,

And the second begins when you realize you only have one.

The Valuable Time of Maturity, Mário de Andrade,
Brazilian poet, novelist, musicologist, 1893–1945

LATE JUNE 1976, THE WEST OF ENGLAND

The rain was a light summer matter, more a mist than a downpour. Somehow, though, it settled within her, burrowing to her bones. She was shivering, cold and hungry, and she was about to do the worst thing she could imagine. To give up her most precious possession.

It was late in the evening, but the days were long. Long and light. Midsummer. The young woman had been obliged to wait. No spare cash left even for a packet of cigarettes and she was gasping for a fag. She had hung about in the town, sitting in a Wimpy bar, watching the clock for hours with one cup of cold tea, making it last, a bottle of warmed milk to feed the baby, until the darkness began to draw in. Then she had set off in the rain, which had returned, falling more heavily as she strode, speeding to her destination, three miles outside the centre of the small market town, to the Catholic church.

There, she hung about outside the lychgate, pacing nervously, rubbing at the damp on the end of her nose, stamping her feet, drawing up her courage. Her adrenaline was pumping. This was so risky. What if she were to be spotted hurrying up the stone pathway that led to the church, if something, someone, drew attention to her presence there? She was carrying an overstuffed bag hoisted across her back – all her worldly possessions – and the babe in her arms. He was tucked beneath her winter coat, pressed tight to her bosom. She was wearing the coat because there had been no space left to pack it, and when she fled the town, she would need to take it with her.

She had promised herself there would be no tears, no emotion. She was drained of all feelings, and she was resolved. This had to be done. There was no other choice, no alternative solution.

The last of the rhododendrons either side of the pathway were still in flower. Big, fat ruby-coloured blossoms, big as feather dusters, browning at the edges. She loved these flowers. They seemed generous and kind, and the foliage gave her a smidgen of cover as she struggled forward. The priest's house lay tucked away behind the church, which was set in a small cemetery with row upon row of old headstones, most of them capsized. In the distance on the same plot of land, out of sight from her current position, was the convent. It served as an orphanage.

A narrow path joined church and presbytery. When she reached the church she skipped on past the great entrance doors, firmly locked and bolted, and hugged tight to the stone wall. She shot a swift glance about her to confirm that there was no one in close proximity to identify her. Then she rounded the holy building and made for the priest's lodging. A light was on in one of the downstairs windows. His sitting room? She had no idea. She was not a regular churchgoer. She couldn't have said anything about the father's daily routine. An early riser for morning mass, yes, she supposed. Which was when she calculated – worst-case scenario – her boy would be found. She prayed, though, that the priest would hear the ring of the doorbell and discover her son tonight.

A sound alarmed her. A voice. Two voices. Both male. She stepped quickly off the path and pressed herself within the dark-green leafy bush. Someone at the front door. A shaft of light from an inner hallway. A friend or parishioner leaving? She had not considered such a possibility. Foolish, foolish. Her heart was beating fast. It was in her mouth. The rain was pounding against her shoulders. The child, worryingly damp, needed changing. He was growing restless. She couldn't delay any longer. This had to be done. No time like the present.

A man donning a trilby was exiting by the front door, she glimpsed the priest's shadow as he called a friendly goodnight to his visitor, switched off the outside porch light and closed himself back inside. The visitor was whistling as he trod the path, passing her with no inkling of her presence there.

She was holding her breath, desperate to pee, terrified the child would start to cry.

Stealthily, when the stranger was well out of sight, she crept out from the bush and pushed on to the front step. She lifted the boy swaddled in his modest bundle of clothes and grubby wool blanket. With tears flowing fast, she placed him on the step within the cover of the porch, close enough to the door to be out of the downpour. Her handwritten note, a few paltry words, was tucked inside the infant's cardigan. She had no skills with language but she prayed those she had scribbled had not been smudged, erased by the rain. 'Bye-bye, my little darling,' she whispered. 'I wish you the best life.'

The tiny boy kicked his legs and began to whimper. Without another glance she shoved her finger against the bell, pressed hard and, with the speed of lightning, took to her heels, darting out of sight, not waiting to see the priest open the door.

Puzzled to find no one there, the housekeeper, a middle-aged woman, stepped off the porch onto the gravel and peered about her. She shrugged her shoulders, shivering as she turned in the rain. It was then she noticed the living bundle on the doorstep at her feet. 'What in the name of all that's holy have we here?'

CHAPTER ONE

The Present, the South of France

Celia Grey was brushing her teeth, listening to the radio. It was ten minutes past six, sunrise on this August morning in the South of France. Dressed only in a towel, she was leaning over the sink in the recently installed shower room down at the swimming-pool level. The tap was turned off, to save water. The toothpaste hung loose, turning to a thin liquid in the heat. Hot even at this hour. And escalating.

'Hot, hot, hotter.' Celia gargled and spat.

'The temperature today along the coast will reach thirty-five degrees centigrade,' the male radio voice was cautioning.

'Every year *plus en plus chaud*,' muttered Celia. She had a habit of talking to herself when she was stressed or super-busy.

The lack of rain – not a drop since the beginning of April – was causing the soil in their vineyards to dry out. Cracks were materializing all across the land. This, in turn, resulted in heavier demands on their irrigation systems. It was also threatening an earlier harvest for the grapes. So many challenges. Plenty on her plate.

But first up was the grand party she and Dominic were organizing.

Sweltering days and nights ahead to welcome a houseful of guests, descending within the next few days. All the bedroom windows would be thrown open looking out upon clear navy skies speckled with stars. Their sprawling old manor house, known to locals as *le château*, though it bore no resemblance to a castle, except that it was constructed of stone, had never been fitted with air-conditioning. Most of the rooms couldn't even claim double-glazing. Celia and her husband, Dominic, had never been especially bothered. The building's thick stone walls did their job reasonably efficiently, keeping the interiors cool throughout the summer months, warm and cosy in winter.

The guests attending their upcoming house party could take advantage of the pool, dive in, beat the heat, lounge on sun-beds on the terrace between cocktails and long lazy lunches. How bad was that? She closed her eyes to imagine the scenes as she patted her mouth dry with a facecloth. She rinsed her toothbrush and placed it back in its glass, screwed up her face and stared at herself in the cabinet mirror, lifting a hand to the wrinkles that spread out from her green-gold eyes. She sighed, a heavy exhalation. Oh, but she was old, and *getting older*, yet she was as keyed-up as a girl off to her first school dance. A flurry of that excitement brought a smile to her freckled features. Their upcoming celebrations promised days of friendship and laughter. Friends, companions, colleagues, many not seen since before the ghastly pandemic, tucking into sumptuous meals. Loved ones and neighbours gathered together to celebrate her and Dominic's achievements here on the estate, the success they had made of her late father's floundering wine business.

Ten years. It was an auspicious milestone.

Against all odds.

She let slide to the tiled floor the towel that had been wrapped around her, pushed it aside with her toe, wriggled into one of several bathing costumes kept hanging on pegs in the washroom and, arms clutching her small frame, trotted out onto the stone-tiled pool surround. Three steps down and she was in the water, floating on her back, arms outstretched, inhaling the aromatic scents of the unfolding summer morning. In the distance from across the terraces, sweet notes from an accordion drifted her way. Celia smiled. Old Henri was in the vegetable gardens, collecting eggs and playing *chansons* to his hens.

She spun over onto her stomach, kicked hard and began to swim. Back and forth, length after length of breast-stroke, while absorbing the golden sunrise on her face, its rays stealing through the branches of the umbrella pines and cypresses. Those trees had been growing for more than a century on the sloping piece of land that encircled the generous-sized swimming-pool.

Celia's mind was spinning from one image to the next. To-do lists for the upcoming party.

Her early-morning dips, while Dominic was at his desk, scribbling away in his top-floor library, and their small team of helpers was gearing up for the busy day ahead were one of Celia's most jealously guarded pleasures. This solitary hour gave her peace and quiet to reflect upon her decisions. Over this last decade she had become such a worrier. Swimming brought order to her chaotic thoughts, allowed her to set out her timetable for the upcoming days. There was a lot at stake. The party was as much a business affair as it was pleasure. She couldn't afford any hitches.

Showered and dressed, damp feet slipped into striped espadrilles, Celia scooted back up the stone stairway towards the rear of the house. Henri, their loyal gardener – well past retirement age, but he wouldn't hear of it, and in any case who was there to replace him? – was making his way towards the kitchens, proceeding at a snail's pace. His straw hat, turned upside down, was cradled in the palms of his hands. Same as every morning. Eggs were his cargo, the freshest and finest from his laying hens. Because Henri was a widower and lived alone, most of his morning's haul ended up in the kitchen of the main house.

Daisy, Celia and Dominic's old Collie, was waiting at the top of the steps, wagging her tail excitedly as though she hadn't seen her mistress for days. Celia gave her a kiss on the head, then lifted her arm to greet Henri. '*Bonjour, Henri!* How many this morning?' she called, in her almost impeccable French.

'Eleven.' He grinned.

'That's excellent. *Merci.* Let's hope those girls provide plenty for the weekend. Nothing like fresh eggs for our guests' breakfasts.'

The dog rose. Long in the tooth, she set off at a trot following Celia. Together, they approached the table under the *magnolia grandiflora* where Dominic was seated, coffee in hand, reading his newspaper. Daisy collapsed at her master's feet, panting contentedly. No matter how busy, Celia and Dominic made a point of having breakfast together. During the summer, they ate at one of the outdoor tables. During the colder days, *le petit déjeuner* was laid in the conservatory.

Celia valued these precious moments in one another's company, even if she didn't care to eat much before noon, especially in the heat. In spite of the exercise, her appetite hadn't woken up yet, whereas Dominic enjoyed a hearty start to his day: eggs from Henri's hens, boiled or poached, toast with homemade jam and fresh fruit. When in season, Celia and Henri picked the fruit from the kitchen garden. The jams and compôtes were made on the estate, by Magali, the housekeeper and cook.

Celia kissed Dominic's forehead and settled alongside him. He placed his newspaper on one of the empty seats, poured his wife some black coffee, no sugar, then buttered two slices of warm toast in readiness for the eggs Magali would deliver any minute now. Celia sipped her coffee and picked at a croissant while they chatted through the immediate needs of the estate and their plans for the day. Dominic intended, he said, to write until lunchtime. He was in the middle of a scene and wanted to get it finished. 'No disturbances, please. And you?'

'I'm driving to the airport after breakfast.'

'Really? Who's arriving so early in the week?' Dominic frowned.

If either of them was forgetful, Celia swore it was him.

'I told you, darling, Thomas and Sean.'

'Who?'

'Our new volunteers.'

Celia was off to collect two young men, both strangers, who were booked to stay with them for several weeks during the second half of the summer.

'Do you know anything about these chaps?' Dominic had

enquired, when she had first announced her plan. 'I mean do they come with references or a good word from friends?'

'No, 'fraid not.'

'Friends of friends, then?'

'Not even that, darling. I found them on one of those internet sites for casual helpers.'

'What – like a dating app?'

'An internet thingy where "the host", that's us, offers board in return for work experience. The idea being they help out on the land, we sleep and feed them, and no money is involved.'

'Good Lord, Ceely, I hope this is wise. There's a lot at stake if it all goes belly-up, my sweet.'

'Claude suggested it. He needs extra help, Dom. It's common practice, these days, he said, especially on family-run farms. Don't pull such a face. It'll work out swimmingly. You'll see. Let's be positive.'

Dominic was not convinced. Celia had an irritating habit of doling out invitations to every stranger under the sun. She rarely gave proper consideration to her offers but, in this instance, he had decided to reserve judgement until he'd met and assessed the young men.

'It'll leave you plenty of time to concentrate on your new play and I can get on with everything else, most immediately the party arrangements. And poor Claude . . .'

'What about Claude?'

'He's struggling to keep the vineyards in good order with no hands to help him.'

Dominic scratched his forehead. The news of these arrivals had made him tetchy. It had completely slipped his mind that two unknowns were flying in today.

'Where are my eggs? Damn it, if this goes wrong, Ceely, I'll be the one called in to sort out the problems, not Claude, me, and I have enough on my plate.' Including new plans afoot that he hadn't yet discussed with Celia.

Celia and Dominic, although comfortably off by most standards, were counting costs, like everyone else. Covid had put a bullet through the heart of their earnings. Both were in their sixties. Both still worked, for the pleasure of it as much as the income. Dominic was a playwright – theatres everywhere had been closed during Covid; no performances meant no royalties. Celia had been a rather well-known actress in her younger years but, as was common for females, the roles had dried up as she had matured. Nowadays, the phone was silent, the offers non-existent. These days she ploughed her energies into their wine business, the vineyard estate she had inherited from her parents.

Twelve years previously, Dominic had written a stage play with a leading role for a fifty-something actress. *Journey to Starlight* had been conceived as a vehicle for his wife, Celia.

And a rollicking good role it had been. Regrettably, the play had been panned by the critics and the production had folded before it reached London.

Artistically, it had been bitterly disappointing, and a public humiliation for Celia. Financially, it had been a crushing blow for the pair of them. Throughout an illustrious career, *Journey to Starlight* remained Dominic's only flop. In her darker moments, Celia still worried that she had let her husband down, that with another actress in the role the play might have succeeded. The venture had cost them every last cent of their savings. The debts had caused her many sleepless nights. Escalating interest and bank charges added to the nightmares. Celia had been terrified. How were they to pay it all off? Eventually, to satisfy the creditors, she and Dominic had sold their home, an elegant two-bedroom maisonette in Primrose Hill, which Celia had adored.

With pretty much nothing left, they had packed their remaining possessions into their sole vehicle, Celia's ancient convertible Volkswagen, and set off for the South of France, to Les Roches du Soleil, the rambling, run-down mansion and vineyard that had belonged to her parents. It had been intended as a temporary solution.

For several reasons, they never revisited that chapter in their lives. Celia had sealed it off. A dark and painful period in what had become a struggling marriage.

Magali arrived with the eggs. '*Bonjour*, Celia. Dominic, I've made you an omelette.' She plonked the plate before him. 'Cheese and tomato. We've a ton of tomatoes and kilos more to be picked. Ripening too fast in this heat. I've asked Henri to leave the rest on the vines for now. I've no place left to store them, what with all the extra provisions stocked for the upcoming weekend, and I'll have no time to make chutney this side of your celebrations.'

'Magali, will you pack me some eggs, please, to take to the lodge for the new arrivals?'

Magali nodded. 'I'll ask Henri to walk them over for you while you're at the airport.'

'Splendid idea, thank you.'

'This smells delicious, Mags, *merci*.' At the sight of breakfast Dominic's irritation was appeased. He took up his knife and fork with glee.

Celia watched him. He had settled so satisfactorily to the life out here. The elements, the customs of Provence. He was a different man from the Dominic of a decade ago. Transformed. When they had crossed the Channel with what was left of their possessions, they had been barely speaking. It had been touch and go, their marriage, their future.

Tamping down the bitter memories, Celia turned her attention to the views. This beautiful eighteenth-century manor house, surrounded by its hectares of vineyards, was set within the sloping lands of the Esterel. Their grounds extended all the way to red-rock cliffs that faced out over the sea. Celia had always regarded her parents' bequest as the best thing to have happened to her, healing several overlapping heartaches. How many times had she silently thanked them for this most generous and timely gift, for her good fortune? It had rescued her.

The failure of the play had been far worse for her, she still believed, than for Dominic, who had continued to write and find outlets for his work. Much tougher for an actress to revitalize her career, and at such a distance from the hub of theatre-land activity. Of course Celia could have chosen to sell the estate – it had been valued at a considerably higher price than their Primrose Hill abode. It would have discharged all their debts, left them with cash in hand and their London home. Dominic had proposed this option, tried to persuade her to agree, but Celia had refused. She couldn't bear the prospect of relinquishing her father's legacy and his life's dream. 'I can't sell it. I'm going to France. For a while, at least. Will you come with me?'

'France?'

'Just until . . .' Until what, when, she'd had no clear picture.

'Until we're back on our feet,' Dominic had stipulated.

No permanent arrangement had been envisaged. Nothing chalked out besides negotiating their lives back into less choppy waters.

15

Against the odds, Celia and Dominic had moved on from their flop, the strains and heartaches it had caused their marriage. They had adapted. The London housing market had been buoyant. The Primrose Hill property had been sold for a healthy sum, all their debts cleared honourably, while the precious funds that had remained, a matter of a few thousand, had been converted to euros and transferred to France.

The wine-making enterprise, which, due to Celia's late father's ill-health in his widowed declining years, had been sinking into neglect and debt. It had required a massive amount of hard physical slog and a new vision with cutting-edge strategies to drag it into the twenty-first century.

Both she and Dominic had questioned whether they had the stamina and the wherewithal to learn the trade and then stick at it. They were not agriculturalists, they were theatre and TV folk down on their luck. This vineyard had been intended as a temporary hideaway, a lick-our-wounds-quietly-out-of-the-public-eye in a rather beautiful, if threadbare, bolthole.

Until Dominic had undergone what he laughingly described later as his Agrarian Epiphany. His flash of enlightenment. 'Celia, what say we stay on?'

'Are you serious?'

'Yes, let's do it! Let's make a go of it!' he'd declared, once they had rigorously studied the paperwork, the Excel sheets, after months of meetings with bankers, agronomists, the notary, neighbouring farmers, vintners, lawyers, and after they had spent weeks hiking the hillsides, getting fit, growing to love the early mornings and the fresh, gentle air while acquainting themselves with every inch of field and grove on Celia's inherited estate. A resplendent patch of, in places, hard, rocky terrain that had so fortuitously become hers. Theirs. Row upon row of stark brown shoots fetching up out of the red earth.

And then came the first days of spring when the buds began to appear. Creeping into April, the leaves, a pale electric green, unfurled.

'You won't believe this, Ceely, but there are days when I swear I can hear these plants breathing. When the wind whistles through them and ruffles those tender shoots, it's as though they're chanting.'

Celia was dumbstruck, stunned by Dominic's jubilation. It was as though he had been reconditioned, rejuvenated.

During the warm early-summer days when the birds sang and the sky was so blue and wide, the fruit clusters started to emerge, tiny green beads peeping.

'Inflorescences – what a marvellous word and what a spellbinding sight.'

Plump clusters of miniature grapes, Nature's miracle, its promise, ahead of the hot, dry days when the wind whipped and the soil shrivelled to dust clods. Even then the shrubs were growing heavy with their clumps of juicy black berries.

'My God, just look at those beauties!' Dominic had whooped.

He was a new man. Look at him, marvelled Celia. He's reborn. She had closed her eyes, buoyed up, feeling a warm if tentative rush of happiness, daring, for that precious moment, to believe there was hope for the pair of them.

The quality of the wine Celia's parents had produced was average by any standards. The greater portion of it was sold to the local cooperative for a few francs, later euros, a litre. Dominic, always one to rise to a challenge and fiercely ambitious by nature, had decided he and Celia, with a team of experts, Claude at the helm, could do a darn sight better. 'We could make something special of this place. I mean, it's a paradise as it is, but how much more satisfying if the wine was also remarkable.'

Celia, still stinging from the hurts of London, silently worried. Watching Dominic step into the role of gentleman farmer had brought her some reassurance, but what if the fracture in their marriage she had discovered in London should prove to be as deep, as irreparable as she had originally feared? What if that same temptation should beckon Dominic back? What if this backbreaking but blissful existence should prove to be nothing more than a passing flirtation with

18

Nature? Everything was at stake. They were in no position, financially or emotionally, to take another gamble.

Providentially, Celia's cares had been groundless. Building upon her father's ambitions had turned out to be significantly more successful than she had dared to dream. She and Dominic had stayed on and, importantly, they remained together. They had turned their fortunes around.

'Ducks to water, that's us,' Dominic had declared with relish. As long as it didn't infringe upon his precious writing hours, he revelled in the running of the wine business, threw himself at it with a lusty force, and Celia had felt reassured when witnessing his new-found passion. As for her own professional life, well, that had been the price she'd paid.

CHAPTER TWO

'In the early years, Les Roches du Soleil wasn't much of a money-spinner, in spite of its acreage. We were scraping a living, battling to keep afloat, but after ten years of bloody hard labour and dedication, our profits are on the increase. Thank Heaven. Each year we build on our previous achievements. And since last autumn, we've started to sign contracts with outlets in the UK and a rather smart restaurant chain in Tribeca, New York . . .'

'That's exciting.'

'It is indeed, Sean. The quotas are modest, but we're doing our damnedest to expand that growth.'

Both men in the car with Celia were listening intently. Thomas was moving his head from side to side, staring out of the window, seemingly lost in his own universe.

'So, there you are, that's us in a nutshell. We're a very small team, working ourselves to the bone, living a dream we had never dreamed.' She laughed. 'Your contributions over the next weeks will help us enormously, so huge thanks in advance for coming on board.' Celia was still smiling as she signalled left to leave the A8 motorway. 'Anything you need, let me know and I'll do my best to deliver.' On the slipway, she slowed down for the road toll booth, *le péage*, before turning right at the first roundabout onto a winding lane that would lead them up into the sun-baked hills. Her two passengers, one beside her and the other in the rear, asked no questions. They seemed to be assimilating the topography around them.

Both young men had arrived that morning on the same Heathrow to Nice British Airways flight. The older of the two, the dark-haired Englishman seated at her side, was in his mid-thirties. Too handsome for words, had been her silent observation when she'd first caught sight of his tall, lean figure striding through Customs, a heavy backpack pressed against broad shoulders and a guitar-case hanging from his right hand. He spotted her, waved confidently and called her name, 'Hi, Celia! Celia Grey, it's me, Tom Fletcher!'

She'd lifted an arm in recognition of his greeting, delighted to have found him.

'I recognized you instantly.' He smiled. 'You're as lovely off screen as on.'

The compliment had thrown her. She had dropped her gaze, fussing with her hair, staring down at her leather sandals purchased at the Arab market in Marseille, her varnished, well-pedicured feet. She was trying to recall. Had she mentioned she was an actress? (And, let's face it, pretty much a retired one at that.) She had used her married name in all correspondence, hadn't she? Dominic's name, Millar. Not her stage name, which was also her birth name.

'Well done, Thomas, for getting yourself here. Lovely to meet you at last. Sean hasn't come through yet. We'll just wait for him.'

'Call me Tom. Wow, I'm such a fan.' He had grinned, then started to hum, beating the flat of his hand against his thigh.

The other, Sean, seated now in the back – she was watching him in her rear-view mirror – was staring out of the window, disengaged from the conversation or listening passively. He was younger, mid-twenties, still at university, less assured. He had barely said more than five sentences. A red-haired Dubliner, who upon first encounter had momentarily let go of his case to shake her hand. 'Pleased to meet you, Mrs Millar.' The words had been spoken softly, shyly.

Both men had beards, the scruffy, fashionable models that covered the lower half of their faces without being moulded or shaped. As though they had simply forgotten to shave. Celia had never found it an attractive look, but perhaps she was just old-fashioned. It sort of suited Thomas.

The men had never met before and she had never met them. All three travelling in the car were encountering one another for the first time; all three were planning to spend the next four to six weeks in each other's company. Celia had high hopes that it would work out splendidly and that she wasn't taking any risks. Whatever Dominic's scepticism, she was determined to be optimistic.

'Sean,' Celia glanced again into her rear-view mirror to draw the attention of the pensive Irishman, 'I mentioned to Thomas . . .'

'Tom.'

'. . . to Tom. I mentioned to Tom before you cleared Customs that a fierce, dry heat has been our fortune for these past weeks. The meteorological chaps keep promising rain, but so far no sign of it. And now the temperatures are set to rise again. Can you handle the heat? The work will be strenuous and you'll need a hat. If you haven't brought one, we have stacks . . .'

'No worries. I'm from Dublin. We're used to fierce heat over our way.'

Celia frowned, nonplussed, returning her eyes to the road. She didn't want to miss the exit.

'Holy moly, take a look at that view!' exclaimed Tom, pointing through the windscreen.

'Amazing, eh? My father never stopped singing its praises. He fell in love with land and landscape on their very first trip. I remember him describing this climb from the airport on the introductory tour he made here with my mother. He went on about these seascapes for weeks.' Celia beamed at the recollection.

'When was that?'

'Coming up to fifty years ago.' Celia had just turned seventeen when her parents first found Les Roches du Soleil. 'A distant memory.'

The Land Rover was approaching a sharp uphill loop in the road. The track had narrowed to no wider than single access. Ahead was a parking spot, strategically chosen for tourists to take photographs of the sweeping panorama. It was also used for giving way to descending traffic. Celia stopped, slipped into neutral, offering her companions their first opportunity to appreciate this local wonder: the Riviera hinterland. Laid out at their feet was a carpet of jutting rocks, olive trees, green oaks, pines, palms. It spread wide and rolled in a gentle fashion all the way to the bays and inlets of the Mediterranean where a silver-white stripe across the sea's horizon glistened in the sunlight.

With the engine idle, the cicadas were audible. The sawing beat of summer.

'Remarkable, *non*?'

'Magic.'

'I was joking about the heat in Ireland. If I have to walk this, it'll kill me.'

'Think you can get used to it, Sean? Remember to drink plenty of water.'

'Yeah. I best give the whiskey a rest until I get acclimatized.'

Celia shot another glance into the mirror and grinned. She had a comedian on board. 'The road gets even steeper for a bit, so hang on tight.'

They crawled the ascent, engine whining. She pushed the stubborn gearstick from first into second. Sweat was trickling down the back of her legs, bare beneath her long cotton skirt. 'As I mentioned in my emails, you'll be housed in the same cottage. I hope that's fine? It's a stone lodge, really. A little isolated but spacious and, big plus, you're right by the sea.'

Tom whistled. 'Great stuff.'

She swung off the narrow tarmac onto an unsurfaced track that steadied, then levelled off. 'We call this the Devil's Trail.'

Stones kicked and spun under the wheels, several hitting the carcass of the well-travelled Land Rover.

'Are those the Alps?'

'They are indeed.'

The flank of mountains Sean was asking about was rising majestically at some distance to their right. They were travelling westwards through desert scenery from which all colour seemed to have been leached. The plants were desiccated rags.

The men stared but made no comment.

'Months of drought and our unforgiving Provençal sun.'

Tom wound down his window but such a cloud of dust flew at him that he quickly shut it again.

'Don't worry, the estate is not as remote or as infertile as this, but, as I said, no rain since April. Even during the winter months the wet days were few and far between. Several of the coastal towns near Marseille have imposed water bans.'

'Climate change, eh?' muttered Tom. He began to whistle again as though giving tune to his thoughts.

Both men, peering through the windows, were surveying the terrain. It was a dustbowl, the soil cracked, the grasses wilting.

Celia was trying to identify the tune Tom was humming, but she was not familiar with it. 'From here on, the scenery gets softer, more habitable. Our land boundary starts somewhere here, though the entrance gates are about five hundred metres further along. I'll stop there to collect the mail. As you can see, the road is flatter and then it's downhill for a bit. Our land extends west and to the coast. Inland is where the vineyards are planted.'

'How many acres have you?' Tom asked.

'Close to forty hectares of vines laid out in lovely geometric rows. You'll spot the first vineyards soon. Plus, we've forest land above. Then there are the terraces and gardens tucked round the main house. That's the manicured bit. It's not all as bleak as it looks from here.'

'That's good to hear,' came the voice from the back.

Celia drew the Land Rover to a halt outside the main gates. 'Bear with me.' She jumped out to retrieve a clutch of letters from the postbox. Hopping back in, she said, 'OK, let's get you both to the cottage and then some food.'

CHAPTER THREE

'I suggested that once they've settled in, they walk over and join us for a light lunch. I'll ask Magali to lay the table under the magnolia. It will give you an opportunity to meet them. They seem really nice, both of them. Between you and Claude, you can decide the duties best suited to their individual capabilities.'

Dominic and Celia were alongside the swimming-pool. He was cleaning its pale blue interior, a weekly chore that he wasn't fond of, preferring to be in his library out of the heat, writing. His Panama hat was sticking to his brow, irritating him. He lifted it off, tossed it on to a sun-lounger and wiped his sweating forehead with the back of his arm.

'There's a devil of an amount of brush and cuttings to clear. With no burning allowed, it'll have to be chipped. One of them can crack on with that. I'll take them on a tour of the fields and give them a twenty-minute tutorial on what's involved in growing vines. If they last a month, they'll be here ahead of the harvest.'

'Which would be marvellous.'

'Better to do the tour before lunch if they're ready. Then we can all relax and get to know one another. Will they be joining us for all meals?'

'I don't see why not.'

'When are the party guests due to start arriving?'

'Sal's first. She and Frank expect to be here Thursday evening. They're driving over, Eurotunnel from Dover. It's going to be a long haul if this heat keeps up.'

'It'll be splendid to have her here before everyone else.'

Sally was Dominic's daughter, his only offspring from a previous marriage that had ended in his late thirties, several months after he'd met Celia.

'Yes, always willing to lend me a hand and full of brilliant ideas.'

Celia had not been married before. A dedicated career girl, she'd convinced herself. There had been short-lived affairs, but she had shied away from commitment. Her first relationship, when she was twenty, which she never spoke of, had left her bruised and damaged. The 'David Episode' was how she remembered it, though she tried never to think of it.

She had lacked confidence, trusted no one outside her family, until Dominic came along. He had been the rock upon which she had built her future.

Celia had been thirty-four when she had first set eyes on Dominic, five years her senior. Their introduction had taken place at the BBC rehearsal rooms near Shepherd's Bush: a reading for a television play for one of the prestigious Screen One slots. Script by Dominic Millar. Celia's role had not been the lead but it had certainly been meatier than a cameo.

Plastic cup of BBC coffee in one hand, rolled-up script in the other, Dominic had entered the rehearsal room and chosen a seat for himself at the top of the table alongside the director. Celia found herself instantly drawn to the playwright. She'd observed his graceful movements, the thoughtful brown eyes beneath bushy brows. His physical appearance had put her in mind of the poet laureate, Ted Hughes. Dark-haired, powerfully built, like a splendid farm horse. So sexy, she'd muttered to herself.

He seemed not to notice her. His head was bowed towards the script, hair flopping over his forehead – he swept it back every few minutes with the flat of his right hand, which held a pencil as though it were a cigarette. Every so often he scribbled a note in the margin.

Celia was stricken with stage fright at finding herself in such formidable company, more so once she'd admitted to herself that she was attracted to the playwright. Feasting her eyes on him, studying him at the far end of the table, her heart seemed to be lifting out of her body, taking flight.

She had adored her role and had been thrilled to bits when her agent had called to say she had been offered it without an audition or screen test.

It was some months later, during a delicious moment of post-sex pillow talk, she had learned from Dom that he had cast the vote for her. The director had wanted a different actress. Dominic had been persuasive and won the day. Won the girl too, as it turned out.

After the television play had been recorded, cast and crew had gone their separate ways, but she and Dominic had continued to meet. He took her to dinner at Lemonia, a Greek restaurant in Primrose Hill village – he lived in Gospel Oak or somewhere close by. They talked. They talked as though it was their last opportunity. She no longer remembered the subjects of those conversations. Everything. Nothing. Enthralling. Their lives, their pasts, although Celia had never uttered a word about the 'David Episode', the long-buried, painful chapter about which, even today, she felt a debilitating shame.

They talked until they became aware that the restaurant staff were washing the floors around their feet, and no other diners remained. They walked, climbed to the summit of Primrose Hill by starlight, still talking as though everything had to be said, spilled out, shared, unencumbered. On the crest of the hill, where it was chilly, they set themselves on a bench, side by side, torsos touching, finally in silence. It was growing cold. Dominic wrapped an arm around Celia's shoulders, pulled her close. They stayed that way for what must have been hours, tucked tight, burrowed into one another, shivering in the night air yet elated, watching the dawn break over London.

A few days later Dominic took her to lunch in the pub on the corner by the hill, the Queen's. He had a wife, he told her. They had one daughter, Sally, whom he adored and wouldn't, 'for the world', do anything to hurt. *Besotted* was the adjective he used to describe his feelings for his girl. He talked about Sally frequently, but rarely mentioned his wife, skirting round her existence as though deftly cutting her out of the plot. 'Haven't you ever thought you might like children, Celia?' he quizzed her once, out of the blue.

The question took her by surprise, an arrow through her heart. She dragged her thoughts from the past, the memories of David. The loneliness that had enveloped her. 'No, not really, I mean, you know . . . working as an actress, never the right time, not met the . . .'

'And never married?'

She shook her head. The ache inside her was overwhelming, threatening to peel open and reveal the depth of her wound.

She was falling in love with Dominic, but she must not. She must not sleep with him, not this married man. She must not throw herself into another dead-end affair. Imprudent, foolish, dangerous to lay herself wide open. It would be she who got hurt. She, alone, in her single-person flat crying by the open fridge door.

And then, as if from nowhere, out of the blue, sitting on the grass on a windy afternoon on Primrose Hill, blossoming daisies encircling their feet, watching couples flying kites with their children, shrieking and tomfoolery, Dominic had asked her to marry him.

'But what about . . .?'

'We're done,' he'd smiled sadly, 'long done. I love you, Celia.'

The newspapers had busied themselves into her relationship with Dominic. It had gone a bit public when the word had leaked out. But once they had married, legalized the affair, the journalists had lost interest, as they inevitably do . . .

'Ceely! Are you daydreaming? I said, why don't I drive over to the cottage now, invite the chaps on a tour, throw in a little wine-tasting to welcome them?'

'Claude says there are repairs needed to the roof of the tasting barn.'

'Precisely. I can point that out to them while we're there. You never know, one of them might have roofing skills!' Dominic was scooping up the car keys.

Celia gathered up the batch of mail she'd collected from the letterbox and headed off to her first-floor office. 'Party preparations for me. See you for lunch. Ask Claude to join us and don't forget your hat or you'll fry out there.'

CHAPTER FOUR

While the newcomers were exploring the estate with Dominic, Celia was closed away in her den. Unlike her husband's capacious library one storey above where she was now, Celia's work space was very modest: a converted dressing room barely larger than a linen cupboard, but it possessed a generous window that faced out towards the mountains and distant olive groves and let in masses of light. As always during the hot and sticky months of the year, the window was flung open to welcome in the fresh air and birdsong. On this particular midday, though, in spite of the tranquillity the corner usually afforded her, Celia's head was spinning. She felt giddy, knocked off kilter by the correspondence she had just received.

Her phone lay silent on her desk. Alongside it, resting within fingertip reach, was a one-page letter. She drew it centimetres towards her, read it again slowly, surveying its sparse contents in disbelief.

She picked up her iPhone, stared at its darkened screen, wondering what her next move should be, then let it slide back to the desk. Should she telephone him or reply by text?

Your letter has been forwarded to me in France . . .

Or should she ignore his communication? Of course not. How could she possibly ignore it? But she could wait, hold fire, say nothing yet . . . calm herself first.

It was as though she had been hit by a cricket bat. She retrieved the letter, handling it gingerly, contemplating its tone. The words were discreet. If it had been opened in error by someone other than herself – Dominic, for example – he, they, would not know, could not discern, the significance of its contents.

The text was simply stated, ink-penned not typed. Nothing dramatic or threatening.

In the left-hand corner at the bottom was a +44 mobile-phone number. The United Kingdom. She could respond or she could ignore it. Tear it up right now, throw it into the wastepaper basket. Persuade herself she had never received it, that this man, its sender, did not exist.

But why would she do that? He was part of her. Yes, indeed. Her eyes were drawn to his message one more time and a tentative smile broke out across her face.

My dear Celia,

This is David. Does my name mean anything to you? I

hope you remember me. I am getting in touch with you after decades of lost time in the hope you might want to meet up. Would you like that? I cannot describe how much such a get-together would mean to me. Perhaps you feel the same.

Or perhaps not.

Please, Celia, dear Celia (may I call you Celia?), feel free to ignore my reaching out, if that is what you prefer. If your heart is unable to open up, to accept me, I can't deny that I will be disappointed, of course I will, but I'll understand and I will respect your decision for privacy on this intimate matter. And I promise, if you don't answer this note, I will not attempt to make contact again.

Yours, David

PS Hawksmith.

PPS I am sending this via your agent as I don't have your contact details. You live in France, I believe? I have been thinking about making a short trip to France. If you are not too busy, I could pop by. What do you say?

D

Dear God. David. It really was David. After all these years.

Once upon a time, she had dreaded the possibility of this day. That he might appear from out of nowhere, knock at the door. Feared it from the very core of her being. Conversely, there had been occasions, rare, when she had asked herself about him: where he was, how he was getting along. There had been moments, fleeting, when she had mourned the absence of his company in her life.

And now?

It had been so long. Was it too late? How could they begin at this stage in their lives? David Hawksmith.

What sort of a man had David matured into?

A kind, erudite human being? It would seem so. Thoughtful, judging by the words in his correspondence. She drew the note closer to her, lightly brushing it against her bosom. She was still trembling.

After her first moments of prevarication, Celia decided that she would not ignore David Hawksmith's request to meet. Preposterous and cruel even to consider it. She typed a text, carefully copying the number at the foot of the page into her phone:

Dear David, My goodness, what a . . . Well, this is a bolt out of the blue! To hear from you like this. Unfortunately, I am not in London, not in the UK at all. As you so rightly surmised, we are living in France. However, I feel sure that at some point we can find an opportunity to . . . to, well, to say hello. Goodness me! Yours, Celia

She reread it, erased it instantly and tapped in a second attempt.

Dear David, This is Celia. What an extraordinary surprise. To hear from you so unexpectedly. Of course we must meet. We're throwing a party here at our vineyard. It's short notice, I realize. Saturday, this weekend (12 August). Why don't you come? PS As you guessed, I don't live in England.

She closed her eyes and pressed Send.

Within the time it had taken to type the text, the message signal on her phone pinged. It was from him.

Goodness, he's keen!

Celia! How marvellous to hear back from you. I would like that very much, thank you. What are you celebrating? D

And then:

I will need an address, D

PPS I have never been to France. D

What had she done? She hadn't thought this through. Had it been rash to invite him, a stranger, to her home before talking with him face to face, before getting the measure of him? After all, he could be anybody.

David, are you on an iPhone? May I FaceTime you?

'Fraid not, sorry.

While Celia was puzzling the problem, her phone made an unfamiliar buzzing. It startled her. She looked at the screen, read his name, David Hawksmith. She accepted the call and there he was. 'Hello.' He smiled. 'Don't look so baffled. It's What'sApp.'

Her heart was beating fast. She stared at him, at the small, insufficient image of the man. Mid-forties, and he was handsome, rather rugged. There was a disconcerting amount of background noise as though he was standing in a busy street. She wanted to ask, Where are you? And decided against it.

Neither spoke. They continued to look deep, penetrate the screens, appraising one another. The image, the reality of the present. Across the miles, the distance of time. The decades that had passed, separating them . . . For one embarrassing moment Celia felt a tear spring up in the corner of her eye. She hastily brushed it aside. She recalled the ache that his absence, in those very early days, had caused her.

'A party in France?' he said eventually. 'Sounds so grand.'

She chuckled, rubbing the skin at her throat. 'I'll send you the address after this call.'

'What are you celebrating? It's not your birthday.'

'Not my birthday.' She shook her head. 'Goodness, what are we celebrating? Good question. First, importantly, the close of our first decade of wine-making. We, my husband and I . . .'

'Dominic? '

'Yes, Dominic.' David knew about Dominic. 'Well, we've lived over ten years in France, it's been . . . been hard-going,' she stuttered, 'but we're turning the corner. And . . . and . . . it's coming up to thirty years since he and I met. Way back at the BBC.' The memory caused her eyes to sparkle.

David was listening, drinking it all in, watching her silently. The ghost of a smile broke his features.

'Any excuse, really. I love parties, David—'

'Party girl, eh?' he butted in.

'Mm? Yes, and it's been ages since I've thrown one, even a decent-sized dinner party. Bloody Covid.' She was starting to waffle, drew herself back. 'Would you like to join us? It won't be huge. Well, it'll be quite big. You know, a gathering of cherished friends, family, loved ones . . .' She hesitated, tripped over her words, before moving hastily onwards, conscious of his possible reaction. 'There will be a handful of business colleagues as well, a few of our most loyal customers and clients and a sprinkling of villagers. That's about it!'

'Thank you.' His gaze was roaming over her face as though he couldn't quite believe he was in her presence at last. Celia Grey.

'You might enjoy it. I mean . . . you know, if you can come.'

'I'll be there. Wild horses wouldn't stop me. You don't know how long I've dreamed about this.'

It had been an informal invitation, made on the spur of the moment, the natural thing to do, after decades of silence and because he seemed a decent, kind-hearted soul. So why not?

It was a typical Celia response to the moment. *Why don't you join us?* Occasionally regretted later.

And what would Dominic say?

'I'd love it if we could spend some time together, Celia.' And David added hastily, as though he could read her fears, 'It's never too late.'

Even through the screen she could see the twinkle in his eyes. A gaze that seemed familiar, yet so foreign. But she was being fanciful. Who was he, this soft-spoken, rather bashful young David Hawksmith who had made contact with her out of the blue in a handwritten letter sent via her agent with *Confidential* written in ink at the top of the pale blue envelope above the London address?

A male voice was calling to him. He swiftly turned his head. 'On my way, mate! I'd better get on. Don't forget to send the address. See you . . . very soon.'

She nodded and he was gone. She was staring at a blank screen. No one there, no David.

She felt elated. And terrified.

Lord, was she making a terrible mistake?

———

Celia had been sitting still for too long, mulling over her exchange with David. The likelihood of his imminent arrival. It was a little alarming. Not the fact of his coming – she was excited at the prospect of meeting him, getting to know him – it was the silence that was troubling her. The silence she had allowed to grow around his existence.

Her skirt was sticking to the chair, her spine damp from the heat. She should carry all her paperwork downstairs to the conservatory and spread it out on the table there. She didn't need a lot of space but it would be airier, more cheerful. When she and Dominic had first moved there, he had bagged a study on the south-east side, the rear of the house, with oodles of *étagères* for his books and files. Celia had agreed it was the ideal retreat for him, peaceful, protected from the rowdiness of house activities. (And back then she would have done anything to keep him happy, to keep him . . .) Dominic had been writing in his library earlier while she'd been at the airport. He was on a roll, he'd said, a new play on the go, and 'at a relaxed pace', he claimed modestly, he was preparing his memoirs. A theatrical autobiography his agent, Blake, had been encouraging him to tackle.

When he returned, after lunch, she would request a few moments of his precious time. Knock on his door. He got cantankerous when disturbed, but it was essential he hear her story. She must relay to him the facts about David Hawksmith.

David Hawksmith.

She was still holding David's letter.

What if David should turn out to be a bore or completely out of tune with the rest of their guests and clients? She mustn't lose sight of the fact this party was also a business affair.

She regretted now that she had not confided in Dominic way back when they were first getting to know one another. There had been ample opportunities over the years. It had been a senseless and unnecessary omission. Dominic would have taken the whole business in his stride. He would not have judged or criticized her. Too late now. Or no, because very soon David and Dominic would meet, face to face, spend a weekend together under this very roof.

If David turned up, of course.

She tossed her pen on to her disorganized desk. It came to rest on top of all the scraps of paper, the bills and quotes for this and that, the lists – changes of plans, rethinks, costings – scribbled over dozens of times with her multi-coloured Bic biros. Lists and then more lists. She should go and help Magali put some lunch on the table. The men would be back any moment now from their tour of the vineyards and the wine-tasting barn. She had almost forgotten about them, but hoped it had gone smoothly, that Dominic and Claude were happy to work with Tom and Sean.

If one of them had a current driving licence – had she asked this during her Zoom interviews with them? – she could delegate the task of collecting guests from the airport and station. Shopping, too, once they got to know the favoured bakers and butchers . . . Yes, these two might prove to be a Godsend.

But lunch first.

And then an imperative: break the news to Dominic about the arrival, the existence, of David Hawksmith.

CHAPTER FIVE

Celia was two rungs up a stepladder, deadheading the wilted blooms on her precious rosebushes. It was a super display that scaled the stone wall alongside the conservatory. This tucked-away courtyard, edged with rosebeds and mighty terracotta pots planted with a dazzling array of scarlet geraniums, was one of her hideaways. She loved it, often found herself here when she was – as now – troubled. She took great pleasure in nurturing the fertile corner. Watering, pruning back the growth, such activities helped her bring perspective to her anxieties.

This was a shaded spot to the west of the house. The conservatory was inside, a bright, comfortable living area for the wetter, darker days, used almost exclusively during the winter. They rarely ventured into it at this time of year because it was suffocatingly hot when the sun beat down against the massive panes of glass.

Celia had equipped the tiled courtyard with four vintage

wicker chairs and an iron and glass oval table. It was well appointed for enjoying a late-morning cup of coffee or an evening glass of wine. Here she idled away hours, labouring over the accounts, reading, keeping herself occupied during the solitary hours when Dominic was immersed in his play-writing. Thanks to the old stone walls of the main body of the house and this modern wing of glass, it was well protected against all but the fiercest of weathers. Even so, she had taken the precaution of wearing her sunhat.

'Celia!'

Lost in her musings, expecting no one, the unfamiliar voice startled her. She had been deliberating upon the best way to introduce the subject of David to Dominic who'd told her after lunch that he didn't have time for her at present: 'I need to work, we can talk later.'

'Five minutes, please, Dom. It's rather important.'

'Later.'

She spun about, nearly losing balance, and discovered Tom at the foot of the ladder.

'There you are.' He grinned as though their encounter there was the most natural and intended event in the world.

'You surprised me.'

The unexpected arrival looked a little dishevelled in tired old shorts, laced-up hiking boots and, well, little else. Bare torso, broad shoulders.

She frowned, waiting.

'Let me help you with that.'

'With what? No, no, thanks, I'm fine.' The heat was making her giddy. 'My, it's hot.' She stepped down from the ladder, placed her woven basket, half filled with browning rose petals, on the table and laid her secateurs on top. Releasing her spine after all the bending and stretching, she stood to her full height, which was a good foot shorter than Tom's.

Hands pressed against her broad-brimmed hat, she gazed up at him, bemused by his appearance. 'Were you looking for me, Tom?'

Tom was smiling broadly. His eyes were dark as carob pods. Dancing eyes that shone out from an open face. His hair was unruly, sticking upright in several directions all at once, rather like a straw man.

She was puzzled, disoriented. 'Or . . . you're probably looking for Dominic? Sorry, but you won't find him about at this time of day. He's at his desk, sealed off from the world. You'll never catch hold of him during his "creative" hours. Even I have to wait till he resurfaces.' It was her own frustration she was voicing now. 'Shall I point you in the direction of Claude's office?'

Tom shook his head. 'I don't want anything at all. I was strolling about, getting a feel for the place, when I spotted you on the ladder and thought maybe I could lend you a hand. Thought it'd give us an opportunity to chat.'

'That's very kind but it's – I enjoy doing this. My speculative time when I've lots on my mind.'

Which she certainly had.

The buzzing of honey bees drew Celia's focus to the herbs growing in a hedge alongside a low stone wall. They were feasting on the sage and parsley, which, thanks to the shelter there, were almost permanently in flower. 'It's a relaxation for me.'

'I get that. A kind of meditation?'

'Sort of.' She was hoping Tom might just wander off again, leave her to her ruminations. She had texted their address to David Hawksmith with the party details, but she should have run all this by Dominic first. Blast that he was always so otherwise occupied and unavailable to her.

'I'm a bit like that about certain chores, especially those outside in the fresh air. Like I love to paint garden furniture or strip and restore wood.'

'That's nice.' She had moved to the table, was pouring herself a glass of iced water. Her cheeks felt damp and sticky.

'I could give a lick of paint to your shutters, if you like. I noticed they're looking a bit sorry for themselves.'

Celia screwed up her eyes, glancing up at the row of wooden shutters ranged along the first and second floors of the three-storey manor house. 'Actually, I rather like them faded and flaky. Shabby chic.' She laughed. 'Characterful.'

'Sure, sure. I do too. Not a criticism. I was just offering to . . . Well, I want to show gratitude for the opportunity you're giving me to hang out in this amazing place with you two guys for the summer. Sean – he's sleeping – said the same.'

'Oh, I'm delighted. We've never done this before, invited complete strangers to work with us.' She took a sip of the chilled water. It tasted so refreshing. She couldn't offer Tom any as she had only brought out one glass.

'It's pretty standard, these days, booking people from the internet. Everyone does it. There's no real risk.'

She lifted her basket from the table, readying to return to her task, to the lower canes of the bushes. 'Well, that may be so, perhaps, but we haven't previously. I suppose we're, Dominic and I, well, a bit old-fashioned.'

The way Tom was watching her, the depth of his gaze, made her feel a little uncomfortable. It was as though he was poised, readying himself . . . wanted something.

'Apologies . . . must get on,' she muttered.

Since she and Dominic had taken up residence on the estate, distanced themselves from London, she was out of the habit of being in the company of younger men. She was no longer surrounded by gorgeous young actors full of charm and patter. Like so many middle-aged women, she felt invisible in male company. Impossible to gauge how one was perceived, if noticed at all.

Several petals drifted to the tiles at her feet. 'Nonsense, you're timeless, Celia, like your films.' He unhooked the basket from her wrist and bent to scoop up some fallen flowers before handing it back to her. Close to, she she saw that he was a little older than she had originally guessed. Late thirties, forty? Still young, of course. Had she even asked his age during their Zoom interview?

'This heat is quite something, eh? Why don't we finish this together and then you can take me on a tour.'

'Oh, I don't have—'

'If you have time, that is. I don't want to intrude. Dominic drove us round the vineyards but it would be awesome to discover some of your favourite spots too. How about you take me to a lovely swimming cove?'

She had masses to do, to think about. But, clearly, Tom wasn't going away . . .

A little later they abandoned the basket, packed tight with withered roses, placing it on the iron table, and set off in the direction of the sea. Celia was feeling a little lighter, less agitated than she had felt after her exchange with David Hawksmith. Tom was easy company. Mostly he just hummed.

He hummed while they walked and when he wasn't humming he was whistling. Was he filling in the silences? Was he ill at ease, as unsure in her company as she was in his? It was only when she asked him how he earned his living in his 'real life' and he confided he was a composer that she understood.

'You're writing music in your head?'

'Film scores mostly,' he added shyly. 'Only a few have sold so far and even they haven't been used yet. It's tough. I'll send you a link to some of my recent compositions. Maybe you know someone who could . . . It'd be fab to hear your feedback.'

The bay Celia was guiding Tom to was a twenty-minute hike but it was a favourite of hers when she had time to swim in the sea, not often these days. They had reached the cliff's edge. It plunged to the water.

'Spectacular,' he crooned.

'Paradise Cove, they call it. And no one comes here, aside from a handful of locals. Well, it's a climb if you want to go to the beach.'

'Let's do it.'

'No . . . I really must get back. I need to see Dominic . . .'

'Ten minutes. Come on.'

The narrowness of the creek caused the sea to be a little rough as it drove itself inland in white curls and beat against the shore. Here, the rock was not the pale limestone so typical of the Mediterranean but a dark red. Rocks as red as rust.

She hadn't been intending to dedicate so much of her afternoon to . . . well, frivolity. She had urgent matters to resolve.

David. She must find time with Dominic. Prepare him for the shock of . . .

Tom brushed the flat of his palm against her bare freckled arm and began his descent. After the first step he swung back, grinned, winked and took off. The steps were less than half a metre wide, hacked out of the face of the escarpment, when, by whom, Celia had no idea. The centre of each was smooth, polished by centuries of foot traffic. There was no hand-rail. It was essential to take care.

She watched Tom, bay-bound, gliding without hesitation. She hung back, then decided to follow.

After a small leap, he hit the pebbles and set off, loping, rangy and slender. His naked shoulders were changing colour, burned by the sun during their walk. She raised a hand to her face to wipe away the perspiration. The heat was like a screen coming in off the sea. Her cheeks felt flushed, also reddening. Her fair complexion meant it had taken her several years of living on this coast to acclimatise.

Tom, a short distance from her, dropped to his haunches. He was sorting through pebbles, making a selection. Standing to his full height, he raised a muscular arm and spun a smooth

53

grey stone into the turquoise-blue water. Away from the shore, the sea was as still as an ice rink. The stone skimmed, bounced and bounced onwards, throwing up a whorl of water shaped like a crown as it slipped out of sight beneath the surface of the calm sea. At each ricochet, Tom lifted his arms wide in a gesture of triumph, throwing a glance back to Celia with a winning complicit smile. His hair was curling in the salt air, his face growing bronzed.

'We should have brought our bathing togs.' He laughed, tossing his head backwards. His jubilance was infectious, his bright, easy manner untouched by life's knocks. She envied him.

'I should get back,' she muttered, more to herself than to her companion, who in any case was out of earshot unless she yelled.

A pair of gulls overhead swooped close. One dived to the shoreline and gobbled a discarded rind of dried orange peel. Tom was hoofing it back across the cove, following the curve of the damp sand, making sure not to get his boots wet in the waves, occasionally hopping like a small boy to avoid a more adventurous splash.

'Do you swim, Celia?'

'Every day.' She smiled, turning her back to the water, to Tom, taking her first step towards the foot of the stone tread that snaked the cliffside.

'We should come back tomorrow, as the sunrise hits the Med, and have a dawn dip. There are none of the great waves of northern Cornwall here, which are such an inspiration for my music. Still, it'd be awesome. Gentler sounds, other rhythms.' He was looking all about him. Then he threw back his head as though conversing with the cobalt sky, the occasional cloud. Listening to music only he was tuned in to.

Celia turned away, spun on her heels and began the ascent. 'I'll leave you here,' she called. 'You can find your way back. If you fancy it, join us for dinner. Invite Sean. Otherwise, see you in the morning, bright and early.' She lifted an arm in a casual wave, stepping determinedly upward.

'Wait, I'm coming with you.' He was bounding in great strides, arms swinging, ascending from the sand to the stones until in a flash he was behind her.

Before they separated – he to follow the winding dust track through the vineyards to the lodge and she back to *le château*, she learned from Tom that one of his reasons for accepting the summer job was that he had recently broken up with his girl, a long-term relationship.

'Sorry to hear that.'

'It's been rough. I need this time out,' he confided. 'Thank you,' he whispered, wrapping his arms about her and hugging her tight. 'Plus I was dead keen to meet you. I know we have so much in common. Catch you later.'

Striding off through the green fields bespattered with blackening fruits, he was singing at full volume. She watched his receding figure for a moment or two. The hug, its spontaneity, had bowled her over. She could have wept. She was thinking of David. The lost years.

CHAPTER SIX

By the time Celia came into view of the house, dusk was chasing at her heels. She was sprinting the last hundred metres, trying to catch up with herself after her unexpected and not unpleasant outing with Tom. She paused, stood for a moment, breathless, slipped her mobile phone out of her shoulder-bag, wondering whether Dominic had been trying to find her, and discovered an unread text message.

Celia, we will be arriving by train into Cannes on Friday morning. Train from Paris due in at 11.13 a.m on 11th. I hope the early arrival does not inconvenience? All seats were booked for Saturday, 12th. (High-season weekend, apparently.) If a problem, I can check us into a little B&B for the first night in Cannes and we can make our way up to your estate on Saturday afternoon as originally discussed. Do let me know. Yours, David

Celia stared at the message and reread it several times, frowning. It was not the announced early arrival that wrong-footed her, though that too, of course. Would Magali have prepared, aired and made up all the bedrooms by Friday? Mental note to self: ask her in the morning. No, it was the 'we' that nonplussed her. The invitation she had extended to David had not included a companion. Of course, it had not specifically excluded a wife or plus one. Was he married? Even such basic information she had not thought to find out. Celia had simply assumed, should David accept the invitation, he would be travelling over alone.

In her mind, the box room on the top floor had been marked down as his for the weekend. She would have to rethink that. Offer him and his travelling companion, wife or partner, somewhere a little more commodious given that this was his first time to their home. Perhaps Sally, Dominic's daughter, and her husband, Frank, would agree to squeeze themselves into the box room for a brief spell. It would only be for three nights, the long weekend. They could relocate afterwards when David and Other had headed off. Sally was always so accommodating. Who could wish for a more amenable stepdaughter?

No sign of Dominic. Damn. Instead, Celia hotfooted down to the pool for a swift pre-twilight dip. The cicadas were at full throttle, a frantic orchestra ceaselessly rehearsing. The air was still, hot, muggier. Not a whiff of breeze to slacken the burden. The sky had grown cloudy, overcast. It looked as though a storm was threatening. Oh, yes, please, anything to break up this heaviness. But there would be no rain. Every day they waited, prayed for the promised downpour, but the heavens never delivered. The earth was desiccated; plants were withering. It would not take much to torch the vegetation and then it would combust like a tinderbox. In her mind's eye, she pictured hectares of burning land. Every landowner's seasonal nightmare. Tragically, forest fires were a common occurrence down this way throughout the summer months.

She was thinking about the party: they would have to take every precaution throughout the weekend. The spit turning, clusters of guests, many smoking in the garden, candles flickering. A barbecue on the go. She would have a word with dear Henri, ask him to prepare all the hosepipes and connect them to the water sources.

She had hoped to have her talk with Dominic before drinks and dinner but he was still encased in his study, catching up on the hours he had devoted to touring the estate with their new assistants. She pictured Tom hurling pebbles. Head thrown back, listening to the notes of Nature: celestial songs, sea shanties. She envied him his youth, his openness to all that lay ahead of him. Unlike her, he was not burdened with a secret so foolishly buried.

CHAPTER SEVEN

'I think you picked those two young men for their charm and good looks, darling,' Dominic observed amicably.

Well, she certainly hadn't, but she couldn't deny they were a handsome pair.

She and Dominic were lounging side by side on on a couch on one of the upper verandas. Daisy, the Collie, was asleep at their feet. Just the two of them, their first moment alone since breakfast. They were enjoying a post-dinner glass of chilled white wine from their own *cave*. She caught the soft hoot of a tawny owl hidden somewhere in the trees surrounding them. She loved their calls, found them reassuring. The heat had lessened with the setting of the sun. Even so, it remained wretchedly warm. Oppressive, no matter how many cold showers or swims she indulged in.

Tom and Sean, who had dined with them, had said their goodnights and headed off on foot in jaunty fashion to the lodge, which they claimed was ideal, perfectly comfortable.

'Well done, Ceely. It looks as though your internet search for manpower will prove to be a success. Early days yet but I have a good feeling about both of them. Claude must be delighted.'

At least she'd got that right. She was on tenterhooks worrying about how best to broach the subject of David Hawksmith. Somehow the explanation of the newcomer's imminent arrival seemed insurmountable and she couldn't decide where or how to begin to fill the gaps.

'I thought we might chat through the guest list before we turn in,' she said breezily. Dominic yawned, lifted his bare feet on to the low glass table in front of them and crossed one foot over the other. 'I'm tired, my sweet. Off to bed when I've finished my wine.' He was watching the stars, eyes peeled for the Perseid meteor shower, even a lone shooting star or two. And this was the year of Jupiter emblazoning their nights with its splendid displays so close to the earth and the moon.

'I know, challenging to be writing endlessly . . . It's . . . There's just one . . .'

Dominic briefly closed his eyes. It had been a taxing day. 'Ceely, I've got a lot going on that needs my attention. These endless discussions about party logistics, you manage it all so perfectly. Let's leave it in your capable hands.'

'Well, two guests actually whom you—'

'We've been over it several times already. I'm perfectly happy with the list, darling. If you've added a stray or two, as is your wont, that's fine by me. We'll accommodate them.'

'His name is Dav—'

At that moment Dominic's mobile, on the table by his feet, began to sound and spin. He leaned forward and swept it up in his right hand, switching his glass to the left. 'Bit late for callers,' he muttered, squinting at the screen. 'Oh, it's Sal. How lovely. Hello, darling, all well?' Dominic placed his half-finished glass on the table and lifted himself from the nest of cushions, phone to his ear. He had turned his back on Celia. Stepping over the snoring dog, he wandered away towards the iron railing.

Celia downed the remaining wine in her glass and stood up. She was ready for bed too, drained after a day of revelations.

Dominic was laughing, deep in conversation with his daughter. The moment for her disclosure had wriggled away. It would not be tonight that her past was revealed.

Damn it.

Before she went to sleep she glanced at her phone to reconsider the message from David, which she hadn't yet answered. She would do so first thing in the morning. Surprisingly, she found a text from Tom. A link was attached.

Have a listen. I wrote this during Covid when life was in turmoil for many reasons. Thanks for dinner and a memorable outing to your patch of paradise. I long to hear your thoughts on my music. Tom x

CHAPTER EIGHT

The stone lodge – it didn't have a name – where Tom and Sean were now based was a brisk twenty-five-minute walk from Les Roches du Soleil's main residence. It was the most remote of all the estate farmhouses, of which there were four. On foot, it was a sloping approach along red-earth paths that cut through several of the vineyards, so attractive now with their green leaves and dark, pendulous fruits. The two-bedroomed cottage had been constructed in the early 1920s on a flat, sandy clearing, metres from the edge of a steep seaside cliff.

The position was inspiring. No one, thought Celia, could fail to appreciate its uniqueness. The rear windows, including the one in the attic, which had been converted into the second bedroom, were seaward-facing. Aside from a few pine trees, there was little to screen out the view: the Mediterranean unfolding in all its splendour. Total sea and beckoning horizon.

The lodge had unfenced-in yards, front and back. Out front, two mature stone pines, possibly planted when the cottage was first constructed, acted as a natural shade for the residents. Celia had installed an outdoor wooden table and two chairs beneath one of the pines. A summer dining idyll.

At the back the yard was desolate. Nothing much grew there besides wind-slaked thyme, gorse and a few other maritime shrubs. Cross it some forty steps and you reached the precipice, cliff's end. Here, twenty metres below the headland there was a small horseshoe bay, rocky and pebbly with patches of sand, similar to the one Celia had taken Tom to the day before. Unfortunately, this one was accessible only by boat because, unlike Paradise Cove, no stairway had been carved into its rock.

The thrash of waves against mighty boulders was ever present, merciless, as was the mewing of the overhead gulls as they wheeled and circled. That was this land's end's soundtrack, along with the wind. Celia loved it. She had often thought, if she'd been gifted with her husband's literary skills, she would have bagged this outpost for herself, claimed it as her isolated haven. The peace! She had never understood why it had not appealed to Dominic. 'Too far to walk every day,' he had reasoned.

Consequently, the cottage had stood empty, slowly crumbling from weather and sea-salt erosion, during the first eight years of their tenure until they had earned sufficient funds to renovate it. It was a task Celia had taken on with gusto. Even so, it was still only occasionally inhabited, used for holidaying guests when the main house was overflowing. This was the first time it had been put to tenanting temporary staff. If it worked out with the lads, Celia thought, she might consider the solution more frequently. Heaven knows, they needed the extra hands.

Today she was not walking the rusty-red paths. She was driving to the lodge, delivering provisions purchased in the local village grocery store, the only *épicerie* this side of their nearest town, Saint-Jean-en-Forêt. Her route, grandly named the Coast Road, was little more than a shoelace of tarmac with plenty of weeds growing either side because it was so rarely travelled. It was just about wide enough for one car, inching forwards dangerously close to the precipitous drop. Celia bit her lip, focusing on the road ahead. If she as much as glanced over the escarpment, down towards the incoming breakers, she'd lose her nerve and spin out of control.

She was making the journey to deposit food and household products at the cottage along with a note she had scribbled earlier. According to Dominic, Claude had taken the men with him to one of the vineyards to start the big clear-up of the dried-out mounds of cuttings from pruning.

She parked the Land Rover, yanked hard on the cranky old handbrake and jumped out. A gust off the sea greeted her, lifting her shoulder-length ginger hair, which she hadn't had time to tie back that morning. It cooled her neck and face; a refreshing sensation. According to her phone, the outside temperature was registering 36°C. Punishingly hot. One of the boxes she was about to unload contained six bottles of San Pellegrino mineral water. The tap water, fed from Alpine springs, was uncontaminated, perfect for drinking, but it was nice to have the fizzy option on hand too. She knew the door was unlocked because she had not given the men a key. She had mislaid it, which, of course, had disgruntled Dominic, causing cross words between them.

'Don't make a fuss, please, darling. No one's going to traipse all the way over there to steal . . . steal what? And their privacy is guaranteed just by the position of the place.'

Dominic judged it inconsiderate. 'It's disrespectful to go barging in,' he berated her. 'Why didn't you hang the key on the rack in the hall, along with all the others? I installed the wretched thing precisely for this purpose, to avoid you misplacing every key on every conceivable occasion. And to lessen the time I spend searching for them. Sometimes, Celia, you're exasperating.'

Even the copies, and copies of copies, went astray.

Such had been his frame of mind at breakfast. She had downed a swift coffee with him after her swim, then scuttled off.

Still no disclosure on the subject of David. The days were galloping ahead. Friday, with David and his companion's arrival, was hurtling towards them.

She kicked open the lodge door, clutching the heavy grocery box in both hands, staggering with the effort. Sweat was breaking out along the column of her spine beneath her loose cotton shirt. She very nearly lost her balance tottering over the threshold. The back windows were wide open. A horizontal sheet of incoming air blasted her. She was thinking how welcome it was when the door behind her abruptly slammed. It made her jump. Through the open windows, she could hear the distant waves rolling, bouncing against beach and rocks. A pale blue cotton shirt, swaying slightly in the draught, was hanging from the back of one of the dining chairs, jeans thrown across the sofa. From a small travelling speaker set on the dining table came instrumental music: a delicate melody. Might it be one of Tom's compositions? He must have left it playing all morning. She'd better have the 'saving energy resources' conversation with them when she next saw them. The notes were pleasing, though, if a little sad. Rather tender. When she had time, she should listen to the link Tom had sent through to her.

When she had time!

She dropped the box with a thud on to the kitchen counter and took a beat to catch her breath, then lifted out one of the plastic bottles, which she slid into the fridge to chill ready for their return.

Glancing towards the breakfast table, she saw that two mugs had been forgotten there, one with a spoon standing up in it, and two plates with toast crumbs. As she stepped from the open kitchen towards the front door, she heard voices.

Sean opened the door. Tom was directly behind him. Both wore scruffy shorts and were flecked with dust and leaves.

'Celia, what a surprise.'

'Oh, sorry if I'm intruding. I'm bringing rations.' She gave an awkward laugh, which they didn't pick up on.

'I'll unload the rest of the shopping and leave it on the step outside. You can bring it in yourselves. Apologies for barging in.'

She exited the cottage and beetled towards her vehicle. The sun beat hard against her head. Where had she left her sunhat? On the kitchen work surface in the lodge? She was dragging the two remaining boxes, one after the other, to the step where she deposited them in the shade. They contained butter, two litres of long-life milk, a couple of cheeses, Camembert and Roquefort, and bacon rashers. Henri had already brought the eggs. Hearty breakfasts for the working pair. All these should go directly into the fridge before the sun and heat griddled them. The door was slightly ajar but she didn't knock. 'Rest of the food's outside,' she called.

As she stepped up into the driver's seat, about to gun the engine – her hat was on the passenger seat – she heard Tom calling her.

She turned her head uncertainly.

'Were you looking for me?'

She frowned.

He was barefoot. His hair was rumpled. 'I thought perhaps . . .'

'I was bringing supplies.'

He nodded. 'Thanks for stopping by with all this grub. Catch you later.'

'See you both for dinner,' she called in response. Tom was bending to gather up the first box. His torso rippled with muscles as he stretched out his arm and waved. Celia thrust the gear into reverse, causing the wheels to spin on the shale track. She wouldn't mention this incident to Dominic.

CHAPTER NINE

When Celia returned from the cottage, she learned from Dominic that Sally's call of the previous evening had been to inform her father that she and Frank were obliged to postpone their trip. Frank had tested positive for Covid so they were housebound for the foreseeable future. Their quarantine would cross over Celia's party weekend.

'Oh, no! What bad luck. Did you send them my love?'

'Wretched news.' Dominic agreed. 'I told her to come and stay as soon as they're clear of this bloody virus. It's not going away, is it?'

'I'm so disappointed.'

'We'll have an *à quatre* family celebration later. It'll be far jollier. Certainly more intimate. I told her you've invited the world and his wife for the weekend. Every day the list gets longer.'

Celia almost choked on a mouthful of bread. She and Dominic were grabbing a hasty sandwich outside on the terrace in the shade. Her mind was spinning. Sally's unexpectedly vacated room could be given to David and his companion. Or if for some reason the Hawksmith pair required separate quarters, his companion could have the box room and David could go into Sally and Frank's. Perhaps this unforeseen development from Sally could be turned to advantage. Poor Frank, though, and she was disappointed that she wouldn't benefit from Sally's organizational skills in advance of the festivities. There was still so much to do.

Celia was scribbling lists, gulping water, ignoring her food, a sure sign that she was panicking. 'What have I forgotten?' She was still fretting about David. She must broach the subject now. It was this minute or probably never.

Dominic was chewing his ham baguette, perusing the pages of *Le Monde*, his preferred daily paper, which he still had delivered to the letterbox at the gate every morning. 'I doubt you've forgotten anything. Do calm down, darling.' He was cradling a glass of chilled beer, his elbow resting on the table alongside him. He was in his own world, as he frequently was when immersed in writing a book or script. Some days, like now, it was almost impossible to get through to him, as though they lived on different planets, as though they were strangers.

She had to get this worry off her chest. 'Anything interesting to report?' she asked, in an attempt to draw her husband's attention away from the print.

'Mmm? Oh, did I mention that when all this jollying is over, I have to pop to London? Possibly week after next.'

'*What?* Before the harvest? No, you didn't. That's bad timing. Is this about your book?'

'TV interest in an old play.'

'How exciting. Which one?'

'Let's talk about it when there's something to it. Unconfirmed chatter at this stage.'

'Oh. Well, I can't wait to hear more.' It irritated Celia when Dominic was secretive. It woke up old insecurities.

'Oh, and I forgot. Jacques was on the phone . . .'

'Who's Jacques?'

'For Heaven's sake, sweetheart, the butcher. He tells me you've ordered an entire sheep along with trimmings for the spit-roast and dozens of sausages for the barbecue. We're supposed to be keeping a brake on our funds, Ceely.'

'That is a gross exaggeration, Dom. And why do you always take his side?'

'He also mentioned you've invited him and his family to the celebrations. Is there anyone you haven't invited, my darling? The guest list seems to be getting a little out of control.'

Celia's stomach lurched. 'Actually, I did want to talk to you about one other guest. It's not someone you . . .'

While Celia was gearing herself up yet again to unburden herself of this long-buried story, Magali came marching out onto the terrace, full of purpose, her sleeves rolled up to her elbows, hands deep in her apron pockets. 'Sorry to interrupt. Celia, there's a gentleman at the door asking for you. He says he has a delivery.'

Celia physically sagged. 'What now? No one in the South of France delivers between the hours of twelve and two.'

'The fellow says he's come from Menton and didn't manage to make sense of your directions. He's complaining that he's been turning in circles for half the morning and has missed his lunch-break.'

'Offer him a glass of something cold and a plate of bread and cheese, will you, please, Magali? Thank you. Sorry, Dom, I'd better deal with this.' Celia rose from her chair and hurried into the house, through to the front door, leaving Dominic with his beer and *journal.* She was silently cursing. Dominic was still blithely ignorant of her unannounced guests.

The delivery that had interrupted their snatched lunch came in a small open-back truck crammed with fruiting lemon trees. Celia had purchased twenty from a marvellous nursery in Menton specializing in the propagation of every conceivable variety of citrus fruit. (The new postmistress in the local village had given her the name of the citrus-farming brothers.) Menton, nudging tight against the French-Italian border, was an enchanting hilltop city, renowned for its unique climate and spectacular lemon farms. Celia's order had been for the Four Seasons variety, a sweetly scented tree that fruits and flowers all year round. They were a little more expensive, of course, but Celia dreamed of that fragrance wafting across the warm evening air, hypnotizing their guests with its perfection while they chatted and laughed, consuming and imbibing, all the while complimenting Dominic on the fine quality of their house wines. Afterwards, to justify Celia's extravagance, the trees were intended as a permanent fixture for the estate. Celia knew exactly where they were to be planted. Close to the wine-tasting block where all visitors could enjoy their perfume.

But that was later. She would give her mind to their installation in the weeks beyond the party. In time for this autumn's season of *dégustations*. In the meantime, the trees, each standing at close to two metres high with gloriously spreading aromatic branches, were destined to enhance the evening's gaieties.

Celia's plan, her vision, was to place the trees in two rows on the lawn beneath the swimming-pool, ten to each row, with a spacing of a metre between each tree. The two rows, set three metres apart, would create a natural al fresco dining area where long trestle tables and chairs were to be assembled. In her mind's eye, the makeshift dining 'room' would be festively lit with dozens of candles on the tables, fairy lights and lanterns hanging from or threaded through the branches of the trees. Sally, Dominic's daughter, was a TV production designer. She would have made a perfect job of these decorations. She had such style. It would have been spellbinding. But Sally was not going to be here. Celia would have to organize the embellishments herself.

CHAPTER TEN

Lorries and vans were climbing the driveway, one banking up behind the next in a chaos of deliveries, disgorging chairs, lanterns, hunks of lamb, and all conceivable party paraphernalia. Dominic locked himself into his library, insisting that he was not to be disturbed, thereby depositing the supervision of everything on Celia's shoulders.

On the Friday morning Celia called in Tom and Sean and left them in the able hands of Henri and Magali. Their task was to prepare the only bit of garden the estate maintained as a manicured lawn. It was a leafy rectangular patch, measuring some four hundred square metres, fringed by imposing centuries-old cypresses and umbrella pines. It was situated three terraces down from the main house, one level beneath the pool. It was accessed, as was the pool, by a pair of magnificent curving stone staircases that descended, like semi-closed wings, from the rear of the main house. The heads of the two staircases were decorated with a pair of weatherbeaten

Greek goddess busts. Celia had discovered the sculptures at a flea market in Nice soon after she and Dominic had moved to the estate. Their style was not exactly in keeping with the eighteenth-century mansion, but Celia didn't give a hoot. The 'girls' were graceful additions, embellishments, she claimed, and she adored them.

The grand dinner party or 'spit-roast banquet', the highlight of this mid-August holiday weekend, to be held on the fast-approaching Saturday evening, was to be located on this lower lawn. Celia calculated they were catering for somewhere in the region of sixty at the main event. It had been her intention to use several of their trestle tables, rustic and easy to transport, placed in one uninterrupted line between the lemon trees. An authentic Mediterranean ambience. Under normal circum-stances the trestles were brought out of storage just once a year, when they were set up in the vineyards for the grape-pickers to lunch at during the harvest. Outside harvest season, they remained stacked in one of the larger barns alongside the courtyard.

However, when Sean and Tom, with directions from Henri, carried them into the yard, Celia saw that they were way too scruffy for the coming weekend's more upmarket purposes – and she couldn't justify buying a new set of tables. Dominic would hit the roof. Their extravaganza was already over budget. As an acceptable alternative, she had ordered crisp white linen tablecloths from Cannes to hide the damaged wooden slats and create an illusion of elegance. The day before, she had taken delivery of seventy foldable chairs – on hire, Dominic was relieved to learn.

Having given detailed instructions as to how she wanted the furniture laid out, Celia jumped into the Land Rover and set off at a roar for the railway station in Cannes to meet the 11.13 a.m. TGV train from Paris. It was twenty to eleven and she was running embarrassingly late. A couple of kilometres along her route she realized she had forgotten her handbag. Her phone was in it. Blast! Too late to turn back.

It was a twenty-five-minute journey. For the first stretch she drove along the bumpy track that led from the estate, meeting almost no one until she hit the outskirts of the coastal town and the holiday weekend traffic. David would wait, of course he would, but it wasn't great to come hurtling down at a quarter to midday without warning him of her delay.

She sped into the station forecourt. Slowing to a crawl, she peered out of the window in search of David and Other. Parking was prohibited except for a swift drop-off or pick-up. The municipality had become impossibly strict and the fines were steep. It would have been more prudent to park in the neighbouring multi-storey but she assumed David and his wife or girlfriend would be outside the station.

No sign of David and friend.

Behind her, frenzied hooting from an impatient driver.

'Oh, for Heaven's sake, show a little patience!' she yelled, shifting the gear stick into second, then crossing into the taxi lane to exit the station. She almost collided with an approaching bus she had not spotted in her rear-view mirror. The driver let out a long, angry hoot and barked something out of his window.

'Keep your shirt on! I'm sorry. *Désolée.*'

And then, from the far corner of her vision, she spotted him. Was it him? She was fairly sure . . . Yes, it was. It must be. On the other side of the street, installed outside one of the station cafés. 'David!' she shouted frantically, out of the window.

Horns honking from several directions, growing more impatient, drowning her voice. 'David!' Damn it. She couldn't stop here. She was obliged to leave the station forecourt and go back round the block. It was a circuitous route that could take ten minutes, bringing the time to midday. How rude she must appear. 'David!' There was so much noise, bustling activity. No reaction from the waiting man.

He had taken off his jacket and was sitting in his shirt sleeves, staring at his phone, scrolling for an update from her, no doubt. She pulled the Land Rover out of the station, seeing then that the small table he was perched at was occupied only by him. No one else. At his side, partially stowed between the plastic table legs, there were two pieces of luggage. Had he, after all, decided to make the trip alone? She felt a sense of relief at this possibility. By now she was on the street that turned left from the station, turning left again at the open market – chock-a-block with cars and shoppers. From there, passing several halal butchers and *pâtisseries orientales*, sticky cake shops, the direction was once more left, where the road ascended. The cars were nose to tail. It could be fifteen minutes before she dropped back down to the station forecourt and cafés. The delay was making her jittery.

A clear run sailed her onwards; she was back in front of the Gare de Cannes in eleven minutes, chugging to a halt directly alongside where David was still sitting. It was illegal to park at the kerbside. Even so she nudged the car tight to the pavement scratching the wheel's metal hub as she did so. Damn. At least she had left space for the cars behind to overtake. She leaned over, engine still running, stretched across the passenger seat, wound down the window and bellowed David's name. He turned, brows creased, and then a wide grin broke across his features, an expression of amazement when he caught sight of her. 'Celia!'

'I can't stop here. The police'll skin me alive. Sorry to be so disgracefully late.'

David threw a glance towards the cramped interior of the scruffy little coffee shop with its display of garish photos of kebabs and omelettes, intended to entice newly arrived tourists.

'Gillian's gone to the loo, and I need to pay for the coffees. Can you give me a sec?'

'Of course. I'll grab your bags, throw them in the boot.'

Celia leaped from the car.

There he was, standing now. A surprisingly tall man, and broad – she hadn't expected it – arms hanging woodenly at half mast preparing to greet her. As they drew close, they knocked awkwardly against one another, muttering apologies. Suddenly he made a grab for her, yanking her into a tight embrace. Celia could hardly breathe. His body was trembling, his heart hammering. Her own emotions were almost choking her.

'God, it's good to meet you at last, Celia. You can't know . . .'

She couldn't speak, face pressed into his damp shirt.

'I'll fetch Gill, pay for the . . . Be right back.'

David bumped into Gillian at the entrance to the café. She was coming out, wiping her hands with a paper towel. He said a few words and hurried inside. Gillian turned her attention to the table and then to Celia, who was now at the rear of the car dragging not two but three heavy bags. What on earth were they travelling with?

Gillian approached, hovered, watching Celia as she bent and hauled, without offering to assist.

'Hello.' Celia smiled. She propelled the second bag deeper into the boot. 'I'm Celia.'

David's companion was surprisingly young. An offbeat creature, with a nose-ring, her hair was cropped short, a boy's crew-cut, except that most young men didn't sport such fashions these days. Down here their heads were shaved, their beards bushy and Middle Eastern, like Muslim priests or mullahs.

'Yeah, Dave mentioned you.' The newcomer spoke with a pronounced Cockney accent.

Celia had been expecting a partner closer to forty, closer to David's age, but Gillian couldn't have been more than twenty, twenty-two at the outside. 'Welcome, Gillian, to the South of France.'

'Shall I climb in the back?'

'You decide.'

'Dad'll want to sit beside you.'

Celia almost keeled over. 'Sorry, did . . .' The heat, the rushing, the stress to arrive here on time. 'Sorry, did you say *Dad*?'

'Yeah, Dave's my . . . he's my dad. Didn't he say?'

It was then that David reappeared, his face split with a nervous smile, an apprehensive glint in his eye. 'Good, so you've met.' He lifted his jacket from the back of the plastic chair and opened the front passenger door. 'Am I going in the front?'

A white police car was approaching, blue light spinning. 'Quick, get in.'

Celia made a dash for the driver's seat on the busy roadside, after closing up the rear. 'Let's skedaddle before I'm booked.'

Her passengers were lost in their own worlds. Celia took advantage of their silence to get to grips with this mind-blowing turn of events. Gillian, in the rear, was engrossed in her phone while David was staring out of the window, tongue-tied or taking in the view, the majesty of the landscape, as the SUV climbed. Celia, scrabbling her thoughts together, was at a loss. Where to begin? Her hands gripped the wheel. She wondered why her guest hadn't thought to apprise her of the fact that his companion was his daughter. Was there a wife? A mother somewhere – of course, there had to be. And how much did Gillian know of her father's past? What had he told her? Who was Celia in their story? What role did she play?

How in Heaven's name would Dominic respond to all this?

The girl seated behind her was her *granddaughter*. She hadn't yet come to terms with the unexpected appearance of her *son*! Her son, who was a grown man, a stranger she hadn't set eyes on for forty-seven years.

This invitation had been a miscalculation of judgement on her part. It was not that she didn't want to become acquainted with these people. Of course she did, very much so . . . but the timing was all wrong, out of synch. Now, with sixty or thereabouts for dinner on Saturday, including important clients . . . There were so many questions. So many holes, gaps, in all their narratives. *And* there was Dominic. Dominic, who had still not been informed about this almost inconceivable change in his wife's circumstances.

She shifted the gear to third as they chugged off the road, and swung the steering wheel hard to the right, scaling a sandy track. A light-red powder rose from beneath the tyres, temporarily obscuring the view. Her heart was in turmoil. What on earth was she going to say to Dominic? Would they all get on? Could they make a go of it?

'It's not much further now. Do you know the South of France, David? Speak any French?'

He shook his head. 'Not a word. Well, except *bonjour* and *merci.*' He laughed nervously. 'I haven't travelled all that much, to be honest, Celia. We went to Spain once for our holidays, didn't we, Gill? But that was . . . oh, more than ten years ago. Only time I've been out of England.'

'Alicante, it was. I was nine.'

'Yeah. You built that extraordinary sandcastle. Fantastic, it was. Even the local mayor came to see it, remember?'

Gillian, behind them, put a cigarette into her mouth and lit it. There was little Celia objected to more than smoking, and smoking in enclosed spaces was her *bête noire*. She wound down her window. A cloud of fine dust blew in. She closed it again. 'I'd prefer it if you don't smoke.'

'Gill, put that ciggie out, please, there's a good girl.'

Gillian sighed theatrically. 'Don't nag me, Dave.'

'Gill . . .'

She wound down her window, and stretched out her arm to jettison the smouldering butt.

'Don't!' yelled Celia. Both heads turned towards her, bewildered. 'Apologies, sorry, I didn't mean to shout, but, look, look at the land. It's dry as an old dog's bone. That burning stub would cause a forest fire in seconds.'

'Oh, bugger, sorry.'

'You weren't to know, Gill. There's an ashtray in the front, pass it over. Your father can extinguish it.'

Which David did.

Celia took a deep breath. As soon as they were home she would show Gillian to the box-room and install David in Sally's regular spot. Immediately after, she'd go in search of Dominic, badger him till he listened. No matter what he was engaged in, he must hear her out. She had to get this off her chest. Top priority.

CHAPTER ELEVEN

The new arrivals stepped out of the car. David was blinking in the hot pale light, gazing about him, wonder-struck, glancing this way and that, taking in the grounds and the handsome stone mansion house, which rose three storeys high. He let out a whistle. 'Hell's bells, Celia. It's a palace.'

Celia was opening the boot while the English pair, turning in slow circles, continued to marvel at the grounds and exterior of the house.

'You've got a pool. I spotted it from the lane. How fantabulous.'

'Well, this is pretty special. All yours, is it, Celia?'

'I'm going for a swim.' Gillian took off, loping over the parking stones, bounding towards the front door.

'Don't you want to take your bags to your room first?' Celia called after her.

'Dave'll grab them. I'm going in the pool. Woo-hoo.' She didn't turn back as she sprinted into the hall and out of sight, heading towards the rear of the house.

'She'll find her way. Gillian's very capable.'

'Where's her mother? Are you and she . . . ?'

'We're divorced. Not much contact between us these days. Old story. I'll bore you with it another time . . . So much to talk about.'

Celia nodded. 'Sorry to hear that.'

David shrugged, tugging at the lapels of his jacket. 'It was a while ago, Celia.'

'I wonder you didn't mention Gillian when we talked.'

'I hadn't intended to bring her, and then . . . plans changed and, well, she was dead keen to come. Is her presence a problem? It looks like a pretty large house, plenty of rooms.' He chortled awkwardly. 'You could run this place as a hotel.'

Celia silently chided herself. She hadn't intended to be dismissive or rude. 'No. Of course not. Yes, plenty of rooms. She's more than welcome. After all, she's my . . . Well, it's all . . . I look forward to getting to know her, both of you. It's simply that it's a great deal to take in.' Celia was standing with her head bowed, sandalled feet prodding at the gravel.

Opposite, bags closed about his boots creating a mini barrier between them, David studied her. His mother. 'I hope I haven't, you know, overstepped the mark. I've been so looking forward to this, Celia . . . Bursting with excitement. Since I wrote, since we chatted on the phone, since years . . .'

There was a note of panic, of uncertainty in his voice. 'I don't want to, you know, get it wrong.'

Celia lifted a hand and rested it tentatively on his arm. 'You haven't. You're very welcome here, David. Why don't we get all this luggage inside? I'll show you to your room. It's too hot to stand about out of the shade. We need to find you a hat. Then you and . . . your daughter can make yourselves comfortable. Let me know if there's anything you need. Why don't we all reconvene out on the back terrace for cold drinks? Half an hour? How does that sound?'

Ten minutes later, heart palpitating, Celia's forefinger was tapping gently on the door to Dominic's study. It met with no response. She heard him sigh loudly, an expression of his impatience. He took great exception to being disturbed while at work and very rarely answered unless pressed.

'Dominic, it's Ceely,' she insisted.

'I'm writing.'

'I know, but . . .'

No response.

'Dominic?'

'Can't it wait? Half an hour.'

'No, it's urgent.'

'Oh, very well,' he growled.

She turned the metal handle in the old oak door; it creaked as it unfastened. The smell of old books hit her as she stepped inside. A woody, vanilla-like odour, which she loved and found comforting. She clicked the door behind her, sealing out the rest of the world. 'Sorry to interrupt the muse.' She smiled apprehensively.

'You look good in that light green. It suits you, complements your lovely locks.' He placed his fountain pen on his desk alongside its navy leather case. 'Come and sit down.'

Even before he had encouraged her, she was crossing the room, settling herself in Dominic's beaten-up grandfather chair of well-weathered leather. It dominated the corner beside the fireplace, which was so rarely lit except in the dead of winter. She pulled her feet under her long cotton skirt, curling herself tightly into the cushion as though she were preparing to hibernate. The chair creaked as she shifted her bottom backwards. Her husband watched her, studying her pretty freckled face, her untamed hair flying in all directions, damp from exertion and the clammy weather outside.

'Still hot?'

'Sweltering.'

'Your presence tells me this is serious.'

She nodded. 'It is.'

He waited.

'It was pea-brained of me more than anything else.'

'*Pea-brained?* That's an odd choice of word.'

The open gaze of her green-gold eyes had always melted him. One of the things he loved best about her. And he did love her, always had, no matter the past. The mistakes, which they had never touched upon. Such a delicate loveliness she possessed. It was her insecurities that let her down, forced him to keep a distance lest she swallow him with her doubts and misgivings.

'My behaviour, I mean, was pea-brained.'

'Oh?'

'Not to have confided in you way back. Honestly, I can't think why I didn't.' She was gazing at him now with such intensity, almost terror. 'I always trusted you, knew you loved me, that I could . . . count on you, but . . .' A frog caught in her throat. Another, a very different, more recent, memory usurped her train of thought, of that year when she hadn't been able to count on him, when she had dreaded losing him, when she didn't trust him, when he had drifted out of reach and she had feared he would never find his way back to her.

She began to cough. 'Sorry.' She was struggling, pulling herself back to the here and now, to the reason she was in this room, disturbing Dominic's train of thought, his work.

'Need a glass of water?'

She shook her head.

He gathered his hands together, elbows resting on his reddish-brown mahogany desk, awash with hand-scribbled sheets of paper: his magic carpets of inspiration, he called them.

'Out of the blue . . . Oh, God, Dom, I don't know how to tell you. A thunderbolt from my early life has arrived.'

He steepled his fingers, waiting.

Shoulders tight, she was staring at her younger self. Celia, naive, barely an adult.

'Let's hear it then, Ceely. Whatever this dark secret from your youth is, the skeleton in the cupboard.' He allowed a small smile, as though mildly amused.

She rubbed the heel of her right hand into her eye and took a deep breath. Even though she was safe here in this room with its shelves of books, seated close to the man she loved more than any other person in the world, she was trembling. 'Many moons ago, long before I met you, when I was twenty and it was summertime, I got myself involved with . . . with . . . well, the wrong sort.'

'The wrong sort?' Dominic frowned, leaned back in his chair. His eyes, pools of chocolate brown, were soft and forgiving as he gazed upon his lovely wife. She was such a small-framed creature, delicate for one with such a big heart and mighty passions. 'I'm sure this is nothing we can't handle, darling. You whip everything up into a storm.'

'I know you think I overreact, dramatize things, but this is . . .'

'Go on.' He smiled in encouragement.

'A gang of young men. Always kicking around together in a crowd in our town. One in particular I hung out with. If I'm honest, I was besotted with him. He was, like all of them, no good, but I couldn't see it then. He was handsome in a loutish kind of way. I would have described him as charismatic, but I was . . .' She fell silent and let out a long sigh. 'I was foolish, blind.'

Dominic rubbed thoughtfully at his chin. 'And you've bumped into him somewhere down on the Croisette in Cannes and, being big-hearted Ceely, you've invited him for the weekend's get-together. Well, there'll be plenty of lamb.' He laughed.

'Please, Dom, don't patronize me. Bear with this, let me . . . recount the tale as it happened.'

He was rather taken aback by her solemnity and her simple frankness. 'Apologies, my heart. On you go.'

'They were a gang of thieves. Worse.' Celia cleared her throat again, a tear rolled down her cheek. 'Saturday nights, we'd stroll aimlessly – well, I thought it was aimless – through the town. Suddenly, they'd slip stealthily into action. A car might be stolen. A motorbike. Me riding pillion, we roared off into the night. A shop window displaying television sets was smashed, items grabbed, glass in shards on the pavement.' Celia scratched her nose, replaying mental images from an era long buried.

'Were you involved in these thefts?' This was a little more serious than he had envisaged. An entirely other patina to Celia.

'Aside from climbing onto a stolen bike once, no, not at all. I was horrified when I began to get a sense of the gravity of what was going on, terrified of the consequences. The risks involved. At first I tried to ignore everything. All I wanted was to spend time with Terry, be in his company. Then I begged him to stop. To walk away from the others while he still could. "They're criminals," I wept. Terry scoffed, mocked me. He judged me a prude, brushed me roughly, physically away from him. He slapped me. Then he . . . he started to hit me.'

'Dear God.'

'He grew more violent towards me. He boasted he'd never get caught. Called me "chicken". In fact, he was the ringleader.'

Dominic frowned, taking the story in. 'Why didn't you stop seeing him?'

'I – I loved him, or thought I did. I was infatuated, I suppose, but I promised myself I'd keep away, never go near him again, run away from home, leave Bristol if necessary and then . . . then . . .' Her words dried.

'And then what?'

'I discovered I was pregnant.'

'Good Lord, Ceely, why have you never mentioned any of this?'

She shook her head. 'Stupid, stupid of me. I thought . . . thought I'd lose you.'

'Well, yes, that was pea-brained reasoning. How could you have doubted the depth of my love for you? Anyway, what happened?'

'I tried to persuade Terry to marry me. Of course he had no intention of making such a commitment. Told me in a brutal way that he didn't love me, that I meant –' she took a breath '– fuck-all to him. It was my fault, he said, that I'd got myself "knocked up". He ordered me to get rid of it or I'd be forced to deal with the consequences on my own. "Don't count on me." He threatened to stop seeing me. Of course I was devastated.'

'Dear God. What a gent.'

'I didn't know where to turn. My parents were away, here, on this estate. It was a couple of years after they'd bought the place. I was completely alone. Pregnant, broken-hearted and petrified.'

'My poor sweetheart.'

'Terry and his cronies were plunging themselves into ever more serious crime. An old man got battered, seriously injured, beaten with an iron bar when they broke into his shop. He tried to defend his till. He nearly died, spent weeks in intensive care in the hospital. It was on the evening news. In all the local papers. The search was on for the thugs who had committed the crime. I felt so ashamed, harboured thoughts of going to the police, hatched a plan to turn Terry in. I knew I had to break free. I knew it was dangerous but Terry's hold over me was too compelling, and he threatened me physically. I had nowhere to turn, I . . .' Celia picked at the sleeve of her blouse. She chose not to mention even now to Dominic how overwhelmed she had been by Terry, the force of her feelings for him, how desire had swept her along, left her without critical resilience. Even at twenty, she had become a shadow of her true self. She had grown weak, sick. And it had taken her years to rebuild that confidence, that sense of self.

'Go on, Celia.'

'I feared confiding in my parents who, in any case, were, as I said, over here, or our family doctor. Eventually, out of desperation and because my pregnancy was advancing, I confessed the bare bones to my father almost as soon as they stepped off the plane. He listened without a word of judgement. Then, obviously, inevitably, I poured out the whole sordid story to both of them. Mummy was equally forgiving. Looking back, I think she'd suspected some problem was brewing. Instinct had warned her.'

'And the unborn one?'

'I'd left it too late for the alternative. I gave birth to the baby, christened him David. Well, there was no baptism service. He was just a few days old when we gave him up to a local convent for adoption. My parents arranged everything.'

Dominic picked up a small tube of mints, put one into his mouth and began to suck it. Since he'd stopped smoking, years ago, the mints were a reflex when he was stressed, needed to think, or was blocked with his writing.

'Why on the eve of our celebrations are you pouring out this saga now?'

'David's here.'

'Here? You mean *here*? You stayed in touch?'

'I've never known anything of what happened to him, no details of his life, not even his name, aside from David, of course. I had more or less – I'm ashamed to admit this but, well, I'd put aside all feelings for him. You know, he was submerged in my past. A time of my life I'd wanted to break with. Then, out of the blue, at the beginning of this week I received a letter from him.'

'This week?'

'The note included a phone number. So, I made contact. And, well, you know how I am . . . I invited him to the party.'

'That doesn't surprise me.' Dominic helped himself to another Trebor mint.

'I collected him from Cannes railway station this morning. He's here.'

Dominic turned his head towards the window. He sat deliberating for what seemed to Celia an eternity. 'And you know nothing about where he's been educated, how he was brought up . . . whether he's a decent sort?'

'Not yet, no.'

'I see.'

'I'm so sorry, Dominic, to lay this on you, on us.'

'Well, we must make your . . . David welcome. Of course we must. That goes without saying.'

'And . . .'

'There's more?'

'He's brought his daughter with him. I wasn't expecting her.'

'Daughter, I see. And wife?'

Celia shook her head. 'They're divorced.'

Husband and wife sat in the room lined with books, shelf upon shelf of stories, of plot twists, of unpredictable endings. They were silent, lost in thought, both contemplating this new scenario and its impact on their present and future lives.

'Well, Ceely, my darling, for an actress of such meticulous timing, you could have played this one better.'

'Forgive me, Dominic.'

'Nothing to forgive, my dear. I'm just reconfiguring the landscape. A son and a granddaughter have appeared from out of nowhere while a grand soirée is looming for some of our most essential wine-purchasing clients.'

'I've been trying to break it to you for the last few days . . . what with Sally and Frank being ill and everyone so busy, though . . .'

'Is there anything you know about him?'

'Not very much.'

Dominic ran his hands through his hair, breathed in, sighed. 'And the daughter?'

'Nothing. I was unaware of her existence till this morning. She looks like a rather pretty boy but that's not uncommon, these days, is it? We've hardly exchanged a word.'

'You're certainly full of surprises, my love. Right, then,' he rose from his chair, tossed the mints onto his desk, 'I think I can safely say that that my writing's finished for today. By the way, what happened to his father, the Terry chap?'

'He died in prison. Or so I read. It was all ages ago.'

'In prison, I see.' Dominic rubbed his face and stood up. 'Quite a sordid history. Well, I'd better go and say hello to this . . . son. Introduce myself to – to your family. I'll see you downstairs.'

CHAPTER TWELVE

The soft click of the door, then silence. Celia's face dropped into her hands. Alone, she remained curled like a cat on Dominic's fireside chair. She wanted to give him space to take in the situation and, frankly, she felt too drained to move. It was her fault. She could have managed all this with far more grace, slowly welcoming her kin into their lives, finding a warm space for these strangers, accepting them proudly as her own. *If* they proved to be decent people. Poor Dominic.

She stood up and wandered over to his desk. He still wrote with a fountain pen. Only once that stage was completed did he feed his material into his computer and print it out. He never spoke about his work in progress, never discussed its subject. He was entirely private about his process, though Celia was always the first to read the finished product before it went flying off to Blake, his agent in London.

She ran her fingers over the pages without reading or even taking in the jumble of jotted words, the lists, character notes, plots. Then she drifted to the window, which looked out over the back of the house to the pool and terraces beneath, to a neighbour's olive-clad hills in the blue distance. She stood on tiptoe to take a good look at the lawns where the furniture was being arranged. Magali had left all the new linen cloths in neat piles ready to be secured to the table tops. As Celia's gaze roamed the grounds, her attention was caught by a figure at the pool, lying on her back on a sunbed under one of the open parasols. It was Gillian, topless, sunbathing in her knickers, her clothes in a heap on the wet tiles at her side.

'For Heaven's sake!' Celia pressed her face hard against the glass. Dominic's den was two storeys up from the ground floor and the pool was one level lower. Was her eyesight playing tricks? She glanced to and fro, wondering whether Tom and Sean were still working in the vicinity.

Might David be in his room unpacking or had he and Dominic already bumped into one another? She should find them. She had no problem with nudity. She and Dominic frequently skinny-dipped at the weekends when no one else was about or late in the evenings before they turned in for the night, but today the house and grounds were busy with people. She judged Gillian's behaviour a little inconsiderate. Lacking respect. Or was that old-fashioned?

Oh dear, first the cigarette and now this. She didn't want to begin her relationship with this unexpected, unannounced grandchild by issuing a list of dos and don'ts, a host of criticisms. Nonetheless, something would have to be said.

Celia made her way down the stairs, rounding the two flights until she reached the back kitchen and pantries, where Magali and Béatrice, a teenage girl from the village who worked at the estate from time to time, were surrounded by baking dishes, flour and sugar bags. The space closely resembled a ski resort. Magali had requested help for the weekend and Celia had given her *carte blanche* to choose two assistants for the preparations and one more for the dinner service, if required. Young Béatrice was the first of the team. She was a plump soul of sixteen or seventeen. Her face was dark pink, shiny and sweating from the heat of pots boiling, steam lifting from beneath the lids.

'Oh, Celia, you remember Béatrice, my cousin Josephine's youngest? She's agreed to lend a hand again this weekend.'

'That's very kind of you, Béatrice, thank you. It's lovely to see you. *Bienvenue.*'

'*Bonjour, Madame Celia.*' The girl bobbed a curtsy, which made Celia fight back a smile.

'We're making cakes,' sang Magali with pride. 'Or tarts to be more precise. A selection of puddings.'

'Marvellous. I hope someone's collecting those delicious apricots in the walled garden. Henri says they're as ripe as they're going to get. The birds will nab them if we don't harvest soon. Why don't you take a couple of kilos home with you, Béatrice, for your family? There are far too many for our purposes even with a party imminent.'

Béatrice said she had begun her morning at seven. She had walked up from the village before the heat 'bit her'. And, yes, her first chore had been to pick apricots with the gardener.

'She's managed nine kilos, another two of almonds and a few peaches. The baskets were laden, but the peaches are not ripe enough yet for these desserts,' explained Magali. 'I might find another way to use them.'

'Well done, Béatrice.'

The girl's moist pink cheeks positively glowed with pride. 'We fed the chickens too, and collected nine eggs. The old man plays music to his plants and animals.'

'Magali, have you seen Dominic?' Celia, engrossed in all the kitchen news, had forgotten Gillian and David.

'In the winter drawing room with that tall fellow who's just arrived.'

'How about ice cream? Or sorbet? Would the peaches serve for that if we boil hard and add lashings of sugar? cried Béatrice, pleased as Punch with her inspiration.

'Sorbets! Delicious in this heat and spot-on for dinner parties.' Celia smiled.

'I fetched them a chilled bottle of rosé at the boss's request.'

'Clever you, Béatrice. Yes, let's have a sorbet for an in-between course. Magali, can you hunt down the ice-cream maker? I haven't seen it all summer. Stored somewhere safe, no doubt.'

'I'm pretty sure I know where it's hiding. In the second pantry, if my memory serves me.'

'We'll have a late lunch, if that works for you both. Something simple. I don't want to take up your precious baking time. Salad, cheeses, cold meats will do the trick. Can you lay up for four, please, Magali? On the terrace above the pool. Thank you.' Celia stepped backwards out of the kitchen. 'God, those tarts smell delicious. Well done, both of you.' She winked and hurried along the back corridor towards the drawing room, where she heard the soft hum of male voices deep in conversation. She knocked lightly. 'May I come in?'

'Of course, darling. Silly to ask.'

Dominic's tone had softened, she was relieved to hear.

The two men were seated either side of the fireplace facing one another in the wing-backed chairs she and Dominic used during the colder months when the room came into its own. Between them, Daisy was sleeping peacefully on a rug. Each man had a glass of rosé at his elbow on the occasional tables beside the chairs. David half lifted himself from his seat as Celia entered.

'Ready for a small rosé, Ceely?' asked Dominic.

She shook her head. 'I'll hang on, thanks. Please, do sit down, David. No need for ceremony here. I've asked Magali to prepare lunch on the terrace. Will Gillian want to eat with us, David?'

'Why not? She's down at the pool or was a short while ago.' David bent towards the Collie and stroked her head. The dog nudged closer to his arm and rested her muzzle on his shoe.

Celia threw a glance in Dominic's direction. Had he caught sight of David's daughter sunbathing? Had anyone noticed her by the pool? Celia had expected Magali to remark upon the newcomer's attire or lack of it, to be surprised or a tad shocked by the semi-nudity, but perhaps she'd been too busy to pay attention.

'David's been filling me in on his past. He grew up in Kent on a small hops and livestock farm near the sea where his parents were tenant farmers. Isn't that so, David?'

David flashed a glance at Celia and nodded.

'I confessed that this has all come as a bit of a surprise. Still, it's a pleasure to welcome you into the family, David, even at this late stage.'

Celia, now perched on a small leather ottoman, swung her attention towards her son. Her son, her granddaughter, this was all going to take some getting used to.

'I hope we aren't intruding? I – I hadn't realized we were, that I am . . . a secret.'

'You're not. Not at all. It's lovely you're here. We're enormously looking forward to getting to know you, aren't we, Dom? Gillian, too, of course. I wonder if I might just ask, David . . . I spotted her a short while ago by the pool . . .'

'Gillian loves to swim and a pool of her own is a luxury way beyond our more humble lifestyle. I hope you don't mind that she just dives in. All this . . .' he waved an arm about '. . . well, it's a bit of a fantasy, really. We weren't expecting such grandeur. Of course, given how famous you are—'

Dominic coughed and swallowed a mouthful of wine.

'That's what pools are for. Diving in. You might just mention to her that it's – erm – probably best if she wears a bathing costume or a bikini, when there are people milling about.'

'What?' David let out an embarrassed guffaw, tugged uneasily at the open neck of his pale blue shirt. Celia noticed it was slightly frayed at the collar. 'I'm sure she hadn't intended to offend or shock. I'll have a word with her.'

Dominic was refilling the glasses. He winked at Celia as he stood up and took a step in David's direction to pour the pink wine into his glass. 'Yes, better you do. We have some very handsome young chaps on the premises at present. It's all very casual here, but possibly not quite that relaxed. And our septuagenarian gardener, Henri, a longtime widower, might have a heart attack.'

Each of the three laughed politely. Dominic was certainly making an effort on his wife's behalf. She wanted to kiss him. Celia lifted herself from the stool and rubbed her lower back. 'Right, let's get lunch rolling. Dominic, shall we say in ten minutes on the magnolia terrace? You bring David. I'll try to find Gillian. Anything you don't eat, any food allergies, David?'

'It's all looking too good to be true.' He grinned. 'I'm sure the grub'll be equally fantastic.'

'Lunch is usually very simple but I'd better know for dinner tonight. Our doctor will be turning up at some point. Here in time for apéritifs, he's promised. Accompanied by his latest wife. Third or fourth, we've lost count. He's Italian, speaks impeccable English so no worries on that score. He'll be driving over from San Remo where his elderly mother still lives.'

'I'm no trouble. Anything you put in front of me, I'll devour. Gill's a no-meat girl, I'm afraid. Vegetarian, occasionally vegan, bit uptight about it all, but I'm sure she'll find something that will keep her happy. In a paradise such as this, how could she not?'

Celia was silently wondering whether Gillian would prove a bit of a headache. She smiled encouragingly. 'I'll ask Magali to rustle up an omelette or a burrata salad with our neighbour's olive oil and tomatoes picked from the vines by Henri this morning. Don't worry, she won't go hungry. The fridges are groaning, all set for tomorrow. See you both shortly.' And with that Celia hurried from the room, back towards the kitchens. There was still so much to organize.

She decided to run down to the pool first, to ask her granddaughter to get dressed for lunch. Granddaughter? That bizarre girl? It seemed so implausible. When Celia reached the deck with the sunbeds, there was no one, only the outline of a wet body on one wooden lounger, and the relentless droning of cicadas out of sight. The parasols were fluttering. A breeze had picked up, but it did nothing to disperse the sultriness of the early afternoon. 'Gillian!' Celia's trained voice rang out.

The girl's clothes had gone so perhaps she had returned inside. Had anyone shown her which room had been assigned to her? Should Celia go in search of her? She had wanted to check the table, ask dear, patient overworked Magali to add a cold vegetable dish or an omelette to the menu, but would Gillian refuse eggs? Celia pushed her hair off her hot face. They didn't need this extra stress.

Where had David's daughter disappeared to? Might she be roaming the corridors, lost? Celia decided it was remiss of her not to to show her guest, relative, where she was to sleep. Common hospitality.

Having made up her mind, she retraced her steps up the stone staircase, past the goddesses, swerving to the left. Hearing an engine start, she glanced back across to the lower lawn. Henri was on the *tracteur tondeuse*, their splendid John Deere ride-on mower. He was giving the grass, sad and dry from lack of rain, a final trim before everything was locked in place for the Saturday-evening festivities. Oh, it was going to be magical. Already, the two rows of lemon trees added a southern Mediterranean ambience to the scene. Perfect. Sean, the young Irish student, who was revealing himself as a sensitive and industrious soul, was skipping between the lemon trees with a long hosepipe, watering them. They were standing in the ghastly black plastic tubs they had been delivered in.

Celia stopped in her tracks. Where were the elegant vintage terracotta jars she had ordered from her friend, Pierre Cluzy, a well-known potter living in Vallauris? The pots or jars were intended as containers for the trees for the duration of the party weekend before they were moved elsewhere for planting. Had they even been delivered? How had she overlooked this important detail? She had no memory of signing for them. Might Dominic have done so and failed to mention it? Celia turned again from her ascending path, back down the staircase towards the lawns.

She must ask Henri about the terracotta pots. If they hadn't been delivered, she would be obliged to cover the hideous containers: they were far too ugly to leave exposed. She descended two steps. In the far distance, she caught sight of

Gillian sitting cross-legged like a Buddha in the shade, back upright against the trunk of one of the umbrella pines, fully dressed in the clothes she had arrived in. Surely they were damp.

Celia lifted her right hand high to the pure blue sky, waving it frantically above her head. Her bracelets rattled and glinted as her arm swept the horizon. 'Gillian!' No reaction. The girl couldn't hear her. Celia let drop her arm. Leave her be. She'd find them for lunch if she was hungry. Otherwise, better she make herself at home at her own pace, in her own fashion.

She, Celia, needed to be cool and composed about this unlikely addition to the family. But what a huge weight off her mind that Dominic had accepted David with such good grace. Celia was deliberating now about whether to go back up to the terrace, so lunch wasn't delayed, or step down to where Henri and Sean were working and find out about the terracotta pots. She decided to return to the house. She'd telephone the potter when his *atelier* reopened after the midday break. Meanwhile, a bite with the others, and a much-needed glass of wine. It wasn't even two o'clock; she felt limp, as though she had been on the go for days.

Hardly surprising. It wasn't every day one acquired a new family.

CHAPTER THIRTEEN

Dominic and David were already installed at the round table, legs outstretched, relaxing in the shade of the magnificent centenarian *Magnolia grandiflora*, which was in full blossom. Daisy, who appeared to have taken a shine to David, was pressed against the arm of his chair, prodding him with her paw for yet more caresses. The men were engrossed in conversation. Evidently Dominic had found a point of contact with his stepson. Stepson! It was all so improbable. Aside from Celia's short car journey with David earlier, she had barely spoken to him. Too busy, occupied, but wasn't there also an underlying dread of unlocking this relationship, of picking it apart?

Disclosing the existence of Terry Strait to Dominic earlier had unearthed a host of painful memories, all, until today, neatly sealed away. Terry's violence towards her and the years it had taken her to rebuild, to heal herself.

At the time, so long ago, she had felt grief at the loss of her baby boy, of course she had, but it had also been with a sense of relief that she had given him up for adoption. At twenty she hadn't been prepared for motherhood. Most of the turbulence and despair she had suffered in those years had been seeded by Terry and his acts of cruelty. The cold realization that she had meant nothing to him, that their relationship, her love, had been of no matter, that the knowledge of a child, his child, had sent him spinning into a violent rage, had withered, diminished, her. She had convinced herself that he was a young man of vigour and potency, blocking out the facts. She had denied the reality: Terry was sadistic, a delinquent who had taken pleasure in hurting others, in causing pain. Most especially the suffering he had inflicted on Celia.

Now a grown man had walked into her life. Forty-seven years old. She still remembered his April birth. Of course she did. Terry's son. Might David have inherited any of his father's traits? The violence, the lack of social responsibility? Terry's criminal streak? Was it in his DNA? Thus far, David had shown himself to be considerate, thoughtful, ill at ease, perhaps, but certainly not cocky or cruel like his father. Of course, it was early days. Little of the inner man had yet been revealed.

Dominic beckoned her towards them. 'Ceely, we're waiting, come and join us.'

'On my way.'

David turned his head. His face lit up when he saw her. He was a handsome, imposing man. His physical appearance had taken Celia by surprise. Several inches taller than his father, broad-shouldered with big solid hands, a working man's hands. He bore no likeness to Terry, or none that she could recollect, but she hadn't known Terry in middle age. Neither did David take after her. He hadn't inherited her colouring or her lightweight build, her Titian hair, freckled complexion. Her porcelain looks. David was a sturdy, muscular bloke who, as far as she could tell, resembled neither of his parents.

Aside from the lack of physical similarities, his manner, personality, also seemed dissimilar. Mother and son in name, a kinship stamped on a form, a sheet of paper, lost for ever.

No deep emotional attachment had kicked in from her side. Should it have? Should she have experienced a significant life-changing hit deep down in her solar plexus? A sort of cheesy light-bulb moment, causing much hugging and tears, as you might see in a film?

Mum!

Welcome home, Son!

Did she lack the prerequisite maternal instincts? Was she cold, heartless?

And then there was Gillian. Granddaughter, dear God! An oddball or just an ordinary modern young woman? Celia doubted there would be a smooth path forward for either of them.

As she crossed the terrace, David watching her every step, she was debating whether she was capable of giving this a go. Of embracing this new and, frankly, ill-matched family?

She arrived at the table. Dominic was pouring her a glass of wine. He was not the easiest of partners, but she felt an overwhelming gratitude to him for taking David on, for engaging with the newcomer who, from today onwards, would be a fixture in their lives.

The perfume of the waxy white-cupped magnolia flowers humming with honeybees took her breath away, diffusing her nagging doubts. 'Oh, my word, that scent is fabulous. David, do you like flowers? Do you know anything about plants? Since we moved here, I find myself getting excited every single day about this or that tiny discovery.'

'Sit down, Ceely, relax.'

She was babbling, giving no opportunity for anyone to respond. 'Lord, I'm starving. Ah, perfect timing, here comes Magali.'

Magali was approaching along the path that led from the kitchen. She was carrying a laden tray, taking her time.

'Here, Mags, let me take that.' Dominic stood, his white linen napkin falling to the stone-tiled terrace.

Celia swooped to her husband's feet and gathered it up, refolding it and setting it to the side, while Magali offloaded a variety of dishes onto the immaculately shaded table.

'Heaven's above,' muttered David, eyeing the plates of food.

'You must be starving,' Celia chipped in. 'Did they serve you breakfast on the Eurostar? Appallingly, they don't on the French lines, not even in First.'

'We stayed in Paris last night. Got the early train down this morning. Grabbed a couple of croissants at the station.'

'I've brought another bottle of rosé and the corkscrew,' said Magali. 'And some chilled San Pellegrino for you, Celia.'

'Marvellous, thank you. We might only be three but let's leave the extra setting in case.' She picked up the clean napkin laid for Gillian and handed it to Dominic.

Magali nodded. She was cutting bread. The knife she was using was so impressive it might have been a scythe. She held the loaf tight to her bosom and sawed at it, brown slices falling like early autumn leaves onto the breadboard. David watched, spellbound.

'Gillian's off somewhere communing with Nature,' Celia informed her lunch companions.

'She'll be taking all this in then, preparing a sketch or two, no doubt.'

'Oh, does she draw?'

'Draw? She's fantastic, studying at the fine-art college in Kingston. I'm a very proud man. Why do you think we have so many bags? She's lugged all her paints and brushes along with her so she can work here. It's been a bit of a palaver.'

'But how marvellous. I look forward to seeing some of her work. An artist in the family . . . that's splendid.'

'I've a talented and famous mother who used never to be off the telly whom I admired and adored even before I knew, erm, the facts, and now Gillian's all set to make a name for herself.'

Celia lowered her head.

Dominic reached for the bottle in the cooler. 'More wine, David?' He smiled.

Celia spoke to Pierre, the potter, on the telephone directly after lunch. He confirmed that the delivery would be made at the latest on Saturday morning. She was dismayed. 'That's cutting it fine, Pierre. Any chance you could make a huge effort and whisk the jars over here this evening, no matter how late?'

'My driver's called in sick. Well, it's his wife. But I'll see what I can do.'

'And we look forward to welcoming you and Ghislaine for dinner tomorrow evening. Don't forget.'

'How could we? No one throws a party like you, Celia. And it's been too long, what with all these lockdowns. See you tomorrow.'

On the matter of the pots, there was little more Celia could do, but over lunch an idea had been hatching. IF the antique pots remained absent, who might be capable of designing some paper covering for the black tubs? Well, it would have been Sally, of course, but as it turned out, fortuitously, there was now another artist in the family. It had occurred to Celia, as she listened to David sing his daughter's praises, that this could be the ideal opportunity to reach out and create a bond between herself and her granddaughter.

After she had put the phone down, she headed up to Gillian's room on the top landing, where the girl had been directed by Magali, having failed to show for lunch.

CHAPTER FOURTEEN

'Gillian,' Celia whispered, into the wooden door. 'Gillian, are you in there?'

'I'm doing my yoga.'

'Sorry to disturb you. When would be a good opportunity to . . .?'

After several moments of shuffling sounds, the door was unbolted and pulled open.

The women surveyed one another.

'Sorry to disturb.' Celia noticed Gillian's face was beaded with sweat and flushed, her prominent cheekbones slightly burned. She had caught the sun.

The girl stepped backwards, drawing wide the entrance to the room. 'Come in.'

'I do apologize. I had no idea . . .'

'Why would you unless Dave warned you? It's no big deal. Don't look so concerned. And sorry I was topless by the pool, didn't think. Dave sent me a text. Told me to keep my kit on. It's just so hot.'

'Your father says you're a painter.'

'Yeah, I am.'

'I might have a small assignment for you, if you'd be willing to help me out.'

Gillian, in stretchy shorts and tank top, threw herself onto the single bed and tucked her bare feet beneath her thighs in a meditative pose. Celia hovered by the door. There were clothes and plimsolls and boxes of various shapes and sizes everywhere. The floor was engulfed in the contents of Gillian's two bags. Several rolled-up canvases were standing upright. Bits of paint-daubed cloth hung from the sill. The window was wide open letting in a stream of air. Where on earth had she found space to practise her yoga?'

'Are you working on something at present?'

'I'm always working on something. Why don't you come in? You look awkward and it makes me uncomfortable. It's your house.'

Celia waded through the chaos to the vintage school desk tucked away in the far corner of the cramped space. There she lowered herself onto a raffia and wood chair. She took a breath and inhaled a whiff of cigarette smoke. Unmistakably.

Gillian had been smoking in here. Celia bit the inside of her lip, forcing herself not to mention it. 'Do you need a larger room? I hadn't taken into account that you might have all this – this material with you. Well, I hadn't known about you at all.' She laughed. It came across as somewhere between a joke and an anxious, rather desperate plea.

'I'm fine here, Celia. What's the job?'

Celia poured out her concerns about the belated delivery of the vintage pots. 'If they're not here by tomorrow morning, I'll need to improvise.'

Gillian listened in silence, watching with eyes that pierced you, following you everywhere, missing nothing, inscrutable in her stillness. In one so young, it was a little unnerving.

'And so I thought of you.' Celia clapped her hands together. 'What do you say?'

'Sure, I could do that. You want me to begin right away or wait and see whether your fancy jars get dropped off? Twenty will take me some time, though. I can't just knock this up in an hour.'

'No, of course not.'

'You want me to paint the plastic uglies in funky colours? You know, like loud and psychedelic? Or do you prefer I try to camouflage them? A more subtle approach. With leaves and plants and stuff? Nature-themed.'

Celia gave it some thought. 'Which do you think?' She was keen that Gillian choose a solution she felt comfortable with.

'Leaves and vegetal matter will take longer because I have to collect all the material first, then work out a design. Create the look. But I think it will be more effective, more in keeping with your glamorous style – you know, the elegant well-dressed house and all the land and everything.'

'I'll leave it to you, then.'

'I'll ask the old gardener bloke to lend me a wheelbarrow and some secateurs, if that's cool with you?'

'Henri. Henri is the gardener. Yes, of course. He couldn't be more accommodating.'

'And I can take bits of branches, maybe a few flowers from wherever I like?'

'Well, yes, within reason. No lopping branches from the lemon trees.'

'I'm not stupid, Celia. Are you intending to pay me for this work, a day and a half's labour?'

'Pay you? Well, I . . .'

'It's a commission, right?'

Celia lowered her head, stared at the palms of her hands, fiddled with her wedding ring. 'I had seen it more as . . .'

'What?' Gillian glared at her.

'Everyone in the family doing their bit to help the party go with a swing.'

'The family! Ha! And if I wasn't here what would you do? How much have you shelled out for the fancy pots?'

Celia lifted herself from the chair. 'I think we'll just forget about it, Gillian. I'd seen it as an opportunity for us to create something together, get to know one another.'

'Fine, no probs. I just want to know where we stand. Cool, I'll do it for free.'

'I'd really rather we forget about it.'

'What – and spoil the design and atmos of the evening with those unsightly planters? You're clearly such a perfectionist and this is your paradise. It'll bother you – the whole weekend you'll be fussing. In any case, they're unsightly. Really jarring. Ha-ha.'

'Yes, they are . . .' Celia needed to get on. She also wanted to terminate this conversation in an amicable fashion. 'Why don't you do what you think is appropriate in the time available to you and we can talk about recompense later?'

'Actually, I don't want any cash, thanks. I just wonder at your sense of entitlement. The poor relatives, let them do the donkey work.'

Celia was winded, taken aback. There was a hardness in the girl's features that conjured up, flashing before her, a cold grey stare that surfaced from a lifetime ago. Terry's face contorted with rage. The memory so possessed her that she couldn't banish it. 'Forgive me,' she was floundering, 'if I've offended you. I was trying to construct . . . a . . . bridge, a way forward for the pair of us. Clumsily done on my part. Apologies.'

'Can I just say something to you, Celia? You know, straight up and to the point.' Gillian pulled her legs out from under her as though she were readying herself for confrontation.

A physical dread stabbed at Celia's heart. 'What?'

'Connecting with you means the world to Dave.'

'Why do you call—'

'To Dad. Yeah, Dad. Personally, I think it's a bit sad, pathetic actually. I mean you're just a rich old lady, right?'

'Well, we're not—'

'Dave's nothing to you. You never tried to find him, did you? To learn how he was getting on, whether life was treating him in a decent way. Did you ever ask yourself whether he was still alive, what had become of him? Your son? Flesh and blood.'

Celia was dumbstruck. Shocked and hurt. A coil of misery rose up within her and caught in her throat. The dredging of a long-forgotten heartache. She fought against it, Terry's rejection of her, his physical terrorizing of her. Her desire to erase the entire episode. 'It's true, Gillian, I didn't tried to find David. You're perfectly correct on that score. There were reasons why . . . but, when David contacted me, I didn't shy away. I didn't refuse to meet him. I picked up the phone and called him directly. And you are both here, in our home. And will always be welcome back because we are indeed related. Please, don't be so angry, Gillian. This is not easy for any of us.'

The girl shrugged, scratched at the white bedcover with her fingers. Her nails were painted navy blue, but the varnish was chipped.

'This is as weird for me as it must be for you.'

Silence.

'Can we give it another go? Start again. I accept I've wrong-footed, and I apologize. I haven't had a lot of practice at being a mother. None, in fact. A stepmum, yes, but certainly no experience at slipping into the role of grandmother . . . Goodness, no. Come here.' She took clumsy steps with her arms outstretched, careful to negotiate the debris on the floor, terrified of stepping on a precious object, breaking it, stirring up further wrath. 'Give me a hug.'

There was no response.

'Please, Gillian.'

Gillian held her position. Her head was lowered, her gaze directed towards her crossed legs, physically refusing to let Celia in. Celia wasn't sure whether the girl was still angry or crying. Celia bent low and locked her arms around the young bony shoulders. It was an awkward position, clumsy. She felt the heat of the girl's body, the confusion, the jangle of emotions. She rested her cheek against the dark cropped head, the hair sticky with gel, which smelled sickly sweet. 'Let's try to be friends, Gill, shall we?'

Footsteps were hurrying along the corridor, up and down stairs.

'How about we try to learn from one another, Gill, across the generations? That'd be a fun challenge, no?'

'Celia! Ceely, darling!' Dominic was calling her. 'Federico's arrived.'

Celia's instinct was to hurry away, extricate herself, but she stayed put. 'Shall we give it another go?'

Gillian shrugged. Celia accepted it as a tentative softening, an accord. She buried a quick kiss on Gillian's still bent head and skipped from the room. 'See you later. We'll have a . . . blast together,' she whispered as she closed the door.

'Federico, Freddie!' Her footsteps tumbled down the stairs, curving the two flights.

'*Ciao, bella*. Sorry we're a little late. The coast road is crammed with *i turisti*. How are you? Beautiful as ever, *bellissima*.'

CHAPTER FIFTEEN

Preparations were afoot for dinner on the terrace beneath the magnolia. Shadows and bats were dancing about the partially laid table in the falling light. Tom and Sean had offered to grill some chicken on the barbecue. The poultry was to be served with a heaving bowl of fresh Italian *fettucine* brought from San Remo by Federico. It was ready for boiling in a mighty cauldron in the kitchen. Tom had suggested it might ease the workload for Magali and her two assistants, who were enclosed within steamy rooms, endlessly cooking dishes for the following evening's banquet.

Wines were being brought up by the dozen from the cellars. This was Dominic's domain: *maître caviste*, cellar master, a responsibility in which he took the greatest delight. Presently, he was underground with their estate manager, Claude, his close friend, ally, the man who had taught him everything he knew about producing quality wines. On this matter, they were brothers, kindred spirits.

Three fridges in the larger of the two pantries were being stocked with two *cuvées* of white wine, both from 2018. One had recently won gold at the renowned Paris Wine Fair, Porte de Versailles. The wine had been singled out by the experts for its delicate hints of the *garrigue*, its 'herbaceous peppery Provençal aromas'. This was the first time a wine from the estate had been awarded a medal, a gold at that. It was another reason to celebrate, to holler it loud to all their clients and buyers. Of course, the news had already been sent out on their bi-monthly Les Roches du Soleil newsletter, composed by Celia upstairs in her tiny office.

The rosé Dominic and Claude had chosen for this weekend hailed from their 2021 vintage, a 'light, unpretentious wine' that could be served with most summer dishes. Several crates of their finest deep, dark reds were also being carried up this evening to settle overnight in one of the pantries. In the late morning the men would begin decanting them, giving the wines time to breathe before being served at the following evening's feast. The reds would be a triumph, both men agreed. 'As gratifying to the palate as biting into a perfectly ripe, home-grown plum,' boasted Dominic, with pride. And both would make excellent companions to Celia's choice of spit-roast lamb, which perhaps, on reflection, was not such a bad option.

Tonight they would be ten: Tom, Sean, Claude and Henri, Federico hanging on the slender arm of his beautiful young

Spanish wife, Valeria, who clung to him as though she feared he might disappear, David and Gillian, and their gracious hosts, Celia and Dominic, who were obliged, though never at the same time, to jump up from their seats to answer questions from the kitchen or make last-minute decisions. Every member of staff, including the small but well-coordinated wine team, was working flat out, but no one objected or complained. A mood of excitement fizzed in the air, fevering the falling light.

Still the jars from Vallauris had not made an appearance. Celia had hoped that Pierre, after their phone conversation, would have found a means of delivering this evening. Instead she had received another call from him, fifteen minutes before everyone was due to congregate for a light, bubbly rosé as a welcome aperitif. He was mumbling a stream of apologies. His driver's wife had gone into labour. The baby was a month early. Of course, no one had foreseen this. The employee had rung in to say that he wouldn't be able to work on Saturday, and would most likely not be available until the following Wednesday.

'I'm going to try to close the pottery early and deliver them myself but it won't be before mid to late afternoon tomorrow.'

'*Merci beaucoup*, Pierre, for your efforts.'

Deflating news, but no more to be done.

Celia's options lay between keeping her fingers firmly crossed that if and when the jars did show up she could organize sufficient hands to settle the lemon trees, still earthbound in the black tubs, into the terracotta jars without any hassles or breakages, at breakneck speed. The jars were heavy, each weighing close to forty kilos; they needed to be transported from the front of the house where the truck would deposit them to the back terrace and, from there, conveyed down the stone stairs all the way to the banquet strip. Tomorrow, Saturday morning, the trees were to be garlanded with fairy lights, which would make them difficult to manoeuvre. Boughs with electric wires hanging from them might get entangled, or snap. It could all go horribly wrong.

Or she could have another word with Gillian. That was what she chose to do.

In fact, the plan in Celia's mind had expanded.

All it needed was Gillian's cooperation.

After searching here and there, Celia found her in the back living room, sifting through a stack of CDs. 'Don't you guys have Spotify?'

'Spotify? Erm, possibly not. No, I don't think so. Gill, I wanted to ask if . . .'

Gillian was waving a disk of Joni Mitchell's *Blue*. 'I was looking for some Bowie. You must have Bowie. I read that Joni gave her kid up for adoption. Did you know that?'

Celia hadn't and chose to ignore it now. 'Gillian, I was hoping you might design the lighting on the trees as well as decorating the black plastic horrors.'

Gillian, dressed in jeans, black ankle boots and a crisp white shirt, tossed the CD onto the floor next to the chair where she was seated. Celia resisted the temptation to pick it up and slide it back into its cover.

'Sure,' Gillian answered, without fuss.

Celia smiled, observing that the girl had put on some makeup. Her grey eyes were encircled with a darker-grey kohl. She found herself thinking how beautiful Gillian was in a startling, post-punk way. Her skin was so pale it was like powder snow, clear and soft, in stark contrast to her black gelled hair and the heavy eye make-up.

'So, you're putting me in charge of the lighting and the pot decorations. Kind of Mistress of Set Design. Is that the gig?'

'If you're happy to do both, yes.'

'Cool. I'll begin now.'

'Don't be . . .' She laid a hand on Gillian's crossed leg, instinctively thinking to withdraw it. Instead she allowed it to rest there. 'If you begin early tomorrow morning, you should have sufficient time. Shall I ask one of our young helpers, Tom or Sean, to give you a hand with the collection of twigs and flowers?'

'Yeah, that'd be ace. It'll be easier for me if one of the blokes can help with the limbing. If I need a ladder and chainsaw.'

Celia frowned. 'I don't think we need to go as far as lopping branches off trees.'

'Yeah, we might. I've had a really neat idea. I was thinking about it after you left my room. I could start with pine foliage. You know, use it like a base note when creating perfume. Thick bushy boughs of green pine needles with cones still attached.' She was using her arms to paint her ideas visually in the air. 'They'll make it dead easy to cover the black containers. If there's time, I'll silver spray the cones. Then I'll decorate the foliage with lights and softer vegetation. Bring in some contrast, a few of your creamy white roses. It'll be kind of sparkly too. If you've got any canisters of silver spray, that'd be stellar.'

Her enthusiasm awakened in Celia the desire to participate, to go along with whatever ideas Gillian threw at her. 'I'll take a bet that we'll find spray among all our Christmas decorations tucked away in one of the sheds. Anything else you need?'

'Cool. Tell me where to find the decs and I'll dig out the spray this evening.'

Celia rose to her feet and held out her hand to Gillian, which after a moment's hesitation, the girl accepted. She steered her grandchild outside through tall French windows to a courtyard. Crunching on the gravel, they crossed to a *hangar*, erected at the far end of a row of stables.

Gillian popped her head over one of the stable doors. 'You got horses, Celia?'

Celia shook her head. 'Not since before my parents were here.'

'You should have horses. Dave loves them. He grew up with them.'

Without breaking her step, Celia led the way onwards to an enormous barn. Here, she pushed against a heavy door and they stepped inside.

'Wow! This is bloody amazing.' Gillian's head was tilted towards the tiled roof held in place by a skilful criss-cross structure of massive dark French oak beams.

'It dates back to the eighteenth century, same period as the construction of the main house. The stables and all these outbuildings are the originals.'

The ring in Gillian's nose caught the beam of light from outside and glinted as she turned in circles lifting her arms as though about to take flight. 'This'd make the most brilliant artist's studio.' She laughed. 'I think I'll bag it for myself. Can I?'

It warmed Celia's heart to see such pleasure in the girl's face. 'Why not?' She smiled.

'Promise? Okay, let's hit the decs.'

'Blimey, these are heavy. Celia, can you give me a hand here?'

Together, from a row of modern slatted wooden shelves installed during her parents' tenure, they lifted down one cardboard box after another and placed them on the ground All were laced with dust and cobwebs. The side of each carton was carefully labelled in Celia's handwriting: 'Christmas Decorations – 1', 'Christmas Decorations – 2', and then a third, followed by further cartons containing 'Hanging Glass Balls', 'Garlands of Flashing Lights' . . .

'You've got everything, haven't you, Ceely? Your home is the Promised Land, eh? An island of sanity in a world of pain.'

Ceely?

Celia was taken aback. Gillian must have overheard Dominic calling her by his pet name for her. Did she mind that their intimacy had been borrowed? No, not under the circumstances. In fact, she found it rather endearing.

'What's your nickname, Gillian? Do you have one?'

Gillian was on the earth floor, on all fours, arms buried in a box crammed with paper chains, frilly expanding paper bells and other outmoded odds and sods. 'These are all a bit tawdry, don't you think, Ceely?'

'Goodness me, yes, you're right. Christmas baubles from when my father and mother first came here. Probably time to throw them all out.'

'I don't have a nickname. Gillian or Gill's good. I answer to both.'

'What did your parents call you when you were small? They must have had an affectionate, a pet name for you.'

The girl froze as though under fire. 'I really don't remember, Ceely.'

Celia frowned. Plainly, she had touched a raw nerve. Had she or Dominic learned where David and daughter had spent the girl's childhood years? She was combing through previous conversations trying to recall the facts David had furnished. He had grown up in Kent, Dominic had mentioned that. Nothing about Gillian.

They really did need more information.

'Do you still live at home with your mum?'

Gillian shook her head. 'I'm at college, Ceely, remember? We discussed it.'

'Yes, that's right, sorry, we did. Do you have a boyfriend? Someone from college maybe?'

Celia was standing over her granddaughter. Granddaughter. It was still mind-boggling, though she was warming to the idea. She was watching the girl prodding and ploughing through the falling-to-pieces boxes.

'I identify as non-binary, Celia.' Gillian lifted her head and her probing eyes met the older woman's.

'Oh?'

'I'm bi. That's bisexual.'

'I know what bisexual is.'

The girl threw back her head and laughed. 'You look a bit freaked. It's not complicated or scary so don't get twitchy. It just means I don't see myself locked into being a woman who only couples with blokes, though I'm into blokes too. It's pretty straightforward. You're cisgender, I'm not. And that's how it goes.'

Celia shifted the weight on her feet. She felt she was getting out of her depth and wanted to change the subject. 'Found anything?'

Gillian eyed her with an unflinching gaze, before breaking into a grin. 'Moving right along, eh, Ceely? There are no glitter sprays among all this kitsch junk. Push over the next box, if you will, please. I hope you'll be updating your decs. This lot's from the Ark.'

Celia delivered the second load and bent low to help. Together they rummaged through five grubby boxes. 'Bingo! Two canisters. We're in business.' Gillian settled back on her haunches, one canister in each hand as though she were holding a pair of trophies. She shook both to ascertain how full they were. 'We might need to buy more. Or, I'll go easy on the silver detail. How many people do you have here for Christmas, Ceely?'

'Not many, only close family. Some years we have a larger get-together for New Year's Eve. I prefer Christmas to be intimate with loved ones.'

'Loved ones,' Gillian repeated, closing her eyes. 'I'm trying to picture it. Harmony. Laughter. Present-giving.

Where do you place the tree? I bet its humungous, an exquisitely structured blue pine that stands in the great hallway alongside that very impressive flight of stairs that sweeps up all those floors, as though you were in a palace. Who decorates it? You?'

Celia heard voices from somewhere beyond the great shed where they were standing, disintegrating half-empty cartons scattered about their feet. The knees of Gillian's jeans were patched with earth and bits of straw. She was slapping off the dirt with the flat of her hand.

The voices had brought Celia back to the present. She had lost track of the time. 'My goodness, it's after seven.' She had momentarily forgotten Gillian's questions. 'We ought to get back. I need to be there. Will you put away all these boxes for me, then come and join us? Dominic will be serving an apéritif shortly.'

'Can I come back for Christmas, spend the hols here? I could set up a studio in this old barn and I'd decorate your tree for you. We could throw this rubbish out, buy new stuff. It'll be magnificent.'

'What?'

'Can I come and spend Christmas here with you and Dominic? You know, loved ones, family and all that. Merrily, merrily on high.' She jiggled one of the canisters as though it was maracas and she was making rumba music. Her face lit up when she smiled. The silver ring shone in her nose, whose tip was rouged from the sun, and her uneven teeth glistened white but not a perfect white. One of the upper two incisors was slightly chipped, but the look was not unattractive.

Celia, whose attention had been elsewhere, concentrating on the house and her complicated party plans for the morrow, swung back to the girl. There was such vulnerability in her plea that she felt overwhelmed with affection towards her. It hadn't been a flippant request. Gillian had meant it. Belonging. She was looking to belong. This girl was her granddaughter. It was all too extraordinary, but not unpleasing.

'Don't you spend the holidays with your father, or your mother? What about siblings?'

Gillian lowered herself, crouching beside the first container, and started slinging the scattered items back into it, closing the flaps with an edge of anger, or was it hurt? 'I have no brothers or sisters. Just *moi*.'

'But you have your parents? David, your father is . . .' Celia had also been an only child. Perhaps the isolation, loneliness, explained why she had attached herself so vehemently, recklessly, mistakenly to Terry.

Gillian had hauled the first box back on to its shelf and was propelling the second with her feet as though dribbling a football.

'Yeah, my father. Sure. Santa Claus personified. Down at the pub with his mates. Listen, I shouldn't have asked. Sorry for overstepping the mark. I got carried away.' She started to hum 'White Christmas', sounding like an angry wasp.

Box two was now positioned next to its companion. Celia hooked her hand around Gillian's arm. The polyester shirt sleeve sent a teeny electric charge through her fingers. She was filled with unexpected love for her.

'If you'd like to come and stay with us for Christmas then of course you're very welcome.'

Gillian shrugged her arm free. 'You're embarrassed by Dave and me. We're not your type, not your class.'

'That's not fair, and it's not true!'

'You get on. I'll finish these and see you out back in a bit.'

'I mean it, Gillian. Please accept this as an official invitation to celebrate Christmas with us. And I promise to set you up in a bigger room with plenty of space for your paints, yoga mat and everything else you need.'

'Thanks, but no thanks. I don't need your pity.'

'Pity? No, no, you're mistaken.'

'See you later.'

Celia shifted her weight uncertainly, then decided to let the dispute go, to allow the girl's emotions to dissipate. Engaging in conversation with Gillian was like walking on egg shells.

Tomorrow, after Gillian had completed her fine work, the mood would be lighter between them. Surely?

Touch wood.

CHAPTER SIXTEEN

Flames were crackling on the barbecue, hungrily devouring the logs Sean was feeding on to it. One of the hosepipes was at the ready, a safety regulation they always adhered to in case a sudden rogue spark took off. Summer fires were insatiable: one second's carelessness and all was gone. Vigilance was essential.

Celia reached the rear terrace, moving towards her guests. They were assembled in a loose circle with crystal flutes hanging from between their fingers. Everyone was elegantly turned out. Dominic broke from the crowd. He had been in conversation with Claude, their sad-eyed oenologist, who lived alone in the manager's house on the estate. His wife had left him and returned with their son to her parents' village somewhere in the north of France. He rarely saw his boy, these days. As a rule, Claude disappeared after work, but tonight he had accepted Dominic's offer to eat with them. Celia clocked her husband's frown as he strode towards her. 'Where have you been?' he demanded. His question was sharp, accusatory, out of character. 'Did you forget something?'

'No, I—'

'I thought you'd never get here.'

'I was helping Gillian. Why are you so jumpy? *Ah, bonsoir,* Claude, delighted Dom's persuaded you to stay for supper.' She waved. 'What's up?' she whispered, as Dominic arrived at her side.

'You look very beautiful, my love. No change there.' They strolled towards the table and their guests, their bodies occasionally knocking against one another, easy with years of familiarity. Still, Celia had been startled by her husband's cutting tone.

'David's on his own,' she noted, more to herself than to Dominic. The man, her son, was set apart from the other party guests, standing in the shadows, taking it all in. Above him, the open flowers on the magnolia shed their inebriant scent across the final moments of the vanishing evening. Tonight, the perfume was almost cloying.

'I've been doing an internet search, to confirm one or two facts we might discuss later.'

'About what?'

'David Hawksmith.'

Celia's step faltered. Fear shot through her. Like father, like son? A history of violence? She swung her body towards

Dominic and held on to his arm, he whom she loved more than any other in the world. 'What?' She combed his weatherbeaten features. 'What are you saying?'

'Was there any moment when you doubted him, when you questioned the veracity of his claim?'

'Doubted David? You mean, like he's not my . . . Not at all. I was shaken when I received his letter out of the blue. I'd never expected to hear from him, not after all this time, and Gillian, well, she's a little hard-going, zany, but . . . But no, I never questioned his claim, why would I?'

Suddenly, she felt weak, exhausted. The intensity of the day's relentless heat was diminishing. One could breathe, exhale, stand erect, no longer depleted by the force of the sun. Still, Celia's head was beginning to spin. She steadied her hand on Dominic's arm as they advanced, at a snail's pace, delaying their arrival at the table. She had driven herself half insane over these past few days about David and her years of never acknowledging his existence, but it hadn't for a minute occurred to her to question the authenticity of his claim. The details he had furnished up to now, without her requesting any, scant though they were, had given her no cause for suspicion. Why on earth would she fear he was a fraud? In any case, for what reason would someone pose as her long-lost son? What was to be gained? Money? Certainly not blackmail. That would be preposterous. There wasn't a newspaper in the kingdom that would care that she'd given birth to an illegitimate son almost half a century earlier.

She was beginning to feel faint.

'Where's the girl?'

'*The girl?* You mean Gillian? She's putting away some decorations. She's doing her bit for the party tomorrow, helping me out.' Celia glanced back to the open doors through which she had left the house. Music was playing in the living room, barely within earshot. A female singer. American? She was trying to recall her name. Diana Krall, yes, that was her. Canadian. She wondered who had switched on the radio or slipped a CD into the deck. Gillian. It must be, which would explain why she hadn't appeared yet. Should she go in, chivvy her along? No, she'd join them when she was ready. Besides, Celia's presence was required here.

'Shall we leave all this till later?' she begged, *sotto voce*. 'I mean . . . are you sure?'

'No, not at all. I just had a hunch earlier, a nagging voice of apprehension. When he and I were talking he made a remark, a passing comment, which struck me as odd and I thought I'd do a bit of digging before mentioning anything to you.'

'What have you found?'

'Nothing, not yet.'

'Then what is this about?'

'Celia!' Federico was calling her. How debonair he was. Dashingly handsome and such an incorrigible flirt. His new wife was younger, ravishingly beautiful.

'Oh, Dominic, let's discuss it all tomorrow. Coming, Freddie!' she called brightly. 'Or Sunday, not now. Please, let's put all negatives out of our minds for this evening. We can't, mustn't spoil the party, our special celebratory weekend. We've worked so hard for all this. There's so much at stake.'

Celia was an actress. Her role on this balmy evening was that of *la châtelaine*, the capable hostess blessed with beauty and oodles of charm. She was required to be open, to welcome all who entered her domain. Dominic and Claude were the wine connoisseurs but she was the mistress of the festivities and she was beholden to play her part. As to the other matter, disagreeable as the implications of it were, she and Dominic could get to the bottom of it together. They'd winkle out the truth, but not tonight. On Sunday they could address it, call the credentials of the Hawksmith pair into question, if it proved necessary. If there was any foundation to Dominic's suspicions, if she had been duped, they'd manage whatever was necessary. Graciously. Without a scene.

Dominic, tall, strong-featured, still a handsome man, resilient, with his almost full head of greying crinkly hair, bent low to kiss his wife's cheek. 'As I said, you're looking very beautiful, my love.'

'Let's mingle,' she replied.

Sean was dressing the quartered chickens with spoonfuls of dried *herbes de Provence*, as Magali had shown him. Once each thigh, cut of breast or wing was done, he drizzled olive oil over it and laid it on a serving plate ready for Tom to fork it onto the grill. The sizzling and spitting seemed somehow to create percussion to the jolly ditty Tom was singing, rather too loudly, as he cooked and basted. All round them, the shrill song of the cicadas, their final notes of the day, was easing off, settling silently into the darkness. No match for Tom!

Someone had thoughtfully lit the dozens of candles Celia had left in a bowl alongside the barbecue, ready to decorate the table. She smiled at the gorgeous displays. The lights danced softly into the darkening night, bringing a romantic mood and a delicious sense of make-believe, of theatre, to the scene. They had been placed in meandering rows along each of the low stone walls and upper steps of the curving staircase. How enchanting it all looked. Even her prized Greek goddesses had been blessed with candles flickering round their bases.

It was all just as Celia had envisaged it.

'Who did the lights?' she asked Dominic.

'No idea.'

'They're exquisite.'

The hum of convivial conversation greeted their approach. Valeria was in a sundress and low-heeled sandals; the men sported a relaxed casual elegance, all looking forward to a delicious meal. Such perfection delighted Celia, and she would not risk it for the world.

No one must tarnish this flawless scene.

If she had been tricked . . . But, no, such a possibility was preposterous. Over-concern on Dominic's part? He wrote too much fiction. Or might it be that, at this late stage in their lives, Dominic was unable, incapable, of embracing such a secret from Celia's past?

Sean was moving discreetly between guests, topping up glasses with the fizzy pink wine that Dominic had instructed be served tonight and on the following evening to each guest as they arrived. Our 'Welcome Tipple', he described it. A decision immediately endorsed by Claude. This evening, the two men were listening out for the reactions and, importantly, fingers crossed, the compliments.

'I'll take over.' Dominic removed the bottle from Sean, who nodded and slipped back to the barbecue to assist Tom.

'And make sure you pour yourselves a glass,' he called to the young assistants. Clever of Ceely to have found them. They were hard-working, both of them, and personable. He made his way back towards his wife who, caught up in conversation with Valeria, had not filled the empty flute she was clutching. A little too tightly, he noticed. Celia was on edge, but she was way too skilled an actress to let the cracks show. He held back rather than interrupt her. When Federico led Valeria to the edge of the terrace to point out the views from this or that aspect of the estate, Dominic stepped forward and settled his arm around his wife's bare shoulders. 'Shall I get you some wine?'

'In a minute.' She glanced towards David Hawksmith, who was still hovering by the trunk of the great tree as though chained there. 'Poor chap. He seems so out of his depth.' David's sole companion, drowsing at his feet, was Daisy, their elderly Collie, who had certainly taken a shine to him. 'I'm going over to bring him into the circle.'

'Charm him as only you can.'

'Do you really doubt him?'

'Not sure. There's something about him, his manner, I don't feel comfortable with. Some gut instinct . . . but let's give him the benefit of the doubt until, as you say, tomorrow evening is behind us. Besides, if he is genuine, we don't want to have behaved without grace by ostracizing him, do we?'

Celia nodded.

David was glancing nervously at his watch. Was he apprehensive because Gillian had not yet shown up? Or was some other matter troubling him? Where on earth was Gillian? She must have finished tidying the barn by now.

147

Perhaps she had returned to her room to take a shower after scrabbling about on that dirt floor. Celia felt a tight knot grip her stomach. It was so unlike Dominic to nonpluss her, to call an alert when there was little she could do to rectify the situation. A tiny stab of grief passed through her. She prayed there was no foundation to her husband's suspicions. She had been growing fond of Gillian, who was quirky and difficult, yes, but she was vulnerable, too, and extremely bright. Above all, she was creative and Celia admired that. She had begun to feel a positive energy about the connection that bonded them, an optimism about their potential friendship. If they could find common ground their discovery of one another might prove to be a gift. And how jolly, wouldn't it be, to have a granddaughter? Kin of her own. A ready-made family.

'I hope you're wrong,' she whispered, skirting the chattering guests, making her way towards David. A smile, albeit a tense one, parted her lips.

'*Bonsoir*, David. I hope you're getting acclimatized? I see Daisy has befriended you, but why not come and join the party?' Celia slipped her hand through David's crooked arm and gently nudged him out of the shadows. He seemed to be pinioned to the spot, almost trembling. Disturbed, the dog wandered off to the young men at the barbecue.

'Why don't we get you a glass of wine?' Celia offered softly.

'Or would you prefer a beer? It can be a bit terrifying, so many new faces. Let me introduce you to everyone. Claude,' she called.

Claude nodded. He was occupied, replenishing glasses.

'Have you met our marvellous wine master? He first worked here when my parents – your grandparents, David – owned the place.' She was tactfully inching David into the crowd. 'Claude speaks excellent English so no communication worries and, I promise you, there's nothing he doesn't know about producing top-quality wines. We'd be sunk without him. If you're interested, after this weekend is behind us, I can take you and Gill on a tour of the winery if you fancy seeing it.'

'I don't really know anything about wine, to be honest, Celia.'

'Well, it might be interesting for you to discover some of our production secrets. Are you comfortable? I mean the room and everything?'

'It's more than I would have dreamed of. This place, well, you know . . .'

'It's probably all a little overwhelming, I do understand. Well, for both of us. Listen, we'll set aside some time before you leave, just the two of us, spend a few hours together . . .' She was talking in a more intimate and, she hoped, soothing tone. 'There's so much to share, to discover, I'm sure you agree.'

'I brought some—'

At that moment, before David could finish his sentence, a young woman in a flowing olive-green and white frock stepped out onto the terrace through the open French windows. She was prancing towards the table and gathered crowd. Her arms were lifted away from her sides as though she was about to break into dance.

Daisy gave a half-hearted bark, then returned her concentration to the meat sizzling on the grill. Sean surreptitiously slipped the dog a breast of chicken. Celia's attention was drawn away from David. She was puzzled by the appearance of this unexpected arrival, so elegantly turned out. Was there a guest she had completely forgotten about? Someone she had invited on the spur of the moment, as was her wont, then accidentally blanked from her mind? It was only as the figure drew closer, as the lights illuminated her face, that Celia recognized Gillian. Gillian utterly transformed. Gillian with the gel washed out of her hair, which was brushed into a softer, more Audrey Hepburn look, swept back behind her ears. The lightweight dress lifted and fluttered as though it were sewn from the wings of dragonflies. From a distance, Gillian exuded the confidence of an entertainer stepping centre stage, excited to perform.

'Christ on a bike!' David's exclamation. 'That's our Gill. Look at her. Who would have thought it?'

'She looks so graceful. So sophisticated,' murmured Celia.

Gillian was making her way, more gingerly now, towards her father and Celia, her eyes wide with a look of uncertainty, almost a plea for validation.

She was wearing a pale rose lipstick, shimmery green eye shadow and black mascara. Thankfully, thought Celia, she had removed the dark circles of kohl. This was a softer, more conventional makeup, a far more feminine, fair-lady image. Of course, Gillian might protest that this was Celia's old-fashioned taste. Point taken. Still, to Celia's eye the elegance suited her. It was immensely flattering.

'Come and join us,' Celia called, arm raised, driving David at her side a step or two forward. 'David, you should be the one, proud dad, to introduce your daughter to our friends. She's certainly the belle of the ball.'

Heads turned as Gillian skipped to the far side of the barbecue. The two lads, still at the grill, followed her slender frame with nods of approval. Tom raised a glass, winked at her and let out a long, low whistle. Desire had been awakened, thought Celia, hardly failing to notice the expression on Tom's face. Oh, to be young again.

As Gillian drew closer, Celia's attention fixed upon her swan-like neck. It was flounced with a magnificent gold locket and chain that Celia recognized instantly. 'What the . . .?' She frowned. 'You're wearing my necklace.' The accusation was spoken before she had thought to restrain herself.

Gillian's right hand reached up to the golden pendant and she stroked it tenderly. The ring in her nose had not been removed. It was at odds with the rest of her appearance. 'I borrowed it. Hope you don't mind. It's so gorgeous, I couldn't resist. Seems a pity no one's showing it off.'

Celia was stupefied. Anger shot through her. She was intending to wear that very precious necklace for the following evening's grand soirée. 'But where did you find it? You must have gone into our bedroom. Rifled through my jewellery box.' She realized then that the dress Gillian was wearing also belonged to her. 'You've been through the wardrobes too.'

Gillian had helped herself to all that had taken her fancy from Celia's belongings. Had she also trespassed in the guests' rooms? Valeria's suitcase, perhaps? Celia felt a rising panic. The bedrooms were never locked. Why would they be in her private home?

Had Dominic's misgivings been accurate? Were these two a pair of robbers, posing as family, here to carry off whatever took their eye?

'I've never seen you in anything so . . . lavish,' remarked David, who apparently had not fully comprehended, if at all, what his daughter had been up to. 'You look bloody marvellous, our kid. Quite the movie star, just like your gran here. Could be cast from the same die.'

'Thanks, Dave. Thought I'd get in touch with my feminine self for a change,' grinned Gillian, still fiddling with the chain, a twenty-two-carat gift from Dominic for their twenty-fifth wedding anniversary. A gift to shore up their marriage at a point when their lives had been on the rocks, when Celia believed she had lost not only their London home but her husband too. A painful time best left buried.

'You don't think it would have been good manners to ask me first? What you've done could be construed as stealing.'

Gillian's steel-grey eyes fell coldly on Celia, a pick through the older woman's heart. Tears were rising. '*Stealing?* I didn't stick the stuff in my backpack and do a runner. I've only borrowed it. I wanted to make you proud of me, Celia. I wanted to look classy so you'd show me off to your posh mates as your chic granddaughter. I was making an effort. Playing my part for you and for Dave.'

Celia took a deep breath struggling for composure, her heart racing. 'Gillian, go back upstairs, please, and return the locket to its case in the jewellery box where you found it.'

'Why?'

'Because it has sentimental . . .' Celia swallowed, grappling for the appropriate words. 'If you cannot grasp why what you've done is inappropriate, Gillian, then, please, just do as I ask. Keep the frock on for this evening. We can discuss the rest later. Before there is a scene, I am asking you to return

153

upstairs and do as you are told,' she repeated, with managed calm. 'Before Dominic sees you're wearing the gift he bought for me.'

A large tear rolled down Gillian's cheek.

Before Celia could muster any further words, soften her reactions, the girl swung on her heels and marched towards the French windows. Heads turned, observing her departure, but apparently no one had caught the acrimonious tone of the exchange.

David, at Celia's side, was clearly confused, clueless. 'I don't understand what the problem is.' His face was squeezed into one big troubled frown. He looked as though the world had imploded and no one had warned him about it. He reminded Celia of a rejected bloodhound. She felt so sorry for him. 'Did she borrow something she shouldn't have? She looks terrific, though, doesn't she?'

Celia tapped her hand on his wrist. Edging away, she said, 'Try to mingle, David. I'll be back. Everything's fine.'

As she passed Dominic, who was refilling glasses and pointing people to their places at the table, she pressed her hand into his chest and whispered the same, 'I'll be back.'

Magali and young Béatrice were approaching, bearing two hefty bowls of crisp fresh salads, a groaning platter of the best French cheeses and a silver bucket clinking with ice cubes. Another woman from the village, in her late thirties, whose name Celia couldn't recall right now, had joined the team. She was struggling, balancing five bottles of chilled mineral water in her arms. David stepped swiftly towards her, hands outstretched, to take them. 'Here, let me.' He smiled. A wide open smile.

Suddenly from the music system within the living room a piercing blast of dissonant sound.

What on earth . . .?

Someone had changed the CD, which was emitting horn music at full volume.

The chicken quarters were ready. Tom was trilling the news to all and sundry while removing the succulent cuts from the barbecue, placing them on the serving dishes garnished with fresh sprigs of rosemary and downy sage leaves, while Henri was helping to put plates on the table. Claude was uncorking a bottle, Dominic another, his from the lighter of the house reds. As he worked Dominic was recounting a tale from his vast repertoire of anecdotes to the assembled party. 'Have I told you about the time when . . .?' He was keeping the mood buoyant, the evening swimming along satisfactorily. He gave a nod of reassurance to his wife's disappearing frame as, brow furrowed, she glanced back to him. Barely a beat later, he returned to his story. It was followed by an expected roar of laughter, hands clapping appreciatively. He had delivered the punch line.

CHAPTER SEVENTEEN

Celia, at a canter, vanished into the house. She reached the living room, which was deserted. The music was blasting. She hurried over to the system and muted the volume. Hastily, fingers fumbling, she pressed eject and drew out the CD, selected another from the library rack, Oscar Peterson's *Night Train,* and slipped it into the player. The door into the hallway was wide open. She hurried through it and up the stairs to her and Dominic's bedroom where the door was also gaping. As soon as she entered, her eyes were drawn to the gold necklace lying like a coiled snake on their white linen bedcover. Her jewellery box on the dressing-table was unfastened. A few bits and pieces, a bracelet of no real value, a rather pasty ring from earlier more theatrical days, had been tossed between her hairbrushes, lotions and creams. The entire room reeked of her perfume, an invisible haze of Chanel No 5. Makeup brushes deposited willy-nilly. Her hairdryer dumped on a stool, cable and plug hanging loose, the cheval mirror turned to a different angle. She couldn't tidy all this now. Later. Her priority was their guests: the meal was being served.

But first, one other task . . .

She returned to the corridor, fastening her bedroom with its key, which usually lived on the inner side of the lock. Once all was firmly latched, she continued up one more flight to the second floor where Dominic's study was situated. She confirmed that it was securely locked. A few doors further along was the box room where Gillian was housed. It was wide open. All lights left on. Celia took two tentative steps inside. Empty, lifeless. Her white and olive-green dress lay on the floor, abandoned among the mayhem, like a parachute or a cloud come to rest. Nothing had been tidied away, nothing tucked into a place. The windows yawned, giving access to the evening midges and moths attracted to the blazing bulbs. Several were fluttering around the bedside lamp. The door to the shower room had also been left open. A damp bath mat lay on the floor. Underwear jettisoned beside it.

'Gillian?' No answer. All was hush. Futile to call in the hope of . . . It was obvious the room was vacant. Where had Gillian disappeared to?

Beyond the window, Venus was rising, a beacon of radiance, glowing over the ancient blue hills of the lower Alps. Jupiter was on full display too. Celia took a step, drawn by the planets' brightness. Outside, some distance below, rising peals of laughter and animated conversation. Dominic hosting. Wine flowing. Glasses clinking. She knew that her absence would be remarked.

Had she overreacted?

Gillian was probably downstairs by now, hobnobbing with the guests, keeping her father company, the necklace returned, the incident forgotten. Celia's gaze roamed the room, scanning it for anything suspicious.

Dominic's doubts had spooked her. Had her responses been over the top? Had he sown mistrust?

A thick well-thumbed sketchbook lay on the cane seat of the chair by the school desk. Celia decided to scribble Gillian a few hasty lines, just in case she was hiding somewhere, cradling her upset:

Apologies if I overreacted. Please come back and join us for supper. We can discuss this misunderstanding tomorrow. I am excited at the prospect of us getting to know one another. I hope we can be friends. C.

She flipped the sketchbook cover, expecting to find a blank space to write her message, but within the pad – a journal? – there was a series of photographs, each glued to a separate page. Beneath each one in coloured inks was written her name, CELIA GREY, followed by dates: May 2012, September 2004, and more. Seven photos in all. Her professional, her family name. They were followed by a collection of theatre programmes. Towards the centre of the block was a cluster of reviews, for theatre and television shows. A rather flattering portrait of Celia ten or more years younger stared back at her. It had been taken before the disastrous outing with Dominic's play, before they went into rehearsals, before their lives, their marriage, had spun off-kilter.

Next page, a photocopy of a news-printed photo of her and Dominic on their wedding day. They were in Eversholt Street standing outside the Camden Town register office, holding hands. One of Dominic's fingers was softly brushing her shiny new wedding ring. She was beaming, luminescent. His name, Dominic Millar, was underscored with several black ink lines. And the date of their wedding written in by hand. 'What in Heaven's name is all this?'

Celia riffled onwards through the pages fast, faster, back and forth, snatching at the images. Incredulous. Snippets from her life. One section included the most damaging of the reviews for the play with which she and Dominic had suffered such a financial blow. A few lines from various critics' lambasting had been highlighted with a yellow marker pen.

Celia Grey stalks the stage with an air of desperation.

Ms Grey never appears comfortable, never fully inhabits her character.

Without her husband, the talented Dominic Millar . . .

A younger actress might have . . .

A younger actress? Had Celia's despair, her heartbreak, been so evident, so crystal clear? The ignominy.

Those painful, excoriating reviews. Even today, she saw every one of them in her mind's eye. Relived the devastating moments when she had first read them. Each week, another city, on their tour to London. Each week another hammer blow to their aspirations, to her professional dignity.

And what of the other, the more profound hurt, the private story not exposed here in the press reviews? The chapter no one else knew.

The worst of all rejections. The potential loss of Dominic when she'd seen . . .

She closed her eyes briefly, walling out the memories. Not now. She must not return to those past days. Not tonight.

She blotted the bead of a tear forming in the duct. She had guests to charm. And tomorrow business clients to win over, contracts to secure for their vineyard. She and

Dominic? They were on the up again, enjoying a winning streak with their wines. She must celebrate that. Their life together was different, less physical, less intimate. Inevitable: they were older . . .

But why would Gillian be hoarding all this information, burrowing into Celia's life, giving emphasis to her failures with a marker pen?

She dropped on to the chair, the scrapbook open on her knees, no longer capable of writing her message of reconciliation. She was shaking. Tears rose again, stinging. She brushed the varnished fingers of her left hand against her lashes in an impatient attempt to put an end to this foolishness, to avoid mascara smudges on her face. Her ebullience and pride in all that she and Dominic had created here, their fight back, the rebuilding of two damaged lives, her happiness at their achievements, suddenly it all felt as though it were being targeted, and might at any moment deflate like a punctured balloon.

She did not want to be reminded . . .

Was her existence, her and Dominic's, under some threat?

The heartaches she and Dominic had lived through during those gruelling eighteen months, her public failure, the pain, it all came swirling back. It's true what they say. You can receive a hundred glowing reviews but it's the bad ones, the cruel criticisms, that go right to your heart and cling to you.

They stick like tar. The ones that mark you out as a failure, a has-been. Past your sell-by date.

Celia had built, was constructing, a new, successful existence. She missed the world of entertainment, show business, theatre, achingly so, but she had found a substitute here and a means of expressing her talents. And she had not lost Dominic. The fire and passion might have gone from their relationship, but they were older now. What could she expect? They were content together, weren't they?

Slowly, she replaced the book on the desk, closed it, rested her fingers there for a moment longer, inhaled deeply, bringing to power all her theatrical training, and then she rose with determination. Tripping over abandoned items, she crossed back towards the window. An ashtray spilling with cigarette butts sat on the small table. Gillian had been smoking in bed. She glanced about. Where was the yoga mat? Nowhere to be seen. A fabrication? Part of the disguise she and Dominic were being sold?

Could she trust this father and daughter twosome? Were they on the level? Or was Celia's imagination running wild? Were the notebook, the collection of photos and news articles nothing more than a grandchild's desire to learn everything about her lost family?

She felt tired, confused.

But if Gillian's intentions were honourable, why highlight the negatives?

Outside it was warm, suffocatingly still. Celia took another deep breath expanding her lungs with fresh clean air, unclogging her emotions. It was a glorious mid-August evening, a little too hot, but blessed. Blessed like all others. Except for these stupid nagging doubts.

A cry rang out in the distance. Far from the house, beyond the outbursts of laughter and merriment. The screech of a short-eared owl. That eerie blood-curdling sound. It sent a shiver up Celia's spine. And there it was again.

She stood still, back rigid, among the chaos of possessions, belonging to whom? Who was this young woman? She was keeping a check-list of Celia's past, intruding upon her history. A stranger? Somebody not related to her at all?

CHAPTER EIGHTEEN

The next morning, Celia was up at dawn plunging into the pool, making the most of the breaking of the day. The rising sun greeted her with the dewy scents of pine and rosemary, promising the gift of an unexplored day. And what an important day it was to be. A banquet to enliven the hearts of friends. How many months had she been preparing for it?

The evening before had turned out to be a lot of fun. So much laughter. The joviality had helped to calm her tensions, even though Gillian had not reappeared – or not to the dinner, at least. At the last minute Celia had seated herself alongside David, closing the gap where Gillian was to have been placed. It had not been a good moment to quiz David who seemed, during her absence, to have brightened considerably and had slipped into the swing of things admirably. Neither did she intend to mention her findings to Dominic. Not yet, not until this evening's jamboree was behind them. In any case Dominic had been fast asleep by the time she had eventually climbed into bed at close to two a.m.

After their supper had drawn to its successful conclusion some time around midnight, Celia had made her way to the kitchens to lend her loyal team a hand with the tidying up, using the time fruitfully to talk through any last-minute concerns or queries about today's upcoming event. Encouragement and special thanks were afforded to Magali, Béatrice and Adèle, the latest addition to their team. Instead of heading off to bed, Celia had hung on, weary but glad to wind down in their company, which was good-natured and a wee bit risqué. She listened with amusement to the gossip bellowed across tables and sinks. Their giggling, their lighthearted observations on this or that outfit or hairstyle, or overheard snippets of conversation. Béatrice confessed with high emotions and much patting of her heart with the flat of her hand that she had been dangerously close to swooning, to dropping a plate of stewed apricots, when Tom winked at her.

The others agreed that he was *trop beau*, too handsome for words, and quite the catch.

'*Et il a un tête,*' observed Magali, which translated as 'he has a head', common parlance for saying he was intelligent.

'And what about the new fellow? He's taken a right shine to you, Adèle.'

'Don't talk rot, the pair of you,' Adèle riposted shyly.

Astonished, Celia turned her attention to Adèle who was releasing a barrette from her hair, letting it fall to her shoulders.

'He's a hulky bloke.' Béatrice sniggered, fingers pressed over mouth.

Adèle waved a hand, chuckling. 'Stop the tomfoolery.'

It was time to vacate the kitchens.

'*Dormez bien et, encore, mille mercis,*' Celia repeated several times. She was about to climb the stairs, drag her exhausted body to bed. The dishwashers were humming, uneaten food had been packed away, all the surfaces sponged down, everything left pristine. The trio were folding their aprons into a drawer, donning jackets for the starlit twenty-minute walk to their homes lower down the hillside. None had brought a car. All three lived and had grown up within walking distance of one another in the closest village to the estate. Celia had offered to drive them but they had shaken their heads, saying the fresh air would do them the world of good.

'A bit of exercise never hurt nobody.' Plump Béatrice's philosophy.

However, watching her stalwarts yawn and stagger while wearily kicking off their espadrilles, changing into sturdier footwear for the trek downhill, Celia drew back from the staircase and insisted, 'Girls, I'm driving you. I won't hear a word of protest.' She would not leave them at this ungodly hour to descend the mountain.

Days earlier, Magali had been invited to stay over during this hectic weekend in a small flat above the stables but the housekeeper had preferred to return to her terraced house, its façade painted ochre pink, where her retired husband, once the owner of the one and only *tabac* and post office in the village, and their loyal Jack Russell along with their son, Pascal, awaited her, even if she was obliged to be back at her post before seven the following morning.

Celia went in search of the car key. The trio of women piled into the Land Rover as she fired it up. Even at past midnight, the outside temperature was tipping 27°C.

'Rain's forecast.' Adèle yawned. She was squeezed into the back alongside Béatrice, the pair of them whispering like schoolgirls.

'Forecast but won't bless us,' observed another. All were too dog-tired to debate the subject. Still all vociferously agreed that the weather could keep its dirty tricks to itself and guard its distance till after the festivities.

Celia slowed to peer through the wide-open window before deciding to pull over. The sky was remarkably clear, stars and planets blazing in every direction. Venus was hanging low and bright, like a satellite of the waxing moon. Distant Saturn was visible, and a surprise close-up of the giant ringed Jupiter. This was the sky that guided Celia as she motored back up the hill alone after depositing her helpers in the village square, where all but a few feral cats were silent and in their beds.

She stepped out of the Land Rover, shook her shoulders, releasing the tension in her neck, her aching spine. The sunless, moon-bright air caressed her cheeks. It smelled so fragrant. Thyme, meadow saffron, juniper and a host of other wild *garrigue* shrubs greeted her. Their heady aromas, specific to the region, were always more intense at night. She leaned against the side of the vehicle, peering heavenwards, inhaling the resinous, herby bouquets floating on the warm air. The rocky red earth gave a unique tang to the Les Roches du Soleil estate wines, which was partly why she so revelled in these perfumes.

Jupiter, so close, seemed almost within her grasp.

There were some excellent stargazing spots at this altitude between road and sea, along the path that eventually led to the stone lodge. Tonight, though, she was too whacked to venture any distance. She and Dominic sometimes strolled out here during the long midsummer nights to observe the Perseid meteor showers. Occasionally, they'd encounter inhabitants from the village or others living in more remote surroundings, everybody taking advantage of the late-night drop in temperature when you could breathe and move about the earth without the sun's oppressive intensity.

A crack of laughter caught Celia's attention, disturbing her musings. She turned her head in the direction of the cliff's edge. Two, no, goodness, three people were lounging on their backs in the tufts of drought-frazzled grass, giggling. One was convulsed with laughter. She hadn't spotted them before because they were low to the ground and possibly because she hadn't been expecting anyone. Another round of laughter and a female voice started to chatter overexcitedly in English. It was Gillian. Celia couldn't make out her silhouette and certainly not her features but her distinctive voice carried on the still night air. Was her father with her, and a third person? Someone she and Dominic knew? Or someone they weren't acquainted with? An intruder? An accomplice? Celia was tempted to steal along the path to identify the other members of the threesome, but decided against it. If they spotted her they would think she was spying. In any case, she needed to get home. Dominic, if he woke, would be perturbed by her absence at this hour.

Another explosion of laughter and she caught Tom's name, followed by his attractive Cornish drawl. He rose to his feet, unsteadily. He had a bottle in hand. Wine from the estate, more than likely. He was singing at the top of his voice. A rich tenor. Gillian stumbled to an upright position. She was swaying, clinging to Tom's shoulders to keep her balance.

They rocked drunkenly in each other's arms. Her body, flying backwards, opened to his. Celia supposed the third member of the party was Sean. And a moment later, he leaped up, steadier, more in charge of his faculties than his companions as he went off in the direction of their digs. Tom and Gillian were now kissing. Her head was thrown upwards as he bent low to her face, her lips, her swan-like neck.

Celia spun her attention elsewhere, to the view she knew intimately: the limestone hills, the pine forests, boulders, bush-covered slopes that she could barely make out now, but they were pictured in detail in her mind's eye. She turned to the Land Rover, pulled open the door as quietly as she could so she didn't draw attention to her presence. Once in her seat, she waited until the couple broke apart. Still holding hands, they teetered downhill, towards the lodge.

When they were out of sight, she fired the engine, pushed the stubborn gearstick into first, and fast-tracked for home.

After her swim, during breakfast with Dominic, Celia kept silent about her discoveries from the evening before. She worried they would fuel Dominic's speculations. And she needed time.

Dominic mentioned only that he would respect her request to set aside the subject of David until the weekend was behind them. Until then he would keep his reservations and suppositions to himself.

Instead, they talked of more pressing business. Radishes.

'Might their flavour be too peppery? I'm thinking about the bubbly rosé you and Claude are proposing to serve.'

'No radishes, Ceely,' Dominic pronounced. 'Strike them off the menu, for Heaven's sake.'

Celia crossed them off her ingredients list and made a note for Magali.

'We want to tantalise the tastebuds, not overburden them,' continued Dominic. 'Such a silky, tender wine will be better partnered with crudités of chicory, celery and carrots served with an aubergine and herb dip.'

Yes, that would be simple and ideal. 'Aside from crudités, there will be slivers of Serrano ham on cocktail sticks intercut with melon, plus our fig and olive compôte.' Magali had made the compôte the previous autumn. 'We're serving it on thin slices of toast.'

Dominic nodded approvingly.

'And canapés of *foie gras*.'

The menu was settled. Both were satisfied on that score and Celia was keen to get cracking.

There was still so much to put in order, last-minute tasks such as dressing the tables, now firmly secured as one long surface beneath the shade of the overhanging citrus trees. With

Gillian's errant behaviour, the problem of the black plastic tubs arose again. Celia was deliberating about whom she might rope in. Who had even half an hour to dedicate to this unforeseen duty? Sean, ever at the ready, was the first to spring to mind. Where was he? Assisting Henri in the vegetable gardens, almost certainly. They would be collecting wheelbarrows of fresh produce required for this evening's menus. Béatrice and Adèle would be waiting impatiently to wash and prepare the greens and salads. They would also be responsible for scrubbing the root vegetables, the potatoes, peeling the home-grown onions and garlic, essential for the lamb, which still awaited its garnish.

Clearly Celia could not steal Sean from Henri, who was growing too frail to achieve all that harvesting, hours with a pitchfork, on his own. Who else could she ask?

David? Where was he?

Celia sped down the stone steps, past the busts of *Athena* and *Daphne* towards the lawns where the black pots stood. Someone had already given the citruses an early-morning dousing. Sean, no doubt: he was consistently prompt at his post. The grass was browning, exposing cracks in the dried earth. After its cut yesterday it was looking rather too parched, but she and Dominic had decided to refrain from irrigating it further. Their water reserves were running low and even for registered agriculturalists, such as themselves, water was to be used sparingly.

As she reached 'the banqueting level', she noticed that stacked on the trestle tables were the fifteen boxes of fairy lights she had purchased online. They surely hadn't been left out all night? She turned, puzzled as to who might have brought them down from the scullery cupboard. It was then she spotted Gillian standing at the foot of one of the umbrella pines alongside a ladder resting against the tree's scaly trunk. A wheelbarrow stood close by. Gillian, in men's shorts and a midriff-revealing tank top, was gesticulating, calling to someone in the tree. A chainsaw began to whir. Celia glanced upwards and spotted Tom. A branch dropped to the ground with a light thud.

Celia hurried to where the young couple were working. 'Gillian!'

The chainsaw started up again, drowning her call. She ran to where her granddaughter, or whoever she was, was yelling instructions to Tom. As she drew close, a second limb hit the earth missing her by a hair's breadth.

'Ceely, move away. You'll get hurt.'

'Tom!' cried Celia, ignoring the girl. 'I'm not sure these lovely trees should be pruned.'

'We're only snipping the tips of a couple of the lower branches, those that barely catch the sunlight. Half dead anyway.' His sinewy arm was raised above his shoulder, pointing upwards and exposing tuffets of dark hair in his armpits and across his naked chest. 'Nothing to worry about, Celia. Afterwards, we'll go for the cluster pines and leave these lovelies to themselves. There are half a dozen or so of the clusters growing along the cliff ridge on the way to our lodge. I've seen some good foliage we can lop off for Gill's purposes.'

'Are you helping Gillian with the decorations then?'

Having descended the ladder, Tom was heaving it away from the trunk. He was in a pair of worn brown shorts that hung loosely from his abdomen, revealing the elastic waistband of his black underwear and the brush of dark hair on his slender belly. His body was lithe, sweating, covered with bits of pine and sawdust. His hair was matted but his dark wood-brown eyes shone and danced.

'Gill asked me, if that's not a problem. It'll only be a couple of hours. I ran it past Dominic and he was onside.' His eyes locked with Celia's and she found herself turning to the lengths of sawn tree, unable to meet his gaze.

His music.

'Of course . . . Good idea, thank you.' She hadn't listened to his music. It had slipped her mind.

'I'm going to start threading those fairy lights through the branches on the lemons shortly. Once Tom knows the vegetation I want for the pot exteriors, he'll cut it for me. Then he can return to his own business.'

'Excellent. I'm glad you have someone to help with all this, Gill. Delighted you still want to be involved . . .' Celia trailed off. In her mind's eye, she saw herself standing in Gillian's room: the scrapbook with its underlinings; the borrowed dress abandoned on the floor. In her own room, the necklace out of its box. 'By the way, have you seen David this morning?'

'He was feeding Henri's chickens. Now he's digging potatoes, preparing them for the kitchen.'

Gillian had shuffled towards the tree, settling companionably alongside Tom. Their bodies were centimetres apart. Celia recalled the image of them on the hill, well after midnight. Their secret intimacies. She pictured the sketchbook with the yellow-highlighted passages from the theatre reviews. Snatches from her past squirrelled away, like withered flowers pressed between the pages of a novel.

Why?

She was at a loss.

When had Gillian requested Tom's help for today? When they were star-gazing? Did it matter?

Tom lifted the ladder and straddled it across his shoulders. 'Better get on.' He smiled with a wink. 'Catch you later, Ceely.'

Ceely.

'We all must get on. Thank you, Tom. I'm very grateful.'

He strode off, leaving the two women alone, face to face. For a moment they eyed each other without a word. It was Celia who broke the silence. 'Thank you for going ahead with this. I wasn't sure how I was going to manage.'

Gillian's face was bare, fresh, pale as milk, her hair flat against her skull and damp from exertion. Perhaps the most natural Celia had seen her. Idiosyncratically beautiful. 'You look . . .'

'What?'

'At ease,' she said.

'*What?*'

'Relaxed. Happy. Less . . .'

'Uptight? Well, you certainly haven't contributed to that,' their young guest retorted.

'You mean because I was angry you went into our room, breached a private space uninvited, dug into drawers, leafed through cupboards, and helped yourself to my belongings?'

'Coming, Gill?' Tom calling.

'On my way! I didn't *help myself* to anything. You're overreacting.'

'I came looking for you . . .'

'To apologise for being so cruel?'

'To discuss it.'

'Gill!'

'Got to go if you want your party to look fantabulous. See

you later.' And with that, Gill loped off, in her red Converse, arms dangling loose at her sides, towards Tom. He was waiting for her with a broad grin on his handsome face. As the girl approached, he broke into heavenly song.

CHAPTER NINETEEN

Sixty or thereabouts were gathered beneath the stars, seated around the long trestle tables exquisitely dressed now with damask linen cloths, pure white flowers jutting high in slender vases, and vintage multi-headed candelabra. A tender side of lamb was roasting on the steel-framed spit, sizzling juice and promise. Every so often, the crank was turned by Henri with sterling assistance from young Sean. Even without a common language, they'd formed an affable and efficient partnership.

At regular intervals Magali appeared, on hand to baste the impressive cut of browning meat, while Claude and Dominic had assumed their roles as sommeliers. Glasses were being replenished, new bottles uncorked. The sparkling rosé was slipping down a treat.

'Next year's award winner, Dom?' called someone.

'Fingers crossed.' Celia smiled nervously.

The mood was exuberant, merry, as dusk fell about the motley crowd.

Even the insufferable heat had had the decency to make itself scarce, replaced by a comfortable drop in temperature. 'Oh, I can breathe,' cried several.

A barn owl swooped by, noticed by a few.

David had been commandeered – or had he offered his services? – to help in the kitchen, a role he seemed to engage in with relish. Celia watched him and his light-hearted interaction with the squad of busy women. The language hurdles and misunderstandings between them were the source of peals of laughter and much gaiety. She had a sneaking suspicion that he really had taken a shine to Adèle. She was strikingly attractive, voluptuously built, with jet-black hair, the loveliest of the trio. A trio that was now blossoming into a bustling, rather jolly quartet, David being the fourth. He was assisting with the ferrying of cutlery and crockery up and down the flights of stone steps from house to banquet level. He was more at ease, observed Celia, more in command tonight than he had been since his arrival.

Celia, complimented by everyone, looked radiant in an ankle-length cream silk dress. It had a scooped neckline with two thin straps holding up the bodice and was lightly ruched at the back. Her reddish colouring was set off by gold and amber drop earrings that swung as she turned her head, with the locket and chain Gillian had 'borrowed' the previous evening. Her hair was pinned back in a loose chignon. She was flitting from one end of the extended table to the other, ensuring that every guest was being served all that they desired.

The village mayor, Olivier Aubert, looked equally resplendent in his double-breasted purple waistcoat and watch-chain. His jowled features hung like melting tallow. Dominic had insisted that Olivier be placed at the head of the far end of the table. His beaming wife, Désirée, seated to his right, was decked out in a daffodil yellow shift. She had arresting blue eyes and was as plump as a Toulouse sausage.

A delicious breeze was blowing in from the hills and lower mountain ranges set north of the property where their pine forests flourished. These timbered inclines looked down upon the volcanic slopes and valleys where Dominic and Celia's magnificent vineyards were planted, protected from the fierce winds of the north by the mountainside and warmed from the south by the heat of the Mediterranean sun. The breeze brought with it a medley of ambrosial perfumes, inhaled and appreciated by most who were gathered around the table, The majority of the guests could identify them because they had grown up with them. Each had known Les Roches du Soleil since childhood. Some, the more elderly, had worked on the estate in previous times. Others were boasting that their parents or grandparents before them had been employed as day labourers to crush the grapes by foot. All present, chattering over one another, were recounting tales of bygone eras, when they were tots who'd barely learned to walk. Memories were being shared, embellished. Some had accompanied their parents daily, arriving on wagons drawn by mules during the annual harvests to collect the grapes and deliver them to one of the local winemaking cooperatives.

Better days, a few claimed. Others hotly disagreed.

Oh, but we should bring the horses, the mules back.

Do away with petrol. Bah to warmongering Russia.

For the most part, the stories hailed from before the mid-1970s when Celia's parents had taken over as proprietors. The Greys were the first foreigners to take possession of the estate. For some, the arrival of the British had been met with suspicion. Those who distrusted foreigners perceived it as the beginning of the end for the Provençaux and their traditional way of life. But there were others, plenty, who welcomed the newly installed owners and offered them support, Henri and his wife, Claude and his family among them.

'Oh, but so much has changed since those days!'

A host of tales were spun, discussed, enhanced, rectified, argued over, all in an amicable if sometimes heated fashion.

Those were the good old days. Yes, indeed, nodded solemn or smiling heads.

Celia turned her attention from the debates. David was still up and down the stairs, helping with the service. She should insist he find his seat, unwind, get involved. Or perhaps this was his way of participating?

Modern changes, most at the table agreed, were the real cause for concern. The climate was hotting up, weather patterns askew. Drought. All agreed that the worsening water issues were disturbing. It was no longer a question of one's neighbour filching from next door's well, cheating on his boundaries, shifting the demarcation markers. No, no, those old tales were piffling, compared to today's issues. All fell silent contemplating the challenges.

Wine replenishments were called for. Claude was on his feet again, at the ready.

These days, water was rationed. In summer, without private wells or agricultural licences, you had to make do with next to no water access. What in the future would be their irrigation rights, and the financial impact of keeping your crops alive? The livelihood of every local gathered would be affected . . .

On they discoursed, knocking back the excellent vintages, helping themselves to more crudités, another mouthful of *foie gras*, while the lamb was roasting, promising a succulent repast. The aroma of the olive-oil-basted juices was causing stomachs to rumble. A toast was made to their friend and neighbour, the olive farmer, Sébastien.

While they waited patiently for their food, Celia was fretting: the main course was taking longer than she had

hung on a hanger and returned to Gillian's room. A small envelope accompanied it. Inside a card with the address of the estate embossed in burgundy and in Celia's handwriting:

You look stunning in this dress. I hope you will accept it as a gift. Thank you for your marvellous stage-dressing skills. Celia

She was fully aware that her gesture might be rebuffed, that the volatile girl might use the offer against her in some way. She was half prepared for it, but she was determined to heal the rift. She wanted harmony in her home. Whoever these two people, this father-and-daughter couple, turned out to be, she was growing fond of them. Or perhaps her emotions were coloured by her joy at this extravagant repast knitting together so seamlessly. She could not deny that Gillian's decorations were spectacular – several had remarked upon them – and certainly contributed to the magical mood of the soirée. The only pity was that the decorated tubs were hardly visible because they were at ground level. The lights dancing through the lemon boughs, however, had given birth to an illuminated avenue. It was as though the dining area had been transformed into an enchanted sweetly scented arboretum.

'The dress fits you perfectly. I'm glad you decided to wear it. Are you enjoying yourself?' she asked.

The first dinner plates, each graced with two slender slices of tender pink lamb, were being delivered to the table, starting at the far end with the mayor and his wife. Madame Aubert had been diving into every platter offered to her and was already piling potatoes on top of her meat when a noise like the combustion of flames erupted from somewhere not too far off, followed, moments later, by a loud thud. The interruptions drew everyone's attention, stunning the assembly.

Dominic, positioned at the other end of the table opposite the mayor, rose immediately. Celia, without waiting for Gillian's response, stood erect, a frown dissecting her lovely features.

'What was that?'

'A clap of thunder?'

'No, it wasn't, but what a blessing if we were in for some rain.'

'We certainly need it.'

'But not tonight. No one wants to spoil a good shindig.'

'Nature playing its dirty tricks again.'

Dominic hurried to Celia's side. Both were squinting towards the north-east, to the far reaches of their terrain, to where the explosion or combustion appeared to have come from. Illicit hunters? Hunting was forbidden during the summer and it was heavily controlled. In any case, this was a private domain.

'It didn't sound like gunshots.'

'Besides, the infiltrators would be trespassing.'

'If it's illegal hunting, you bring 'em right here. I'll book the blighters as soon as turn round,' bellowed the mayor, rapping his knuckles against the tablecloth.

Désirée Aubert patted her husband's arm. 'Blood pressure, dear,' she whispered, and popped a potato into her mouth.

The main course plates continued to be delivered. Béatrice and Adèle, sweat clustering on their shiny foreheads, fearing the succulent lamb would get cold, were hopping back and forth between the spit and the diners, who were now returning their concentration to their food.

Magali and Henri were carving as though their lives depended on it, Sean and Tom forking the meat onto the plates.

'Shall I come and help you?' called David to Adèle.

'No,' she replied, 'sit down.'

Celia, observing the pair, wondered whether he had disclosed to anyone the nature of his relationship to the owners of the estate. She certainly hadn't.

Dominic, still puzzled by the explosion or whatever it was, hovered uncertainly before returning to his chair. To his left was Madame Madeleine Boyer, the stylish wife of the proprietor of one of the finest five-star hotels in the South of France. Theirs was a magnificent belle époque property set along the coast on a windy promontory this eastern side of Marseille. In its time, it had played host to kings and queens. Madeleine's husband, Alexandre Boyer, was a loyal and important customer for Les Roches du Soleil. He was already discussing orders with Dominic for their next season, the months leading up to and including Christmas. No deal would be struck this evening, of course. The couple were staying over. Breakfast would be the moment to conclude, before they set off in their open-top roadster en route for the Var.

Dominic made his way back to his seat, topping up several glasses as he passed, throwing out a light quip or two, frothing the mood. Many of the diners were moving to the reds now, the ideal accompaniment to the fine meat. Claude was doing the honours.

Someone, elsewhere, over on the left, proposed a toast to Jacques, the butcher, who rose to his feet, nodded, blushed and settled down again.

Celia was scanning the horizon. No signs of warning lights. And, most importantly, no flames. Not likely it was a wildfire. Still, the disruption had caused alarm, even if all appeared quiet now. Hesitantly, she turned her attention back to the company, to Gillian who was refusing a plate of meat from Béatrice. 'I only want veggies,' she was explaining emphatically to the puzzled village girl, who shook her head, not comprehending, then parked the plate in front of the next guest in line, Pierre Cluzy. Celia lightly brushed Gillian's back, then made her way to her own chair to the right of Dominic.

The disruption had been forgotten. Conversations were back on track, knives and forks clattering against white porcelain dinner plates. Laughter rose, hitching itself to the darkening hours, before drifting off into the ether. The matching white dishes steaming with garden-grown vegetables were being handed back and forth. The mayor's wife was salivating over her second helping of pink meat. She let out a raucous guffaw at a remark made by someone south of her seat and slapped her hand against her mighty bosom. 'Oh, my word!' she trilled, nodding approval to Claude at his proposed top-up.

Tom gave old Henri a light slap on the back and jogged to his chair, chilling alongside Gillian. Celia found herself observing their ease and delight in one another's company. Any and all futures were possible for them both. Gillian barely resembled the punky girl who had got off the train just thirty-six hours earlier. Sean and Henri were still at the spit, quenching their thirst – hot work cooking on flames – with chilled bottles of beer. They must have organized them earlier with one of the girls from the kitchen. Or Magali, yes, she would have considered old Henri. As she always did. How many years had they worked on this estate? Magali had been employed by Celia's mother, but Henri had spent his childhood with his parents, living in one of the stone bungalows, long before the Greys had taken the keys to the property. He might possibly have been born on the estate. Celia wasn't sure.

She was still worrying about that blasted disruption. Should she ask dear, willing Sean to hike up the hill and do a quick scout about? Only to the forest entrance, no further. Just to set everyone's mind at rest. She whispered her intention to Dominic, who, under his breath, told her to leave it. Let the lad have his dinner. 'It'll take him the best part of a quarter of an hour to reach the track at the foot of the forest. It's not a fire or we'd have spotted the first of the flames by now, and I doubt it's trespassers. It's most likely a boulder that's broken off the mountain, rolled downhill, crashed against something, a pine tree most likely. We can do a recce in the morning. Relax, enjoy your fabulous party. Congratulations, darling.'

There was a brief hiatus while the plates and used silverware were whisked away. Under normal circumstances, as was the custom, the same cutlery would be used for the cheese. Celia, though, had agreed with Magali earlier that, as this was a special occasion, they would be replaced for salad and *fromage*. The mood was cheerful, voices were at a higher level than earlier, cheeks pinker. The empty bottles were being stowed discreetly in crates out of sight. The crates were being stacked high, then higher. A light apple sorbet with a hint of peach was being served to refresh the palate after the meat. This was Béatrice's masterpiece. She had been rummaging about in one of the cellars the previous afternoon and had chanced upon several kilos of apples stored the previous November.

Claude was in motion again, pouring the darker of the reds for the cheeses. There were tarts and apricot flans to follow. Celia was pacing herself, keeping her wits about her. She had switched to water an hour or so earlier. She would enjoy a glass of crisp white with a modest helping of flan. Dominic was preparing to say a few words, not a speech, simply a few words. A *merci beaucoup* for the wonderful decade they had enjoyed here in the South of France, the help and expertise that had been so generously given. A subtle mention of their first award, jealously won in Paris. A triumph for this lesser-regarded *terroir* of Provence. Once the staff had served themselves helpings of food and everyone was devouring their delicious sorbets, 'an inspired addition', he would rise to his feet and deliver his few words, first in French, then a truncated rendition in English.

It was as he was pushing back his chair that the second disturbance occurred. A mighty crack, a crashing, a snapping of cumbersome vegetation, hefty branches, then a high-pitched groan and a booming thud, followed directly by another thud amplified to the heavens. Several shrieking sounds followed, almost screams, as though small animals were being slaughtered.

'Lord almighty.' The mayor's wife was blessing herself, making the sign of the cross.

Might it have been a screech owl that had been disturbed in its nocturnal hunting? Or was it something more sinister?

'What in the name of . . . ?'

'There's murder afoot!'

'Don't talk silly, Désirée,' barked the mayor to his wife.

Sean was on his feet. 'Shall I go and take a look?' he called, from further down the ranks.

He had been seated alongside Pierre's wife, Ghislaine, who was nervous at the best of times and looked now as though she were facing a ghost. 'Goblins of the night making their mischief,' she whispered, to anyone who was daft enough to listen. Most knew better than to pay her any attention. 'We're none of us safe when they get loose. They eat babies.' Her fingers were tugging at her coral necklace. Those close to her were giggling at her foolishness, hands covering their lips.

'Would you, Sean? Shall I send someone with you?'

'I'll go,' volunteered David, who was on his feet, removing his jacket, tossing it untidily on to his seat while Celia and Dominic exchanged a quick glance. Was this wise?

'Shouldn't it be Tom? He knows the geography of the land a little better.'

'No, David, please, we'll send someone else.' Celia stood, calling across a jumble of plates and glasses.

'I'm on my way,' he insisted. 'Let's move, Sean.'

Before Dominic could respond, Sean, followed directly by David, was loping across the dried-out lawn. Daisy, the Collie, mistaking this for a game, was padding after them. The pair were ascending the stone flights of stairs, shoulder to shoulder, striding two steps at a time. Twenty years older than Sean, David was remarkably fit. Soon the men were out of sight. The dog, panting, gave up at the top of the staircase.

Still no sign of flames on the hillsides.

'Should I call the emergency services?' Celia whispered to Dominic.

'Of course not. It's a minor forestry disturbance. Sounds worse than it is. Wind amplifying the damage.'

To lighten the mood, revitalize the party spirit, old Henri rose from his seat, took up his battered accordion and began to press agile fingers against the bass buttons, the keyboard. French *chansons*. Firm favourites with this crowd. Jacques Prévert's 'Autumn Leaves'. The evergreen notes wafted in and around the candlelight, easing the anxious faces, seducing the guests' attentions back to their food.

'Stuffed to the gills but I can't let this go to waste.'

'What a spread.'

'I love that tune. Bravo, Henri.' This was Tom, humming along to the melody, breaking into song, encouraging the chorus.

A spattering of applause among the clatter of cutlery, the splash of wine into emptied glasses.

'Dominic,' called the mayor, 'I'd say you've got trees down. That'll be pines snapping. I've heard in some parts of the uplands they're going over like ninepins. It's the *sécheresse*, these interminable months of aridity. The trees can't take any more. In all my years, I've never known the drought get this bad. No rain to dampen the dried-out earth, to hug those roots.'

'Old Olivier's got a good thought there,' called one of the wizened women. She lived with her son in a couple of rooms in a half-crumbled watermill. 'Earth's so damn dry there's nothing left for the roots to grab and those pines are so wretchedly shallow-rooted.'

'Or could it be rockfall? Seen it many a time. Rocks careering down the mountainsides causing avalanches, crushing everything in their wake. They'd kill a man in a second.'

Celia took a deep breath, thinking of the two who had set off into the darkness. Were they safe? 'We shouldn't have let them go,' she muttered to Dominic. 'At least Sean knows his way around a bit, but David not at all.'

Dominic waved away her concern impatiently.

Henri continued to play his sweet tunes. Hints of Juliette Gréco, Édith Piaf. There was no sign of a fire in the forest, which would certainly have mustered the assembled crowd to their feet, and would justify calling in professional assistance. Instead, Celia gave a signal for the tarts and flans to be delivered.

Celia, eyes darting back and forth, was watching for the return of Sean and David, but they were nowhere to be seen yet. If they had found anything untoward one would have raised an alarm. Under the circumstances, it was wiser to lean back and relish the rest of the celebration. Tomorrow morning they could gather together a search party, if necessary, to discover what had triggered the eruptions.

Dominic rose to his feet, made his speech with characteristic equanimity and humour but perhaps a few words briefer than he had originally intended. Nonetheless, there was laughter, a sense of neighbourliness and good humour from his well-fed audience, followed by plenty of applause and a cheer or two.

Claude was proposing to wash down the desserts with a final flute of the light-pink bubbly, or a Farigoule *digestif* – a liqueur made on their premises but not sold commercially by the estate. Its main ingredient, steeped in pure alcohol, was

Provençal wild thyme, reaped from the hillsides all about them, the *garrigue*, the bosky Mediterranean scrubland. A dash of caramel gave the drink its golden hue. Served chilled with ice cubes, it was refreshing, but Celia settled for a small quantity of dry white wine. A well-earned final glass to toast the assembled caucus and round off the evening. She knew in her bones that the party was a triumph.

Alexandre Boyer, to her right, his head thrown back, was laughing heartily, a glass raised, preparing to toast his hosts. A warm feeling washed over her. She felt sure that this evening would be recalled and talked about far and wide for many months to come.

Decision-making on viticultural or land matters would be that much easier for Dominic to achieve, to encourage others to action, after this evening. The foundations for accord were being cemented. Those who mistrusted the Millars because they were foreigners might look upon them after this evening with kindlier, less judging eyes. Celia knew all too well that they would never be accepted by the Provençaux as natives but their farming methods were garnering respect and their results were envied and admired. Fingers crossed, the wines, the latest vintages for sale and to order, would also remain in the memories of those present on this enchanted starlit evening.

CHAPTER TWENTY

The party was breaking up at a leisurely pace. Monsieur the mayor was hauling Madame from her seat while she snickered and tittered and hiccuped. Once both were upright on their short, sturdy legs, they were shaking hands, exchanging *bises*, the traditional kisses to the cheeks, with their neighbours and friends, both new and old. A pool of people surrounded Dominic, slapping him on the shoulders, promising to call him regarding their next order, bestowing compliments upon him for the sterling results he and Claude had achieved.

'Your best vintage to date.'

'An award well deserved.'

'You are giving this region a name to be proud of.'

'Organic wines will be your next challenge.'

Celia was embracing one departing friend after another, waving goodnight while also signalling to her team to escort the sleepy overnighters to their rooms. Travel bags had already been deposited in the two suites taken by guests.

Her feet and back were screaming. How she longed to kick off her shoes, to disappear for a late-night moonlit dip, but she couldn't unwind just yet. One couple or another might call for missing towels – she sincerely hoped not – or some other small item overlooked, forgotten, even though she had checked the rooms twice that afternoon. More importantly, and the underlying reason for not being able to ease off yet, there was still no sign of David and Sean. Had someone thought to furnish the men with lamps? Why hadn't she called to them, as they hurried away, to nip into one of the sheds and pick up a couple of torches?

Gillian and Tom were standing together in a purposeless fashion. He, with his arm across her white-and-olive-green-clad shoulders. Celia suddenly felt a flood of irritation towards them. Tom should have been the man to hike to the forest, not David. But he had eyes only for Gillian. It was remiss of him but now was not the moment to chastise.

Celia turned her attention to Henri, who was on his knees at the spit, making certain that not a single ember was left smouldering that could be carried by a late-night gust of wind, a spark spinning off out of control.

'Tom,' she called, 'give Henri a hand, please. And when you've done that, carry the crates of empties back up to the sheds. Magali will show you where to stow them.' Her tone was sharper than she'd intended and she registered, but ignored, his puzzled expression. He gave a friendly salute, muttered under his breath to Gillian and took off at a lick to assist Henri. Poor old soul must be shattered. She should drive him home.

'Henri, time to stop. I'll give you a lift.'

'Just finishing here,' he answered in his fading voice.

'No, there's an army of us here to tidy up. I'll fetch the keys. See you by the car, and don't forget your squeezebox.' She grinned. 'How clever of you to bring it along. Tom, when all's done, please switch off the tree lights at the electricity box, then unplug them. Make sure there are no candles left burning. Not a flicker to catch, understand? I'm counting on you to check thoroughly.'

He nodded, still perplexed by her abrupt manner.

Hoisting the skirt of her frock above her ankles, she hurried up the steps. On her way, she'd let Dominic know where she was going. Voices echoing everywhere, people wishing each other goodnight. *Bonne nuit. A bientôt.* Dominic was out front, waving off various cars, directing this person or the next on their way. Magali, who looked as tired as a flogged mule, came to inform Celia that she and her troupe had wrapped everything up for the night and they'd be making their way down to the village.

'Wait, I'm taking Henri and I'll come back for you all.' This was one of those moments when Celia cursed that she and Dominic had only the one vehicle aside from tractors and various wine-hauling machinery. It had been a decision made during the earlier hardship years and they had never got round to reconsidering it.

Magali thanked her, assuring her that there were plenty from the sumptuous supper who owned cars and lived in the village. Each of her small team had a ride home. 'I'll be back to make the breakfasts and do the tidy-up at seven.'

'Seven thirty is perfect. We'll all need a little lie-in. And take Monday and Tuesday off. Bless you, thank you for everything. Tonight was a huge success, mainly due to you three.' She kissed Magali on both slightly damp cheeks, gave a thumbs-up to the wilting women, grabbed her shoulder-bag and strode off in search of Henri, who was hauling himself up the last few steps of the stone stairway, accordion under one arm.

The night was clear, flooded with starlight. The navy-blue sky was as though it had been polished by the wind, which was gaining in force. Glancing beyond the windscreen north-east to her right, Celia observed a bank of rising clouds sailing high above the forest. 'That looks threatening.'

'Gusts are whipping,' observed Henri, as they bounced in the motor along the dust track. The ripening vines either side of them were swaying and bending. 'We could be in for a mistral, a blaster at that. When I looked in on the bees this afternoon, they were hunkering down, preparing for fierce weather.'

'It's funny how they know.'

'Oh, those girls have fine instincts, better than any news channel.' She heard the mirth, the warmth in his voice.

'It was that young British lad who spotted them, returning to the hives.'

'Sean? Yes, he's very observant.'

'No, not him. The tall fella. Says he had hives when he was a kid.'

'David?'

'Nice chap.'

They travelled on in silence, a tired satisfaction, Celia wondering about David's childhood.

She dropped Henri at his cottage, thanked him profoundly, 'and for the music. It always wins them over.' She insisted that aside from strolling to the main house for a square meal and some company, if he fancied it, he was to give himself a restful Sunday. 'You've earned it. Thank you for everything.'

'When that young David gets back remind him that he's promised to visit the bees with me tomorrow. The hives on the higher hills. I want to set off soon after light. And next week we'll tackle those forestry problems. Don't you worry your head, Celia. All will be well. Get some sleep.'

'What would we do without you? *Bonne nuit*.'

He tipped his brown felt fedora, like the gentleman he was, then held tight onto it. His accordion was swinging from one shoulder. One gust and his hat would be sailing heavenwards. Remaining where he was, he craned his neck, squinted, surveying the sky. 'Bad weather definitely coming in,' he predicted, before shuffling the last few metres to his front door.

Celia, stifling a yawn, followed his bent frame until he was safely inside his empty house. He was surely lonely. It was possibly why he refused to consider their proposals for retirement, even though he was nudging eighty. He'd stay on in the house, of course. That went without saying. Asking him to leave the estate was out of the question. Since Liliane, his beloved wife, had passed away a decade earlier, he'd lived there by himself, save for his broods of chickens, ducks, half a dozen goats (tethered far from the vineyards) and his treasured bees. Liliane had been the minder of the livestock in the early days, but Henri had always been the beekeeper. She'd died a matter of months after Celia and Dominic had taken over, so they had never really become acquainted with her.

The day would come, though, when Henri could no longer work. And then what? They would be lost without him.

It was after one. Celia reversed the Land Rover, turning it in the narrow lane, to make the short journey back to her bed. Too late for a swim. She was bone-tired, yearned for sleep, tranquil in the knowledge that their celebrations had been the best of fun and, fingers crossed, a professional success.

She crawled forward in quiet contemplation, thinking how pleased she was she'd chosen this evening dress. It had worked well. Buying a new frock, when this one had been so rarely worn, would have been an extravagance. Her thoughts switched to David. What a trooper he was. She hoped he was safe in his room by now.

A shadow moved in the headlights. Someone ahead walking the track, his back to her, moving slowly in the direction of the main house. Too short to be David or Tom, it could only be Sean. Unless it was a trespasser, an illegal hunter descending from the forest? She prayed not. He didn't appear to be armed. Where was her bag, her telephone? A moment's panic. It must be Sean. She flashed her headlights. The figure turned. It was Sean. He waited, a dejected air about him.

Why was he alone? Where was David? Had something happened?

CHAPTER TWENTY-ONE

'Jump in,' she commanded.

Sean's sandy hair was solid with sweat, standing erect. 'Thanks.' His body and clothes gave off a kind of peaty smell as he climbed aboard. Not unpleasant. Of decaying leaves, compost. Perfumes of the forest. Of Ireland too, possibly. His movements were heavy, weary. His face was dusted with perspiration and a light coating of the rust-red earth the Esterel region was famous for. Ancient volcanic soil. The young man let out a deep groan as he slumped back in his seat and closed his eyes. Celia rammed the gearstick into third, pushing the motor onwards. 'Are you all right?'

He nodded, eyes still closed as though he were napping.

'Where's David?'

Sean shrugged. 'Dunno.'

She was alarmed. 'Sean!'

'We separated.'

'Why?'

'David's idea. Thought we'd cover more ground individually. I went left, he took the path to the right.'

'The steeper route? But that's insane. He doesn't have the first notion of the lie of the land here, the pitfalls. I hope he had no thoughts of climbing to the upper forest? It's so dense, and at night . . . We only intended for you both to take a scout, a swift reconnoitre, to confirm there were no fires. And no trespassers or arsonists.'

'We saw no fires. All was calm on that score as far as I could gauge. And I didn't spot a soul.'

'That's reassuring.'

'But when I circuited the western section of the hill's base, I came face to face with a monster of a tree. It had fallen directly across the path, cutting off all further access. Lying on its side. Celia, the trunk's girth was fecking taller than me. I'm not kidding. I mean, I'm no giant, but even so . . . Further up the rise, its roots were jutting skywards, like some mammoth gargoyle or a predator out of *Avatar*, more than twice my height. I've never seen anything like it. Keeled over, its canopy spreadeagled all the way beyond the base of the wood's perimeter. It's mangled a section of your fencing along the higher reaches of that top vineyard. You know, the sloping one? Claude said it's where your Mourvèdre grapes are growing. It's crashed into the field, like an out-of-control plane, demolishing the vines as it landed. I'd say you've lost a couple of hundred plants from your stock right there.'

'Dominic won't be pleased.'

The field Sean was referring to was close to a hectare in volume. It produced some of their finest black grapes and the fruits had been ripening nicely. These grapes were used for the best of their estate rosés, their top-selling wines. Celia could clearly remember the year Henri and Dominic, with a welcome hand from Claude, had cleared that overgrown field. Blitzed it. It hadn't been touched since her father had become sick. His illness had made it impossible for him to continue to manage the estate. Dominic, with able assistance from the other two men, had dug up the old withered stock and replanted the entire expanse with fresh young saplings of the Mourvèdre variety. The work had been crippling, making sure that every main root from the old plants had been removed.

Claude had heartily recommended this shift to Mourvèdre. 'It'll liven up your rosé remarkably,' he had promised. 'I tried to persuade your father to do it ten years back but he was no longer fit enough. It's still the best solution.'

How right Claude had been. The following spring, or the one thereafter, once many bottles had been sold and their coffers replenished, they had installed the wooden fence Sean was referring to. Dominic had spent more than a couple of months driving the pickets into the rocky ground.

'Damn, about the fence.'

'It's difficult to be more precise about the damage without daylight. My phone battery died, so I couldn't investigate further. Once I reached the tree that blocked the path I turned back. I had to find the track by the moon. It got real scary. I heard a fair amount of grubbing about in the undergrowth.'

'Like what? Might it have been David or a poacher?'

'No.' Sean chuckled. 'Wild boars snuffling about. It freaked me, though. Feared one of the mothers'd charge me. If she'd reckoned I was after stealing her young, I'd have had no chance.'

'Jesus, Sean, none of that sounds like good news.' Celia was worrying about David. He'd never find his way in the dark. Should she deposit Sean, then try to find him herself? But where to begin in the middle of the night? She would need to change her shoes, take off her long frock. Could David have made his way under his own steam back to the house? How self-sufficient was he? If the battery in his mobile phone had also died, he could be stumbling about with nothing more than an occasional beam of moonlight, veiled within the forest, to illuminate his path. Nobody would hear him if he yelled for help.

'Did David have his phone with him?'

'I guess.'

'You didn't hear him calling?'

'Not at all, or I'd've looked for him.'

She tried to picture the moment David had taken off, but her brain was tired, fuzzy. Had she and Dominic acted irresponsibly? They should have stopped him volunteering, rushing away like that. 'Do you want to come back to the main house and I'll fix you some supper, make you a cup of tea, or shall I drive you directly to the lodge?'

'The lodge'll do me grand, thanks, Celia. There's food in if I fancy a snack. Doubt it, though. A shower's what I'm craving and a few hours' beauty sleep. You're probably on your last legs yourself.'

She threw a glance at him. 'I am. We really appreciate everything you've been doing to help us.'

'I'm having the best time.' He grinned. 'If I were back home, I'd be in the taproom at my local, the Dead Man's, serving bar food and Guinness to the tourists. And they've seriously cheapo wine at that bar. One sip and you and Dominic'd keel over. This is real adventure.'

'Well, let's hope we have no more adventures for tonight, eh?'

Celia drew into the front yard, switched off the engine and let her hands drop into her silky lap. She yawned, turned her head towards their dear old manor house. The night, the building, all was still, many bedroom shutters closed, other rooms in darkness. She sat motionless, too bushed to shift herself. Her feet were killing her. She was out of the habit of wearing heels, even low ones. She should have changed into loafers before driving Henri home.

Should have, should have . . .

There was not a soul in sight, of course not. Doors locked, everyone tucked up. With the possible exception of David. Dominic would have retired – she had told him not to wait up. She regretted that now because she was thinking they should send out a search party. But, first, she should slip up to David's quarters to confirm whether he was there or not. Might Dominic have seen him, spoken to him before turning in? When she'd dropped Sean off at the lodge, before she'd been obliged to take the coastal track back in the dark on her own, scary enough in daylight but treacherous at night, she'd asked Sean to check with Tom. She had waited by the car, strolling up and down, stretching her legs while Sean went in to find his housemate and, if he was still up, bring him out. Celia was guessing that Gillian was more than likely in there with Tom. Wouldn't she want to know that her father was safe and not still out on the mountain?

'There's no one here,' Sean said, as he stepped back out of the front door. 'I knocked a couple of times, but he's not responding. Knocked pretty hard at that. He'd have heard, for sure.'

Rather than walk back to the lodge after the party, the pair must have settled for Gillian's single room.

'Thanks, Sean. Get some sleep. Come up to the main house whenever you feel like it, join us for breakfast.'

Sean nodded. 'Will do, Celia, if I don't sleep all day. Take care on your drive back.' He tilted his head skywards. 'Looks like a storm's coming in.'

She watched him close the lodge door as she turned the vehicle and inched her way forward, haunted by the plummet seawards if she made a wrong move.

CHAPTER TWENTY-TWO

Safely home, she climbed out of the car, lifting her ankle-length skirt so she didn't trip in the darkness, and glanced heavenwards. It was close to three, judging by the moon's trajectory. The sky was starry and clear. The wind, though, had a bite to it, knife's edge, and it was gaining in force. From the direction of the mountains came long, low rumblings, like distant thunder, but she had no faith it would deliver the desperately needed rain.

The front door was bound to be locked. She made her way round to the side of the house, to where Dominic kept a key hidden. It gave access to the kitchen entrance. Weary as she was, she feared she would not sleep until she knew that David was safely ensconced in his bed

She climbed the stairs to the first floor in her bare feet, slingback pumps in her hand, not wishing to awaken any who slept lightly. David had been allocated Sally's room. This meant tiptoeing past her and Dominic's quarters as well as one set of their visitors, the Boyers from the Marseille hotel. Federico and Valeria were on the second floor. The old wooden boards, polished to a dark honey hue, creaked noisily no matter how softly Celia trod. She bumped clumsily against the skirting board. Exhaustion, not wine. Sally's was the last door to the right. The room faced out to the front of the house. When Celia had glanced up from the car, its shutters were open but it was in darkness. When she reached it, she knocked softly. The door opened of its own accord having been only lightly latched. She hesitated. 'David?'

No stirrings from within.

'David.' She spoke his name a little more forcefully throwing a glance back along the corridor, concerned another door might open, folk disturbed. She hurried into the room. The deadness of the silence, save for the escalating wind outside, confirmed that no one was present, not even a sleeping someone. Beyond the windows, the higher branches on the tallest of the conifers, 'the venerables', were creaking and groaning like the timbers of a sailing ship abandoned at sea.

She switched on the main light. It glowed harshly, stinging her tired eyes, acclimatized to viewing the world only by candle or moonlight. She squinted, raised a hand to her face, shut her lids tight, then opened them to readjust. The room was, as she had suspected, vacant. It was remarkably tidy, not a handkerchief askew. The bed was neatly made. A medium-sized holdall was perched on a chair by the small round table, positioned against the window. She had placed the chair there some years ago for Sally. It was an ideal spot to enjoy a morning coffee or to read during the scalding hours of the afternoon siesta.

Sally loved this nook. She considered it hers. To all intents and purposes, it was. She even kept a few summer clothes in the wardrobe. One year she had stayed for several months after the break-up of her first marriage, before she had met Frank and embarked on a new, happier life. She had claimed this as her haven. During those months, she had painted the tiles in the shower cubicle a lustrous Persian blue and decorated the walls of the sleeping area with delicate illustrations of flowers and plants. Natives she'd collected from the surrounding Provençal hills during afternoon hikes, sometimes alone or sometimes with her dad and Celia. After she left for London to rebuild her life as a solitary divorcee, emotionally stronger than when she'd arrived, Celia had chosen to keep the decorations. Since then, it had been deemed 'Sal's room'.

Way back when Celia's parents were still alive, this had been the room they had assigned to their daughter – 'Ceely's hideout' – and later to Celia and her boyfriend, Dominic. (How relieved they had been that she had finally met someone 'grounded'.) Summer holidays, Christmases,

New Year. Celia still looked back on those visits as special, happy times in the embrace of her kindly ageing parents. They had never wavered in their support of her. Especially over David.

David.

David had not returned.

She should wake Dominic, telephone the emergency services. Send out a search party. Where else might he be? Might he be downstairs in the winter drawing room, where Daisy had her basket? Calming himself with a much-needed tipple? It was worth a try. If not, she'd rouse Dominic. They couldn't ignore this. She scooted as stealthily as she was able back along the corridor, down the stairs, flitting on bare feet to the drawing room. Daisy was curled up in her basket. No one else present. So hard of hearing was the dear old soul that her sleep was not disturbed by the appearance of a silhouette at the half-open door. The grandfather clock struck the half-hour. Celia spun on her heels and returned upstairs. Should she climb one storey further and warn Gillian? She was reticent to knock. Tom was there too. A little intrusive? She'd hold off for the moment.

Somewhere outside a shutter loosened from its latch slapped against a window frame, then hammered relentlessly against the building's stone façade. The wind was howling. Damage was afoot. Inside the master bedroom Dominic, no matter the furies outside, was deeply asleep. Celia crawled up onto the mattress and perched alongside him, tenderly stroking his upper arm.

'Dom.' His body shook and repositioned itself. She poked at his back. 'Dom, wake up, please.'

It never failed to amaze her how deeply he slept while most nights she lay at his side worrying about everything under the sun. 'Dom.' Now she shook him gently by the shoulder, bare because the sheet had fallen loose.

'What? What?' he grumbled, only half conscious.

Beyond the window a branch cracked and crashed earth-wards, taking smaller boughs with it. The storm was pounding at their walls.

'What?' Dominic rubbed at his face, surfacing. 'Ceely,' he managed, frowning at her fully dressed state.

'Dominic, it's David. He hasn't returned from the forest. We need to look for him.'

'What time is it?'

'I don't know. Half past something.'

'He's probably in his room.'

'I've been there. He's not. Please get up. We must do something.'

'For the Lord's sake. He's bound to be somewhere. At the lodge. I don't know! Come to bed, Ceely.'

Celia refuted the possibility of the lodge, relating her

encounter with Sean, re-confirming that she had been to their guest's room and had done a swift recce downstairs.

Dominic hauled himself to his feet, hair awry, still barely awake.

'Put some clothes on, come and help me.'

He stumbled into their en-suite bathroom in search of a dressing-gown, cursing and coughing all the while.

They sat with the wakened dog, who was bemused by their presence at this ungodly hour, sipping steaming mugs of tea. Dominic was party now to all the facts. He had telephoned the emergency services, still muttering curses under his breath. They had informed him, as if he wasn't fully aware already, that the region was on red alert.

'I told you, Ceely. We have to wait it out. You might as well come to bed, get some shut-eye.'

'I can't sleep, not knowing where he is, or what's happened to him.'

'We haven't even established yet who these people are.'

'Dom . . .'

'Well, what do you *know* of them?'

'Whoever he is, if there's been an accident on our property, we let him go. We have a responsibility!'

Dominic placed his unfinished tea on the side table, rose

and held out his hand to his wife, whose face was contorted with fear and panic. 'Come on, you old sweet, we're not arguing about this now. Depriving yourself of your beauty rest won't help anyone. To bed, I insist.'

Celia found it impossible to quiet her mind, wide-open eyes staring at the ceiling where the weather was creating an animated shadow play. She tossed fitfully one way, then the other. Eventually, after Dominic had slipped into his dreams, she sneaked from their bed, deciding to wait out the storm in David's room. There was no real logic to this choice, but she felt closer to the man, as though she were drawing this stranger or son towards her, coaxing him to refuge. And when he did return, she'd be there to minister to him. Being in his space might help her to allay the horrors that were seeding themselves within her.

Once in the empty room, she crossed to the window in a heavy, somnambulant fashion, shifted David's Gladstone bag to the floor and settled on the chair. From there she could keep watch. Outside on the gravelled driveway, near where she had parked the car earlier, stood a hare. Far from its habitual feeding fields, it looked lost, perplexed, as though about to be blown off its feet. Celia's mother used to encourage her to make a wish when they spotted a hare – it would bring them good luck, she'd promised. Celia briefly closed her weary eyes and wished for David's safe return. She barely registered anything except the violent swaying of the trees, bending as though wrestling. Even from within, the windows firmly shut, she could hear their moaning and creaking.

She gazed out at the night sky, her mind slipping from one stage of her life to another. Even in the years before she had met Dominic, this estate had been her sanctuary. After she had given up the baby, severed relations with Terry, her parents had driven her here and tucked her up in this room. Late April. Springtime. Her emotions had been in rags. All kinds of loss and post-natal blues. The world had turned black, switched off its lights, as though she were living through an endless total eclipse, until she reached here, where the mountains had greeted her with a blaze of colour. Long walks salved her wounds. Mother and father had wrapped their love around her. In the same way she had gathered Sally into her arms and shown her affection during her stepdaughter's darkest days.

And who would ever have imagined that that forsaken baby from a past so long suppressed, about whom she knew pitifully little, would be residing here this weekend? Her own son, her flesh and blood.

Except that he wasn't here.

Had an accident befallen him?

The question delivered her back to the present, to the reason she was waiting in this room as dawn was breaking. She let out a long, noisy yawn. Her body was wilting, her muscles begging for repose.

David must be injured or he would have found his way back. Stumbled over an unseen rock along the pine-needled path, knocked his head, concussed. Some mishap. Anything. A branch torn loose, falling . . .

Dear God.

It was the not knowing . . .

As soon as it was light, as soon as the wind had abated, she and Dominic would assemble a rescue party. David was unfamiliar with this terrain. He was without water, possibly without an operating telephone. Bearings askew in the darkness, exhausted, as was she.

Celia swivelled in the chair to scan the room, the bedside table, looking for a mobile phone. Her shoes were on the floor by the door. There was little else on display. Nothing to give a clue as to the identity of the inhabitant. If Sally had been in residence there would have been pairs of coloured sneakers lined up in a row at the foot of the mahogany chest of drawers, used towels slung from the shower rail, jeans, shirts, sports bras thrown in an untidy pile on the chair where Celia was now slumping.

It was then that she registered David's bag alongside her feet. Its gaping mouth. He had barely unpacked. As though it was not his right to claim the few metres dedicated to him. Celia recalled how he had stood glued to the trunk of the magnolia on that first evening, only Daisy keeping him company. Unlike Gillian, who had strewn her tiny patch with everything she possessed, who had no qualms about entering others' private spheres and helping herself to whatever she fancied. Had David even deposited his washbag and toiletries in the bathroom? Celia bent to the bag. It gave the impression of being full. Her hand touched its faux-leather casing, hovered by the opening. Might his passport be within, secreted in a side pocket? Or might it have been stowed in one of the drawers of the two bedside tables? Her mind slipped back to Gillian, to the scrapbook. The Celia Grey scrapbook. Might David also be travelling with such 'keepsakes', if that was how one described such memorabilia? Her heart began to pound. Fear, discomfort, culpability, at the prospect of plundering someone's private affairs. What would Dominic say to such a trespass? Dominic, who was suspicious of these newcomers, who didn't trust them. Celia lifted her head and glanced at the door, irrationally expecting David to stroll in and catch her at her reprehensible act. But didn't she have a right to know who this man was, who these people really were? If Dominic had doubts, was it not Celia's duty – well, perhaps not duty, but her prerogative – to uncover the truth?

Was this man her son? *She believed he was but she'd better know.*

Her hand crept to the interior of the bag.

Nosing through the private affairs of a house guest was unthinkable. It was wrong on every level . . . but this was a little bit different, wasn't it?

Closing her eyes, as if to shy away from her disgraceful behaviour, she prodded, encouraging the bag to open wider, to give her access. Her hand sank deep, fingertips touching t-shirts, underwear. She lifted herself from the chair and dropped on to her haunches. Her heart was skipping beats. She was too worn out for such an adrenaline rush. Working feverishly, she stabbed deep beneath the shirts. Both hands now, fishing for a purse, pouch, or travel wallet. Nothing. Sleeves, buttons, a belt buckle. Did she dare turn the holdall upside down and tip everything on to the floor? She realized that the overhead light was on. If David should find his way back from the forest, if he should glance upwards from the driveway and spot the light in his room . . .

Celia staggered to her feet and sped to the door. Spinning this way and that, trying to decide . . . She turned on a bedside lamp and flicked off the main switch. The lamp emitted a softer glow. While at the bedside, she pulled open the drawer to the console. It was empty. She hurried round the foot of the bed and did the same on the side closer to the shower room. This one was not empty. A thick packet was wedged into the drawer. A document, a file? She grasped it between both hands and worried at it until it was free, trying not to damage the padded manilla envelope.

She was in possession of a thick folder, stuffed to bursting, possibly weighing a couple of kilos. She eased herself onto the bed. To open the folder she had to uncoil a piece of string wound round a two-pronged metal clasp. Slowly, battening down guilt and impatience, Celia unravelled the string and flicked the flap free. Inside was a collection of loose papers and envelopes. Assorted sizes. She turned the folder upside down and decanted everything onto the bed. There were dozens of envelopes. Each one sealed. Dates written on them in Biro. Photos, David, 1985, Parents, 1979. Et cetera.

Dare she unseal one of the photo packs?

She glanced up at the door. What if he appeared now?

She had come this far: she had to confirm David's identity. It was essential to refute Dominic's suspicions.

Before she set the buff folder on the console, she checked that nothing had been left inside. A passport-sized portrait was caught at the very bottom in the inner lining. It was of David. She turned it over to see whether anything was written on the reverse. His signature or a name perhaps. It was blank. The photograph appeared to be quite recent. A new passport applied for, for this trip to France? She set it on the bedside table and stared into it.

Her son.

Or not.

But yes. Surely yes. She wanted it to be so. To claim him as her own flesh and blood.

Drawing one leg up onto the bed, she swung herself towards the recollections scattered beside her. A swift search, shifting papers, overstuffed envelopes, revealed no passport, no identity papers. No driving licence in evidence. Obviously, he had entered France with documents so they must be somewhere. She glanced back at the bag still on the floor at the edge of the rug across the room, then returned to all that was dispersed here.

A yellowing sheet of paper, foolscap, folded in two drew her attention. Opened, it was a threadbare photocopy of a form, a receipt, with handwritten entries, but so ancient was it that the ink had faded to a rusty brown. The heading was the address of a Catholic convent, an orphanage, in the west of England. The small town close to Bristol where Celia had spent her early years. Beneath the address there was a telephone number with an outdated STD code, defunct since the early nineties. She scanned further down the page.

Name: David Grey.

Date of birth. Here, filled in by hand, was 26 April, the day of her son's entry into this world, which she, of course, knew by heart.

Followed by this was the date when he had been accepted

into the above-mentioned establishment. This was recorded as 30 April, four days after his birth. She felt her stomach clench. It was accurately recorded. Her eyes scrutinized the flimsy sheet. There was, unsurprisingly, no mention of Terry – Terence Strait. The newborn had been given up by Celia's parents. The dotted line that required the father's full name had been left blank. Had she ever revealed Terry's identity? She could no longer remember. At some point she must have told her parents. Either way, it had been their family name that was registered as the child's. The baby had been received into the orphanage as David Grey.

Hair, blond. Celia noted that it was several shades darker now.

Eye colour: light blue.

Weight, four pounds, two ounces.

She had forgotten how frail he had been. She had glimpsed her child just once, with his few strands of wispy straw hair, before he was taken away. She had been requested to choose a Christian name for her son but that was the extent of her claim over him. He had been spirited away from her moments after the birth. (The stab of that moment as she watched the infant being carried from the room. It stung her even now.) No feeding, no cradling, had been deemed best for all. That way, attachments couldn't be formed. The severance was kinder.

All those years ago, her shame at being a single mother, the stigma, the neighbours, the Church. An overwhelming despair had swamped her, fuelled by Terry's callousness and the ache she had felt at the privation of that teeny, unknown newborn boy. All she had craved was to die.

Her parents had brought her here to France to recuperate. To this very room. Day followed day. Early summer brought a caressing heat that warmed the chill in her heart and inevitably, eventually, the ache, the raw, confused emptiness, had thawed and healed. Almost. Towards the end of that same summer, she had left for London, setting off for drama school, where a whole new existence had opened up for her. David Grey had been tucked away, allocated a secret place in her heart. She had admitted to no one the existence of the tiny delicate creature whose skin she had never touched, whose cheek she had never been given permission to kiss. Slowly, as the years drew further away, the memory of him slipped from beyond her orbit. He became a ghost, too distant to reach. He had been the one breath of life in a landscape of ugly memories.

In Celia's confused young universe, David had been a mistake. Her sin. Taken from her because she did not deserve him and was not capable of raising him. Elsewhere, everyone had promised her, David would be given better opportunities.

The little boy had been adopted, awarded a new name and a new life. Of this life, Celia was entirely ignorant. The sealed envelopes alongside her must contain the clues to those missing years. She picked one up from the bed. Dare she open it? She decided not. David had brought them with him for a purpose. To share them with his true mother? She would be patient. Discovering them together would be a step towards building their relationship. Bonding. Forgiveness.

She and David had not yet spoken of those decades. There had been too much to address over the party weekend.

But they had time.

When he returned from the mountain.

The important point was that this man, this shy human being called David Hawksmith, *was* her son. A surge of happiness rushed through her.

Might David have suffered sorrow throughout the long years? Loss? Abandonment? Had his adoptive parents, Mr and Mrs Hawksmith, been attentive and loving towards him? Celia prayed they had been kind. Were they still alive? At what point had he discovered his biological mother's identity? Throughout these decades, Celia had never tried to find answers to these questions.

She laid the photocopy of the registration paper on the bedcover. A tear rolled down her cheek. It might have been hot oil, it singed so deeply. She felt immeasurably tired. Beyond the windows, which were rattling, beaten by the wrathful wind, boughs were splitting and birds wakening. The first of their morning chorus was being sung, or was that the wind hissing and whistling? If she didn't close her eyes, she would keel over. She allowed herself to collapse gently backwards, head against the soft downy pillow, which smelled faintly of David's aftershave, and to drift off. Her heart was so burdened. She feared the weight of her mistakes might bear down upon her and crush her of strength. Rest would soothe. Then, later, when it was light, they would track down David. There was so much to tell him, so much to learn, so much to make good. Repair. A future to build together. But first, a nap.

CHAPTER TWENTY-THREE

Celia opened her eyes, heavy with sleep, a deep, dark sleep of forests and winds, of lost beings trapped, of fallen branches, trees on the move, rolling, cracking, snapping, of owls screeching into the night. Where was she? An unfamiliar room. Sally's room. She was fully dressed. Her creamy clothes crumpled.

Her fingers brushed against papers, a flurry of which slid, spilling like a waterfall, from bed to rug.

A crash of thunder split the sky overhead. She glanced about her.

And then it all came flooding back.

She scrambled off the bed, dipped to the floor. Snatched up the documents, thrust them clumsily together, and stuffed them into the folder and then the buff envelope, which she pressed back into the drawer. She rose to her feet. Bare feet. The movement caused her head to spin, giddy as though hung-over. Her shoes? By the door. She had to get out of this room.

It was all coming back, the events of the night before. Was David still missing? She glanced towards the window. A louring sky. Dark, ominous. Was it dawn, pre-dawn? Or was this light caused by the menacing weather? What time was it? Had she slept minutes or many hours?

She took a deep breath to steady herself, tiptoed to the door where she scooped up her sling-backs. She peered into the corridor. No signs of activity. All was curiously still.

She plunged the length of the corridor, pushed open the door to her and Dominic's suite and disappeared inside. She had expected to find Dominic still in bed, had intended to slip out of her clothes, discreetly so as not to disturb him, and climb in beside him. But the bed was empty and had been made. The scent of Dominic's aftershave lingered, as it always did following his shower. He was up and dressed. She needed to know the time. Where was her bag, the habitual home for her phone? She could text David, she was thinking, as she climbed out of her dress and tugged off her underwear, heading naked to the shower. Outside a mighty clap of thunder, followed by another. The old windows were rattling. A sudden downpour of heavy rain slapped against the panes. RAIN! The prayed-for rain, the rain they had begun to believe would never fall again. Her party was over, their lands would be irrigated. This was a very good omen. All would turn out well.

CHAPTER TWENTY-FOUR

It was a quarter to eleven when Celia descended the stairs, although she had no notion of the lateness of the hour. Showered, presentable in jeans and a loose rose cotton shirt, she was less tired, more optimistic, ready to face the day and her houseful of guests. To spend time with David, talk, connect, share moments from their separated pasts. Embrace the man who was her son. He was safe, she felt sure of it. How could Dominic have fed such doubt into her? And why did she always prepare for the worst scenario?

'I smell fresh coffee,' she muttered, as she made her way into the conservatory, which served as a breakfast room on such tempestuous days. The rain was assailing the window panes, running in wide rivulets to the earth outside where small stones were spinning in ever-deepening puddles. Her beloved climbing roses had broken loose from the iron skeleton of this glass extension. They were rocking back and forth, bouncing against an overflowing metal pail forgotten on the tiles.

There was no one at the table. No friends, family; no Dominic, and no David.

'Dominic?' she called loudly.

Only Daisy, curled up beneath the table hiding from the terrifying weather. When she saw Celia the dog dragged herself to her feet whimpering and rubbed her flank against her mistress's legs. Celia bent low and gave her a hug. 'Dear loyal girl,' she whispered, kissing her ear. 'Nothing to be afraid of.'

Out of the corner of her eye, Celia spied a tiny leak, a dribble of running water, entering through a hairline crack in the conservatory's structure. Mental note to get it fixed before autumn set in.

Dominic was sprinting along the passageway from the kitchen. He had a tea-towel draped over his arm.

'Where the hell have you been?'

Celia was taken aback by the force of his words.

'I thought you'd gone out, foolishly got yourself stranded in the storm, but when I saw the Land Rover . . .'

'Where is everybody?'

They were speaking over one another, questions, exchanges, tripping at the same time.

'The Boyers left last night.'

'Oh?'

'I hotly advised against travelling but they insisted. He

texted me his order. It's substantial, just what we need, Ceely. Well done.'

'But what about David, did he make it back? Where are the others? Is Gillian still upstairs?'

The rain was beating so ferociously against the glass roof that they were obliged to raise their voices.

Dominic frowned. 'There's no one here except us. Well, not that I'm aware of. Federico also left last night, soon after you set off with Henri. Said to thank you for your marvellous hospitality. Magali hasn't appeared. I doubt she could have made it up the hill without being blown sidewise. And, obviously, Henri didn't deliver his eggs. Where have you been? I didn't hear you get up.'

'I was . . . looking for David.

Dominic stared at her in disbelief. 'You went out in this?'

'Don't shout. I . . . I went back to his room, to see whether he'd returned and . . . and . . .'

'And?'

She hesitated, scratching at her throat. 'He wasn't there. I'm dying for a cup of coffee. Any left?'

Dominic's eyes were roaming her face. 'I'm not sure I'm following the logic of this. If he wasn't back in Sal's room where have you been?'

'I fell asleep.'

'In his room? We don't know who this man is, Celia!'

She ignored the rant. 'We need to find him. Let's drive to the forest.'

'Don't be ridiculous! We'd never get through. The lanes – everywhere is flooded.'

'He must have been trapped on that hill all night. I can't imagine the condition—'

'I'm sure he's taken refuge somewhere. At the lodge with the others.'

'He wasn't there when I dropped Sean back. Sean claims he last saw him in the forest before they got separated.'

'Splitting up was irresponsible.'

'Please call the fire brigade.'

'We telephoned them, remember? I can't keep pestering them.'

'Things might have changed. We have to do something. Shall I contact them?

Dominic sighed. 'Let me deal with it.'

'Report him as missing.'

'If you're certain.'

She nodded. 'The emergency services will find him. I'm going to wake Gillian. She'll want to know about her father.'

No helicopters could take off. The force of the wind would blow them off course. Celia and Dominic were cut off. The internet went down. The electricity disconnected, but even after Dominic had rebooted it at the mains, it instantly died. 'It's not our power. It's the entire sector. We'll have to wait it out. Where's that granddaughter of yours?'

Celia shrugged. 'I knocked twice. They must still be sleeping, or . . .'

'They?'

'She's with Tom. They seem to have taken a shine to one another.'

'Good Lord!'

Celia smiled. How unobservant her husband could be on occasion. And he a writer, one who made his living observing other people, charting their emotions.

'Well, leave them be. There's nothing she or anyone else can do right now.'

'Oh, Dominic, I keep picturing David hurt. Leg trapped beneath a fallen tree, or . . . He's been out there for hours. Frozen, soaked. We really must get up a search party.'

'Ceely, you heard what they said at the fire station.'

'There must be *something* we can do. I should wake Gill.'

'Leave her where she is. Please. I couldn't deal with any histrionics.'

At that moment, the overhead light flicked on and then off again leaving them in semi-darkness. Celia stood up from the table, where she had guzzled two cups of black coffee, one directly after the other on an empty stomach, and walked through to the kitchen annex in search of candles. They had cartons of them packed away, purchased for the party. She carried a small box through to the conservatory, placed half a dozen in candleholders and began to light them, several on the table. 'There, that's less gloomy. Hard to credit that only yesterday I was worrying about a forest fire and now here we are in a house that's about to sail away on a river of mud.'

'You fret about everything, Celia.'

'I'm concerned, that's all.'

'Well, as there's nothing to be done, I might pop upstairs and catch up on a spot of writing. Would you mind?'

'Mind what? Being left alone?' She shook her head. She was so frequently left alone. 'Daisy's here. Have you seen my bag? My phone's in it. There might be a message . . .' She had crossed to the windows. The wall of glass looked buckled, distorted by the streams of rain slithering and snaking to the ground. Like crazy mirrors at a funfair. All perspective distorted. She felt blasts of damp air force themselves between the iron joints near her feet. She was listening to the gusts lashing their fury on the coast. Month after month of drought and now this. A monsoon.

'Dominic?' She was staring out at the inundation. Puddles swirling and spinning.

'Mmm?'

'What was it that made you doubt David's authenticity? He is genuine, you know. I found his adoption paper.'

'Did you? Online?'

'When I was in his room.'

'You didn't go through his personal belongings? Celia!'

Celia felt her guts constrict. She had known Dominic would disapprove. 'No . . . Well, not all of them. I came across it accidentally in the bedside drawer.' Not quite the truth, but . . . 'He's genuine. I wonder what caused you to doubt him.'

'He and I were talking on that first afternoon in the sitting room. On reflection, I can see that he was obviously nervous, out of his depth – he does seem to be rather ill at ease in our company. Remember how he stood by the magnolia the other evening, stiff as a sawn log? I think in the first instance I misconstrued his rather sheepish behaviour and took it to be guilt. And he made a passing comment about being born in Kent whereas I understood from you that the birth had taken place somewhere near your home town in Bristol. Is that correct?'

She nodded. 'His adoption paper is specific and accurate. He's carrying it with him. The address, not far from Bristol, is written at the top of the page. I might give the convent a call when all this has settled, confirm it.'

'A wise move.'

'Or send them an email.'

An almighty crash of thunder sounded. Lightning struck overhead, sky splintering, delivering to the glass room for a matter of seconds, seconds repeated, an eerie zigzag opaline light.

Daisy began to whine, curled and trembling beneath a chair. Celia beckoned the petrified animal to her side.

'I hope this doesn't get any worse.' She shivered. 'Calm, Daisy-girl, nothing to fret about.' She shrugged her shoulders, feeling a chill. She ought to find herself a woolly jumper or pashmina.

'The vines won't take kindly to too much more of this. They won't withstand rain of this force. Pity the poor grapes.'

'Don't go, Dominic – would you mind?'

'What?'

'Stay with me, will you? Keep me company just till the worst of it is over. I feel a little, well, scared, to be honest.'

'Silly you.'

'I know. Even so, please stay. Wait with me . . . When the storm's over, I'll drive to the lodge and ask Sean, Tom too, when he gets up, to come and help me look for David. I'll check in on Henri while I'm about it.'

Dominic, who had been hovering by the door, returned to the table and sat down. He glanced about for something to read, to occupy himself. He was not a man who tolerated indolence. 'I shouldn't think it'll last for too much longer.

Another hour, two at most. Too fierce to be sustained. But I agree, not pleasant. I dread the damage to the vines. Still, nothing to be done for the present and nothing to be afraid of. Come and sit down, Ceely, stop agonizing. Relax.'

They settled at the table with the freaked dog nudging against their thighs, desperate for caresses and reassurance.

It occurred to Celia that it was a rare moment, almost unique, that she and Dominic were together doing nothing. A silent intimacy that had slipped out of their relationship, both always so occupied, so engaged in their pursuits. Keeping at a manageable distance all that had never been spoken about, all that had put a wedge through the heart of their marriage.

She lifted a hand tentatively and placed it on his arm. Dominic turned to her, gazing into her face. He was tense, tight.

'Are you angry with me?'

'Foolish woman, about what?'

'The appearance of David. My rather late revelation.'

She could tell instantly from the way Dominic attempted to dismiss the question that some level of antagonism was festering. 'Of course not,' he responded brusquely.

'Then what?'

Silence.

'What?'

'Why didn't you confide in me years ago instead of making me look like a darn fool when the chap turns up out of the blue? A stranger purporting to be your flesh and blood, and I knew nothing of his existence, Ceely. And now I discover his rather insalubrious pedigree, and still I'm obliged to welcome him here, make conversation with him and that idiosyncratic daughter.'

'Dom, you know as much as I do.'

'Not true! You knew you had a son, that's all I'm saying. The circumstances. And you never thought to share such a significant episode with me.'

'Might it have changed something . . . if you'd known?'

Dominic sighed, drummed his fingers against the table and heaved himself to his feet. 'I'm going to serve myself a glass of wine,' he mumbled, leaving the question to drift unanswered in the damp air.

CHAPTER TWENTY-FIVE

The rain continued without respite, lashing at the walls and windows, battering with the muscle of an army readying for invasion. Gillian and Tom had made no show by lunchtime. Celia asked herself whether she should knock again or leave the pair to their privacy, their lazy hours in bed. She recalled her early days with Dominic in London. How they had loved their Sundays together in bed buried within a cave of weekend newspapers.

Celia hadn't actually been into Gillian's room. Well, not since she had found the scrapbook. Was now the moment to mention the scrapbook to Dominic? Probably not.

The electricity seemed permanently to have given up the ghost. In spite of the daytime hour, due to the louring skies, darkness enshrouded the old house. The grey clouds belched rain, sheets and sheets of never-ending impenetrable rain. The rooms felt damp, chilly. The walls seeped a mustiness, an odour, and somehow, to Celia's mind, a long tamped-down sadness enveloped it all.

She pictured her mother lifting a china cup to sip her tea, smiling benignly, or reaching to polish her precious artefacts on the mantelpiece. She recalled the last days here with her lonely, frail father before he was moved to the hospital in Cannes and the house was left unoccupied.

An intangible, inexplicable grief was descending upon her. A sense of loss. She lacked the stamina, the resilience to fight it. Imagine if she didn't have Dominic. If his presence was just a space remembered. She closed her eyes to banish such an unpalatable scenario.

She had nearly lost him once . . . fought hard to win him back, was still fighting, every day. But she mustn't entertain such memories now. She must pull herself together.

The kitchen hobs were gas-powered, should Dominic and she fancy a bite of lunch, but Celia couldn't face food. She paced the conservatory, staring out of its wall-to-ceiling windows. Staring into a void.

'Hungry?'

Dominic sipped his wine, shook his head.

Lunchtime came and went. Only the antique grandfather

clock in the hall, another of Celia's late mother's finds, chimed the hour.

At twenty past two, Dominic took himself to the sitting room to read yesterday's newspaper. He muttered as he left the room that he might light a fire, not because it was cold, though Celia was feeling shivery, but for the cheeriness, to counter the humidity, offset an accruing mood of bleakness.

Like shadows lengthening, their spirits were sinking, alone together, trapped in this unlit house at the edge of a grey sea.

A little light-headed from insufficient sleep and no sustenance, and to shrug off the desolation taking hold, Celia forced herself to activity. For the second time that day, she climbed the two flights of stairs to Gillian's room and knocked. Then once more. Silence. 'Gill? Gill, it's Ceely, Sorry to disturb you . . . both. OK if I come in?'

The room was vacant, as hauntingly lifeless as David's had been the previous night.

Where could she be? Disappeared into thin air.

It was as if this father and daughter duo had never really existed, as if they had never turned up here, claiming kinship. Were they nothing more than figments of her imagination? Ghosts from an unnavigable past. Except that, unlike Gillian's father's room, this one remained an unholy mess.

As Celia had made her way along the corridor, she'd heard a loud and rather alarming thwacking sound. Gillian's window had been left gaping, and it was slapping back and forth, threatening to break loose from its hinges.

'Oh, for Heaven's sake!'

Oh, yes, this girl definitely existed!

Celia stepped into the room. Rain was pitching itself across the sill and spitting onto the vintage desktop where the scrapbook lay, untouched since Celia had returned it there. She crossed to secure the window, shoving at it, beating it with her fists, forcing it because the damp had caused the wooden frame to swell and stick. The precipitation outside seemed to be lessening. Its fury subsiding. Too late for the scrapbook. It was probably ruined. Its cover was sodden.

Had the bed been slept in? Impossible to tell from the cold white hillock of scrambled sheets.

If Tom and Gillian had not spent the night here or at the lodge, where were they? In some other place, with David? She crossed to the unmade single bed, perched on the mattress and pondered the chaos, the mysteries of the twosome. The dress Celia had given to Gillian was nowhere to be seen. Her note with its envelope had been opened and lay discarded on the floor. Was Gillian, wherever she might be, still wearing the dress? Celia scanned every surface. In search of what? She had no idea what she was looking for. A key, a clue to unlock the puzzle. But there was nothing, no item, indicator, that sprang out at her, or drew her attention. A passport perhaps? No sign of one. She refused to dig about in the drawers, so rose from the bed and made her way back downstairs. As she reached the ground floor the front-door bell began to ring, the knocker hammering too.

'Might that be David?' she called, as she hurried across the hallway.

David, at last?

Two young men with frayed expressions in excessively damp uniforms were waiting on the porch. *Les pompiers*, the firemen, who were the core of all rescue operations in France.

'Madame Millar?'

Celia nodded.

'Your husband called us several hours ago. Registered one of your party as missing?'

Again she nodded.

'Impossible to get through until now,' was the explanation for their tardy arrival. Celia invited them in. Apologies for wet and muddy boots, dripping attire. They compromised, advancing no further than the foot of the sweeping staircase.

'Which of your party is missing?'

'A British guest, here for the weekend. He doesn't know the area.' She decided against mentioning any family connections. Better not, at this stage. In case . . .

'Our helicopter fleet is grounded, impossible to take off,' the men explained. 'No aerial rescue operation can be mounted until the winds have died down.'

'There must be something . . .' It seemed imperative that some action was triggered. She was clutching at the front of her blouse. Her head ached.

'Wind's force is still too high, currently ninety-five kilometres per hour. But we can access some areas with four-by-four vehicles. It depends on the terrain, of course.'

'Please. Let's do that, then. I fear for our . . . friend's well-being. Unless he's found . . . So many hours exposed to . . .'

'Does he suffer from asthma, migraines, any allergies?'

Celia had no idea. She hadn't even considered such handicaps. Gillian would probably know, but where was she?

Dominic had appeared, was standing at her side. 'I'd say there's been some mudslide, rockfall, due to such an excess of rain and yesterday's winds. There are narrow tracks but no roads to reach the summit. We suspect there might be several trees fallen, possibly closing off the approach after last night's earlier gusts.'

'There are trees down everywhere, Mr Millar, landslides, roads cut off, barricaded, cars submerged two metres and more in water.'

'Dear God.'

'Several villages in the lower Var have been declared danger zones. Emergency services are doing all they can. We're stretched to the limit. Already three fatalities reported.'

'Oh, sweet Lord,' mewed Celia. David, wounded, trapped, had been the recurrent image in her mind, but she had not contemplated the possibility of death.

'And the motorways?' Dominic was thinking about his clients. 'The Boyers,' he muttered to Celia. They had texted him from the road but had they made it safely back to their hotel before the weather had grown so savage? It had kicked up so fast. 'I'd best call their Reception.'

But the landline was dead and there was no power to charge his mobile.

'Where's your phone?'

'I can't find it,' she confessed.

'For heaven's sake, Ceely!'

'The motorways, the A8 and A7, are open, but deserted. Tempest warnings are being transmitted on all radio and TV networks here in the south-east. Of course, plenty of households are without electricity so the message is not necessarily getting through.'

'There are advantages to being positioned a little higher inland. Less flooding perhaps,' one of the two young men, the softer-spoken, offered in an attempt to reduce Celia's evident distress.

'Please, can we get started?' she urged. 'I'll come with you. We can take the road for part of the stretch, if it's not closed, but after that it'll be off piste all the way.'

Dominic laid a hand on her arm. 'I'll go,' he stated coolly. 'It'll be tough, darling.'

'Your husband has a valid point. We might need the extra pair of hands to heft fallen branches, displaced rocks, clear paths as we advance.'

'It's too dangerous, Madame.' The younger of the two spoke again. His dulcet tone was firmer this time. 'Right, let's get some details. Then we'll radio head office to send a reserve scout vehicle. We'll also book a helicopter for as soon as this is a feasible operation but, as I say, the winds are not on our side yet and we're overstretched at present. Resources overextended.'

Dominic led the two men through to the conservatory where the candles offered some subdued lighting. He ran up the stairs two at a time to his office to find all relevant paperwork for the property, which included every inch mapped, surveyed and registered. Legally, the estate belonged to Celia – her inheritance – but he kept hold of, occupied himself with, the filing of all the official documents as a precaution against her mislaying any important papers. From such documentation the firemen would be able to begin to pinpoint the necessary areas of exploration.

At last, thank God, something was happening.

CHAPTER TWENTY-SIX

The rescue operation had been underway for more than two hours, as far as Celia was aware. The men, all of them, were still absent and she prayed their search had not been abandoned. As each hour passed, the force of the rain diminished. When she gazed out of the window, she was greeted by a soft summer downpour. It boded well for success, for David's recovery, which swelled hope in her heart. 'They will find him,' she muttered.

The darkness began to break up. Glints of light filtered through the bank of clouds that hung low over the house. She pressed her face to the window. The grounds outside were a swampland. Water was running off the guttering and whooshing noisily down the drainpipes. Its force was astonishing, fast-flowing into drains already saturated, adding to the mire that lay beyond the windows. If she ventured out, she'd need wellies.

At some point the electricity sprang back to life. She ran through to the sitting room, switched on the television, tuned in to a local station. The footage was shocking, harrowing: images of the devastation caused by the torrents everywhere along the coast and inland. Higher in the hinterlands behind Nice, some nine hundred metres elevated, one village had lost every house built on the banks of its ravine. They had just crumbled into the river beneath. The pictures seemed too incredible to take on board. As though the town had been constructed from cardboard. Down at the coast, the reports were equally grim. Swept up by the swell of crashing waves hitting beachside roads, cars had been carried out to sea. Drivers and passengers locked inside their vehicles had perished. Encased, imprisoned, drowned.

In the beachside city of Nice, the waves rose two storeys high. Broadcasted warnings stated: 'Stay indoors, keep off the roads, far from public zones.' The forecast predicted that the foul weather, a freak storm, was blowing itself out. But caution remained essential. Not for several decades had a natural disaster of this magnitude been suffered in the Alpes-Maritimes. Discussions, debates on climate change ensued. Celia switched them off and paced the rooms.

Could a man out there alone survive such elements?

Her son.

The weather was calming, but there was no news from Dominic. No one had returned. Celia, who was beginning to go stir-crazy with the uncertainty, decided to drive to the lower vineyards. She left Daisy sleeping soundly in her basket, a bowl of food at her side. First to check in on Henri, in case Claude or Sean hadn't already managed that, and from there to the lodge. Somebody, somewhere must be privy to a minimum of information.

The car key was not in the hall on the pad. She cursed herself for never remembering to replace things where Dominic insisted they should be left. She pulled on a pair of climbing boots because, try as she might, she failed to locate her wellingtons, usually in the gunroom. Quilted jacket donned to keep her warm and dry, she sprinted through the remaining rain, sinking into puddles, to the car where she found the key in the ignition. The engine turned over without a hitch. Reversing, gravel spinning, she proceeded, worrying now that she should have left a note in case Dominic returned while she was out. She wasn't intending to be away for long and decided against turning back.

Jets of water flew up around the tyres; plumes of spray broke against the vehicle's carcass. Her descent was cautious, never exceeding second gear. The driveway was perilous. She feared she might skid, lose control. Her pulse was beating low in her body, her breathing uneven. Beyond the windscreen, a curled ray of gold broke through the anthracite clouds. How its rays shone.

She wound down the window. The air was a nosegay of Nature's fragrances. The vegetation was soaked, sated. On the positive side, groundwater levels had been replenished after months of drought while on the other hand there was shocking damage on the surface.

She descended towards the first of their vineyards, progressing along the track at a snail's pace. The dark-red earth, usually a dust bowl, had been transformed into a mud bath. Damaged vines greeted her. She braked cautiously, drawing the Land Rover to a halt. The destruction was heartbreaking. The plants in this field were also grown for their rosés. So much hard work wiped out. Purpling fruits drowning in a brown lake.

This field was one of their newly planted prides. A massive investment, two winters back, it had been producing well. This autumn would have been its second harvest. Did the fact that the plants were young make them hardier? Did they possess an innate ability to survive this deluge? Would Dominic and their skeleton crew be obliged to drain this immense field? How else could they give the roots a chance to dehydrate, restore themselves, to avoid rot setting in?

These were Claude and Dominic's areas of expertise, but Celia was sufficiently well-versed to understand that the waterlogged roots, deprived of air, were susceptible to root rot. Acre upon acre of lifeless vineyards. You work the fields, invest emotionally, and grow to love them. They become a part of you. It wasn't just about financial loss, though that, too, of course.

She switched off the engine and leaned her face out of the open window, heartbroken at the carnage.

The moist air was invigorating after months of scorching heat. She opened the door, about to step from the car, when the thrum of an engine drew her attention. She peered heavenwards. A helicopter was progressing from the south-west across the grey-speckled sky, beating a path towards the pine forest. The emergency services? Had they found David? Was this chopper to airlift him out? She must get on.

A brief stop at Henri's found him in his yard, shovelling debris from the path. He had seen no one but had been out to the back, checking on his fowl and goats. Earlier, after the storm had passed, he had walked to the walled vegetable garden to confirm that his hives had not blown over. His bees were fine. 'They stayed indoors.'

Celia was delighted to hear it. When Henri assured her he was perfectly content on his own – what a relief to be able to breathe fresh air again – she took her leave.

'If you need help . . .' he called after her.

She shook her head, preferring to leave him in peace.

A late-afternoon sun had broken through, brightening the storm-washed world. The perfumes unlocked from the trees and the Mediterranean shrub-land were intensified by the recent rain.

Certain plants, as they dried, were discharging wisps of steam, like recently extinguished candles. For safety's sake, Celia chose to park the Land Rover and cover the remaining kilometres on foot. The coastal track with its precarious drop would be a mess of mud. She pulled over and switched off the engine, wondering what she might learn from those at the lodge. It was then she noticed her shoulder-bag with her mobile on the floor behind the driver's seat. Might there be a message from David? Unsurprisingly, it was out of battery. Even so, she shoved it deep into her pocket and took off.

Due to the treacherous condition of the paths, it was early evening by the time Celia eventually arrived at the clearing in front of the stone house. She caught the distant slap of water against rocks, but otherwise, all seemed calm, untroubled. Out front, to one side, close to one of the great pines, were two canvas chairs, blown over, soaked. Alongside them, on the ground, a candleholder with candle, soggy and useless. The place was so still, it seemed abandoned. Celia knocked and waited, distracted by the antics of a parasol butterfly fluttering round the apices of a large rosemary bush planted near the door, still rich with its lilac-blue flowers. Late in the season for these blossoms, she was thinking, as the door behind her was unbolted from the inside and opened. She swung about with a smile, fully expecting to be greeted by Sean. Instead, she found herself face to face with Gillian.

Neither woman knew immediately what to say.

'Have you moved down here?' Celia's opening remark was harsher than she'd intended.

'I stayed over. Tom and Sean are not here.'

'Oh?'

'They joined the search party. Dave's missing.'

'How long have they been gone?'

'Couple of hours. Dunno. Dominic and two blokes in uniform needed their help.' Gillian remained on the far side of the door jamb, leaning inwards as though readying to close the door at the first opportunity. She was wearing men's clothes – loose khakis way too big for her, rolled up at the ankles and tied at the waist with a red paisley scarf, a baggy red check shirt. Celia vaguely recalled having seen Tom in this outfit.

'May I come in?'

Gillian shrugged. 'Your house.'

Celia flinched. Was the girl only so ungracious with her or was this confrontational manner a trait she nurtured? She stepped inside, pulled off her damp quilted jacket and paused in the tiny hallway to tug off her filthy boots. Against the wall were several pairs of heavy work shoes. Tom and Sean's.

She moved into the room. The dining table was cluttered with dirty plates and dishes. A bottle of their estate wine, empty, stood among the dregs with three used glasses. It was one of the whites served at the party.

The door to the lower bedroom was ajar. She glanced in that direction but could see little through the gap besides a T-shirt abandoned on the tiled floor.

Gillian was clearing space at the table.

'Do you want a glass of wine?'

'No, thanks. I'm driving.'

'Tea, coffee?'

'A glass of water would be perfect, thank you. It's quite a hike when the tracks are so boggy. I walked part of the way to avoid the coast road, treacherous after the storm.' She was feeling disconcerted, threatened by Gillian's attitude. And the fact of her presence here. Had Gillian and Tom been in situ when Celia had asked Sean to wake Tom up? Had they been avoiding her?

Gillian, her back to Celia, was at the sink rinsing wine glasses, then pouring tap water into one.

'I'd love some fizzy if there's any left.'

'Champagne?'

'Sparkling water, please.'

Gillian sighed, made a play of emptying away the tap water and crossing to the fridge. She pulled out an unopened bottle of San Pellegrino and carried it to the table. The damp glass left a ring where the younger woman put it down. 'There you go,' she said, pitching herself backwards into one of the dining chairs. She had been smoking. The remains of two cigarette butts had been pressed into a half-eaten egg yolk abandoned on a plate.

Celia bit back her disgust. She unscrewed the bottle cap, poured the fizzy water and downed a mouthful. 'Are you worried?' she asked.

'About what?'

'Your father. He's been up on that hill as far as we know since late yesterday evening.'

'Sean's showing them where they parted company. Dave can't have gone too far from there. They'll find him. He's pretty strong and fit.'

Celia asked herself whether Gillian really believed her father would be safe, or was she putting on a brave face, unwilling to reveal her vulnerability? 'May I ask why you call your father Dave and not Dad? Or is this very old-fashioned of me? Sorry, if I come across as out of date, not in tune with the young and your more modern ways. My stepdaughter, Sally – you would have met her this weekend but for Covid – she always refers to Dominic as her dad, her father, but she's a generation older than you.'

Gillian glared at Celia with unblinking eyes.

I'm yammering like a parrot, Celia berated herself silently. Gillian picked up a small plastic packet from the table. It contained tobacco and white filters; all that was necessary for the rolling of a cigarette. She began to dribble particles of tobacco onto a leaf of paper so flimsy it looked as though it might disintegrate. This she licked and stuck in her mouth. Celia tried to remember whether the girl had been smoking a roll-up in the car. Or were these Tom's? She hadn't noticed that Tom was a smoker. Or perhaps they were used for making joints, smoking cannabis.

Gillian picked up a lighter, a fluorescent green supermarket purchase, from the table and lit the cigarette.

'Is this going to freak you?'

Celia received the question as a challenge, an act of defiance. She shook her head, managed a smile. 'Go ahead.'

But the exhalation of smoke made her nauseous. She hadn't eaten. She was tired, fraught. It had been a very long twenty-four hours. She lifted the glass of water from the table, noticing the liver spots on her hands, more marked every time she paid attention to them. Gillian with her navy-blue bitten fingernails was studying her, weighing her up. Her pale, fresh face, inset with those extraordinarily penetrating grey eyes, brought Terry to mind. Terry Strait had had grey eyes. Mean, cruel eyes. Cold. Gillian's were neither mean nor cruel nor cold. They were heedful, cautious, alert. She struck Celia as perceptive, sharp-eyed. Rude, ill-mannered, yes, but not cruel.

'Tell me about your mother. Where were you born, Gill?'

Gillian coughed on an inhalation of smoke, or guffawed. 'Are we back to the inquisition? I was born in London, South

Woodford. If you don't mind I prefer not to talk about my mum.'

'Why not?'

'Because it's depressing. She has a rotten life.'

'I'm sorry to hear that.'

'Why should you care? You never gave a shit about Dave, never bothered to find out how his life was going. Your own son, for Christ's sake.'

Celia winced at the swearing. It came across as unnecessarily violent. 'Let's talk about your dad, then. Shall we? I'd like that. You seem very close.'

'Jeez, what is this? We're all on tenterhooks for Dave's safety, Celia, sick to the stomach with worry, and you're grilling me.' Gillian rubbed at her nose with the base of her thumb. The pierced ring in her nostrils jiggled. The cigarette between her fingers released a stream of smoke. It caused her to cough again. She lifted herself off the chair. 'I need to pee,' she said, rising. 'Excuse me.' A fork clattered from the table to the floor. Gillian paid it no attention. She was pressing the partially smoked cigarette into the remains of the egg before giving it a final twist.

'Well, let's hope Dave'll be back soon, Gill, that he's not hurt. We're all concerned for his safety.'

'If you want to wait here, that's up to you.' Gillian crossed to the bedroom and disappeared behind the closing door.

Celia let out a long, hopeless exhalation. She took a sip of water, scooped the fork off the floor and asked herself whether she should hike back to the car, make her way to the rescue base, find the men, offer to help. Or should she clear the table, do the washing-up, sit it out in this untidy house until there was news? Until Gillian reappeared. She placed the fork on the ashtray-plate, hating herself for being so inadequate. Why could she not manage this situation with Gillian better? Why was David's daughter so aggressive towards her?

Better to forget the washing-up and just go home.

CHAPTER TWENTY-SEVEN

The light was fading. Bats were swooping, circling over the terraces. A pair of crows flew by the windows, cawing like witches on broomsticks. It was close to eight.

A loud, incessant rapping at the front door crashed into the dying of the day. Celia, alone in the conservatory, ran to open it. Sean burst in.

She sprang backwards, shocked by the state of him. Puffy-faced, as though he'd been crying. Hair damp, slicked tight against his skull. He was covered with bits of brush and dried leaves as though he'd been in physical combat with a bush. His clothes were drenched, like a second skin plastered to his body. 'What? What is it? Have they found David?'

'The medics are at the base of the forest. They're preparing an airlift out. We've been clearing a landing strip. All of us at it. It's taking for ever. The others are still there. I thought I should come and get you.'

'So they found him?'

The young man shook his head, incapable of further speech.

'For the love of . . . Sean, what's the news?'

He was crying now, his face buried in his hands, sobbing like a child. Celia stepped in to him, gently easing his face free, wiping tears with her fingers. She wrapped her arms about him, pressing his wet body tight against her bosom as though he were her son. Her son. A massive all-encompassing hug. Sean was hot, sticky, shaking. She felt his tears on her cheek. He was heaving. Shock, exhaustion, pain?

'Breathe,' she whispered. 'Breathe, Sean, then tell me everything.' She led him into the hallway.

'Dave was in an unholy state,' he gasped. 'There was so much bl-blood. He's lost litres. Unconscious. I thought he was dead when I saw him. One of the emergency team seems doubtful he'll pull through.'

'Oh, God.' She felt herself go weak. In her worst gut-churning moments throughout this interminable day she had not envisaged anything so bad. That David was hurt or weakened by exhaustion, yes, hypothermia, possibly, but not this. In her mind she had refused the possibility of anything so grave.

'Are you sure you didn't misunderstand what the fireman said?'

'I don't know . . . Perhaps. I d-don't think so.' Sean buried his face in her shoulder. 'Jaysus, Celia, the blood on the earth. It was like a fecking abattoir.'

She took this in silently, and then, 'It would appear worse, more dramatic, diluted by all that rain.' She drew the lad tighter to her, as much for her own solace as his.

'There's more,' he mumbled.

'What more?'

'I – I ca-can't say it.'

'Sean.' She pushed him to arms' length so he was forced to face her. A slick of his red hair was glued to his forehead. They were standing in the high-ceilinged hallway, barely acquainted yet facing the consequences of a calamitous accident. 'What more, Sean? What could be worse than David's . . .? Oh, my God, no.' Why was Sean here delivering this news? Why was Dominic not at her side? 'It's Dominic, isn't it? Where's Dominic?'

The young man blubbered.

'Dominic – Sean, tell me!' She was fighting against exploding emotions. Her mouth felt as though it were jammed with metal. A taste to make her throw up. Her stomach was lurching, her inner clock spinning out of control.

The boy, no longer a man, a child in the face of events too horrible to witness, was choking. 'Calm yourself,' she whispered, 'Come and drink some water.'

His face was blotchy and damp. He wiped it, dragging the back of his wrist across his mouth. 'They've put him in an air ambulance.'

'David?'

'No. Dominic.'

'Why? Is he accompanying David? I don't understand.'

Sean shook his head.

'Where's Tom?'

'Gone back to the lodge to tell Gill about her dad. Dominic's hurt, Ceely.'

This was beyond any nightmare.

They were disturbed by a second, less overwrought knocking.

The same pair of young uniformed officers who had arrived earlier in the day. Now bedraggled, wrecked by the exertions of a seemingly ceaseless battle.

Without a word Celia invited them in, led them through to the sitting room where Dominic's newspaper lay on the seat of his chair. Neither of them wanted to sit but she insisted. 'I'm making tea for Sean, can I offer . . .?'

They shook their heads. They were here to report and to make sure that she was fine until a doctor could be called to her.

'I don't need a doctor,' she snapped. But should she call Freddie? 'Sorry, apologies, overwrought, forgive me. Please give me the news.' It was an overlong vigil. Everybody's nerves were fried.

David had been unearthed higher up the mountainside, above their original search area, where several trees had crashed southwards, falling over one another creating a wigwam of broken trunks. They had found him there, within the tent of tree trunks.

'. . . hard to understand why he had climbed so far into the forest. He was unconscious when one of our colleagues found him. Soaked, of course, from the rain, and there is a rather nasty gash on his head. Quite deep. The hospital will furnish all details about the impacts of the accident. We suspect he may have slipped, smacked his head against a rock . . .'

'Or a falling trunk hit him. It's impossible to be more precise at this stage. He has lain a long while without assistance.'

'Heavy haemorrhaging. I'm sorry to report. Do you know his blood type?'

Celia shook her head. Her fingers were scratching her chin. Might this information be noted somewhere in his room? Should she go and look for it? 'Is he being treated by an emergency crew until he can be lifted out?'

'He's on his way to hospital now. The paramedics are with him, doing all they can.'

'And Dominic? What's happened to my husband?' She had no desire to show herself as unsympathetic, but Dominic . . . She needed news.

'He tripped over a root or stump, tumbled down the hillside. He was moving too fast, anxious to get back to you to break the news about the other gentleman, I would guess. Without X-rays, a proper examination, we don't know the extent of the damage. Possible internal bleeding. He was conscious when the helicopter came for your guest. They needed to get the other out first as his injuries are more serious.'

Her heart punched at her chest. 'Where have they taken him? Both of them.'

'One of the major hospitals at the coast. Cannes would be the first choice, if there are any vacant beds. It's been a weekend of casualties. Otherwise they'll go for the closest available.'

'One of us can drive you there.'

She nodded. 'Give me five minutes, please.' She'd call Freddie first. Get him to administer a tranquilliser for Sean. And then the hospital . . .

So many of the arterial roads were flooded and blocked off that gaining access involved several circuitous deviations. The journey seemed to take for ever. It was dark: night had fallen by the time Celia stepped out of the car in front of Accident and Emergency at the Simone Veil Hospital. It was situated a few kilometres inland of the French Riviera coast in the urban sprawl, amid pale pink apartment blocks in the heart of residential Cannes. Retirement heaven.

Outside, ambulances were lined up in a queue disgorging other victims of the floods. Medics were running to and fro bearing stretchers, yelling instructions, their voices bouncing off the howl of the wind batting against windows and shutters.

David was already in theatre after a series of X-rays and tests. Dominic had been assigned a bed and prescribed a sedative. It was unlikely he would be seen by a doctor before the morning. His condition was not deemed critical, though it was too early to draw any firm conclusions. Due to the catastrophic damage caused by the storms, the staff were burned out, overtaxed. The waiting rooms and corridors had a harassed, troubled vibe about them. Trolleys were being wheeled purposefully to and fro, nurses in white Covid face masks hastening from one spot to another, clipboards clutched between fingers, caps askew, tiredness etched on their young faces.

'Please may I see my husband?' Celia was at Reception. She had been standing for some while in a long line.

'I'm sorry, it's past visiting hours.'

'I've been here, waiting.'

It might be a breach of hospital rules, but Celia would not budge, her expression insisted. The receptionist sighed, rang up to the ward, which was on the second floor. 'Please put this on. You cannot access any part of the hospital unless you are wearing one.' She was handed a mask. 'Take the lift. Ask the night sister. I am not in a position to—'

'*Merci.*'

Celia was at the lift and had pressed the command button. The lift was moving up and down between other floors. 'Where are the stairs?'

'Be patient, Madame.'

Eventually, it landed with a light whisper at ground-floor level. The doors opened. A trolley transporting a middle-aged grey-haired man, eyes closed and skin as sallow as a church candle, was wheeled out. He was attached to a drip. Thankfully, nobody Celia recognized. She averted her gaze, took a deep breath, jumped into the *ascenseur* before it took flight without her, donned the obligatory mask and hit the button for the second floor.

Neon lights. Dark-grey, pleated curtains encased in white frames on silent rubber wheels screened off the individual beds so the patients were hidden from view.

It could have been any hour. Eternal night. Limbo day. A man's loud snoring drew her attention. Certainly not

Dominic's though he was prone to snoring after a few drinks. A junior nurse pushing an empty wheelchair inched towards her, asking whether she could be of assistance.

'I'm looking for Dominic Millar. I believe he was brought up to this ward sometime this evening.'

The young woman, barely older than Gillian, frowned, swallowed a yawn. 'The name doesn't ring a bell. Any idea at what time?'

Celia shook her head. 'Within the last couple of hours. It wouldn't have been earlier.'

'Are you sure you haven't mistaken the ward?'

'Second floor. I was directed here. Are there more wards on this level?'

'This is the only male unit.'

'Then this one.' She was trying to remain calm, but was beginning to lose her rag. Disquiet, fatigue. She shot a glance back along the central corridor. 'He's got to be here,' she insisted.

'Let me check the register.'

The nurse took off. Celia waited obediently at the far end of the long rectangular ward housing, at a guess, some thirty patients.

She was attempting to scan the faces in each of the beds, but many were concealed behind the mobile curtains. The overhead lights were harsh, unforgiving. How could anyone rest? She closed her eyes for a second. She felt as though she hadn't slept for days. Her weariness was beyond description but her apprehension, her terror, was off the scale. She wanted to lower herself into a wheelchair and remain there until she could walk out with Dominic. She could barely lift a limb, and now the wretched lights were triggering a headache. Still, she wasn't budging. She needed to be reassured that this was a minor accident, that whatever had befallen Dominic was mendable and that, before long, he would be back home where she could care for him.

The nurse was hunting through a stack of blue files on a small white wooden desk in the central aisle. She glanced back towards Celia with a look of consternation. And then she seemed to hit on a clue. She trotted off purposefully in her black lace-up shoes to one of the furthest beds along the left side of the ward. There she wheeled back the curtains and picked up a clipboard hanging from a pale-green iron rail, the footboard of the single bed. The man buried beneath the sheets was prostrate, on his left side with his front facing the far wall. Even from behind Celia recognized Dominic's full head of hair. Yes, it was him. Her heart rose. Gladder of spirit, she sped down the central aisle meeting the nurse halfway.

'I can confirm Mr Millar is here. Bed twenty-three.'

Celia attempted to move on past the nurse who raised her arm, blocking her passage as though she were a railway signal.

'He's sleeping. He's been given a sedative and painkillers. He needs rest. Visiting hours are between nine thirty and eleven o'clock tomorrow morning.'

'For God's sake!' Celia cried. 'I want to see him now. What is he being treated for? How serious is his condition?'

'Madame Millar, you are disturbing the other patients. I insist you leave or I will be obliged to call the ward sister.'

'Please.' Celia drew a deep breath, attempting calm, to overcome this human obstacle with reason. 'I need to see my husband, just a glimpse. Then I promise to leave. He's had an accident and I don't know anything about the magnitude of it. Is he awake? Has he had a heart attack or was it just a fall? Please.'

'I have already informed you that Mr Millar has been administered a sedative. He isn't able to talk with you.'

'One minute, just one minute, I beg you. Then I'll go.'

The nurse sighed, then strode back towards the lift and the wheelchair. 'I didn't see you nor give you permission.' Her parting words, curtly delivered.

Celia was at Dominic's side. A blue metal chair had been left close by. She dragged it over to his bed.

'Dominic,' she whispered, laying her hand on his blanketed buttock. 'It's Ceely, can you hear me?' She perched on the blue chair and waited. His eyes were closed. No scars on his face from the fall, no damage that she could assess, but, also, no response. As the nurse had predicted. His breathing was heavy, slow, but not struggling. Celia glanced towards the lifts where the weary young woman was biting back her agitation. Celia's time was running out. 'Can you hear me, Dom?' she repeated. 'Please, make a sign.'

Dominic slumbered on, oblivious.

'I hope you can hear me.' She staggered to her feet, swimming with exhaustion, and laid the back of her hand on his cheek, stroking it. 'See you in the morning.'

When she reached the staff member, she murmured her apologies. 'Thank you for your patience. Do you know what his condition is?'

'Stable, but speak to the doctor tomorrow. I am not at liberty to discuss the patient's circumstances.'

Celia nodded. 'Of course; *bonne nuit. Merci encore.*' The lift doors were open. As Celia stepped inside, the nurse leaned in and pressed the button for the ground floor. Celia's last sighting of Dominic was sealed off by the closing doors.

'David Hawksmith. He was admitted this evening. I was informed earlier that he was undergoing tests. Please can you give me an update?'

'Let me search for his file.'

'Thank you.' Celia glanced at a round white clock hanging on a plain white wall. It was after midnight. The reception area was deserted. Or, no, there was a bank of seats behind her where a trio of silent people were slumped. An elderly Arab couple, shoulders brushing, she wearing a black hijab head veil and a blue anti-Covid mask. The other, two seats distant from the Maghrebis, was a middle-aged Caucasian woman, plump, stoic. Celia fancied she was also a mother, awaiting news of her child. All three had their heads lowered. All three enduring the hours.

The receptionist was scrolling through various documents on her ludicrously antiquated computer, back and forth, clicking at an external mouse to reveal more lists. It was taking an eternity. 'Mr Hawksmith's in recovery after his procedure.'

'I see, thank you. Do you have any information as to how the, er, procedure . . . ?'

The receptionist shook her head. 'None of this is available to me. In any case, it's confidential.'

'Is there a night doctor on duty, an emergency staff member, someone I could have a brief word with? I believe Mr Hawksmith's condition might be critical, I would be grateful to know how the—'

'Staff members are only authorized to discuss the condition of a patient with their next of kin.'

'That's me,' Celia blurted. 'I'm his mother. David's . . . my son.'

The receptionist eyed her with surprise, a twinge of suspicion.

Celia nodded, confirming the fact. She had surprised herself.

CHAPTER TWENTY-EIGHT

It was Monday, a little after midday. Celia had just returned from her second visit to the hospital. She was in the garden standing beneath a diluted blue sky. It lacked the usual intensity of midsummer. The grounds were still drenched, the air moist, but she was grateful for the break, the fresh air.

The positive news was that she would be returning to Cannes around five to collect Dominic. X-rays to his head, torso, ribs and hips, had shown no internal damage. Even so, it had been a bad fall for a man of his age, a shock to his system, with external bruising and scratches on legs and arms. The examination had revealed an ankle fracture. It was a simple tibia break but had caused swelling and some tissue damage. There was also internal bruising in his lower leg and foot. Happily, nothing warranted keeping him on the ward. He was hobbling, could not put weight on the damaged leg, but with rest, it would improve over the next few days.

David's condition, on the other hand, remained vulnerable. To visit him, Celia, had been directed along a low-lit corridor where all doors she passed were firmly closed. At the far end she found herself in front of a wall, the top half of which was glass. There, from a protected distance, she stood looking in on her son. The upper half of his torso was raised. He was in a high bed. His head was swathed in bandages, eyes closed, barely stirring. The elevated half of him was hooked up to a junction of wires, connecting to tubes and bottles. Clear liquids were dripping from the bottles and feeding into both of his arms. On a large screen attached to the wall behind him, a series of lights flashed on and off.

The sight of him had been alarming. She'd wanted to yell at him to wake him up, to beat her fists against the glass. It was impossible to untangle the emotions that were pitching back and forth within her.

She took a step, descending to the terraces behind the house, making her way past the swimming-pool towards the lawn level where the party furniture was still in place. There was not a soul about. Everywhere was strangely silent. Eerily still.

Under normal circumstances, Gillian and David would have been leaving. Celia had promised to drive them to the station for the late TGV to Paris where they were booked on the Eurostar. Celia hadn't seen or spoken to Gillian since the previous afternoon's altercation when she had left her in the lodge, closed away in a bedroom. After picking up the fork from the floor, Celia had put on her boots and departed without a goodbye, without resolving the disagreement.

She sighed now, recalling their fruitless exchange.

She supposed that Tom was with Gillian, keeping her company.

She was silently debating as she tripped down the steps whether she should pop to the lodge before she returned to Cannes. Why not take Gillian with her to the hospital? She would surely be eager to visit her father.

Celia was taking it for granted that Gillian would not be heading to the UK today. If necessary, she could help her sort out the changes to the tickets.

Might she offer the girl a more comfortable, airier room? Would that please her? Most probably she would opt for remaining at the lodge, keeping her distance from the main house, rejecting Celia, whom she clearly despised.

The realization stung.

Where was everybody? She called, 'Hello,' but no voice answered, no life stirred. Magali had been given two days off so no help in the kitchen today. Even so. Celia continued descending the terraces, until she reached the 'banqueting lawn'. And there was Henri, dear loyal Henri. He waved to her. 'I'm just dismantling the spit before it starts rusting,' he called, shaking his head at the chaos the storm had caused. 'Sincerely sorry to hear about Dominic. Thank the Lord it's not more serious.' His rheumy eyes smiled encouragingly at Celia as her foot landed on the grass. It was like soft felt beneath her trainers. Water bubbled up from below the surface.

'What a shambles. Hard to believe we partied here so recently.'

Henri nodded.

Impossible to take on board how everything had changed in just one night. The wine-stained linen cloths were sodden. They had stuck like a layer of skin to the planked wood. Celia decided to bundle them up and carry them to the laundry room. When Sean and Tom appeared, she'd instruct them to dismantle the tables, stow them away, in preparation for the grape-pickers' lunches during the upcoming harvest. It would soon be upon them. If there was a harvest.

How many acres of crops had been damaged? What quantity could be salvaged? Claude was out now in his Duster inspecting each and every field. He'd promised to report back by the end of the day. Dominic would have accompanied him if the accident hadn't befallen him. What if they were to lose the better part of this season's crops?

She crossed to the head of the table where Dominic had presided over the festivities less than forty-eight hours previously and began to gather up the used napery, rolling everything into an expanding snowball as she proceeded. She arrived at the chair where David had sat. His jacket, she noticed now, was tucked there. She recollected the moment when he'd pulled it off, tossed it aside and shot away. She rested the ball of laundry on the table and picked up the blazer. It was soggy and threadbare, more than it had appeared when he'd been wearing it. The lining was still in a reasonably decent condition. There was a flat object in the inner pocket. His telephone? She flung aside a sleeve and turned over the jacket to access the pocket. Two spanking new British passports. She slid them out and tossed the jacket onto the linen. The first belonged to David Hawksmith, identity details all matching what she already knew. It was stiff, its pages possibly never opened. Only one visa stamp: his entry into Europe. A post-Brexit requirement for passage from Britain into Schengen countries. This visit to the South of France was obviously the document's first outing. David must have applied for it specially to visit her, to spend time with his long-lost mother.

Even before he had received her invitation.

She felt tears rise and fought them back. Why hadn't she or Dominic stopped him, overridden David's offer to hare off without a clue as to where he was going? It had been an expression of his willingness to help. To play his part as a member of the family.

She set aside the passport on top of the jacket and held the other, unopened. Gillian's, obviously. It possessed the look of newness, same as her father's.

Henri called to her. He had finished with the spit. 'I'll get the young 'uns to cart this load of metal back up to the sheds after lunch. You want me to begin on the tables?'

'Erm . . .' She glanced the length of them, her mind elsewhere. 'I haven't cleared off this mess yet, but you could wipe down the chairs. They're being collected tomorrow. I'd better get on with this lot. Henri, please, don't stack or carry the chairs. Let the lads do that.'

She always worried that Henri took on more than he was capable of. Whatever would they do when ill health or old age forced him to stop?

With her mind refocused on the tasks to hand, she picked up David's passport again and pushed it with Gillian's into her trouser pocket. She scooped up the jacket and bundled it with the globe of damp washing.

'I'll have to make several trips,' she called, as she set off with light, quick steps towards the house. 'I can't lug them all in one load. If I find Sean or Tom, I'll ask them to come and help you.'

She'd pop the jacket on a coat-hanger back in David's room. It would need steam-cleaning when Magali or Béatrice returned.

What time was it? She wanted to drive to the lodge before she collected Dominic. She'd hand both passports to Gillian for safekeeping. Otherwise she was bound to misplace them.

When she returned indoors, her mobile phone was ringing. She could hear its irritatingly cheerful ditty but could not locate it. It was where she had left it earlier, on a side table in the hall beneath a lovely antique mirror that had belonged to her mother. She retrieved David's jacket, tossed the tablecloths into a basket in the laundry room and darted through to the front of the house.

'Hello?'

It was the hospital. Dominic would be discharged at three p.m., earlier than originally booked. He required a wheelchair for the immediate future, she was informed, which, of course, would be supplied by the health services, to be returned when he no longer had need of it.

'Shall we send him home by ambulance or would you still prefer to collect him?'

'I'll be there.'

The time on her phone registered ten to one. She hadn't eaten anything today, barely a morsel yesterday either. She'd grab a quick sandwich, drive to the cottage, she had no mobile number for Gillian, and, from there, they could set off together directly to the hospital. A time-consuming detour but she felt it was essential Gillian be given the opportunity to look in on her father.

After tearing off a chunk of baguette, filling it with slices of goat's cheese, pouring a tumbler of water, Celia settled at the kitchen table. She lifted the two passports from her pocket and placed them alongside her lunch plate. Before she'd taken a mouthful, her phone rang again.

It was Claude.

'Not great news, Celia. Serious cleaning up required and sooner rather than later. Three of the fields are waterlogged. We'll need machines to drain them. Is Dom home yet?'

'Not yet. 'Fraid he can't walk.'

There was a brief silence while Claude took in the ramifications of this. 'Mmm, well, that's a blow.'

'It's only a matter of days but it'll delay you. Do you want me to organize extra hands to get those fields drained? I can ask in the village.'

'You've got enough on your plate, Celia. Let me handle that. There's a couple of chaps I can rope in.'

'Excellent, go ahead, rustle up the casual labourers and hire whatever equipment is necessary. We'll find the funds. Thanks a million, Claude.'

It was as bad as she'd feared.

She rang off and bit hungrily into her lunch. A glance at the phone screen told her it was a quarter past one. No time to spare. She lifted both passports and tapped them against the table as she chewed. She hadn't looked inside Gillian's. David's was the top one. She slid it aside and flipped open the cover of the second. An unexpected photograph of Gillian stared back at her, looking softer, girlishly pretty, the ghost of a shy smile and shoulder-length hair. The youthful expression suggested the picture might have been snapped a year or two earlier. Even so, hers was also a brand new document.

Issued in July, London. Earlier this summer.

It was the name that stopped Celia mid-mouthful.

Gillian West. Born in London. Grey eyes, no birthmarks cited. Twenty-three years of age.

Gillian West.

Gillian Susan West.

Why do you always address your father as Dave, never Dad?

Celia flipped to the last page. Relatives or friends to contact in case of an emergency or accident. Lorna West was cited as mother, with an address in South Woodford and a mobile number. No other friend or relative declared.

No Dave. No Dad.

Celia closed the passport and pushed away her plate. Her hunger had vanished. So, this young woman was not David Hawksmith's daughter? Following that logic, neither was she Celia's granddaughter or any other nature of relative. Who was she then? Why was she here? Dominic's early doubts, were they on the mark?

Celia took a swig of water, determining to set off immediately. No time to lose. This latest revelation was troubling.

CHAPTER TWENTY-NINE

The girl, the twenty-three-year-old woman, Miss West, was seated in one of the canvas chairs to the side of the lodge. Her face was turned upwards drinking in the rays of the returning sun, eyes closed, until she became aware of Celia's Land Rover drawing to a halt. She was listening to music, a thin tinny sound drowned by the waves hitting the rocks beyond the cliffs. At her side, poised on the second chair where her feet in the red Converse were also resting, was a small amplifying speaker, the one Celia had spotted on the table the first time she had brought food to the lodge.

Celia stepped out of the Land Rover and strode purposefully in Gillian's direction.

Gillian ignored her approach. She had registered it, of course she had, but Celia could tell she was choosing not to react.

'May I sit down?' Celia pulled the chair towards her as Gillian hastily removed her legs, grabbing hold of the hand-sized speaker and tossing it into her lap.

A swarm of midges moved sideways, spinning in circles a few feet above the heads of the two women. Celia dismissed them with an impatient flick of her hand.

'Where are the men?' Her tone was sharp.

Gillian shrugged. 'Working, I s'pose. Claude called for them hours ago. They were gone before I got up.'

'I'm driving to the hospital to collect Dominic. You want to ride along? Look in on your father.'

Gillian pulled at her lips with tobacco-stained fingers, puckering them as though unable to make a decision. Her nails looked freshly bitten: the skin on her fingertips was pink and raw.

A bumble bee landed, humming busily on a nearby rosemary bush.

'I need to leave, Gillian. Are you coming?' Celia had decided not to mention the name in the passport yet.

'Is it going to be ghastly?' Gillian stood up. Her voice was quavery. She tossed the speaker onto the chair she'd been sitting in, disconnecting it from her phone. 'I'm not sure I can handle it.'

'That's why I waited before asking you along. He's sleeping. Hasn't regained consciousness yet. Or hadn't this morning. Let's go. Better than wringing your insides out here. We can talk in the car.'

———

Celia reached down into the pocket in the door, yanked out the passports and dumped them in Gillian's lap. 'I found these. You'd better keep them safe. You'll need them when you're ready to leave.'

They were pitching down the hillside. It was a precipitous drop, but the old Land Rover was holding steady. Celia was keeping a keen eye on the road as they sank in and out of water-filled potholes, dodging the spray and shale. It was laborious going, and she wanted no further accidents. Both women were staring ahead out of the mud-spattered wind-screen while the wipers beat back and forth in a futile attempt at keeping the glass clean.

After a while Gillian spoke: 'Train's this afternoon.'

'I'm assuming you won't be on it?'

No reply.

'You're welcome to stay on until *your father*,' Celia gave emphasis to the words, 'is able to travel.' She shifted down into second as they approached the track's end, crawling towards the junction where they joined a tarmac road.

'Ceely?'

'What is it?'

'Is Dave going to get better?'

The car swung hard to the right. The bumpiness smoothed out. Trees lined the roadside, their leaves dappling the windows. The car was slipping in and out of shadows. In the distance, a silver-white stripe lay across the sea, like spilled mercury.

'Is he, Ceely?'

From the position of the lodge, to exit the estate and reach the coast, they were obliged to travel inland, then turn south following signs to the coastal city of Cannes. It was a round-about route and challenging even in fine weather.

'He was stable when I looked in this morning.'

'Sean says he's got no chance. He's lost so much blood.'

'The blood loss would've appeared worse, diluted by the rain. I'm optimistic, but I haven't managed to speak to his consultant yet. Perhaps we can do that together.'

Gillian made no response. She lifted her right hand to her mouth and began gnawing like a rabbit at the skin on her right index finger.

Celia fought back the urge to yell at her to stop.

They advanced in silence, reaching the outskirts of the city. There, they were caught up behind coils of hooting traffic, roaring motorbikes weaving in and out of the impatient vehicles descending towards the internationally famous resort.

'Almost there. We've time for a quick visit to your father before I collect Dominic.'

'Dave's not my dad.' The confession was blurted out, a desperate admission.

Celia's attention was drawn to a motorcyclist who had clipped the passenger mirror, knocking it off kilter. She observed the incident without anger. Her attention was torn, but she kept her mouth shut. She hung tight, hoping that Gillian would open up now, disclose the facts, expand, confide in her.

Within all the challenges Celia was currently facing, what she most needed was to know who these people were. If they were not father and daughter, not her relatives, who were they? Because she cared. She had allowed herself to offer her home and her heart to them.

She turned into the street where the hospital was situated. Less than a kilometre to go but, with speed humps and vehicles banked up on both sides, negotiating the narrow passage was tricky.

Celia concentrated on finding a spot where they could leave the car and walk. Coming back she would be pushing Dominic in a wheelchair so it shouldn't be too far from the hospital exit. She crept forward at a snail's pace. Someone ahead on the right pulled out. Celia signalled, bagged the space, before making several awkward attempts at reversing. She switched off the engine, rested her hands in her lap and sat in a cool, steely silence. The scrapbook spun to mind. Its unkind highlights. This woman at her side had breached her bedroom, helped herself to precious, valuable items. Paraded about in Celia's clothes. Behaved rudely, unkindly towards her. And she was not her granddaughter? If David, whom Celia was growing fond of, was not Gillian's father, who was he?

Gillian started to cry. A wheeze of misery bled out of her mouth. Was it for real? Play-acting? Celia was at the end of her tether. Dominic had expressed his doubts and she had spurned his misgivings. She felt she was in deep emotionally, making commitments.

'Well, if David isn't your father, who are you?'

Gillian coughed, rubbed at her face. Celia waited.

'Actually, I wish he was. You know, I really wish Dave was my dad. My own was a right bastard.' She sniffed. 'Vicious.'

An image of Terry Strait raising a fist flashed across Celia's consciousness. That spectre of shame, not daring to speak out, caused her heart to race with long-buried angst. She lifted her right hand and reached across the gearstick to rest it on Gillian's leg. She stroked her softly. 'I'm sorry to hear that, Gill. My father was a jewel. I was blessed. He saved my bacon on more than one occasion. But I know about violence. No one should be victim to it.'

'Ricky West. He left my mum when I was three. I barely remember him. Don't care if I never set eyes on him again. Mum says he was brutal. Used to knock her about when he came home from the pub with a few pints in him.'

Celia winced. Distant memories of a raised hand bearing down on her as she cowered against a wall, mercilessly slapping her into a corner where she was trapped. His full force on her. David's father. When she was pregnant with David. How terrified she'd been for the safety of the unborn child.

She struggled now for breath, incapacitated by all that had happened.

'And David?' Her voice sounded unsteady, full of insecurity. The question she did not voice: *David wasn't violent with your mum, was he? Please tell me he doesn't take after his father.*

'Dave's a top bloke, married my mum when I was about seven. They weren't together all that long. She was too far gone by then. Divorced before I was a teenager. Twelve, I think. At least he married her. None of the others did.'

'Too far gone?'

'She drinks. Never stops. Can't seem to pull herself out of it. Ricky West's fault. It'll do for her at some point. I live in dread of that call to say she's topped herself or, you know, croaked it. I told you, she's having a rotten life.'

'So, David is your stepfather?'

'Not exactly. Well, yeah, used to be. More like a grown-up best mate, I s'pose. He doesn't ever see my mum, hasn't for years, but him and me, we stayed in touch. When I got a bit older we started meeting up from time to time. He'd take me to the cinema, buy me gifts for my birthdays, not that he's got oodles of money. He looks out for me, though. Got my back. He encourages me with my painting and stuff. Convinced me to try for art school, which I'd never have dared do otherwise. I wish he was my dad.' She dropped her head, cupped both hands over her face and sobbed with shocking force. 'I hope he isn't going to die.'

This caring, loving man is my son, Celia was marvelling. 'So do I. Let's go.'

There had been little change in the patient's condition. He was resting. Healing.

The two women were waiting, standing side by side in the reception area at the Hospital Simone Veil because Celia had requested a brief word with David's consultant, who was in the building. He had been located, a message sent through to him. It was twenty to three. The air smelled pungent, of disinfectant, formaldehyde, as Celia would have expected, but also a citrus scent. Was it flowing through the air-conditioning system? An essential orange oil to calm the nerves of those facing the worst?

Celia took in the scenes around her. A short, squat Arab woman whose face was only partially visible was mopping the floor, water sloshing. She paused to pull a rag out of a bucket at her feet and polished the leaves of a tall rubber plant. Celia had never been fond of rubber plants. They seemed unreal, joyless things. Grown for hospitals, public venues, never homes. Brightly coloured flowers would be less oppressive.

She glanced at the clock. Her spine was beginning to ache, stiff from tension and handling the old Land Rover.

Dominic would be upstairs waiting for her, impatient to return home. He would have hated every minute of being out of control, bedridden, wasting time, as he would judge it, away from his library. He'd never been a good patient. Gillian was sniffing and biting her nails. Celia was desperate to tell her to cease, but refrained. 'Put your mask on, Gillian, please,' she whispered, then closed her eyes, fearing she was developing a mild headache.

'We don't have to wear them in England. Not any more.'

'Well, here you do. Put it on.'

The lift doors slid wide and a tall man, impeccably dressed in a white medical coat and highly polished brown shoes, stepped out. He was in his forties, dark-skinned, handsome with a flattish nose as though he had once been a boxer, and with a generous head of jet-black hair. He spotted the women and strode confidently towards them. 'Mrs Millar?' Celia nodded. He gave his name and shook her hand, offering a bow of the head towards Gillian, who shifted a step or two backwards.

'Your son is stable, Mrs Millar.' His voice was reassuring. Deep and velvety. Hypnotic. 'But he has suffered a trauma.'

'Was it a fall?' Celia was trying to respond with equal balance.

'I doubt it. The accident has caused a depressed skull fracture, which is a significant head injury. As far as we can ascertain, a heavy object hit or landed on him. It has crushed a portion of the cranium.'

'Oh, God!'

'It sounds worse than it is.' He smiled.

A whimper from Gillian. Celia's head was reeling. She was kicking herself, wishing she hadn't brought the girl. It had been an ill-considered decision. 'But he is going to recover?'

'The extent of the injury and long-term outcome are almost impossible to gauge at this early stage. Obviously we're doing tests to know whether there might be any long-term damage. We have closed up his wound, stemmed the haemorrhaging, minimized the risks as far as possible . . . It's a matter of time and patience now. We're doing everything we can, please rest assured. He's comfortable and not in pain.'

Gillian, half hidden, like a shadow hovering behind Celia, burst out crying. Ugly heart-wrenching sobs followed by a mewling, like a sick dog. Celia wanted her to be quiet. She reached out a hand, groping, fumbling to grip the girl's fingers and calm her. 'What's next? What should we – I – do?'

'Wait. We must give him time. There are no past health issues I should be made aware of?'

Celia shook her head, glanced back to Gillian, who was staring at her feet. 'Not as far as I'm aware . . . I mean . . . he . . . we were separated during his childhood.'

'I see. Well, in a few days I hope to be able better to ascertain what damage there is, if any, to his brain. He's a strong, fit man, and that will go in his favour. I'm expecting he'll back on his feet before you know it.'

In an uncomfortable silence, Celia and Dominic dropped Gillian off at the main gate.

'Would you mind making your own way to the lodge, Gill? I need to help Dominic.'

Gillian nodded and took off. Her face was smeared with black lines from mascara and tears.

After the pantomime of negotiating Dominic out of the Land Rover, along with much cursing on his part, he was settled into his wheelchair. Celia took a pause, a few deep breaths.

'What are we waiting for?' he snapped.

She swallowed any response and pushed him in the heat across the gravel, up the steps, which was complicated, into the house and through to the winter drawing room. Daisy was at the door to greet them, padding along at their side, tail wagging, barking contentedly to have her master home.

There was no roaring log fire, not at this time of year, but the welcoming perfume of pine resin lingered in the room. A stack of dusty cones collected last Christmas was piled high in the grate. The scent was intensified, trapped, because all the windows were closed.

'That girl is like something from outer space. Or a dystopian novel, *A Clockwork Orange*. I don't believe she's your granddaughter, Ceely.'

Celia didn't enlighten Dominic of recent developments. If he knew, he might insist Gillian was sent packing. Beside, he was far too bad-tempered for any discussions. As she'd known he would be.

There was a slight chill in the air. It made Celia shiver, reminding her of the recent deluge, of all that had come to pass over these two stormy days. The tempest that had blown through their lives upending the fragility of house and home. It couldn't get any worse, could it?

She was dead on her feet.

A fly was batting against one of the glass panes, back and forth in a desperate attempt to escape. Celia thought it might drive Dominic mad and hurried across the room to open the window, release it. 'I'm going to get some heating in here.' She was talking to herself more than to her husband, trying to remember in which barn they might have stored the electric heaters, so rarely used. It was humid, not cold.

Magali was not here to ask. Henri might know. The sun was shining outside in the courtyard so the room would soon warm up. She closed her eyes for a moment, allowing the rays of light to brush her face, feed her with hope and encouragement.

'I'll make up a bed down here,' she proposed. 'On that sofa over by the wall.'

He flicked a hand, dismissing the offer. 'I'm fine,' he growled.

'You can't climb the stairs and I am neither able nor willing to carry you and we don't have a moving step thing, so stop being so bloody awkward and ungrateful, Dominic.'

He harrumphed, wrung his hands as though washing them, and pretended, begrudgingly, not to acquiesce.

'Please, don't be difficult, darling. It's only for a few days.' She regretted shouting at him. She allowed herself to be distracted by a cloud of midges outside, circling high above the gorgeous yellow climbing rose, in full flower beneath a heavenly blue sky. Matisse colours, she thought, then heaved the window shut. 'You'll be fine here.'

He stayed silent, acceding with tight-lipped resentment, brewing over her cross words. 'Bring me a glass of wine, will you? Please.'

'Do you think . . .?'

'Ceely, don't start.'

With no more comment, she fetched a bottle from the kitchen and poured him some red. She wasn't convinced he should be consuming alcohol so soon after painkillers and all the other drugs he had been prescribed, but there were only so many things she could argue with him about. She was still mulling over her and Gillian's exchange with Dave's doctor.

'Leave it, will you?'

'I won't.' She returned to the door, bottle in hand. Turning as she left, she said, 'In a few days, this will all be behind you, Dominic. We can't say the same for David.'

CHAPTER THIRTY

Celia was in the conservatory, basking in evening light, a sketch of a half-moon on the rise, candles flickering their warm glow. A paperback set aside, pages pressed to the pine table: she was not in the mood for fiction, unable to grasp the plot. No matter how many times she repeated the paragraph, she still didn't retain a single line of it.

The walls of the house were beginning to feel like a prison, this lovely old family home that creaked and leaked and embraced the broad strips of sunshine creeping into its many rooms. Golden rays spreading across the bedsheets from beyond the windows, flung wide, caressing flesh with strokes as gentle, as heedful as the palm of an attentive lover, into the soft folds of the furnishings, fading the patterns with an intense hot light. This three-centuries-old house had seen both of her parents out. Watched over them in their declining years. Here was where they had lived out their dreams. Her mother and father had been happy here, idyllically so. Her father especially. King of his grape-bearing kingdom.

So, too, had she and Dominic, once they had made a truce with their past, moving on from the emotional and financial damage of London. And the pain they had inflicted one upon the other. At no time did they ever speak about those bruising days. The subject wasn't touched upon. Their way forward had been to ignore, to bury the past.

Or, in her case, to pretend it never happened.

The Silence That Lives In Houses. The title of a Matisse painting Celia was particularly fond of.

Was Dominic even aware that Celia knew what had come to pass? That she had seen with her own eyes the episode unfolding, that she had been witness to his infidelity? The early stages of Dominic turning his heart away from his once-cherished wife to settle his affections elsewhere. She, who had loved him so unconditionally, who had been so grateful for his arrival in her disturbed life. His pacifying presence at her side. That he resented her – if he did – for the failure of the play, his play, was one thing. In itself it was a responsibility almost too heavy to carry. But far worse was that while she was grappling with such public humiliation, Dominic had been falling in love with, into bed with another woman. His head had been turned by another, also an actress, Celia's understudy, Isabelle Carter, who was almost twenty years Celia's junior. The recollection stung her still. Even today, if she allowed herself to fetch up those memories, they caught like a fishhook in her gut.

How she had dreaded the loss of Dominic. At a time when she was at her lowest ebb. They had gambled everything, including their beloved Primrose Hill home. He could have walked away. There was no reason why he should have lingered, should not have begun a new life with Isabelle Carter. Celia had never known or understood why, in the end, he hadn't left her, why he hadn't ended their marriage. Undeniably, at the time, he had been besotted with the younger, beautiful Isabelle.

Throughout the last decade Celia had never mentioned the affair, never replayed that first moment of shock when she had spotted Dominic and Isabelle together in a coffee bar close by their rehearsal rooms in London Bridge. A couple looking so at ease in one another's company, sitting with their arms spread out on the plastic table, eyes engaged. Dominic was facing the door, the glass windows, while Isabelle's back, her lustrous chestnut locks, had identified her. Dominic's big square hand, his writing hand, had reached out gently to caress the tips of Isabelle's fingers. Like the probing feelers of an insect. As slowly, as deliberately as a sequence from a film. That delicate, slightly uncertain touch, seemed, from beyond the window, to ignite, inflame his passion.

While stabbing Celia in the heart.

Until that startling sighting she hadn't suspected anything, had not perceived, sensed, any cooling off of his feelings towards her. It was a fact that he and she had been going through a tense patch in their private lives, struggling through the challenges of the work, mounting his new play, daily rehearsals, mistakes, rewrites . . . So, short-tempered and irrational arguments, yes. Nerves on edge, of course. Highly charged, they were snappy with one another, bickering over breakfast, carping about the tiniest detail. Yes, yes, all of that, but even so, as far as Celia had been aware, their domestic lives had been snarled up in a super-intense work situation. Nothing more threatening. Certainly not this bombshell: infidelity with another woman, an actress, twenty-five years his junior.

Until that lunch hour when, bustling along, hurrying through the lashing London rain, returning from a costume fitting, to arrive at the rehearsal rooms in time for her afternoon call, reciting her lines *ad infinitum* under her breath, she had caught sight of Dominic through the coffee-bar window. She had slowed, stopped in her tracks, puzzled at his presence there, incredulous, observing him. Raindrops falling off her nose. Drawing closer to the window, inching herself to the side, pressed into the shadows of a vandalized telephone box so as not to be spotted. From outside in the swarming rubbish-strewn

London street, she saw that he was in company and she knew instantly the identity of his companion. So noisy was the lane with hawkers and traffic and rain and yelling voices that no one heard her heart begin to crack. Hurrying towards the rehearsal rooms, and then . . . there it was. That moment, theirs, of physical contact. That first glimpse of Dominic's impending infidelity.

Her heart had felt as though it had been snatched out of her and was being squeezed of all life.

During the run-through that afternoon, she had stumbled over her lines countless times, moving from scene to scene as though grappling for breath.

'What happened to you today?' Dominic had quizzed her later over supper.

She had shrugged, brushing it off, unable to confront him. With what precisely?

But she knew.

Pacing their sitting room in Primrose Hill, during one sleepless night after another, Dominic snoring in the next room, she convinced herself that she had been mistaken, that she was blowing up an insignificant chat over a cup of tea or even a cheap eggs-on-toast lunch into ADULTERY. It was nothing, she reasoned. Only her stage fright. Her apprehension. Nothing more threatening. She must not let this flirtation – if even that, but certainly nothing more –

detract from her performance. Opening night was drawing closer. She needed all her steel about her, not in shreds.

The following week, after the show had opened in Manchester to lukewarm reviews, its world premiere, she had picked out the pair in crepuscular light facing one another, bodies close, in the shadows along one of the corridors of the theatre's backstage. Heads an inch apart, leaning closer. Isabelle had the script in her hand.

Of course she did. Discussing the play would be her pre-text.

Celia wanted to run at her, pin the ambitious little hussy to the wall and massacre her. She did nothing of the sort. She buried her heartache while forcing herself to step out on to the stage and give her all. She knew, though, that her performance was deficient. It lacked fire, pizzazz, confidence powering through her veins.

She began to pay more exacting attention, to seek out the signs, the almost imperceptible evidence, which others in the cast were not party to. Dominic's constant proximity to the younger actress, the looks exchanged between them. The longing, the melting in his expression. How those glances had cut Celia! The passion rising, begging to be quenched. Until the day when Celia knew with every fibre of her being that he was about to betray her.

'I need to return to London,' he had told her. 'A couple of pressing professional engagements,' was his explanation. 'Don't worry, I'll be back in time for the matinee on Thursday.'

It was, as far as she was aware, his first lie to her.

Was there also – she prayed there was – a modicum of hesitancy in his intentions? Was he at war with himself? Was there even a slender possibility that he might not go through with this? That at the very last minute he would buckle and not cheat on his 'beloved Ceely'?

After the show that evening, alone at the bar in their Manchester hotel, she drank too much wine, then spent a tortured night convinced that Dominic was not in London. She rang their Primrose Hill landline endlessly. The answer-machine picked up. Her voice. She left no message. Where was he? Still in Manchester somewhere, in the embrace of another. Her pain was intolerable, his duplicity unpardonable.

Meanwhile, as a troupe, they had soldiered on from town to town, city to city, one provincial theatre to the next, living in hotels, digs, out of suitcases, preparing for the grand opening in London. Celia had always assumed that she was alone, isolated in her misery. Reflecting back, had she been blind? Had she been the only one among cast and crew who hadn't speculated about Dominic's affair? Who wasn't party to the gossip?

Dominic had been present far more than was usual for a playwright on tour. It was a new play: that was his justifiable reasoning. Rewrites were expected, extra rehearsals to incorporate the newly penned scenes. The cast and crew were called in to the theatres on a daily basis. At each of these sessions, Dominic was present. So, too, Isabelle Carter, with the three or four other understudies. All sat in each empty auditorium, scribbling notes, readying themselves to take over their role if and when the principal player was unable to perform.

Both Dominic and Isabelle had every reason to be present, though on each occasion they were sitting closer together. Drawn like magnets . . .

And for how many of those touring nights was her husband 'obliged to return to London'?

Was it a fleeting passion, his ego bolstered by the attentions of a glamorous thirty-five-year-old, or was a more permanent relationship budding? Was Dominic planning to leave Celia?

All this, added to those other mortifying moments each week. Tuesdays in the provinces, when the reviews were published in the press, reported on local TV and radio stations. Every week for ten weeks – endlessly, it seemed to Celia. Until eventually, with rotten reviews, poor audiences, the show was closed out of town.

The relief, mixed with her acute sense of failure, when the play – Dominic's play – was scrapped. There was to be no London opening, no premiere in the West End. Exacerbating her sense of failure was now an added concern: insolvency.

Celia and Dominic had invested every penny they possessed in this production. They had tossed the dice and found themselves ruined.

What if he left her now for Isabelle Carter, with her reputation in shreds and not a halfpenny in her – their – bank accounts?

Dominic could and would write again. But who would offer work to a fifty-something actress stepping fresh out of a highly publicized flop?

In this last decade, since their relocation to France, Dominic had authored three theatrical plays; each had been successfully staged. As well, he had been commissioned to write several television scripts. All had been critical triumphs. He had adapted one for the stage, produced at the National Theatre to excellent reviews, followed by a transfer to Shaftesbury Avenue where it ran for eight months.

Celia had been thrilled, delighted for him. His reputation had been salvaged. Almost five years her senior, yet Time was not his enemy.

While she, at fifty-six, what had she been left with? A career in tatters, broke, and a husband sleeping with a woman nineteen years her junior. An ambitious woman in her prime.

In the midst of so much turmoil, timing being the bitch that it is, Celia's eighty-three-year-old father had died in France. Celia had not been at his side during those final hours.

His last days were spent in hospital. She'd made one brief visit to hold his limp, speckled hand, bidding farewell to her beloved father, arriving on a Sunday-morning flight from Heathrow and back the following morning to the UK in readiness for her Monday-evening performance.

And where had Dominic spent that night? He hadn't accompanied her to France.

Richmond, the final date on their catastrophic tour, had been the same week as her father's death. Celia had received the news from the hospital in Cannes, where David lay now, in her dressing room, an hour before curtain-up. One bonus, the only one she could fathom: the cancellation of her contract left her free to take the first flight to France after the play's final Saturday-night performance, to stay on, organize the funeral and be present for the ceremony. Dominic flew over for the service, then back to London the following day.

'Won't you stay a few days? Help me, offer support.'

'How can I, Celia? Look at the mess we're in in London.'

How she had craved him at her side, his loving arms during those raw weeks of grief. But he had grown so distant, glacial. Such hostile behaviour was a side to his personality she had never experienced before. As though she were a stranger, as though he were not the tender-hearted, magnanimous man she had fallen so passionately in love with. She failed to read what was going on with him, within him. Was it anger towards her over the failure of his play? Or had he fallen out of love with her? She was too fragile to demand the truth, to withstand a confrontation. She didn't feel sufficiently sturdy to handle a showdown.

On her father's death, his estate was bequeathed to her. She was the sole inheritor. While, almost simultaneously, their Primrose Hill maisonette had been put up for sale, to cover the professional debts.

'What would you think about us moving to France?' A tentative proposition, barely clarified in her own mind.

'France?'

'What's left of our home here will be going into storage, expensive costs . . . so until we . . .' she had struggled over *we* '. . . till, whatever lies ahead . . . you know, rented accommodation . . . until the next step is clearer . . .'

Dominic had said nothing, frowned. Baffled, taken aback.

'Only for a little while, of course. Not a permanent move.'

She had offered this solution during the final days in their London home. Both of them were dog-tired from packing crates, emptying bookcases, wrapping precious souvenirs of their life together, before the duplex was vacated, signed over to its future owners.

Would Dominic leave England with her or would he stay and build a new life alone, perhaps with Isabelle Carter?

310

'France?' He leaned against the mantelpiece, tapped the toe of his brogue against a carton of books, lost for words. Dominic lost for words! And then he had slipped out. Closed the front door softly behind him. 'For a walk,' he'd said. Maybe he'd stop at the pub for a pint. 'Don't wait up.'

He hadn't returned until the small hours, she wakeful, trying not to stay up, disquiet escalating.

The flat, their half-empty elegant maisonette, had felt as stark, as gloomy, that night as she felt now, this evening.

At no moment did she say to Dominic, 'I know about her. Is it serious or will you give her up? Can we make a new start, rebuild our marriage?' She never once mentioned the woman's name, never implored him to stop the affair. She had only proposed the idea of beginning again, together, at Les Roches du Soleil. A temporary solution until they could afford to repurchase in London.

Those days had been bleak. She had felt forsaken. A brutal autumn. Solitary hikes up Primrose Hill. Hair uncombed, no makeup, exhausted. Part of her had lost the will to battle on. Memories from their early courtship returned to haunt her. The lights of London spread out at her feet. But London had turned its back on her. She had doubted she would ever recover from the loss, the infidelity as well as the excess of negative exposure. Her precious father gone, his strong assuaging arms no longer locked about her. His wise, comforting words silenced, snatched from her. All in a matter of weeks.

She had recovered. Of course she had, as she had recovered from Terry and the 'David Episode'. We always do, don't we? With scars. Scars she kept concealed.

The house, the vineyard estate, the challenges of starting again in such a beautiful but testing environment had kept her occupied, been her refuge, each day mollifying and mending her. Her late parents seemed always present. She felt their spirits in every room, watching over, guiding her.

Dominic and Celia Millar moved on. Isabelle Carter faded from their lives.

The income Dominic was earning from his plays had been ploughed into the wine business. 'My contribution,' was his only acknowledgement of his long-term commitment. And she had been so desperately grateful for it, for him. She told herself, almost convinced herself, that the affair had never happened. It had all been in her imagination.

'Celia?'

She was perched with one leg tucked beneath her buttocks on her favourite farmhouse chair in the conservatory. Face in her hands, tears released, caught in her past.

'I knocked at the back door, and called, but there was no

reply so I . . . Hey, what's happening? Are you crying? Celia, are you ill? Apologies if I'm intruding.'

The voice snapped her back to the here and now, but she was still confused. 'Sorry, what?' She was all at sea.

It was Monday, Monday evening. Or she thought it was. Dominic was napping in the drawing room in his chair by the unlit fireplace, foot with damaged ankle resting on the ottoman, with Daisy his caring nurse. That one glass of wine had helped him to nod off, settled his mood. Celia had made up a bed, after she had eventually persuaded him to sleep downstairs. There was a loo, shower, handbasin across the hallway. There he could wash, and pee in the night if he needed to. She had brought down his toothbrush and other toiletries, had also promised to sleep on the second sofa, close by, keep an eye on him. He had blustered at this, boasting his own resilience, and then conceded.

She lifted her head, bringing her attention back to the present and realized Tom was standing by the inner door. His complexion had turned almost brick-brown from working outside in the wind and elements. He looked remarkably fit, dangerously handsome.

'Tom,' she said, rather stupidly, rubbing furiously at the dampness on her cheeks. 'What can I do for you?'

'Hi, Celia, you look . . . a little worn-out. Well, you must be shattered. Anything I can do?'

'I'm fine, thanks. Fit as a fiddle.' She lifted her right hand and rubbed at her eyes, made a show of stretching her arms. 'Must have dropped off.' She was probably more exhausted, emotionally drained, than she knew. 'Has something happened, Tom?'

He shook his head. 'Everything's tickety-boo. Gillian asked if I could collect some belongings from her room upstairs. I'm not quite sure where it is. Any objection to me zipping up?'

Celia found herself staring at him – a stranger, to all intents and purposes – with his mesmeric, bean-brown eyes. She had for a few minutes forgotten the presence of all the others who were inhabiting her home. The estate was buzzing with the energy of a trio of young people, none of whom she really knew.

'Look, I can see this is a bad moment. I can either try to find the room myself or pop back later. I'll do that, shall I, pop back later?'

Celia was standing up. As she did so, she tottered, stumbled. Tired, faint, beaten down by a mishmash of emotions and memories, her body swung sideways, her hip crashing against the table. 'Ouch.'

Tom strode to her side, took a firm grasp of her upper arms, steadying her. 'Are you hurt? Put your weight on me.'

She shook her head, shuffling backwards, knocking against the chair directly behind her. It caused her to lose her balance a second time. It was as if she were drunk. Punch drunk.

'Hey, careful there.' He zapped his arms about her, pressing her tight against his chest.

She could hear the beating of his heart. It was too much, dizzying. She wriggled inches away from him, releasing herself with clumsy steps. 'I'm fine.'

But she wasn't. He slipped an arm into one of hers and bundled her back to the farmhouse chair. The solid wooden chair had belonged to her father's brother, Uncle Albert, many moons ago. It had somehow found its way here, she couldn't remember the circumstances. It was a comfy, solid place to rest, its arms as wide and sturdy as paddles. She loved it. Felt cared for in it, cradled.

Tom was hovering over her, his proximity unnerving. His gestures were mere kindness – how could he know of her vulnerabilities?

'Shall I fetch you a glass of water?'

'Yes, please. Do you know where the kitchen is?' Was this the first time he had been inside the house?

'I'll find it.' He gave her a reassuring grin and was gone.

She could hear his footsteps, the presence of him, chugging along the rather dimly lit corridor. He was whistling. 'Second door on left?' he sang out. She worried the sound of his voice might disturb Dominic.

'Yes.'

He was back in what seemed like nanoseconds, bearing a tall beaker of cloudy tap water. Droplets were sliding down the outside of the glass. 'There you go.'

She accepted the beaker without a word. Holding it firmly between both hands, downing a long, thirsty swig. She was shaking.

'You've certainly been through the wars. Quite a weekend for everyone.'

She nodded.

He dropped down, long legs apart, onto a chair opposite her, elbows leaning on the table. Face in his hands, staring intently. His gaze was disconcerting, almost too much to bear. The very fact of him, his physicality, disarmed her. 'The other day, Celia, when you came to the cottage . . .'

She felt herself tighten.

'Were you looking for me? Hoping to find me there . . .'

'You mean when I was bringing food?'

His attention drilled into her. 'I thought maybe you'd listened to my music. Liked it, and . . .'

She stared at him, a little stupefied.

'Will you help me, Ceely, please?'

'Help?'

'Talk to Dominic about my compositions, ask him to . . .'

'Tom, please . . .'

'What?'

'Seriously bad timing.' She was attempting to make light of his approaches.

He nodded, hiding his dashed hopes, staring at his clenched hands. 'I thought maybe . . . Did you enjoy the songs I sent you?'

Celia took a beat. 'I haven't listened to them yet, Tom. I meant to, but what with everything else . . . Sorry.'

'Oh.'

'Let's rally the current difficulties, shall we? Then we can all enjoy your music . . . Maybe you could play some to us. How would that be?' She coughed, phlegm caught in her throat. 'How's Gill?' Desperate to change the subject. 'How's she coping with everything?'

'Pretty cut up.' Tom's expression, the consternation in his dark eyes, suggested that he was suffering Gillian's distress in tandem with his own disappointment.

Celia tried not to dwell on Gillian's relationship with Tom. It pulled up a sadness within her that she didn't entirely understand. She wasn't jealous. No, not jealousy. Regret, then, for her own flunked opportunities. Too many years wasted. Pining. Bereft. Loss of the young woman she once was. The years when she had not appreciated her own merits. Her femininity, sexuality.

Her youth was a thing of the past, never to be recovered. What a tragedy then that so many of those vibrant years, when she hadn't grasped the value of her own beauty, had been squandered on that low-life Terry Strait, a man who had been incapable of kindness. Incomprehensible that she had blamed herself for his violent behaviour towards her.

And why had she never spoken to Dominic about his infidelity, cleared the air? Not buried it in her marriage, a thorn to prick her at every turn.

Wasted time.

Still, she wasn't gone yet. Passions flowed through her and called for more than simple kindness. Called for affection and love.

When Dominic was fit again, hale and hearty, when the house was gladder, when David was healed, she would talk to Dominic. Address the past, ventilate it, release it from their lives. Cross the divide. In order to celebrate all the days that remained.

Tom was watching her, puzzled. She put the beaker on the table, shoulders back. 'Thanks for this. Come on, I'll show you Gill's room. If there's too much to carry, we can drive it to the lodge. If she needs any clothes, cosmetics, whatever, tell her to ask. I'm here for her. I hope she understands she can count on me.'

CHAPTER THIRTY-ONE

It was getting late. Celia switched off the call, set her mobile on the side table in the hall, crossed slowly to the drawing room and pushed open the door. She felt a bit chilly. She ought to find her keys and drive immediately to the lodge to Gillian, but could Dominic be left alone? Was he warm enough?

He was asleep, snoring in his favourite chair on the far side of the room, his damaged leg propped on the ottoman. Daisy, also snoring, was snuggled up against his good leg.

Dominic's head was slumped to one side, resting against a deep-green velvet cushion. Should she wake him, try to navigate his weight across the room to the comfier sofa-bed she had so lovingly made up for him hours earlier, or should she leave him be? Might he wake, demanding food? She wasn't hungry, but perhaps she should rustle up a cold plate for him. Leave it on the side table. He'd be a bear with a sore head if she disturbed him and he didn't want to be moved. 'Leave me in peace, won't you?' That's what he'd say. Dear bad-tempered soul. She craved his tenderness, hungered for it. To bridge the fracture, to rediscover who they once were. Those lost intimacies.

The errand would take about an hour. No more. Was it safe to leave Dominic alone for that time or should she telephone Federico, ask him to lend her a hand? Administer a sleeping pill once Dominic was resettled. Sit with him for a short while until he was out for the night. It was late, but Federico would do it willingly. Yes, she'd call him. Before returning for her mobile in the hall, Celia stood over Dominic, partner, husband for more than three decades. She lifted her right hand and stroked his forehead. It was surprisingly warm. Was he running a temperature? Wise to call Federico. Her fingers crept upwards to caress the crown of Dominic's head. His lustrous hair. Less lustrous now than when she had first met him. It was thinning, hairline receding but only slightly, turning silvery now. It suited him, gave nobility to his bearing. He was still an attractive man, masculine, even as he approached his next decade. Women always noticed him, flirted with him, and he basked in the adoration.

She lowered herself gingerly, not wishing to disturb him, on to the broad arm of the Georgian wingback and nestled up close, drawing comfort from the physical warmth of him. She loved this man so deeply, she ached.

Perfectly matched, she'd believed.

Yet she felt – it was fair to say – it had been some years since they had really communicated, truly paid attention to what the other was experiencing. The other's needs. They lived in their separate worlds. Their journey through life at one another's side was both solitary yet companionable. They had built a *modus vivendi* that, to the outside world, could be described as easy-going, kind, considerate and even blessed. Yes, 'a well-matched couple'.

But, she asked herself now, had Dominic also suffered from the chasm that had opened between them? Was he aware of the hurt she had endured? The loneliness she suffered?

Did Dominic still love her? Was he still *in love* with her? Or – the answer to which she possibly dreaded more than any other – *after his affair with Isabelle, after their financial disasters, had Dominic simply settled for life with Celia? A property inherited making their life together the smoothest path forward?*

Tears were welling again. She really needed to get a decent night's sleep. Her emotions were jangled, at sixes and sevens. She was overwrought.

After thirty-something years together were such questions irrelevant? Naive, defunct? Should she simply get on with the business of overseeing their expanding wine operation? Celebrate the positives? Yes.

Yet still she asked herself whether life on this glorious vineyard estate was a compromise for Dominic. During all the hours he sat alone in his library surrounded by thousands of pages of words, myriad stories by gifted men and women who had written about, shared, their intimate joys, sorrows and deceptions, did he lay down his pen on his mahogany table, matching his own existence against theirs, and ask himself: Am I living my best life? Is it too late to up sticks and be on my way?

She and Dominic had never asked one another these questions. They had never had *that* conversation. Before Isabelle, Celia might have begged to be reassured that all was well, that he still loved her passionately. The irony was, of course, that back then it was crystal clear how deeply he loved her. Since Isabelle, it was less evident.

As far as Celia was concerned, Isabelle was always in the picture, lurking somewhere out of sight. She had travelled with them across the water, packed with the bits of luggage that had not been sold to settle their wretched debts.

Because Dominic had never mentioned his mistress, never admitted his infidelity, that he had loved another – even fleetingly, Celia had never managed to relinquish the affair. When, from Dominic's point of view, had their romance been terminated? Before or after he and Celia had set sail for France? Or had it never truly ended? Had it simply been left hanging, marked down as a relationship that could not be continued at this moment? On hold until . . .

Why now? Why was Celia driving herself insane with this surfeit of troubling questions, doubts rising like oxygen in boiling water? Until recently, until the last few days, they had been sealed in boxes in the cellar of her mind.

It could have been Dominic in the operating theatre, not David.

Dominic.

As if within his sleeping state he heard the buzz of her thoughts, Dominic's eyes opened. He squinted, focusing, discovered her there, leaning over him, seated on the arm of his chair, silently weeping.

'What?' he mumbled.

'Shall I move you?'

'What?' He shook his head with mild agitation.

'I have to go out for a while,' she murmured. 'Shall we make our way over to the bed? I'm going to call Freddie to look in.'

He was puzzled, confused. 'Why, for the Lord's sake?'

'I'm going out for a while.'

'Out?'

'To the lodge.'

He frowned.

'The hospital called. David's regained consciousness. He's sleeping now, but the doctor suggested it's a very positive sign. Sooner than expected. He's healing. I must let Gillian know the good news.'

———

Federico and Dominic were perfectly content, demolishing a bottle of the estate's prizewinning white. When Celia closed the front door behind her, they barely registered her disappearance.

She stepped onto the gravel and gazed heavenwards. The stars were out. And there was Jupiter with all its spinning moons winking down at her, giving her the thumbs-up. She grinned. A clear night with a navy sky. Still, too challenging to walk the distance at this hour. She was obliged to drive. That coast road would need time, extra vigilance, and she was still unsteady. Even Freddie had remarked it. 'Shall I prescribe you something, *cara bella*?'

She had shaken her head, feeling sweetened by his presence. Freddie frequently called her beautiful. He knew how to flatter her, put her at her ease. She brushed her cheek for a brief moment against his chest, felt the thread of his expensive shirt and hugged him. 'You're here for Dominic, that's what counts. *Mille mercis.* Don't let him drink too much.'

Eventually, as the waxing moon rose high and bright from behind a bank of pine trees, the lodge came into view, picked out in its isolation by the headlights of her car. It was close to eleven. The place was silent, still. The windows in darkness. Surely they hadn't gone to bed? She rapped hard on the door, but there was no response. From somewhere distant music floated on the gentle night air. She made a tour of the exterior of the house, arriving at the far side where the kitchen windows faced out to sea. She peered in, a sink piled high with dirty dishes greeting her. The upstairs window, the converted attic was open wide. She tilted her head, her neck stiff from driving. 'Anyone up there?'

Only the lapping of waves and a skip of breeze answered her.

Celia turned to the sea, to the mildly sloping shelf of land that led to the precipice. She stepped steadily, picking her way by moonlight around the occasional plants surviving in this sabulous patch, thyme, juniper, wild rock roses, until she arrived at the drop, shuffling cautiously the last few steps. Her head began to swim. She skipped backwards. If she fell, who would know? Here, there was wind. It rose from the bay beneath, carried in from the sea, whorling up the rock-face, like a geyser. Its saline breath rolled against her features, prickly but pleasant, almost thrilling. Boats invisible to the naked eye traversed the distant horizon, their presence signalled by the lights that garlanded them.

Where was everybody? Had the trio gone out? There was nowhere to head for at this time of night. No village bars or clubs to frequent. They would need to make for the coast if night life was what they craved.

Impossible without transport.

Again the strains of a song. Sweet music – a lullaby? – reached her. Where from? She turned to the right, then to the left, and caught sight of a flame flickering. A camp fire on a distant beach. By its diminutiveness, she calculated it must be the best part of a kilometre from her present position. Somewhere in the vicinity of the bay to which she had introduced Tom what seemed like a lifetime ago. Paradise Cove. Access was easier on foot. In the daylight, yes, but at close to midnight when she was unsteady and had news to convey, a high, narrow walkway was too precarious. She hastened back to the cottage and jumped into the Land Rover. With a vehicle the route was more meandering, but it afforded her a sense of protection. Picking up speed, avoiding boulders, pushing along the sandy tracks, lights full on, she reached the headland within ten minutes.

Huddled in the cove, seated peacefully around a camp fire, were her three young adventurers. Tom was playing his guitar. Soft music. A romantic ditty carried beyond the waves on the night air. Its notes tugged at Celia's heart. Gillian was lying on a blanket or perhaps it was a coat, on the ground at Tom's side, curled in on herself, like a seashell. Sean, cross-legged, sat opposite them. He was poking at the fire, feeding it with driftwood. Celia watched them unnoticed for some time. Could she descend the steps by the glow of nothing but stars and firelight? No handrail to protect her? Possibly, but she was reluctant to try.

She lifted her arm and waved. Her voice, her call, evanesced within the wind's flurries.

It was Sean who spotted her. Rather, he was the first to notice the silhouette of a woman high on the cliff-top frantically signalling. From their point of view, Celia realized too late, she represented an urgent messenger at this time of night. She'd had no desire to alarm Gillian, who sat bolt upright when she had been apprised of Celia's presence.

Tom laid aside his guitar and was on his feet, sprinting to the base of the stone stairway. 'Celia! What a fab surprise. Is all well? Come and join us.'

She felt obliged to descend. The light from the moon was insufficient and she feared miscalculating the next step. Tom sensed her apprehension. He bounded up the steps with supreme confidence, taking her hand, guiding her. Then, his arm around her waist, they descended to the beach. It felt good to be protected.

Gillian's shoulders were enveloped in the coat she had been lying on. Her body was hunched in on itself as though she were cold. She remained seated, knees drawn in tight to her chest, while Sean was on his feet, awaiting the revelation. The Irishman hung close by Gillian, alongside the crackling fire, which was throwing out a remarkable heat. On any other night such roaring flames would have rung Celia's alarm bells but after such a deluge the sand and pebbly beach were probably still damp and there was little here to combust.

'Don't be alarmed.' The words were tumbling out of her as she approached. Gillian's face was frozen with the fear of ill-tidings, her huge grey eyes skittering back and forth. Celia's unexpected arrival had seeded dread. The worst communication.

'Not bad news,' Celia called, against the wind and waves, as she drew close. 'It's good, all good. David's . . .'

On hearing the update, Gillian burst out crying, her face pressed into her hands. A release of tension, the strain, the fear. 'When I saw you standing up there, I was sure Dave had copped it.'

'He's very much still with us, making positive strides.'

Gillian let drop her hands and hurled herself at Celia, bear-hugging her as though it were the end of the world and this was the last opportunity to be with her best friend. 'Thanks for finding me. Thanks for caring. You can't know what this means to me.'

The force of the young woman's embrace buckled Celia. She lost her balance and sank to the stones, but instead of getting back to her feet, she surrendered, and cosied herself alongside the fire. Its warmth embraced her. Its crackling took her back to childhood beach barbecues. Tom was at her side, proffering a bottle of red, one of theirs, uncorked, half empty. Or half full. Celia beamed.

'Here, have a swig of this,' he whispered, crouching low. 'And then hang loose. I want to play you my music.'

And that was how Celia spent the fading minutes of what had been a gruelling day. On the pebbles by a camp fire, quaffing wine directly from the bottle, seduced by Tom's compositions. She felt revived, made whole, by his hauntingly beautiful airs and, most importantly, uplifted by the news that David, her son, was on the mend.

The fire spluttered. Sparks shot skywards. In that moment Celia felt her heart swell. Time was fleeting. Oh dear, yes. Still, every second was broad and rich and you could jump aboard, and choose to ride the moment with every ounce of your strength and passion. There was still so much to be enjoyed, treasured and celebrated.

Love, loved ones above all else. Dominic.

She glanced at the sea. Its navy stillness was almost solid, waiting to be broken open, dived into. Her eyes flitted from one to the next of her companions, their faces made rosy by the firelight, transported by the chords Tom was strumming. Each of this trio was a new component in Celia's life and, in their very different ways, an unexpected boon.

She was bowled over by the power of Tom's talent, his flair. It reminded her that life surprises; it bewitches and entrances. Its magic is everywhere, even when it seems to bring you down.

CHAPTER THIRTY-TWO

Celia's head was a little the worse for wear after such a late, but oh-so-jolly evening, and a surfeit of the estate's fine wine. She had missed her early-morning swim, rising only at eight. Too late. Time to get going. Claude, ringing the front bell, had woken her. He was in the drawing room now, door open, with a pyjama-clad Dominic, discussing options for draining the fields. Dominic had also been fast asleep when Claude arrived. Whatever Federico had administered the night before had put him out for the count, but he had woken with a ferocious energy.

Claude announced, as he crossed the hallway, that late the previous evening he had signed on three temporary workers from the village. They were outside in the driveway now, waiting for instructions.

'Are they preparing the harvest? That's early for the pickers.' It was evident to Claude that Dominic was unaware of the extent of the damage created by the weekend storms.

'You need to give them directions, Claude, put them to work. Time is money.'

The pressure was on.

'Does anyone want a cup of coffee?' Celia was calling from the kitchen, while heaping dark, freshly ground grains into a percolator. Water was spitting from a boiling kettle. She was humming happily.

A dredging machine had also been hired, being delivered directly to the site, to one of the submerged vineyards. Who was going on ahead to receive it, sign the paperwork? A responsibility that would habitually have fallen to Dominic.

Magali's son, Pascal, was among the youngsters who had been engaged for the rest of the week. A solid pair of hands, he frequently came up to assist when industry was required, but at just eighteen he was not ready for responsibility, not yet sufficiently experienced to lead a team. Each of the vineyards would require its own small crew.

The place was buzzing with activity. Sean and Tom had agreed to pitch in. Sean had arrived and was waiting outside, but no sign yet of the musical one. 'Why not send Sean on ahead?' Celia called from the kitchen, participating in the conversation from a distance.

Of course, he couldn't read the French contracts so couldn't be expected to sign them. Dominic, with raised voice, was letting everyone know that he was perfectly capable of getting out there, even if it was evident to all but him that this was not the case. 'Someone find me a cane,' he was yelling. 'Grab one from the gunroom. Where's my wife?'

'First you need to get dressed.'

Now the telephone had started ringing. Not Celia's phone wherever that was. Had she left it on the table in the conservatory? Dominic's phone. It was in the kitchen where she was sipping her deliciously strong black coffee with a spoonful of equally delicious lavender honey purchased from the woman who lived in the mill. Celia closed her ears to her husband's ranting and his frustration at his inability to do more than shuffle a few yards. Thank heavens all this would be over in a few days. She dreaded the time when something more serious ailed him, and she was grateful that that day was not this one.

No one had answered the phone and it had started up again. Now it was the landline. She hurried through to the television room to answer it. It was Sally.

'I've rung Dad's number a dozen times but he's not picking up. How did the party go? My Covid tests are still negative so, unless you fear the risks, I'd love to fly over. There are some cheap flights for most mornings this week. What do you say? Frank is happy to fend for himself while he recovers and I'm dying to get away, hate that I missed the bash.'

Celia broke the news of Dominic's accident.

'Oh, no! Were others involved?'

'One.'

'Who?'

'Long story, Sal, not for the phone.'

'Sounds mysterious,' purred Sally, with delight.

Celia needed to be at the hospital. She and Gillian wanted to be there for the crack start of visiting hours.

'Send the flight details. I'll collect you. Come soon. Dom's fine. He's just being a miserable and rather ungracious patient, all things considered. He'll cheer up when you get here. You're his best tonic.'

After the call, Celia was rummaging for the car keys, having again forgotten to leave them on the rack in the hall. She had nearly locked them out of their bedroom the night she had closed the room after Gillian's uninvited infraction. Dominic had read her the Riot Act. There was always so much to think about, objects to remember.

But now she had to get ready, collect Gillian, visit David.

The telephone was ringing, again, the landline, steadily, repeatedly, impatiently. It was bound to be vineyard business. Let someone else do the honours. She was busy. But no one paid the phone any attention.

'Someone get that,' she yelled over the banisters, hopping back into the bedroom, one shoe on. Where was the other? Damn and blast, she'd just taken them out of the wardrobe.

'Celia!'

'Coming.' It was lurking by the bed.

She skipped on down the stairs and was greeted by Claude, harassed, waiting in the doorway of the television room. He was holding the old telephone receiver. 'I'll leave you to deal with this. It's someone asking for Dominic,' he said softly. He handed her the phone and returned across the hall, disappearing into the drawing room to finish his conversation with the boss before getting out into the fray.

'Hello?'

'I'm trying to reach Dominic Millar.'

'Apologies but he's not available at present. Can I help?'

It occurred to Celia then that the caller, a woman, possibly somebody's assistant, had spoken in English. She switched so frequently between French and English that she wasn't always mindful of which language she was conversing in.

'Oh, am I speaking to Celia?'

'That's me, yes, and you are who, please?'

She waited.

'Oh, Blake's assistant! Yes, we've spoken before. How are you?'

CHAPTER THIRTY-THREE

At the end of the morning, after their swift visit to David, Celia proposed to Gillian that they slip off for a bite of lunch. She drove them to the Croisette where beach bars and cafés abounded, where the restaurants with their awnings in tatters were getting themselves back into action after the recent tempest. It was noisy but the fresh sea air was restorative after their excursion into the bowels of the hospital. Teams of artisans on ladders, wielding hammers and drills, were repairing damaged roof beams and timbers. The waves were rolling in fast, beating against deserted beaches. Had the recent gales frightened away the late-summer holidaymakers?

The wind was whipping Celia's hair into her face, catching in her teeth. She led them to a small square table on the sand, at the water's edge. A waitress hurried to greet them, cradling two large menus, which she set in front of them, then disappeared.

Both women stared wordlessly out to sea. The silence lingered.

'It was a bit freaky seeing Dave like that,' Gillian said, after several minutes with no conversation. She laid a box of matches next to her empty plate and was rummaging in her bag for cigarettes. Her bitten fingers were in a shocking state, her cuticles red raw. Celia wished she could encourage her to stop.

David had been propped up on the bed in his private unit, eyes open, groggy, not clearly registering life around him. Still, even given the drugged state of him, Celia had the impression that he recognized his stepdaughter. Perhaps not both of them. She couldn't be sure. Gillian perched on the only available chair at his bedside, leaning in towards him, holding his hand. With her other, she was picking at the blanket as though removing nits. She was talking non-stop, an incomprehensible susurration. Celia couldn't make out a word of what was being shared. She held back at the foot of the bed, fearing her presence might prove traumatic for David. She couldn't have explained why she felt this, but she did.

Did David recall his mother, remember that he had been reunited with her?

The sister in charge of the corridor had been firm about the length of their stay. 'Five minutes, no longer. He needs rest.'

The women had respected the restriction. When Gillian had finally stopped talking, she stood up, bent low over the recumbent figure and kissed him. She had been aiming for his forehead but as it was swathed in bandages, she pecked the tip of his nose, careful not to displace the wires and machines connected to him, or dislodge any of the bottles dripping various liquids into his limbs. David turned his head in her direction. He closed his eyes as Gillian's lips made physical contact with him, then opened them and gazed intently at her. It was the only sign that he was in the company of someone familiar to him. Celia then leaned in and lightly pressed her fingertips against his wrist, clumsily catching a fingernail in the plastic bracelet that was his name tag. 'See you very soon,' she said softly. She had hurried from the room, not waiting for a reaction, stepping on ahead of Gillian.

'Can I have a glass of wine, please?' Gillian asked the waitress, who had returned to take their orders even though neither of them had opened their menu.

'Red, white or rosé?'

'Any.'

This flummoxed the woman.

'We'll have two glasses of a Côte de Provence dry white, please,' Celia requested. 'Leave the menus. *Merci beaucoup.*'

'I'm not hungry.'

'How about we share a pizza? They're very good here.'

Gillian shrugged.

They exchanged few other words before the wine arrived, both staring out to sea, eyes glued on the boats etched against the horizon, thinking about David. The furthest of the yachts had its sails fully hoisted. It was ploughing through the waves at a fair lick.

'Wow, that's impressive.'

'Plenty of wind.'

'What wouldn't I give to be on one of those? Doesn't have to be anything fancy. Just to be out there. Free. Sailing, wind in my hair. I've always fancied a boat.'

'*Santé*,' said Celia, lifting her glass. 'Good health.'

Gillian was already guzzling her wine. 'Oops, cheers. I'm drinking to Dave's recovery. Him being with us really soon.' She raised her glass, toasting an imaginary third person at her side.

Celia was silently calculating how best to tackle the subject of the scrapbook without giving away that she had seen it. Or should she just come clean? 'Shall we talk about Dave?'

'If you like.'

'Is there someone we should contact? A close relative or girlfriend, to notify about his accident.'

'No one I can think of.'

'His place of work? I'm assuming he's employed?'

'Of course he is! We're not down-and-outs!'

Celia lifted her hand, reached across the table. 'Hey, no offence intended.'

'I already called them, explained he'd had a fall and he'd be back soon. Promised to keep them posted. I can do that. They know me.'

'Where are they? In London?'

'I think Dave should tell you about himself. It's not my place to divulge his private business.'

Celia clicked her fingernails against the table. 'I'm sure he would have told me if we'd had time . . . if all this hadn't happened.'

'Nobody's keeping any secrets from you, Ceely. It's just not my place to . . .'

'May I ask how come he brought you on this trip?'

'Do you object to me being here?'

Why was Gillian always so defensive? 'Not at all. It's terrific that you're with us. I'm just interested to know how it came about.'

Gillian took another slug of her wine. The glass was already almost empty. 'Dave talked about you a lot. You know, you're kind of a heroine for him. Well-known, on television, all that stuff.'

'That was a while ago.'

'Even so, when he found out you were his mother, well, he couldn't believe it. Over the moon, he was. Then he was always guessing who his dad might be. Someone really famous, he thinks. A film star so illustrious you've kept it a secret.'

'I certainly don't want to disappoint anybody, Gill, but that couldn't be further from the reality. I was twenty when David was born, younger than you are now. I hadn't even begun my studies at drama school. We lived near Bristol. My parents were in the process of renovating Les Roches du Soleil. They were away in France, looking forward to retirement and—'

'Can I bag that big barn, occupy it as my work studio while I'm here?'

Celia was taken aback by the interruption and change of subject. 'Erm, yes, why not? How about we hive off a section – it's so large. I'll dig out some old curtains for you. They'll give you privacy.'

'Because he isn't going to be able to travel for a while, is he?'

Celia shrugged. 'It's hard to know.'

'Can I crash here, hang out till he gets out of hospital? Then Dave and me can head home together. I don't have to be back at college till October.'

'October?'

'Is that a massive imposition?'

'It's hardly more than a few weeks. I'd assumed that's what you might want to do, wait for David.' Celia smiled. She hadn't in all honesty considered the length of time all this might take. 'You're welcome to stay. I've already assured you of that.'

'It used to get on my nerves how he raved about you,

celebrated mum, glamorous, wealthy, when you'd never got in touch with him. That hurt him.'

'I'm not sure I would have known where to begin to find him.'

'Well, he found you, didn't he? There are agencies, organizations, for that sort of thing.' The anger had risen again. It was always lurking, constricting the pupils of those penetrating grey eyes. 'I thought you must be a bit of a . . . well, a shit. Ignoring your kid.'

'As I understand it, Gill, in the United Kingdom the offspring has the legal right to try to find their birth mother, but I'm not sure the law looks so favourably on the parent.'

Gillian finished off her wine, taking in this information. She didn't argue because, Celia guessed, she didn't know what position the law took on the matter.

'Does he have any family?'

'You mean apart from you and me? Mother and daughter. Well, stepdaughter, sort of. He's never mentioned anyone.'

'He didn't remarry?'

Gillian shook her head. 'He talked about his adoptive parents quite often.'

'Oh?'

'He was incredibly fond of them. His dad used to take him fishing at weekends. They lived on a farm near the coast in Kent.'

'Are they still there?'

'Both had died before he met my mum. They were pretty old when they adopted him. Couldn't have kids of their own.' Gillian lit a cigarette from the Marlboro Red packet she had retrieved from her bag and exhaled the smoke in the direction of the water. 'He's an only child, always been a bit of a loner, he said, worked with the animals in the stables when he was a kid. It's sad but I think you've been his main focus for the last while. He made me a book about you. Loads of plays you've been in, TV, everything. He was trying to persuade me that you deserved my admiration.'

'A book?'

'Yeah, you know a scrapbook with pictures and stuff stuck into it. Not very artistic or anything, but reams of cuttings . . .'

'Really?'

'I don't think he'd read all the reviews or maybe he had and didn't care. Maybe it made no difference to him. I don't know.'

'Why do you say that?'

'Because some of it was pretty negative about you. Like, you know, you're a lousy actress.'

Celia winced. She picked up her wine and took a sip. She was driving. She had only ordered a glass to keep Gillian company.

'I underlined all the crappy bits and gave it back to him but it didn't change his mind. He was determined to make contact with you. It was pathetic – he was like a fawning fan. He *is* a fawning fan. It's embarrassing. I didn't think you'd agree to meet him, but when you did *and* invited him here, he was over the moon. Like, he couldn't stop talking about it. Star-struck Dave. Until he panicked and got cold feet, feared he'd be rejected, out of his depth, so I offered to come along, give him moral support. There you go, that's why I'm here. OK?'

The conversation between them momentarily dried up.

'Can I have another glass of vino?'

'Only if we eat something.'

'No meat or any flesh stuff, then.'

Celia signalled to the waitress, ordered a *quattro formaggi* pizza to share and a second glass of Côte de Provence for Gillian.

'I wouldn't want Dave to live if he's, you know . . .'

'What?'

'Not all right in the head. A vegetable. He'd hate that. You'll have to make that decision for him, Ceely.'

CHAPTER THIRTY-FOUR

When Celia and Gillian returned to the manor house, they were greeted by several pieces of heavy machinery including two manual drainage pumps deposited close to the front door. As well, half a dozen battered old cars were parked in the shade of a small stand of umbrella pines, but there was not a man in sight. Even before the engine had been switched off, Gillian had leaped out, saying thanks for lunch, she wanted to take a look in the barn, do some measuring, figure out how to set the place up for herself. 'Don't forget the curtains, Ceely, I'll be waiting!'

She had mentioned during the ride home that she might make up a bed in the barn, move in there.

Celia had protested, 'I'd prefer you don't do that, lack of sanitation,' but Gillian brushed aside such concerns. If necessary, Celia would put her foot down. She refrained from enquiring why the girl would want to move out of the lodge. She understood why she was less enthusiastic about staying in the box room in the main house, but she had presumed Gillian was comfortable with Tom and Sean. Too small for three, possibly. Should she offer to move her into Sally's room where Dave's belongings still lay, mostly packed? Of course Sally, when she arrived any day now, would prefer her habitual space for herself.

Dominic was alone in the drawing room when Celia walked in. She could read from his bearing that his day had not gone well. Dagger eyes greeted her, as though he held her personally responsible for his incapacity to walk.

'Where have you been?

'Visiting David,' she replied curtly.

'Why didn't you pick up your phone? Claude needs a couple of urgent decisions made. Obviously I can't drive to the fields. In any case, you had the Land Rover.'

'I can make my way there now, if it's not too late. Which vineyard are they in?'

'The field beneath the forest. Half a dozen of the casual labourers are clearing it, chainsawing the fallen trees to liberate the vine stock. They were intending to get those bloody great roots shifted as well, but it's impossible without a crane. Each weighs several tons. And my new fence has been destroyed, did you know?'

'Sean told me it took a hit when one of the old pines came down. I'll drive out there right away. Oh, Blake's PA telephoned. I didn't have an opportunity to mention it earlier. You were busy with Claude. She asked you to call him back. Is this about the TV you mentioned?'

Dominic shrugged. He looked rather sheepish at the mention of his agent, which was curious.

'I'm not sure why you have to be so secretive. I hope it's good news.' She gathered up her bag and phone and strode from the room. Better not forget the phone.

There were six engaged in the clearing up on the highest-lying of their vineyards just south of the forest. Several chainsaws were whirring, putting Celia in mind of that very autumnal activity: pruning back the vegetation after the harvests had been gathered, the grapes had been crushed and were ready for settling. But this was the end of August. It was too early. Their energies should be engaged in cleaning and sterilizing the fermentation containers ready for the arrival of the grape juice. They were now running late with that job. Claude had been occupied with it before the tempest, before these accidents had hijacked his attention. The seasons were askew, the rhythms of the plants provoked, fruits ripening ahead of time and weather patterns extreme, causing almost insurmountable problems for the region's oil and wine producers. All farmers. They were not the sole victims. It was too cold, too hot, too wet, too dry.

And they were one vital man down without Dominic.

She closed the car and walked over to Claude who, with Pascal and a couple of other lads from the village, was heaving and rolling massive wheels of wood: freshly sawn pine trunks. Each circular disc was the size of a lorry tyre and looked as if it weighed several metric hundredweight.

She waved as she approached. Claude raised himself to his full height, rubbed at his spine, beat its base with his fist as though the muscles had gone dead, shook his shoulders and signalled to her. His face was a film of black-speckled perspiration. Kind eyes with creases of worry twinkled through the dirt. He was a good man. Decent. Celia greatly respected him. He had shown her and Dominic immense loyalty over the years. She recalled that even when there had been insufficient funds to meet his wages he had hung on, seen them through, taught them all he knew about the craft. Even now, he went beyond the bounds of duty, mucking in whenever necessary. And this mess was no exception.

'How in Heaven's name will we shift all this?'

He was talking even before she'd reached him.

She paused to take in the scene. Her attention was drawn to the edge of the forest where the root structure of a centuries-old pine, ripped from the earth by the recent winds, was standing upright, balanced on a network of secondary roots. Like a giant circular clock packed with earth and stones, it rose some ten metres above ground level towards the forest's dark invisible heavens.

Higher up, some thirty paces' climb, was a second root, of similar proportions, possibly larger. Its canopy, lying a surprising distance further to the east, had taken younger self-seeded trees with it as it crashed, flattening bushes and vines in its wake. It must have fallen sideways – a shift at some point in the wind's direction? The force of the gales, which had caused the felling of these mighty specimens, beggared belief. Celia progressed haltingly, open-mouthed, surveying the destruction. A humbling sight, and a menacing fire risk.

And David had been trapped somewhere among all this, fighting for his life. Her thoughts returned to Gillian's revelations down at the beach. With what intensity David adored her. His mother. It was a little daunting. Was she up to the task?

The air rising from the gaping craters of earth, where, until just a few days ago, the roots had been peacefully thriving, gave off a sulphurous stench. Dank, musty. Celia instinctively lifted a hand to her face, covering her mouth and nostrils.

There were swarms of tiny flying insects, fungus gnats, speeding close by, flitting in and out of the slain greenery. Their habitats had been upended, deracinated. She let out a heavy sigh. The damage was extensive, appalling. She momentarily held her breath, picturing David caught in this maelstrom. It was a miracle he had survived at all.

'We have two immediate issues here,' began Claude, when he saw that Celia was lost in her own world, impotent as to how best to address the situation.

'I have never seen anything like this,' she murmured. Claude's hands, she noticed, were sticky with resin.

'We've come off lightly, Celia. Seen the news? Inland of Nice, the roads are closed everywhere. Landslides, rocks fallen. Half the mountain has collapsed. Homes disintegrating into powder. One village had its cemetery washed away. Corpses disappeared, swallowed in the fast-flowing river.'

Poor David hadn't come off lightly. Still, Claude had a point. Many in the region had lost everything. Some, their lives.

'Celia, we need to clear the vines of all this spoilage ASAP. The fencing will have to be repaired, probably replaced, but I suggest we leave that till winter when we have time. The imperative now is to release the vines, if they're to be saved, which in any case is questionable. The fruits, of course, are already rotting.'

'No harvest up here then?'

'Not at this level.' He swung on his feet, clad in mud-caked wellingtons, setting his sights on the sloping field, appraising

349

the devastation. This upper area was a chaos of perishing treetops and hurled branches. 'My guess is we've lost some three hundred of the stock plants, conservative estimate, which in bottles . . . litres or whichever way you calculate it, is . . .' He closed his eyes, engaged in his mental arithmetic.

Celia filled him in. 'Ten to twelve bottles of wine per plant, right?'

'From this variety, in a good year, yes. Let's say ten. The sums are less depressing.' He offered her a half-hearted smile.

'So we're looking at a loss of three thousand five hundred bottles of wine right here? None of this includes the damage to the waterlogged fields. Am I calculating this correctly?'

Claude nodded. 'Perhaps a little less.'

'OK, let's be optimistic.'

'Three thousand bottles without a shadow of a doubt.' His expression showed his pain. He was as committed to this enterprise as Dominic and Celia were, had worked it longer than they had. It was his life and livelihood. Claude took immense pride in the quality of the wines, every year making improvements, aiming to produce an exceptional vintage. He respected the land too, thought they should be shifting to organic.

'I'm going to need more manpower, Celia.' He lowered his eyes as though the facts were too brutal. 'I realize that, financially, this is rotten news. If we can rope anyone in. Most casual labour has already been hired by other estates. The more fortunate are already preparing their harvests. Others are in the same bloody mess we're in. Whatever, we can't achieve this without extra hands . . .'

'We'll find the funds,' she promised, even knowing how exasperated Dominic would be when she told him. Her hastily given assurances were always a bone of contention between them. But, right now, she didn't care. Claude needed her behind him.

'The next challenge is what the f—' he bit back the word, a mark of respect to the lady and friend alongside him. 'What are we going to do with all this timber? Manoeuvring it elsewhere will take the logistical expertise and vehicle force of a military operation, while leaving it here is asking for trouble. Massive fire risk and potential wood avalanches.' He scratched his head. 'Stockpiling it where it is might be our only option right now. I need the tractor for the harvests. And transporting all this down the slopes will kill its engine.'

'But it will have to be cleared at some point?'

He glanced behind him. 'No question, but nigh on impossible to negotiate a loaded vehicle on this hill.'

The quintet of men were still hard at it, chainsawing the trunks into manoeuvrable chunks. Sawdust floated in the air like creamy snow. At any given moment, one or other of the team paused to draw breath, to cough the wood chips out of their throats, to spit, glug water. It was exhausting, hazardous work. Within earshot but out of sight, higher up, damaged and rotten branches were still snapping, crashing, thudding to the ground.

'Has everyone been fed and have you plenty of water? I can return with whatever you need.'

Claude assured Celia that supplies were all in hand. 'Magali, bless her heart, is taking care of us.'

'If you're not too tired, why not pop by the house later, after Dom and I have talked all this through?'

Claude promised he would.

'We'll find a solution. With your help we always do.' Celia waved to the employees, gave them a thumbs-up – *Merci!* – then hurried back to the Land Rover. She was calculating as she trudged through the slushy alleys that three thousand five hundred bottles of this fine rosé was a loss in income of some fifty-two thousand euros. On top of that there was the financial outlay, required immediately, to put what they could to rights, hire the extra men, bring in heavy agricultural equipment. Hire a lorry? Purchase a bigger trailer? Clear tons of wood. Plus there were the other fields. The estate had insurances, of course, and they were covered for natural disasters, but the paperwork, the claims ... It would take months. The insurance companies were never speedy when it came to paying out. Plus again, their grand soirée had bitten deeply into the estate's already tight cashflow. She had known it, had been gambling on the return the party would deliver in orders, advance payments, such as the Boyers from Marseille, and the goodwill created among the locals, all of which had been successful, but now they were down to almost zero . . . Bad luck comes in threes, her mother always used to caution.

David, Dominic's ankle, the damaged vineyards. She prayed this was the last misfortune and they could put their energies into reparation. Healing. Rebuilding.

But it would be hard-going.

CHAPTER THIRTY-FIVE

Celia and Dominic were sitting opposite one another in the drawing room. She had thrown together a hasty plate of sandwiches a little earlier and poured them each a glass of red. Her head was thumping. Claude had phoned from the top vineyard to confirm that he would drop by after everything was wrapped up for the evening. The men had done wonders, he confirmed. 'Not a slacker among them.'

Celia's mind was elsewhere now. She was tired, stressed out, but more than that she had been knocked sideways by Dominic's news from London.

'The screen rights to *Journey Into Starlight* have been sold. It's to be adapted for the small screen,' he'd told her, when she returned from the fields.

'Good Lord. Well, that's great news, isn't it? Who's writing the adaptation? You?'

He nodded. 'You understand you can't be involved?'

'Involved? In what way?'

'Reprise your role.'

She shook her head. 'Good heavens, no. Of course not.'

He was fiddling with his glasses in a nervous way. She watched him, puzzled. Of course she felt a smidgen of sadness about letting the part go to another actress. After more than a decade she still considered it *hers*, even if the whole episode had turned out to be a disaster. Dominic had written the role for her.

'Too many mixed memories.' She attempted a smile. She wanted to be excited for him, wanted him to see that she was thrilled by this opportunity. 'In any case, one of us will have to hold the fort here.'

He considered her comments. 'I'll go ahead and accept, of course.'

'No question.'

'Financially, given all the stresses we're facing here, this unanticipated income will come in very handy. A stroke of timely good fortune, wouldn't you say?'

'Indeed. But how extraordinary that after all these years someone should think of it. Especially as it wasn't a commercial success. Who's commissioning?'

She noticed just a moment's hesitation before he replied. 'One of the major streaming networks. Netflix or Amazon, I can't remember which. Blake did tell me. They're all much of a muchness, I expect. They tend to buy outright, he warned, but there will be a decent advance and writer's fees. They're contracting for an eight-part series. It's called a "one-season show". New-fangled titles and lingo,' he said, in disbelief, but she could see that he was pleased. Eyes twinkling, feverishly proud. And far better-humoured.

'That's so impressive. Bravo, Dom.'

Could a two-hour play stretch to eight episodes? She asked herself. It was good news for Dominic, of course it was, and she must view this, as her mother would have predicted, as the first step towards their luck turning. But, even so, she couldn't deny the hunger knocking at her heart. If she were ten years younger . . .

'I hope they choose someone wonderful for my role,' she teased. '*My* role. Listen to me. Do you have any say in the principal casting?'

'Not really.'

'American names, I suppose. Box-office stars.'

He nodded, eyes averted, still wiping the lenses of his glasses with his handkerchief. She knew this man so well. Every bat of his eyelid told a story. Or hid one. And she had a hunch there was more to this . . .

'You know, Ceely, since this was first mooted, before the streaming company confirmed and signed, I had plenty of time to mull the story over, seeing it through a lens, the intimacies of camera, rather than the constraints or epic nature of a theatre. Those late-night scenes, they never quite worked on the boards, did they? And, of course, we can shoot the scenes that are set in Italy in Italy. Venice is never less than magical on camera.'

She was watching him, his enthusiasm mounting. She envied him the artistic journey that lay ahead for him, but it didn't lessen the thrill she felt for him. The gratification he must be feeling now.

'I believe the story will work far better cinematically than it did boxed in on a stage,' he added.

'You're probably right. Your instincts are usually spot on. Wonderful for you that they haven't taken one of their own stable of scriptwriters. Who's the director?'

'Not confirmed yet. Let's keep our fingers crossed it'll be a chap I can work with, feel comfortable with. Of course, I can always . . .'

'Or a woman . . .'

'What?'

'A female director. They're a growing band, Dom.'

'Yes, yes, it could be a female director, of course. I hadn't considered it.'

A ring at the door.

'That'll be Claude. Goodness,' she glanced at the clock above the mantel, 'it's a quarter to eight. He's worked a helluva long day. We are blessed with this crew.' Celia rose, pressed down the creases in her shirt and ran her fingers through her hair. She was pretty exhausted. 'I'll bring him straight through.' She was thinking that she ought to run over to the barn and check in on Gillian. Heavens, she had completely forgotten Gillian, and her promise to provide her with curtains.

'Ceely, send him through. I'll reassure him that we can provide him with all the back-up he needs. That will put him in a perky frame of mind. On your way back, darling, can you grab a bottle of red from the kitchen?'

'Sure.'

'I'll ask him to stay for supper. Hope that's no bother?'

Dominic's spirits had certainly risen since he'd spoken to his agent. She was asking herself why he hadn't mentioned this television offer before. Waiting for the deal to be concluded, she supposed. Or was it because this play could ignite so many conflictual memories for them both?

Claude was shucking off his wellingtons when she opened the door. 'Go on through.' She smiled, resting an arm momentarily on his shoulders. Even through shirt and jacket she could feel the damp of him, the sweat.

'I'm fetching a bottle of red, boss's request. There'll be dinner in a while. Something simple. We're still munching our way through the party leftovers.' The poor man looked shattered, cheeks hollowed, in need of a long hot soak.

'I won't stay long, thanks, Celia, but I'd kill for a glass of wine. We've managed to get those monster trees sawn up. At some point over the next few days, I'll think about how to shift the wood. Henri might have some ideas. Bit of a risk where it is.'

'Well, let me know if I can fix you a snack. I'll be back shortly.'

Across the courtyard in the grand old barn, music. The Smiths, 'There Is A Light That Never Goes Out'. When Celia heaved open the great door, which creaked and shuddered on its rusted hinges, she was blasted by sound, then startled by the transformation taking place at the rear of the space where Gillian was pitched high on the top rungs of a ladder, stretching towards a beam, hanging lengths of cloth.

Celia ambled forwards, taking in the scene. The volume of the music meant that Gillian was almost certainly unaware of her arrival. It gave Celia sufficient time to get the picture. The fabric being used was the ball of tablecloths, the damask napery stained with spilled wine and grease, that she had taken off the trestles after the party, plus a few bath towels and used bedding. Nothing had been washed. To Celia's eye, it was rather revolting. Gillian must have found the laundry room and dragged out whatever she laid her hands on.

It had been Celia's intention to provide Gill with proper theatre curtains, lovely velvet drapes. When she was in her twenties, with her parents' encouragement, she had mounted plays, nativities, musicals, either in here on cooler evenings or during summer soirées outside in the courtyard, where they had enjoyed music, drama and dancing, inviting neighbours near and far to the entertainments. Such a hoot those occasions had been.

Two sets of velvet curtains, one dark ruby and the other a rich forest green, remained from those halcyon days. They hadn't been unpacked for years and were probably moth-eaten by now. Those had been the drapes Celia had had in mind when she'd made the proposition to Gillian. Not the purloining of grubby washing.

Somehow the girl, who was singing along to her music, blithely unaware that she was being watched, had tacked or was pinning all the articles together to create a prodigious, if rather uneven, patchwork screen. It reached from floor to ceiling, with a small gap at the bottom. She was on the ladder hammering the screen's upper circumference to one of the barn's sturdy wooden beams, thus dividing the room into two sections: one larger expanse, where Celia was standing, somewhat alarmed, and a smaller footage, which Gillian had nabbed for her personal atelier.

'Gillian!'

Twice more Celia called before Gillian swung about. She beamed and waved. 'Oh, hi, Ceely. What do you think? Terrific, eh?'

'Can you come down, please?'

Clearly Gillian sensed immediately that her hostess was less than thrilled with her progress. She placed the hammer on the ladder's top rung and descended. The makeshift screen hung at half-mast, like sails that have come unattached from the halyard. Or broken white wings.

As Gillian reached the lowest rung, Celia requested she turn the music down. Gillian tugged her phone from the left pocket of her chinos and directed a command to a large speaker, positioned elsewhere on the floor. The music fell silent.

She turned her attention to her hostess. 'What's up?'

'I was going to give you some curtains.'

'Yeah, but you didn't!'

'Gill, please don't raise your voice.'

'I looked all over the shop, couldn't find you, hung about, and then, after a bit of rummaging, I dug out these filthy old things. Is there a problem with that?'

Celia stared at her feet, hands in her pockets and bit her lip. Was she being uptight? 'I thought we'd agreed that you wouldn't go helping yourself to whatever you fancy without checking in with me first.'

'Oh, we're back to me nicking your jewellery, are we?' Gillian swung from side to side on her feet, kicked one red trainer against the earthen floor. 'I simply don't get you. You offer me something and then you make me wrong for going ahead and taking it.'

'Gillian, I didn't off—'

'I thought this was a neat arrangement. I thought I was being inventive, on the ball, creative, Getting the Job Done,' her voice was rising, 'but you make me wrong, criticize me. Whatever I do, you find a reason why it wasn't the best solution.' She sniffed, ran a hand through her cropped hair, ruffled it, leaving it messier than before.

Celia, head still lowered, raised her hands to her mouth, and cupped her face tightly. She closed her eyes, took a deep breath. Fingers pressing into her cheeks. It was as though she was standing on a tightrope, a gaping chasm stretched out either side of her. There was no map for this and she seemed capable only of wrong-footing. She flat-out wanted this to go well. She desperately cared that David's stepdaughter be included in their family. If David loved the girl, so would she. She had to learn to adapt, be more flexible.

'I tell you what, Gill, stick with what you've got,' she said softly, eventually. 'We don't need any of it immediately and it'll serve your needs perfectly. You're doing a splendid job. I'm going to heat some food. Dom and I will be in the conservatory if you'd like to eat with us.'

And with that, she made her exit from the barn.

CHAPTER THIRTY-SIX

The following day, at Claude's behest, Celia hired several essential bits of machinery – pumps, motors – to facilitate the leaching process. If Dominic could not be in the fields, Celia decided that her presence was essential. Claude and the team required her moral support. The work was hardgoing, disagreeable and filthy. She was unprepared for it.

Sean and Tom proved invaluable. Their rather thankless task was to shovel wheelbarrow loads of silt and decaying vegetal matter. It had been carried along on the rivers of flooding rainwater and had ended up damming the vine alleys. Each was a barricade of compacted mud and squelch. The levels were choking the crops.

As chores go, commented Sean, chirpily, this is 'fecking unpleasant'.

It was slushy and smelly and they were thigh-high in it, but the chaps were going at it with their usual good humour. Tom was leading the team in a chorus of songs from films, which caused much laughter partly due to the language barrier, but was certainly keeping everyone's spirits lifted.

Early the following morning all the equipment used in the recently mucked-out grove was packed up, driven or carried, transported one way or another, kilometres across the estate, to one of the lowest, most southerly of the vineyards. The land was flatter there and, consequently, it was proving more stubborn in its natural release of water and detritus. This inundated vineyard resembled a vast festering pond. A swill of stagnating water and green floating rubbish. It required metres and metres of piping and two high-voltage electric pumps, plus plenty of manpower.

Once all the fields had been leached and cleaned, the soil would need to be tested. It was possible that essential nutrients had been sucked out during the draining process. Each task seemed to create another, but so far, aside from at the foot of the forest where the damage was more serious, they were not looking at digging up or jettisoning the vines. Claude was predicting that these plants would survive. 'I'd say that purchasing and replanting anew won't be necessary. The vines are more robust than I had initially feared.'

'Robust. Oh, that is such good news, eh, Dom?'

Dominic nodded, though his attention, Celia observed, seemed to be elsewhere. In his head he had been transported from the vineyard and was living in the world of his play, his nascent television series. Every time she popped in to see him he was on the telephone.

It was Friday, payday, cash for the daily workers, of which there were now five. Celia drove to the bank in Cannes, and while in the town, she popped in on David.

'He's doing great,' smiled the nurse on duty. 'At this rate, he'll soon be out of here.'

When Celia put her head round the door, she discovered David propped up in bed, wide awake, liberated from most of the wires and tubes. He was devouring a bowl of soup and several slices of toast slathered with butter. Her heart lifted at the sight of him in such fine fettle, the bounce back in his physical strength, even if he still looked disarmingly pale. However, she was less delighted when she realized he did not recognize her.

'Hello, David. Great to see you look well.'

He stared at her with blank, fretful eyes.

'Celia, I'm Celia. Your mo— You're staying with us, remember?'

The name appeared to ring no bells. As far as Celia could tell, David had no idea who his visitor was. Not a clue. Days earlier, she had felt sure there had been a flicker of recognition. Or had it simply been for Gillian?

After this brief encounter, she went in search of the very nice consultant, hoping he could spare her a few moments of his precious time.

'Come in, sit down.'

'Sorry to trouble you. I just wanted to ask . . .'

The doctor served her a beaker of water. 'There are several forms of memory loss caused by TBI, that is Traumatic Brain Injury. It affects some patients more than others.'

'Well, I forget my keys and phone on a daily basis! He might take after me. Or,' she furrowed her brow, 'is there reason to be concerned?'

'In my opinion your son is not suffering from any serious memory difficulties. He's a little confused at moments, which is to be expected after such a setback. He has exhibited one or two signs of short-term memory loss, but really these have been minor. His responses towards the staff and his behaviour in general are giving us no cause for alarm. He knows the nurses, chats with them – well, short exchanges here and there with those who speak English. He seems to be a rather shy man, polite but reserved.'

'Is he aware of what's happened to him?' She was conscious that she was pressing for extra assurances, taking up this man's valuable time, but a doubt was nagging at her.

'It's a fact that he doesn't recall the accident, or the incidents surrounding it. If he doesn't have recall of the accident now, it is very doubtful any of those images or the experience will return. His brain has closed the trauma out.'

'Oh?'

'It's not uncommon and nothing to worry about, Madame Millar. His long-term and functioning memory won't have been affected. Aside from that, there appears to be far less damage than we were initially preparing for. Concussion, minor brain injury—'

'No . . . erm, identity issues?'

The specialist smiled 'Dissociative disorders, amnesia?' He shook his head. 'No, fortunately, nothing so dramatic. David is well on his way to a full recovery. He'll have a scar, of course, but once his hair has grown back . . . He's a fighter, resilient, with good strong responses. A healthy man. And, I understand, he has been perfectly at ease with his other visitors.'

'Other visitors?'

'His two female friends. The younger English one – his daughter? – she was in your company the first time we met. And her companion.'

Celia nodded uncertainly.

'No, provided he has a safe environment where he can rest and recuperate, we will discharge him within the next two or three days.'

CHAPTER THIRTY-SEVEN

Dominic was also exhibiting a more robust state of health, back on his feet, hobbling short distances with the aid of a cane. The stairs were still an issue so his professional world had been relocated from his second-floor library to the winter drawing room, now furnished with all the equipment required for his creative life. Broad-shouldered Tom had carried Dom's computer, with its accompanying wires and gadgets, down the two flights. Once a table sufficiently large for Dominic's needs had been identified, it was transported through from the television room. Sean helped Dominic put all the paraphernalia back together, get it up and running and reconnected to the internet. Sean, they discovered, was a wizard with computers, which Dominic was certainly not. Then, when the machinery was firing on all cylinders, Dominic shooed everyone away and demanded to be left in peace.

Whenever Celia popped in to see how he was getting along, she found him writing furiously, in longhand as was his preferred method, with reams of loose-leafed paper stacked high alongside his right arm, or screwed into balls and thrown into a wastepaper basket by his feet. On several occasions she discovered him conducting Zoom meetings on his desktop screen. The recently signed contract appeared to have given him a new zest for life. Celia hadn't seen him so invigorated in a long while.

The wheelchair had been cast aside, dismissed from Dominic's sight, left folded, leaning on its handles in the hall. It needed to be returned sooner rather than later. Celia had added it to her list of chores for the upcoming days. She'd pop it back to the hospital's medical centre when she collected David.

Meanwhile, Gillian was buried in the barn, her atelier. She and Celia were stepping round each other, keeping their distance, maintaining a détente. Whenever Celia caught sight of her, it was in the courtyard where Gillian was pushing a wheelbarrow loaded with hefty blocks of wood.

'What are you up to in there?' Celia called brightly, on one of their encounters.

'Building a boat,' was the response, which Celia did not take seriously.

Two days later, at the end of the morning, into bright sunshine, blue sky and birdsong, Sally came steaming up the driveway.

She'd flown in and hired a car at Nice airport to save Celia extra hassle. She had evidently picked up during various phone conversations that matters at the estate were tense, to put it mildly. Tyres spinning on the gravel, toot-tooting excitedly as she ascended, she was at the wheel of a snazzy, open-top Fiat, a sky-blue Cinque Cento, her suitcase standing upright on the back seat.

'What's all that hooting?' hollered Celia, from her cramped little office. 'Magali! Magali, is another delivery arriving?' Celia should have been out in the fields, but she had stolen a few hours for herself. She had been searching for contact details on the internet, for the convent that had taken in David Grey all those years ago. The telephone number listed on their form was decades out of date. No website, of course. Her searches suggested the religious establishment might have been sold off, but not closed down. She had written a letter instead, would post it as soon as she could, she decided, haring along the corridor, preparing to deal with whatever new problem had arisen outside. She was hoping to find information on David's adoptive parents. All the information she could garner. If he was suffering memory loss . . .

She poked her head out of an upstairs window and beheld Sally's Fiat drawing to a halt. 'I don't believe it!' She whooped loudly.

A few beaten-up old jalopies parked over to the left under a stand of trees were on view as Sally stepped from her car. She called her father's name, then yelled for Celia. No response. Only the bass thump of rock music hailing from somewhere close by, which was odd, unexpected.

Then Celia was at the front door, arms flung wide. 'Whoo-hoo, you made it!' She and Sally fell into each other's arms. A long, squeezy embrace. 'So glad you got here. How's Frank?'

'Tested negative this morning. Hopping mad at me for skipping off without him. He might follow after the weekend if that suits everyone.'

Arms locked round one another's waists, Celia guided her stepdaughter through to the winter drawing room. 'I'll make coffee while you say hello to your father. Be warned, bear with very sore head.' She winked and disappeared to the kitchen.

Dominic was engaged in a Zoom with 'The Studios', which meant London and various other points on the TV-pro-duction compass. Glancing up from the screen, he caught sight of Sally leaning against the door frame, grinning from ear to ear. He waved, signalling dramatically. 'I'll be done in half an hour.'

Sally blew him a kiss and skipped off to the kitchen where she found Celia with Magali, hard at work as always.

'My God, Mags, that smells screamingly delicious. Don't I

know I'm back in *la belle France* and in *your* kitchen! You and Ceely should have your own cookery show. How are you?'

The two women embraced, old friends.

Magali was slicing and reheating lamb leftovers in a heavy iron pot, throwing in handfuls of garlic cloves, sprigs of rosemary and an assortment of other Provençal herbs and spices.

'That'll keep Dracula at arm's length.'

Celia was brewing a pot of coffee, extra strong, tossing homemade biscuits on to a plate. Sally had set off from her London flat before daybreak and was feeling the tiredness now. Celia explained that since the storms she was out doing what the local farmers called 'a man's work'. 'I'm standing in for Dom. We're in one of the lower fields. Claude has a team of seven.'

'Including my boy, Pascal,' butted in Magali, with pride. 'They're fighting to save the crops.' She was clearly bursting to share the events of the recent days. 'You should have been here, Sal. It's been one drama after another.'

'Really?'

'It's a bit ghastly, actually,' Celia said. 'The flora and fauna victims include hundreds of our vine plants – pretty bad news – plus drowned voles, rats, rabbits, even a sad-looking black bird. Yesterday, I found a gorgeous red fox drowned.' Celia downed her coffee in two swift gulps. 'I'm on my way, lovely ladies. The men need food and moral support. See you for a late lunch?'

'Sounds great. This coffee's delish. I'll take a cup through to Dad. See if I can assist him.'

As Dominic was not available to give his daughter a hug and chat, she delivered him his coffee and strode out into the sunshine across the courtyard. Intrigued by the music hailing from a customarily silent and empty barn, she hauled open the heavy, unwieldy door to take a peek. A rush of Beatles greeted her.

At the far end of the building hung a massive curtain stitched together from what looked like stained sheets. It was lit from the far side. Those lamps created shadows on the drapes as in a puppet show. A female silhouette was leaping to and fro, singing, oblivious to the arrival of any newcomer. The track from the *Sgt. Pepper's Lonely Hearts Club Band* album currently playing was 'Lucy In The Sky With Diamonds'. A firm favourite of Sally's.

'What a gas.' She breathed in slowly. 'It smells great in here.' Another firm favourite of Sally's was the lingering aroma of freshly applied paint. Resiny, oily. Bliss. It reminded her of her own studios. Glue, wood, paints, working chaos. What an unexpected delight. Captivated, she headed across to the curtains and lifted them apart, gently, so as not to dismantle them, merely to create a gap sufficient for her to stick her head through and take an up-close look. There she found a skinny young woman in splotched dungarees. Back to her, balanced on a professional stepladder, she was plastering paint across a vast canvas. Actually, not a canvas. It was an installation, a sculpture, planks fixed together, resting on wooden blocks. They were piled high on top of one another or nailed into formations that created a shape that resembled a giant new moon lying on its back. What it was meant to represent, Sally didn't have a clue, but its dimensions were spectacular. Yes, no, wait, she could see it more clearly if she stepped back, taking care not to tread on or dislodge the curtains.

'Heavens above.' It was a hull, not a moon, a not-so miniature Ark. With a little imagination, the bare timbers represented a boat.

Small pots of paints were scattered in untidy rows on a yellow plastic sheet spread out on the floor. The young woman was wielding high a brush that dripped cobalt-blue paint. Her clothes were marbled and stained with a rainbow of colours. Her short hair, standing upwards in all directions, was aglow with many hues: citron, yellow, buttercup, gold.

The colours already splashed onto the wooden blocks or in stripes along the planks were dazzling. Turquoise, several shades of aquamarine, a sable tone that gave the impression the ark was resting on dark, wet sand. Hoops, rings, coils of gold sprayed thickly, hinting at precious coins, antique jewellery.

'This is bloody marvellous. It looks like a reproduction of the treasures from an archaeological site.' Sally was talking to herself as much as to the young woman who, in any case, had possibly not heard her due to the music, 'With A Little Help From My Friends' now. The young artist was probably not even aware of her presence.

'It reminds me of a Phoenician oar-driven seafaring vessel. Dredged up from a seabed somewhere out in the depths of the Mediterranean.'

Missing pieces, sections of emptiness here and there added to the impression that it was an incomplete object, an ancient, damaged artefact or pillaged watercraft hauled from the bottom of the sea.

'A primitive barge is what I'm aiming for. Obviously on a much more manageable scale than the original sailing ship. I couldn't replicate the dimensions of the real finds, but . . .'

'Why this?'

'My escape route. Well, in my head, at least. Sailing heavenwards into marmalade skies. I was down at the coast recently with Ceely, watched the yachts, was desperate to be out on the water . . .'

'It's mighty impressive.'

'Do you think?'

'I certainly do.'

Outside, as Celia started the engine and began to roll down the drive, she was considering her letter to the convent. She intended to zip to the village and post it right away, before she set off for the lower vineyard, catch the lunchtime collection. Should she have included a photocopy of the original birth certificate? But who was in possession of it? Would it have been her parents or the Hawksmiths? Oh, well, she decided, the letter would have to go off without it. The convent would have records.

Gillian, hands full of wet brushes, still busy on the ladder, swung round to meet the face of the woman who was admiring her artistry. A shortish woman she hadn't seen on the estate before, possibly in her early forties with trendy, undercut bobbed dark-brown hair, clad in baggy orange trousers and a bright-green tank top offset with a heavy metallic necklace. Gillian liked the woman's style.

'A guy who's staying here, his name's Sean, is a marine archaeologist. Well, he's doing his thesis at UC in Dublin. He lent me the most amazing book with loads of coloured pics and illustrations. I thought I'd try to reconstruct one of the finds from an underwater excavation. It was discovered off the coast of Sicily, I think. I mean, it doesn't actually look like this, but the photographs inspired me, flights of fancy and all that. It's kind of taken off from there.'

'What an imagination you have.' Sally laughed.

Gillian grinned. Her eyes were bright and dancing. 'We can all sail away. Some in a pea-green boat or a yellow submarine. Mine's going to be a blue-green galley. Work in progress, of course. I might cut up some of these grubby old tablecloths for the sails. You know, ragged and torn. Shipwrecked. What do you think?'

Gillian watched silently, proudly, as Sally craned her neck and stared upwards, admiring the wooden sculpture in all its glory. 'It's bloody fabulous. I'm Sal, by the way, Dom's daughter.'

'I'm Gill. Dave's . . . daughter.'

'Dave?'

Celia returned from the vineyard later than she'd intended, patched from head to toe with mud. She ran upstairs for fresh clothes, then hurried to the bathroom to clean up. Her feet were soaking, her jeans clinging to her skin. The work was foul. She heard voices, gales of laughter, floating up from one of the lower terraces. French windows open, hands, arms, face covered with soap suds, she caught sight of Sally, down by the swimming-pool in the company of Gillian, who was waving her arms animatedly like a windmill. The girl was clearly very excited. Although she was walking alongside Sally, Gillian paused regularly, turning her whole body sideways, crab-stepping or skipping, all the while illustrating her thoughts with her hands and arms. Sally was screeching with laughter, bending forwards, clasping her stomach to ease the pain of her mirth. Celia, drying herself off, watched them, wondering at their conviviality, before raising an arm and calling to them; 'Let's eat, girls. I'm starving.'

Sally's linen trousers were billowing like golden-orange butterfly wings backlit by the sun as she hoofed it up the stone steps to join Celia. Gillian, Celia observed, had stayed put. One of Celia's Greek busts, *Daphne*, had been adorned with a brown woollen scarf. It hung limply against the balustrades, like a dead branch. She wondered how long it had been there. It must have been Gillian's handiwork. Sally skidded to a halt, puffing.

'Gill not joining us?' asked Celia.

'Says she's got to get to work. Isn't she amazing? Such an imagination. And that boat!'

'Boat?'

I'm thinking of offering her a job. Building sets for one of our shows. She'd be terrific. Who is she? How do you know her?'

Celia avoided the question because she didn't know where to begin. She and Sally had linked arms and were making their leisurely way to the table under the magnolia.

'So, how about Dad's new series?'

'Yes, Netflix calling.'

'Is it Netflix?'

'Not sure. One of those streaming networks headquartered in the States, he said.'

'An eight-parter. He's over the moon. He'll be rubbing shoulders at the awards ceremonies with that bloke who wrote *The Crown*.'

'He told you about it?'

'He's been shooting me endless emails. I've never had so many from him. The most recent arrived when I got off the plane this morning. I popped in to see him twice but he's still Zooming, and looking pretty in charge of it all.' Sally laughed at the idea of her old-fashioned dad vanquishing modern technology. 'He's wangled himself an executive producer credit – did he mention it? Says he's proposed me for production designer, which would be a blast. Just the boost my company needs.'

'But you're doing so well.'

'Sure, working for the Beeb and a bunch of indies who pay buttons. Oh, Ceely, it'd be awesome to get my company on the streaming circuit.' Sally glanced at her watch. 'He should be done by now. I'll just pop in and give him a huge hug. I'll be right back.'

'Still fancy lunch?' asked Celia.

'Famished.' And with that, Sally steamed away.

Celia was alone at the outdoor dining table, waiting for Sally, when Gillian mounted the stone stairs. The girl was about to change direction. A reroute towards the barn, but Celia called to her, 'Can I have a word?'

'Hi, Ceely.'

'Fancy a bowl of pasta?'

'No, thanks.'

'I saw Dave's doctor. They're talking about discharging him in a couple of days.'

Gillian's face lit up.

'The consultant said you'd been in to see him,' Celia added. 'That was kind of Magali to accompany you.'

Gillian frowned. 'Magali? She didn't. Does this mean we'll be going home soon?'

'Well, I don't suppose he'll be fit to travel immediately. I thought he might prefer to convalesce here for a while, what do you think?'

Celia was puzzled. If not Magali, who then?

'He'd rather stay, for sure.'

Gillian's cheeks and chin were a palette of blues and greens, her hair a mess of golden-yellow strands. She reminded Celia of a dandelion in full flower. 'Will you show me your boat?'

'What?'

'Sal says you're painting a boat.'

'I'm building a barge, its framework. I'm using forest wood and some drift I collected from the beach, and I'm painting its wooden blocks. I told you about it.'

'So you did. May I peek?'

'Let's wait till it's further advanced.'

'It'd be fun to see it in progress?'

'I'd prefer not.'

'Oh. Any reason why?'

'I don't want you to undermine me. It's not finished. If you say something negative about it, it will crush me.'

Celia frowned. 'Why would you think I'd do that?'

'Because you do. You put me down, make me wrong. At every given opportunity.'

Celia let out an audible soughing sound. 'I'm sorry, so sorry.'

A goldcrest had landed on one of the magnolia branches just above their heads. It began to chirrup its sweet song. Celia was familiar with the bird: it was one of a pair though she couldn't really tell them apart, or, rather, didn't know the male from the female. She had cared for this one – its crest was slightly more yellow than its companion's – when it had stunned itself flying into the glass wall of the conservatory. She had found it lying on the paved tiling, on its back, its claws curled in the air as though rigor mortis was setting in. She feared it would not be able to right itself and would die. Its marmalade-crested partner had been chirping anxiously at its side, visibly distressed, fearful for the loss of its loved one. Celia had hurried in search of a shallow dish of water, had held the injured bird for a brief second in the palm of her hand to give it warmth, to reassure its panicked heart, and had then placed it ever so gently back on its feet, near the water, in the sunshine. Half an hour later it had rallied and, along with its sweetheart, had flown away. They had shot off like a pair of miniature rockets. How happy it had made Celia.

Ever since, all summer, this teeny creature, little more than a few flying grams, had returned to visit her, seeking her out at various different locations in the garden. When it did, it chirruped to announce its presence. On each occasion Celia ceased what she was engaged in to fill a terracotta plant saucer with water, sufficient for the yellow-crested bird and its spouse.

She wanted to relate this story to Gillian, wanted the girl to understand that she was neither cruel nor hardhearted and that she had not the slightest desire to destroy or undermine Gillian or her work. She valued her, had been hugely grateful for her party decorations and was enormously enjoying her presence here. Well, most of the time.

But she didn't share the story of the bird and its recovery. Instead, she lifted herself from the table, picked up a dish from the ground and filled it with water from a nearby tap, a hosepipe point installed in the stone wall alongside the barbecue. Within seconds the kinglet had swooped to drink, dipping its beak up and down, in and out of the plate, wide round eyes staring. As soon as it had left, the second bird landed at the same spot and also slaked its thirst. Celia returned to the table all the while enjoying the spectacle of the noisy twittering passerines.

Gillian was observing the interaction. 'Funny they're not scared of you,' she commented.

'Goldcrests tend to be quite sociable, not afraid of humans or, at least, not the ones that visit us here. Do have a bite with us. You're very welcome.'

Gillian shook her head.

'Or a glass of homemade lemonade, pressed from our own lemons? Magali's concoction and way too delicious to refuse.'

'Can I have a glass to take to my studio? It's pretty dusty in there.'

'Of course.'

'I'm thinking it would have been more convenient if I'd built the boat outside. The lawn where you had your party, that would be ideal . . .'

Celia was completely taken aback. 'Do you see the boat as a permanent fixture then?'

'Why not? We should do something exciting with it.'

'What do you have in mind?'

'Not sure. I'm cogitating. Am I still invited for Christmas? Sal said she and her husband will be here.'

'Yes, they always come. Well, not during the pandemic, but . . .'

'Great, thank you.'

'I'd better make up a room for Sal. Might you be using your little box space again or shall I ask Béatrice to strip the bed? We could put you in one of the doubles if you prefer that.'

'I'm happy at the lodge, thanks. I like listening to the sea, the waves sloshing against the rocks at night. It's so romantic. Don't hear much of that in Kingston.'

'It's not too cramped?'

Gillian shook her head. 'It's fab. As you won't let me sleep in the barn, Sean's given me his room so I've got privacy. I can stare out of the window, star-gaze. Wishes coming true and all that.'

This information caught Celia off-guard. She had assumed that Tom and Gillian were . . . 'And what about Sean?' she asked. 'Where's he sleeping?'

'On the sofa.'

'Well, that can't be very comfortable when he's working such long hours. These are demanding days for him, filled with rather ghastly manual work. He needs a decent mattress.'

'He's cool about it, don't get stressed. Oh, we're throwing a party. Did Sal mention it?'

'A party? Who's having a party? You and Sally?' Celia silently admitted that she couldn't keep up.

'No, of course not. I didn't even know her before today, though I feel as if we've been mates for years. You know, soul sisters. No, at the lodge. Sean, Tom and me. I'm going to send everybody a formal invite. We were going to have it on the beach with a campfire but we've switched the location because of Dominic.'

'Dominic?'

'He couldn't manage to climb up and down those cliff steps. Or . . . wait! Unless you know someone who has a boat with an outboard. Yeah, of course!' Gillian clapped her hands and did a little jig on the spot. 'Why didn't I think of that before? It'd be gas if Dom arrives by boat. Not my make-believe boat, but . . . Let's arrange that, Ceely, shall we? Catch you later.' And with that Gillian skipped away, forgetting about the glass of lemonade, her mind on her building project or the party, or whatever other fantastical inventions were being seeded in her brain. She was certainly unique. Exasperating, and inspiring.

Celia asked herself whether, if she delivered the promised glass of refreshment in person to the barn, she would be permitted entry and offered a private tour. After a moment's consideration she settled against the idea, fearing the wrath of Gillian or to be accused of breaking some unspoken pact she had been unaware of making. She wanted desperately to heal the rift, the misunderstandings that had grown up between them. She envied Sally the connection she and Gillian had made so immediately. Wiser, then, to respect Gillian's wishes. Instead, she hurried off to Sally's quarters to pack up David's belongings and install them in one of the doubles further along the corridor – where the Boyers would have slept – thus leaving Sally to make herself at home in her own special haven, as she always did.

Every last person on the estate was being furnished with an invitation to Gillian's party. Each had been hand-drawn, individually designed. No two were identical, but each was a single A4 sheet of paper daubed with bright watercolours and loosely scribbled, almost naive, images. Magali found hers on the pine table in the kitchen, inviting herself, her husband and her son, Pascal. Celia was in the kitchen when Magali discovered it.

'*Mon dieu*, whatever's this? Oh, it's that party they've been talking about. This coming Saturday evening.'

There were several invitations on the table, spaced out in the shape of an open fan. One for Béatrice, another for Sally, a third for Dominic, a fourth for Adèle and the last was for David. Each hand-drawn.

There was no invitation for Celia.

'"Seven p.m. Do not arrive late,"' it says. '"On pain of death". Ha, she's a hoot, that girl.' Magali shook her head, thrilled by the drama of it all.

Celia, watching Magali's obvious delight, dreaded the possibility that she was to be excluded. Did Gillian really want to hurt her?

And she felt the hurt.

'Is Sal still with her dad?' she mumbled, to cover her upset. 'Her room's ready. Please let her know, if you see her first. She must've forgotten about lunch.'

Sally had been holed up in the drawing room with her father for the best part of the afternoon. Celia, in the meantime, had cleared out Sally's room and, with the help of Béatrice who, it turned out, was 'walking out' with Magali's son, Pascal, had changed the sheets, hoovered and readied the space. Celia had cut a few of her lovely yellow roses and placed them in a vase alongside the bed to welcome Sally 'home'.

It was a simple shift, moving David along the corridor. He had barely unpacked and the Boyers had only used their room for changing and sprucing up after their long drive. Celia left roses at his new bedside too.

She waited then, fussing about with fresh towels, until all was dusted and prepared, until Béatrice had lumbered off down the stairs to the laundry to deposit the used bedding. Discreetly then, Celia slid open the drawer of the console where David's papers were still secreted. These she removed and, without peeping into his business again, carried them along the corridor to his new sleeping quarters. There she left the file, placed on the counterpane in clear sight. Her thinking was that his precious documents and photographs would jog his memory, would remind him of whose home he was in, his relationship to Celia and this house. *If* there were memory gaps.

When she strode back into the kitchen, Celia found Magali clutching her invitation, one finger moving along a line of text. 'What fun this will be, eh? I hope young Gill's not expecting me to do the cooking. Can we bring the dog?'

'Why not? It's in the open air. May I see, please?'

Celia fought to conceal her sense of rejection. 'How splendid.'

'Gillian asked me to put yours upstairs on your desk. Said she didn't want to go meddling about in there, case you took offence.'

When Celia glanced at Magali's invitation she saw that Gillian had crossed out the address of the party. No longer to be held at the lodge but at the beach, Paradise Cove. With a small PS scribbled in neat black-ink handwriting squeezed in at the bottom: *Dominic scheduled to arrive by boat. 7.10 p.m.*

The girl was never less than enterprising.

'Who has supplied the boat, do you know?'

Magali shook her head, amused. 'She's asked Pascal to get the loan of a fishing boat with outboard engine from one of his mates. Badgered dear old Henri, too, wanting to know whether he has contacts with any of the fishermen who might be willing to act as taxi. Insisted Henri bring along his accordion.'

Celia laughed softly. 'I wonder if she's talked any of this through with Dom, who might not be so amenable. Any idea what the party is in aid of?'

'Her father home from hospital, I expect. Or their leaving party? Yes, that could be it. I'll be right sorry to see them go.'

'Me, too.'

A farewell party. That eventuality had not crossed Celia's mind. She had felt sure they would stay on for a few weeks.

'And we won't be the only ones either.'

As Celia considered the inevitability of their departure, she hardly registered Magali's last comment. When would David and Gillian leave? Early the following week, if David was strong enough to travel? Gillian had confirmed he had a job and a life to get back to. Celia felt panic strike up within her. At the prospect of losing Gillian, she realised despondently it was too soon. This was happening too fast. They still had issues to resolve. And David? Well, David remained a stranger. A son only in name. They had spent practically no time together. There was everything to discover. She felt new purpose with them in situ.

Don't go yet, she was thinking, while asking herself what ploys she might use to detain them.

Throughout the following days, when Sally wasn't beavering away on development ideas with her dad, scribbling notes for him, offering her arm for him to hobble about the drawing room or carry his scripts from table to sofa where he could read over the day's work in solitude and relative comfort, she took flight with Gillian. They sped away on excursions in her rented sky-blue Fiat. Celia spotted them on several occasions throwing their backpacks and bottles of water into the rear of the Cinque Cento and thundering off down the drive in a shower of stones. Laughing, in high spirits. Where were they headed? To buy paint, visit David or simply away on sightseeing excursions? Outings, adventure tours to several of Sally's favourite spots, the beaches, gorges, shaded cafés Sally had first discovered as an adolescent before Dominic and Celia had taken over the estate, when Grandpa and Granny Grey were the hosts.

Sally and Gillian. They were like sisters. *Soul sisters.*

It warmed Celia's heart to see them together, bonding, to witness their exuberance – Gillian, open, vibrant, a member of the family – while at the same time, and Celia was loath to admit it, the sight of them also saddened her. Her emotions were a jumble: they left her confused and dejected because she had not managed this connection with David's stepdaughter.

And because they never once invited her to jump aboard and join them.

Well, they know I'm too busy, she argued with herself. Indeed, she was hellishly busy with estate matters, bolstering and encouraging poor Claude, standing by his choices, decision-making alongside him because it was impossible to discuss anything with Dominic. But it was also a pretext. Celia could easily have played truant from the farm for an afternoon to disappear somewhere lovely, cooler and more peaceful in the hills, with the girls, to walk the shores with them alongside one of the lakes at the Verdon gorges. Share their stories.

Sally loved it up there.

Each time she caught sight of them, they were deep in

conversation. Non-stop chattering. As if there was insufficient time to share every last detail of their lives, to reach deep into the other's heart.

The connection she had craved.

Celia's isolation, various levels of grief, which came as a surprise to her, stung sharply. She had kept herself so occupied over this past decade, she hadn't allowed her feelings any shelf space.

CHAPTER THIRTY-EIGHT

Friday evening: the week was drawing to its close. Dominic, after much shouting and fuss, had shuffled his way with a walking stick to the table under the magnolia where he, his daughter and his wife were about to kick off the weekend with an apéritif. And because it was Friday Claude, with Tom, Henri and Sean, had readily accepted to join the family for dinner and general carousing.

For everyone, it had been a full-on and exacting week, but on all fronts advances had been achieved.

David was to be collected from the hospital the following morning. Disappointingly, Gillian had rescinded on her agreement to accompany Celia, due, she explained, to the level of organization required to get the beach party ready for the following night. As well, she must continue with her hard work on her installation in the barn to which Celia had still not been granted access.

Celia found herself first to the table. She was settling with a book just as Dominic and Sally approached from the house.

For father and daughter, these days of working together were unique, exhilarating and exhausting. They were engrossed in the process of bringing the adaptation of Dominic's play to screen. Scenes were discussed repeatedly. As they were written, they were argued over, tossed aside, rewritten. Each page, each artistic decision or proposal, was being fed back to London, Los Angeles and, as well, to Rome. In the studios of Cinecittà, on the outskirts of the Italian capital, the streaming network had installed a European office; from there the Roman production body would oversee the Italian shooting weeks. London was still involved, but Britain was outside Europe. For financial benefits, at least one partner within the EU was required.

The budgets had been approved.

Dominic was on a high.

The director, a Canadian, was a woman, which, when the news came through overnight, had quietly thrilled Celia even though she was in no way involved in this 'big-budget' television adaptation. Another development was that the TV series was no longer to be known as *Journey Into Starlight*. An executive, unfamiliar to any of them, working out of Los Angeles, had sent a round-robin memo to inform the team that the title would be changed and proposals would be sent through any day now. Dominic had hotly contested this, but he had lost the point. The return argument was that his theatrical title suggested a story whose subject suffered from dementia.

'What the f—!' had been his response to Hollywood. It was ignored.

The most exciting news of the evening was that Sally's role on the series had been approved. 'The bods at the studio said yes. Guys, I'm green-lit!' she yelled to anyone who was listening, which was Celia. She was to head up the UK design team. A contract was being drawn up for her company to crew, build and dress all the interior sets. Sal's title was production designer. The exterior locations, shooting in Italy, would be handled by the Roman team, but Sally would be liaising with them. By coincidence, the costume designer, from Florence, was an old friend of hers. He and she had worked together on several previous productions and had, she said, a 'pretty damn good rapport'.

Show-business was a small, tight-knit world.

Sally had confided in Celia, but not yet to her father, that she was intending to offer a very modest job as runner – all-round gopher – to Gillian, but she was holding her tongue until all the paperwork had been signed and the contract was watertight.

So, the mood when father and daughter arrived at the table was exuberant. Much laughter, exchanging of ideas, followed by earnest debate. Celia put down her paperback and stood to offer an arm to Dominic who, surprisingly, did not wave it impatiently aside. Instead, he smiled warmly at his wife whom he had barely set eyes on over the past few days. He looked tired, she thought, wearier, feathery creases around his eyes, but deeply content.

'Where have you been, my darling?' He winked. 'I've missed you.'

Celia had returned to sleeping in their bedroom upstairs the last few nights. She needed proper rest, not broken nights, as she was spending strenuous hours out on the land with Claude. The last of the casual labourers had been signed off that afternoon. She and Claude had decided that from now on, due to the escalating costs, they, with Tom and Sean, would prepare the fields and winery for whatever upcoming harvest they might manage. This was the first year since she and Dominic had taken over the estate that he had been absent from the picking process.

Dominic had already warned her that he would be leaving shortly for Sicily.

'Sicily?'

'In advance of our scheduled three weeks' shooting.'

The Italian phase of principal photography was no longer to take place in Venice, as Dominic had originally proposed, but along Sicily's eastern sea borders, predominantly in Syracuse. 'Cheaper than Venice and cinematically a fresher look. It will be dramatic, brooding, with the Etna volcano casting its shadow over the backdrop.' That was Hollywood's reasoning behind the location shift.

Celia had made up her mind then to leave Dominic out of all estate affairs until he was free of this commitment. She and Claude could handle it all between them.

The conversation as Sally and her father reached the table was of the score. The Italians were insisting upon an Italian composer and had rejected all other suggestions. So the music had yet to be written. Dominic hung his head and groaned. 'I can't believe this.'

'What?'

'It's the leading lady. She bought the rights to the play. Now she, along with one of the Hollywood producers, is calling the shots,' Sally elucidated. 'She's proposed Madonna to write the score.'

Celia thought a female songwriter was a rather clever idea.

'We need a composer. None of this out-of-our-price-range pop nonsense,' wailed Dominic, throwing his arms into the air.

Celia started pouring a bottle of white. It was casual, her question to Sally, about the identity of the leading lady, a role that once had been so precious even if heartbreakingly exclusively hers. 'You probably haven't heard of her, Ceely. A UK TV star. Not *really* famous outside that world, I think.

Isabelle Carter.' Sally lobbed a miniature savoury cheese square into her mouth and nibbled it, completely unaware of the bombshell she had just detonated. Celia threw a glance at Dominic who was a million miles away. He had not been party to the exchange, lost in his own imagination, pencil moving like lightning, scribbling in one of the notebooks he habitually carried with him. Celia, who had stood up to pour the wine, replaced the bottle in the terracotta cooler, and tilted backwards into her chair. She was stunned by the revelation.

How much of this was Dominic's doing? His choice? When had it first been discussed, decided upon, agreed?

At that moment, the men arrived. Celia's gaze was still fixed on Dominic. She was looking for acknowledgement or repudiation of the fact. How, when, had this collaboration come about?

Dominic was paying her no attention, oblivious to the fact that she had been steamrollered into silence.

The new arrivals were serving themselves beers, grabbing extra glasses from an iron table near the barbecue. Each man had the complexion of one who had laboured vigorously, with satisfaction, and whose skin had been scrubbed by the elements, never mind soap.

Their conversations were animated, also centred round their work. The land.

Tom was saying, 'It was Gill's idea and rather a smart one. What are your thoughts, Claude?'

'Yes, it's obvious . . .'

' . . . and yet none of us came up with it.'

'Of course, eventually it's not down to me and it will be a question of finding the right animal or animals. I have one or two contacts I can call. No idea of the price for such a hire.'

'Plenty of farms must be considering this issue with petrol costs so high and rising,' Sean chipped in.

'Quite a few are making the switch on a more permanent basis.'

Words, exchanges back and forth, were swimming in the evening air, circling with the midges. Above, small black bats were darting almost too fast to be observed.

Celia was still crushed, bewildered.

Isabelle Carter?

The moment had moved on, swallowed by others' chatter and opinions.

Celia, in her own bubble, was chewing on information that impacted nobody but her. And Dominic. Of course Dominic. What had been his reaction to this casting? Had he precipitated it? Had he suggested to Isabelle Carter that she purchase the rights? When had he and she last been in contact?

'Where's Gill?' someone enquired.

The only person not yet present was Gillian, who, according to Tom, was still painting in her atelier.

'I'll go and fetch her,' croaked Celia, who urgently needed to move away, take stock on her own, reconfigure, pull herself together. She sprang up from the table and strode, almost sprinting, round the western flank of the house to the barn where she rapped hard with her knuckles several times. 'Gillian, are you in there?'

No response.

'Gillian, I'm coming in.' She rammed her shoulder against the great door. It shuddered and creaked. The girl was sitting on a stool at the other side of the curtains, legs swinging, talking on her phone, smoking a cigarette.

Celia's first reaction was how easily those hanging cloths clotted with grease could go up in flames. One stray cinder was all it would take. And this old planked barn would be ablaze . . .

'See you soon, then.' Gillian clicked off her phone, took a drag, sensing the presence of another, whom she could not identify because they, unlike her, were not backlit.

'Is that you, Sal?'

'No, it's Ceely.'

Gillian tossed the cigarette on to the earthen floor and ground it out. She stuck her head through the drapes. 'Hi Ceely, do you want something?'

'Is that cigarette properly out?' Celia bit back the question. Instead, she continued her approach. 'Everyone's gathered at the table, enjoying a pre-dinner drink. Your presence is missed.'

'I'll be there in a mo.'

Gillian was about to close herself back into her space when Celia held fast to the gap in the curtains. 'I want to . . .'

'What?'

'I'd like us to have a hug.'

Gillian stared at her with uncertain mistrusting eyes, squinting. '*What?*'

'This impasse that's grown up between us, the misunderstandings . . . It's hurting me, Gill.' She also wanted to say, Forgive me for my foolishness, my inability to get this connection right, but she didn't go that far, didn't dare to open herself up so wide. Just in case. Instead, she slowly, tentatively wrapped her arms round Gillian's neck and shoulders and drew the girl close against her. Gillian did not resist, but neither did she fully reciprocate. Her own arms were folded tight against her chest, pressed up against her girlish bosom. As Celia hugged her, she noted silently that the girl gave off a perfume of smoke and paint and stale food. Or was that the curtains?

———

Outside, back beneath the shade of the century-old tree, Henri had now joined the assembly. Seated on a chair snug against the mighty trunk, he was playing his trusted accordion, a French café ditty, well known to all although Celia could not have put a title to it. Tom was plucking background notes with his guitar. Claude, Sean and Sally were tapping the table top in time to the music, with fingers, a corkscrew, or aluminium beer-can tabs while chatting and sipping their well-earned drinks. The mood was harmonious, easy-going. Gillian ran to join them, clapping her hands. All their faces lit up as she approached. She twirled a full circle, like a ballerina on a box, then plumped herself down alongside Sean, nudging him further along the seat with her bottom. He lifted an arm and wrapped it about her. For a brief moment Gillian rested her head on his shoulder, then jumped up again in search of a beer.

Where was Dominic? He was absent from the gathering.

Celia approached Sally, who was as transported by the music as her companions. Each was begging Henri to play this tune or that, humming bars, laughing at their inadequate French, revelling in an end-of-the-week vibe.

'Have you seen Dom?'

'A call came through. From LA, I think. He went back inside.'

Celia beetled through the kitchen doors along the back corridor where a recently baked fish dish, left to cool, smelled too good to be true. Dinner. She took the precaution to knock on the drawing-room door before entering.

Dominic was not on the phone. He was lying outstretched on the sofa with his legs up on the cushions, head reclining against one of the armrests, his feet balanced on the other. His hands were folded on his abdomen. He seemed reflective, or was he ill?

'Are you cogitating or in pain?'

'What?' His head swivelled. 'Ceely, come on in. Pain? No, not at all, but I am glad to get the weight off this bloody ankle. I've just popped a couple of ibuprofen, waiting for the poisonous stuff to kick in and elevate me to nirvana. Come and keep me company,' he commanded softly. She approached, dragged the ottoman across the carpet to the sofa's head, drawing close to his shoulder and squatted there.

They sat awhile, listening to their own thoughts or to the ticking of the clock on the mantelpiece. Another of her mother's astute acquisitions. Celia remembered her father fiddling for hours with its mechanics, dismantling it, lubricating it. It had only needed a service, he'd explained modestly after he'd got it ticking again. She missed those days. Craved that family life. The love, the company and activity.

Since her father's death, since her and Dominic's disasters in London, she had closed herself into a more solitary, more functional world.

'A tiring week,' she remarked eventually. It was an unnecessary observation, true for both of them, but she needed to lead into this conversation from somewhere, and after ten or more years of silence on the subject, it was impossible to know from which angle to unlock this particular gate.

'Given all that's going on here, a fair amount of shit you might say, this TV project will save our bacon, Ceely. If anything can, this will.' He dug into his trouser pocket, pulled out his mints, and popped two into his mouth. 'I need a cigarette,' he growled.

'Are we that close to going under?' This revelation, its possibility, freaked her, threw her off course.

'No, no, not quite. We've faced worse times. And the deposit for the order the Boyers put through will be paid in a few days. Even so, our cashflow is very tight and it'll be a few weeks before this darn film deal starts to cough up.'

'But aside from bolstering up estate finances, this contract is a real fillip for you, your career. Your status as a writer.'

'All of that, my dear heart. Yes, of course. If I survive the stress of it.' His fingers reached out towards her and without turning his head he searched for her hand, for physical contact.

She closed her eyes, picturing a similar scenario, those same fingers in a café reaching for a different woman seated across the table from him while she, Celia, standing outside, in the rain in the London Bridge street, bore witness to the incident. The overture to his affair with Isabelle Carter.

A single blast of pain tore through her because that same woman had made a comeback into their lives.

Or had Ms Carter never really bowed out? Had she been waiting patiently in the wings? And how much of her had lived on in Dominic's heart? Was this TV series the opportunity she or he or they had longed for? To be reunited.

Celia felt the hurt expanding, scorching her innards.

'I was just lying here reflecting upon the first time,' he murmured.

Her heart skipped a beat. 'First time?'

'Those early rehearsals when I was still feeling my way into this story. I don't want to make the same mistakes again, Ceely. Write myself another flop. I'm nervous, you know. A little insecure. I wouldn't confess it to anyone but you. Not even Sal, only to you. Still, there it is. You being in the public eye, you were centre stage back then, suffered for my misjudgements. You took the rap for it, as Bogie might have observed.' Dominic had attempted a rather poor Humphrey Bogart impersonation, then followed it with a faint apologetic smile.

Her heart had slowed. Her breath refused to draw. She fought back the compulsion to ask him about Isabelle Carter, to unveil, pour out her own damage during that earlier experience. 'Did you blame me? she asked instead. Her voice was faint, lacking the usual timbre of her powerful vocal cords. 'Back then, I mean. Did you hold me responsible for the – our – the play's *flop*?'

He withdrew his right arm. Abruptly. Brusquely. He scratched his face, his chin, rubbing hard. He had let a beard grow, more a greyish stubble, over the days he had been hibernating in this room. She noticed now the air was scented with his aftershave. Chanel, Allure. She habitually bought a bottle for him at Christmas and birthdays. He would never have bothered for himself. Or perhaps he would, and possibly he would have made an entirely different choice.

Another woman, a different Dominic.

'I put the failure down to a number of issues. The play just didn't work. It was, let's say, only half-born, halfway out of its shell. No actress could have given full expression to it. Not you, not Isa—' He spluttered on his mint. 'Not anyone. The story, its dramatic arc, was muddled, incomplete. Only partially fleshed out. With hindsight, I'm clearer about that now. And I must take full responsibility for it. I could see it, and yet I couldn't, if you know what I mean. I was stuck. As a consequence I . . . I made some bad decisions at that time.' He paused, heaved a breath. His clasped hands lifted and fell. 'My confusions drove me to . . .' He felt silent. She waited. He spoke no more, appeared to have abandoned his thought, or the subject entirely.

A tear rolled down her cheek.

Please say it.

She remained mute, waiting, but Dominic did not continue. Did not deliver.

Beyond the closed windows she could hear the muffled sounds of clapping, camaraderie, laughter, music, joy. Henri was still entertaining his co-workers. And then a silence before a burst of enthusiastic applause, before Tom broke into song. Guitar chords, and then that remarkable voice of his. One sustained note. Like an isolated call in the desert. Celia stood up, crossed the room, drawn by the music. She tugged hard to open the window with its ill-fitting, damp-distorted frame, to allow the sounds to flood inside with vibrancy and poetry.

'Who is that, Ceely? Who's singing out there?'

'One of the English chaps. Tom.'

'Who? That Cornish fellow? Well, I'll be damned.'

She nodded and returned to her husband's side, standing over his supine body. Her face, her gaze, remained concentrated on the window and the music, the evening beyond. Her emotional self was with this man who, in spite of everything, she loved profoundly. Slowly, she crouched back on the ottoman and leaned in to Dominic, touched her fingers to his, gently caressing them. 'Tom's voice, it's exquisite, don't you think?'

'It is indeed, but I'm trying to identify the piece and I can't place it.'

'Isabelle Carter,' she whispered.

She had said it, spoken the name. Released it from the cage in her heart.

Dominic made no immediate reply.

'Isabelle Carter was my understudy.'

'I know who she is. What about her?' he barked.

'Sal says she owns this new series.'

'She bought the rights to the play, true, and has sold them on, owns a percentage. A plum role for her talents but hell's bells, Ceely, what about it? No one would have cast you.'

'Don't be unkind! I know that! I'm ten years too old and too many years out of the business.'

'So, why are you bringing the subject up now?'

'Because it's not about me. It's not about the role!'

'Hey, keep your shirt on.'

'It's about Isabelle. I wonder how or why Isabelle came to choose this project. Was it you? Did you offer it to her, suggest it?'

Dominic shook his head uncomprehendingly. 'She's a household name in the UK now, for what that's worth, starred in a few popular family drama series. She's mid-forties – too young for this but, as you say, Ceely, these executives always cast younger. Or in the case of women, they do. They fear older women. Fear their ageing process and their power.'

'Have you seen her, been in touch?'

'Who?'

'Isabelle, Dom. Isabelle Carter?'

'We've spoken on the phone, Zooms recently, but otherwise no . . . not since . . .'

'Not since?'

He was silent. His breath rasped. 'Jesus, Ceely, why are you doing this?'

'Not since the play wrapped? Yes, I remember now.' She bit her lip. 'The week my father died. God, what a hellish week that was.'

There was a lump in her throat, a tightening in her chest. An old, hard anger was rising. Celia knew that beyond the close of the play Dominic and Isabelle had continued to be involved with one other. But for how long? When did their affair end? When Dominic agreed to move to France? 'I've decided to return to my wife. Sorry, but that's how it is.' Or had she, Ceely, been completely blind, naive? Had the affair lingered on, occasional rendezvous in London when he was back in town for work?

Dominic's breathing had become heavier. She watched the rise and fall of his ribcage.

'Ceely, can you move, please? I need to stand up.' His

words were terse. 'This wretched leg is going to sleep, cramps. Here give me a hand, will you? Let's walk. Let's go back outside. I need to get the blood pumping in my veins. That music really is very fine. I've never heard it before. You go on ahead, keep the troops entertained. I'll be out there in five minutes. Need to jot down a thought, a memo to self.'

'Dominic . . .'

'I said I'll join you.'

He was staggering to his feet, his hand pressed against Celia's shoulder, gripping her so tightly, as though she were an inanimate object and the pain didn't matter. Risen to his full height, jigging his leg, 'Must wake the blasted thing up, get the blood . . .' He shifted the back of his hand to her cheek, rested it there. He must have felt the dampness of her skin. The rogue tear. He couldn't miss it. But he made no comment.

'I'll see you outside. Or, no, I might just stay here and catch up on my emails. You go on.' Those were his final words, his conclusion of this meeting. The subject had been closed, shut back into the darkness.

CHAPTER THIRTY-NINE

The following morning, as the engine of the Land Rover was spluttering and shimmying into life, Gillian came haring along the path, flip-flops slapping. She was waving, shrieking, 'Wait, Ceely, hang on!' She bulleted to the passenger side of the car, heaved the door open and pitched herself on to the seat.

'I've decided I should come with you. The guys have instructions. They can handle everything till I get back.' She was breathless. 'Humping the wood and stuff to build the jetty.'

Jetty?

'Good morning.' Celia smiled. 'What a lovely surprise.'

'I lay awake last night for ages – fab evening, by the way, pity Dominic didn't join us. He'd better be there tonight. Yeah, I lay awake listening to the sea and I was thinking, I can't let Ceely do this alone. After all, I brought Dave here.' Gillian chortled. She was in a surprisingly upbeat frame of mind.

Gear rammed into first, they took off. The wheelchair was knocking against the metal interior as the car rumbled down the hillside. Engine and chair creating a cacophony of sound. To be heard above it, they were obliged to shout.

'It's Saturday so I fear we'll run into a fair amount of traffic, which is why I'm setting off early. To beat the Cannes shoppers. The fruit and veg market is a big weekend attraction so I prefer not to get caught in the congestion on the outskirts of the city. I don't want David to be hanging about waiting for us, fearing we're not coming. And I have to return this chair. Maybe you go on in to him, keep him company, while I sign this thing off and whatever other papers need my attention, OK?'

Gillian nodded. 'Sure.'

They rode on towards the highway in silence.

'I need a fag,' muttered Gillian, hand rummaging deep into her overstuffed bag.

'Not in the car, please.'

'Even if I open the window?'

'Sorry, no.'

'God, you're such a stickler for rules, Ceely, lighten up.' She bobbed her head and sang, 'Light up, lighten up. I want to light up.'

'Ten more minutes and you can have a cigarette while you both wait for me. Sit outside on one of the benches. No one will moan at you there.'

'Have you thought about what's going to happen?'

'About what?'

'Dave. I hope we can stay on with you. He can convalesce here by the sea. He loves the sea.'

Celia tapped her fingers against the steering wheel, stared at the taillights of the braking car ahead. 'I hope so, too. Let's wait and see how it pans out.'

'None of this was his fault, Ceely, you know. None of it.'

Close to an hour later, Celia tracked down father and daughter seated in the fresh air surrounded by a curtain of ferns and geraniums in a pretty quadrangle with a small fountain, the hospital garden. They were huddled tight on a bench in the sunshine, deep in conversation. Gillian was dragging hard on a cigarette, doing all the whispering, as though plotting some conspiracy. Her right arm was hooked into David's left. The sun was shining on their backs and shoulders. His hair had been shaved where the wound had opened his skull and where the stitches remained. It was less dramatic in length than Celia had feared. Otherwise, he looked to be in fine fettle.

'Here's Celia,' muttered Gillian.

'Hello, David, good to see you on your feet again. How are you feeling?'

He stepped forward to shake her hand. Celia, hesitant, took his and squeezed it. 'Sorry about all this fuss,' he said. 'The inconvenience I've caused.'

'We're delighted you're safe.'

They set off walking, almost strangers side by side.

On the journey home, Gillian, who was wedged into the back tight alongside her stepfather, was recounting to him her adventures over the past days, the construction of her ancient boat, which they might move into the garden later, and her plans for that evening's party, which, as far as Celia could hear above the wheezing engine ascending the mountainside, sounded mighty elaborate.

'What's the party in aid of?' she called over her shoulder.

'It's a surprise.'

Glancing in the rear-view mirror, Celia noticed the intensity in David's eyes, his level of concentration, grasping for facts.

Gillian needed to be back on site, she explained, when they pulled up out front at Les Roches du Soleil. Off she shot, leaving Celia to lead David inside and up the stairs to his new room.

'I hope you don't mind.' She was explaining who Sally was as they strode along the corridor. 'See, it's only a few doors from where you were. Shall I leave you to make yourself at home? Anything you need?'

He shook his head. 'I can't remember the accident,' he blurted out. 'I remember your party, or flashes, moments of it, but after that my mind's a blank.'

'The doctor said it's quite normal for some patients. No cause for concern.' She smiled. 'Let's have coffee when you're ready.'

He nodded. 'Thank you for this.' He disappeared inside the room.

The house was unusually quiet. It was the weekend. No one working in the vineyards, no vehicles careering up and down the driveway, no helpers knocking, requesting the loo or a chilled bottle of water. No shouts from the yard. Claude was catching up on neglected chores in the fermentation yard. Sally and Dominic were still beavering away in the drawing room, while the rest of them were, well, up to whatever it was they were plotting.

David had not surfaced.

Celia climbed the stairs and knocked cautiously. She heard the creaking of floorboards. 'David, it's Celia.'

The door opened wide.

They stood awkwardly.

'How are you doing?'

'Better.' He stepped backwards, drawing her inside. His hair was dishevelled. He must have been resting. On the bed, spread out all across the olive-green throw, were the contents of the manilla envelope Celia had lifted from the drawer and left in full view for him to find.

'I want to show you . . .' He was smiling, seemed brighter, more certain of himself and his surroundings, more in charge of his identity. 'These,' he said. 'I brought them from England to share with you. It seems like weeks ago. At least I remember all this,' He released a brittle laugh, then frowned. 'I don't want to be an intrusion, Celia. Gill and I should have been on our way by now. We're outstaying our welcome.'

'You're not an intrusion.' Celia slipped her arm through David's and they stepped over to the bed. 'I'm delighted you're here. And looking forward to more time together. Let's see what you've got then, shall we?'

The collection of photographs was prodigious. It included dozens of Polaroids, most a little brownish, beginning to fade.

'My goodness.' Celia lifted one from the pile on the bed. David as a boy on a beach with a bucket and spade, hair and trunks damp. She grinned. 'You?'

'It's Camber Sands. In Kent. About forty minutes from my parents' farm. I loved our days out there. Later, when I was in my teens, I was a lifeguard on that same beach. My first paid job outside farm work. Here, look, here's the lifeguard certificate. David Hawksmith.'

Celia asked whether he had any pictures of his parents and their home.

He offered several with pride. Their smallholding consisted of a modest house with washing on the line at the front. A British car, a well-used Morris shooting brake. Celia stared into her son's past. 'Where was this?'

'Outside Tenterden.'

She selected another photo from the bed. It featured a skinny boy with a front tooth missing, legs astride a docked fishing boat accompanied by a man in his late fifties. The boy was holding high a speckled fish, laughing, triumphant.

'That's me with my dad. We used to fish together off the coast near Dymchurch.' He ran through a list of locations as though Celia could appreciate all these Kentish coastal spots. He was talking non-stop, while she was gazing at a host of unfamiliar details. David was bubbling over with all he wanted to share. She hadn't heard him so loquacious since he'd arrived. Clearly, it mattered to him that she should see all this. He was giving her these treasured memories. The missing years. A lifetime. Years when he had belonged to the Hawksmith couple.

Several of the instant prints showed his parents smiling self-consciously towards the lens, pressed shoulder to shoulder outside their front door. Celia lingered over their features. She felt a rush of longing. Of jealousy too? They appeared good-natured. A kind couple, down to earth, ruddy complexions that had seen many hours of hard work in all weathers. The father was wiry. His face was etched with deep lines, wind-burned. He wore a flat cap. The mother was plumper. Celia almost believed she could pinpoint a similarity between David and his adopted mother. She rested her finger on the woman's image.

'Mum,' David declared unnecessarily.

'Yes.' Would this woman, David's mum, and Celia have liked each other? Might they have got on, found a natural rapport between them? Or would Mrs Hawksmith have judged her harshly?

David was watching Celia intently as she scanned one photograph after another, considering them, while attempting to untangle her own confused emotions. 'That's Jenny and he's Harry Hawksmith.' He recalled adventures, outings they had embarked on, then described the miserable days at school. 'I hated it.' Instead he had loved the great outdoors, scrubbing out the stables, caring for the horses, helping with the technical challenges of ploughs, tractors, cars. And then, on a more intimate note, he confided how bereft he had been after his parents had passed on, his mother fourteen months after his father.

In that respect Celia realized, she and David were similar. Both had thrived on the unconditional love given to them by their parents. 'What happened to this lovely farm?' she asked him.

The farm had been a tenancy, so he'd had no right to stay on. 'It fair broke my heart,' he said. 'And I'd loved being so close to the sea.'

'So you don't live there now?'

He shook his head. 'Not for years.'

She considered how heartbroken she would have been to lose Les Roches du Soleil if her family hadn't owned it. Snatched from her along with the protection and companion-ship of her parents. Even so, Celia was thinking, up until that point, the final loss, David appeared to have profited from a childhood of innocence and untroubled days; all the basics provided by a dependable couple who had been so grateful for his presence in their lives. He had been in safe hands, cherished and cared for.

Loved.

Celia could never have offered him such a felicitous upbringing. It was a fact. Regrettable but true. Not unless she had stayed with her parents, moved to France with them, renounced all hopes of her own life and career. In those early days, when David was a growing lad – sailing, swimming, riding horses – she was still grappling with the violence Terry had inflicted upon her. Her sense of worthlessness. The shame.

She laid the photos on the bed and stroked her son's arm. The gesture caused him to blush. This big man who was so shy and uncertain. 'Thank you for bringing these, sharing them with me. It helps me to know you a little better.'

After all, Fate had done her baby a good turn. These were decent people, thought Celia, who had nurtured the gift bestowed on them. The son they had never been blessed with. 'When did you find out?' she asked.

Towards the end of his mother's life, after Harry had died, Jenny had revealed to David that he was not hers, theirs, in the biological sense.

'Dad never said a word.'

'No?'

'"Davey," Mum said, "there's a matter I need to discuss with you." That's how she broached the subject and then she handed me this.' He picked up an adoption certificate. 'It shook me to the core, devastated me. I'd never suspected, never once doubted they were my proper mum and dad.'

After Jenny died, David had been ejected from the farm and had moved to London. He'd struggled to find a new path forward, a new direction, but he had hated the big city, had yearned for the countryside, the fresh air, the animals. Only in passing did he mention his short-lived marriage to Gillian's mother and Celia didn't pry.

'What about now?'

These days, since he'd escaped the capital, he lived alone in a small flat, two rooms, above a shop in a different borough. 'Sevenoaks, it's also in Kent.' He worked as a mechanic in a garage on the outskirts of the market town. He was satisfied, lacking nothing materially speaking. 'It's not a million miles from where I grew up. Not as pretty as Tenterden, our local town when I was a boy.'

He spoke of Gillian with immense affection. She was the closest thing he had to family.

'Well, after you, Celia. I try to look out for her,' he said, 'as if she were my own. She is in a way. I'd have liked kids,' he confessed. 'Very much. You know, family all around me. I suppose it's what I dreamed of. A wife and kids. A proper brood, with me working the land.'

David's life sounded so empty. It stung Celia to think of him so unfulfilled, so solitary.

While David packed away all his photos and documents, such as driving and heavy-goods vehicle licences, Celia hurried on down the stairs. His lifeguard certificate, swimming badges, his adoption paper signed by Harry Hawksmith when David was two, school reports, technical college leaving certificate . . . He seemed to have hung on to everything; Celia supposed the papers must help to give him a sense of himself. Roots. Belonging.

She rapped on the door to the winter drawing room. 'Who's hungry?'

Sally and Dominic were deep in activity, blithely unaware of everything beyond their own universe. Neither expressed any interest in lunch.

'No time,' Sally called.

Celia and David made sandwiches together in the kitchen. David drank a cold beer as Celia sliced the loaf and he folded in a couple of slices of ham. They smiled at one another coyly. 'Won't eat too much. Gill says there's going to be a big spread later.' He laughed.

'Any idea what the party's in aid of? Gill's being ever so secretive,' she asked him. 'I'm glad it's not your leaving bash.'

'Leaving,' he mumbled, then sighed and bit a mighty chunk out of his sandwich.

She liked him, this solid man, Dave. She had been pleased to share his souvenirs, reaching back into his history. He was a sensitive, good-natured sort of fellow with a tender and broad soul, even if she still could not quite relate to him as her son, her own flesh and blood. She would have expected any son of hers to be more outgoing, more extrovert. Someone who grabbed life with both hands. Not that she had ever considered such a subject before. It amused her, made her giggle silently, the idea that she had given birth to such a hulk of a human being. Quite an achievement, all in all. She no longer remembered what he had weighed at birth. Three or four pounds, no more. Had she ever been told?

'I'd love you to stay on for a while. Would that appeal to you?'

'Wouldn't that be nice,' he riposted, eyes lowered.

She watched him, studied him thoughtfully, then pushed away her lunch, barely touched, lifting herself from her chair. 'Hurry up and finish.' She had a plan. It'd been hatching for a while.

'What's the rush?'

'I want to show you something. You'll need a hat to protect that head wound from the sun. Come on, follow me. I'll fetch one of Dom's Panamas.'

She slipped their plates and knives into the dishwasher, grabbed a straw hat from the old gunroom where there were no hunting rifles but plenty of pairs of wellingtons, hiking boots, hats and walking sticks. From there they set off crunching across gravel, past the barns where Gillian's boat remained hidden, direction seawards along an extended grassy bank, rarely trodden these days. The earth was still a little soft underfoot from the rains, though no longer squelchy.

A solitary building with a sloping roof soon came into view. Even from this distance it appeared substantial, standing alone in the middle of nature. Looking at it now, Celia was reminded of one of Edward Hopper's paintings of Cobb's Barns. The rust-red wooden walls. A vision more arresting here because this southern French earth was also red.

She and David walked in silence, sometimes in single file when the path grew narrow. Overhead, a squabble of seagulls, shrieking and wheeling. Celia paid them no attention. She moved forwards purposefully, excited by the expedition. David, taking big strides, was right behind her, though he paused every few minutes, loitering, squinting skywards, blinded by the light, to watch the birds. 'Gulls always remind me of being a lad, playing on the sand,' he muttered. Next he paused to take in the view, which, to his left, rolled southwards to the opal Mediterranean. He was seeing the breadth and scope of the estate for the first time. 'My God, this is some place, Celia,' he exclaimed. 'Never in my wildest dreams . . . Those views, the colour of that sea. We never get all this in Kent.' He grinned.

The barn was locked, as Celia had expected it would be.

'This was where my father used to hang out, whiling away the hours he wasn't working in the vineyards. His bolthole.'

David tilted back his head and was giving the exterior walls of the outbuilding a once-over.

'My mother collected antiques, vintage stuff really, not priceless heirlooms, but Daddy's passion was . . . Well, wait and see . . .' Celia was tugging at a key, pulling it from her pocket. 'Daddy wanted somewhere to serve as boathouse and general workshop, so he hired a local carpenter to construct this. Sadly, it's been neglected since before he died.'

'The timber work's still in good nick.' David was peering at the joinery, running the flat of his hand over it while Celia fought with the padlock.

'I can't turn this thing. It's jammed, rusty.'

She handed the key to David who twisted and jiggled it until finally he managed to release the lock. 'It needs oiling. I'll do that for you later.' He was pushing hard against the door. It juddered and strained but refused to budge. Finally, with an almighty shove and a kick, David forced it ajar. It growled on its hinges. Cobwebs, hanging like disintegrating bedclothes, waited within. 'Oh, my God!' David bullied at the door again. It yielded to halfway, allowing a shaft of sunlight into the dark-brown space. Thick, dusty, acrid. 'As you say, no one's been here for years.'

In contrast to the cicadas rasping and the mewing of the birds overhead, inside there was a dense almost putrefying silence.

'Any electric here?' he called back, as he stepped within. The palm of his hand was feeling for a switch. The shaft of sunlight exposed circling midges and a window on the far wall, which was shuttered. There was no other source of light except through one broken board high in a corner towards the slanted ceiling.

Celia was coughing at the dust. 'This might not have been such a good idea.' She laughed, brushing her clothes, wiping grime from her cheeks and forehead. 'There has to be a switch, but I can't remember where.'

David found it. He flicked it on and off several times. 'Either the light-bulb is dead or the mains power is not arriving. I can take a look at it tomorrow for you, if you like.'

Tomorrow, that pleased her.

He shuffled inside, attempting to nudge the door further but it was stubbornly stuck. Not another inch. To the left, in a hollow of darkness, was the main expanse of the storehouse.

David pulled his phone from his pocket, tapped on the torch and trained its glare into the blackness. A car on blocks was revealed. An open top, lacking wheels. Alongside it was a smallish boat. Its mast, broken in two halves, was rotting on the oil-steeped floor. Both boat and sports car were stripped of everything, abandoned inanimate carcasses.

'Heavens to Betsy, that's an Austin Healey! My dad used to dream of one of these. Nothing as fancy as this old girl. Our reality was a Morris Traveller.' He laid his hand on the front wing of the long-abandoned car, brushing away layers of dust to reveal its navy paintwork. 'Any idea what this would be worth if it was cleaned up and made roadworthy?'

She shook her head.

'Thirty, forty grand, I'd bet you, Celia. Tragic to let it rot like this.'

'Dominic gets impatient with anything mechanical and I wouldn't know where to begin.' She smiled quietly, leaning inside the space, not too enthusiastic about embracing the dinginess of her father's past sanctuary. She spotted a sun-faded wicker chair, shaped like a bucket. Images sprang up of her father sitting in it outside, reading his several-days-old *Times*, sucking his pipe. Sometimes she'd wander over here, listen to the birdsong, bring him chilled beer and sandwiches, sit on the ground at his feet, legs outstretched in the direction of the sea, back against the warm wooden structure. The memory stabbed her. David's excitement pleased her, counterbalancing the memories.

'Have you still got its papers?' David was alongside the car. He was a boy in an Aladdin's cave.

'I suppose so, somewhere. Dominic would know. I'd have misplaced them if they'd stayed in my possession. It was a miracle I located the key.'

'Look, it's two-tone. Navy and white. Oh, if my dear old dad could have got his hands on this beauty.'

He was speaking of Harry Hawksmith. Not Terry, of course not, nor of her own beloved father whose Utopia this estate had been. Harry, a man she had never known, whose existence she had been entirely ignorant of until a few days ago, who had brought up her son, loved and cherished the boy. Delivered to her now.

How many years since she had been inside this workshop, handing spanners and other tools to her father as he toiled away? Her father thoughtfully puffing his pipe while they chatted. A transistor radio with an adjustable aerial always left on the windowsill or on the ground near the car's tyres, playing softly. She glanced about to see if it was still there but couldn't spot it. He had enjoyed popular music: dance bands, swing, or the BBC World Service.

How many worlds were colliding here?

'A Big Healey. Well, I never. Would you object to me coming back tomorrow and giving the old girl a polish?'

'Not at all. In fact, I was going to suggest that if you're interested, and if you could make the time, you might like to stay on for, well, maybe an extra week or two.'

David eyed her with delight. 'Shall I call my boss? It'll have to wait till Monday now. Request a few weeks of leave, take all my overdue holiday time. If I stayed, I could help you out. I'd earn my keep, Celia.' He grinned.

CHAPTER FORTY

It was approaching seven on the first Saturday in September. Sunset was still a couple of hours away. The warm temperature didn't call for a camp fire, but the ropes of raw sausages and stack of defrosted burgers certainly did. Had vegetarian Gillian shopped for these? Had she popped in to see Jacques, the butcher, and begged him to prepare them for her?

Sean was standing guard over the meat, attempting to keep Magali's Jack Russell from wolfing any of it. The terrier, its incessant barking, was a source of amusement, a topic of conversation for a group of people who were not necessarily comfortable in such diverse company. It was Gillian who had drawn the motley bunch together, staff from the vineyards, kitchens and gardens, alongside villagers and the estate owners. Of the latter, only Celia was present because Dominic, who was scheduled to arrive by boat, had not yet landed.

It was dead on seven.

Celia glanced out to sea, wondering whether this would all go horribly wrong.

Metres before her was was the newly assembled jetty, cobbled together to see Dominic safely on to dry land. It was a temporary construction, which would be washed away or broken up by the waves within a matter of days, but that didn't seem to bother anyone. As long as it served its purpose for this evening. The hired boat was scheduled to dock alongside the makeshift landing stage. Then, with Sally's assistance, Dominic would be able, more or less, to hobble ashore without getting his legs and feet wet or covered with sand. Damp trousers was not the comfort they were aiming for.

The jetty had been fitted together from a haul of the recently sawn wheels of pine ferried down from the top vineyard. The smaller cuts had been filched from a stockpile in one of the barns, wood that had been stored for winter burning.

It was an ingenious concept. Yet another invention masterminded by Gillian.

Gillian had 'borrowed' the estate's tractor with a trailer attached to it for transportation purposes.

Celia, when she heard this from Sean, was less than pleased, but she kept quiet not wishing to put a dampener on these mystifying celebrations. She decided instead to pass the time welcoming guests. It was not her party, but . . .

Béatrice was standing with her mother, Joséphine, and her father, Régis, whom Celia had not met before.

'Régis, a good southern French name,' Celia commented, while kissing him politely on both cheeks.

Pascal was spruced and present, hovering alongside Béatrice. He was giving Sean a hand to feed the fire.

Magali was close by with her husband, Alain, and their fiercely determined little terrier. Henri, sprightly and spruced, had managed to make it down the stone steps. Claude, descending ahead of him, had carried his colleague's accordion. Where was Tom? There he was, guitar slung across his back, flute in his left hand, arriving later than everyone else. He waved and leaped down the stairway. A small woman who lived on the coast at Juan-les-Pins, whose name was Estelle and who was a stranger to Celia, was pacing back and forth, glancing frequently at her phone. In her early sixties with deeply lined features set into a chestnut-hued pixie face, she introduced herself as the wife of Guillaume.

'Guillaume?'

'My husband owns the craft that's transporting Mr Millar,' she explained bashfully.

Celia nodded. 'Not an easy task,' she joked.

'He refused to board at the last minute, your husband did.'

'Oh, no!'

'Took fright. But his daughter persuaded him. Monsieur Dominic is safely aboard and seems calm. They shouldn't be much longer.'

Celia crossed her fingers. Dominic was not fond of the sea. It was one of the reasons, aside from lack of time and funds, that they had never resurrected her late father's dinghy, rotting alongside the Austin Healey. Recalling the visit of that afternoon prompted Celia to search for David, but he was nowhere to be seen.

Estelle's mobile phone sounded. Everyone drew breath expectantly.

'It's Guillaume,' she announced, then went on to relate to the guests that her husband was at sea ploughing the waves.

Sighs of relief.

'Soon here?' begged Gillian.

'Making their approach.'

Gillian, barefoot, dressed in long floaty trousers, a waistcoat and a brightly coloured feather boa was ebullient, punching her arms in the air. Celia was also quietly elated, though she wasn't sure why, except it was a relief that Dominic was playing along with whatever this get-together was about. He could very well have shown his stubborn side and refused.

Sean was now serving wine and offering bowls of crisps to the gathered assembly while Pascal kept a tight grip on the over-excited dog. Dominic had given Sean permission to bring up a dozen bottles from the cellar. Claude had chipped in and purchased another six. Pascal, with funds he'd earned as estate hireling during the past week, had contributed a crate of beer, buried now in the sand, being washed over by the waves to keep the bottles semi-chilled.

There were cushions and a few stools dotted here and there. 'No one needs to be uncomfortable, scratching their bums on rocks,' called Gillian, who seemed suddenly a little unsure of herself. Celia was encouraged to make herself 'snug'. Sean poured her a hefty serving of her own white wine. 'On an empty stomach and all this sea air, I'll be drunk before the evening starts to swing. Oh, well. What if I am?'

'Cheers, Ceely, I'm having an insane summer.' Sean smiled. 'Thanks for everything. We're all having a ball.'

She nodded her appreciation, taken aback. She adored this young Irishman and would be sorry to see him leave. Sorry to see so many leave. They had brought a bright new energy to the estate.

Gillian, who was now pacing up and down at the water's edge, holding her boa high like a sail, was keeping an eye open for the fishing boat. Its passenger was the guest of honour, although Dominic was not party to this fact. Nonetheless, for Gillian's purposes, he was the important focus of this evening.

When there was still no sign of the boat and its precious cargo, she jogged back up the beach. 'How much longer? she pressed. Estelle assured her that all was on schedule.

Celia glanced about her. Everyone was present and correct, except David. 'Where's David?'

'He's with Adèle.'

'Adèle?'

'They've walked to the next bay.'

'Is he safe?'

'Safe? Why wouldn't he be? He's found himself the perfect company. He's in his element. He loves being by the sea and he's over-the-moon happy. I see them! Look, over there!'

'David?'

'No, Guillaume. He's making for shore!' Gillian took off back to the water's edge, waving her arms. 'Look, they're approaching from the headland over there.'

And then, as if a mirage were emerging from the horizon, from between sea and sky, the motorboat rose into view, putt-putting its course in the soft dusk light, rounding the rocks from the neighbouring bay.

'There it is.'

'I see it!'

'Bravo, Guillaume.'

Several started clapping and whistling. As the assembled company gazed on with bated breath, the descending rays of the evening sun gilded the surface of the water. Its calm was broken only by the white spray rising from the vessel.

The guests turned their attention to the makeshift landing jetty. It might have been the docking of the *Queen Mary* in New York harbour on its maiden voyage, such a surge of elation accompanied the advent of Dominic.

What on earth is this all about? Celia was chuckling to herself. Her attention was drawn by Tom who was extracting himself from the crowd, making his way towards a boulder at the outer edge of the small horseshoe bay.

The boat had reached the landing stage. Engine switched off, it was rocking dramatically as Guillaume moored it to the semi-submerged logs. Waves slapped at the hull. Wide-eyed, Dominic was immobile, glued to the spot.

Celia crunched her way to the water's edge, ready to assist.

Sally clutched her father's arm and tucked it safely about her waist while Guillaume stood poised behind his passenger's shoulder. Dominic took a tentative step, yelled, cursed, almost lost balance. The guests gasped. Celia slipped off her sandals and stepped into the waves. Dominic, with Sally's help, righted himself, shuffled on to the wooden quay and then gave a clumsy hop, dragging his leg like a damaged wing, on to the shingled beach.

How vulnerable he is, thought Celia. No longer the titan he once was.

'Hooray!' Gillian, arms above her head, jumped for joy. 'Welcome, *bonsoir*, Dominic. *Bienvenu*.'

Everyone clapped and cheered. Dominic looked bemused, but was clearly mightily relieved to be back on firm ground.

Within no time the small crowd was up by the fire throwing themselves onto cushions, stools, whatever was to hand. Dominic was taken aback by the setting, the *mise en scène*, and Sally was over the moon. 'I haven't swum in this bay,' she was telling anyone who was listening, 'since my early twenties. Dad used to bring me here when we were over from the UK visiting Ceely's parents.'

Dominic shook his head. 'I'd forgotten all about this place. Such a secluded setting, enchanting. When your father took us sailing, we sometimes docked here for lunch and some sunbathing. Remember, Ceely?'

She nodded. 'Of course.'

Dusk had fallen. The fire crackled. Far over to the west of the bay, a quartet of tall, upright lanterns was suddenly illuminated. Tom with his guitar was standing directly in the centre of the pool of light. A few wooden pallets had been joined – nailed? – together to create a flat surface, a dais, a makeshift stage. Was there electricity? If so, where was it being fed from? No one knew, except, no doubt, Gillian, who had stage-managed every step of this. Sally could certainly do worse than offer her a job.

In the distance, the Alps were turning a bruised mauve as the sun deserted them. The scene was bewitching with the pulls and stresses of the waves washing against the shore, a persistent percussion. All eyes were focused on Tom. He struck a note and then, fingers strumming his guitar, he was ready to perform. The chords floated skywards.

David, oblivious to all that was getting under way, was arriving from the neighbouring bay. He and Adèle were clambering over rocks, whenever possible hand in hand. They took in the scene, the expectant faces, the first notes of music, and hurried, scrambling, to find a place, to meld discreetly with the group. Friends, family, stretched out arms to welcome and include David and his companion. Was it Adèle who had been visiting him at the hospital? Celia asked herself and decided that, yes, she was the mystery woman.

David crouched low, shuffling close to Celia. Like every other person present, he was instantly intrigued. Tom's music, his tenor voice, his vocals, each note of his composition was spellbinding. Even the glinting stars were setting the scene, playing their part.

Gillian was frowning at Dominic, dismayed. He was whispering in Sally's ear, while massaging his leg, paying the music no heed, but after Sally had dug him in the ribs with her elbow, signalling him to shut up, he frowned and fell silent.

Applause. Cheers. Refills of wine. Meat was being tossed onto hissing grills, heated by the flames. Sean was the chef, Henri lending him a hand with a word of advice here and there. Gillian was burrowing close up to Dominic. Celia rose to help with the distribution of the cardboard plates and plastic cutlery – choices she would never have made, but what did it matter? The elegance was embedded in the evening, the gathering, a diverse turnout and the marriage of creative energies. All staged within this beguiling Provençal seascape.

Tom, it transpired, had penned the previous composition the day after Celia had brought him to this spot. It was, not unsurprisingly, titled 'Paradise Cove', he announced.

More cheers broke out.

Gillian was eager to inform Dominic of the various details of composition and then to hear his thoughts, to pin him to a decision. Except she never stopped talking. Since Gillian's arrival at his and Celia's home, Dominic had exchanged barely a handful of words with her and now she was seated cross-legged at his feet, focusing all her attention on him. What was she after?

Dominic's eyes were dancing uncertainly in search of Celia. Where was she? There she was, seated by the fire, looking radiant, engrossed in animated conversation with the fellow who claimed to be her son. Not for one second did Dominic believe Celia and David were related. Blatantly not from the same pod.

Hush was being called for again. The next act on the programme was about to commence. Tom was joined by Henri. Both were perched on tall stools on the makeshift podium, playing from an Édith Piaf songbook. The French were enraptured. Béatrice's mother, Joséphine, who fancied she could hold a tune, and after three glasses of wine was more than ready to prove it – little did anyone know that, as an adolescent, she had earned a crust performing in a nightclub in Nice – was humming along, while beating time on the pebbled ground with her floppy espadrilles. Her voice was raw and gutsy, tobacco-fuelled. It drew a cheer, a further round of applause. Tom and Henri beckoned Josie to the stage. She needed no encouragement, grabbed the mike and let rip, enthralling all spectators with her rousing rendition of 'Non, Je Ne Regrette Rien'.

After Piaf came other classics. Jacques Brel was followed as a finale by Charles Trenet's evergreen, 'La Mer'. Henri encouraged everyone to sing along; they belted out the refrain, the sound rising high above the cliffs. It was supersonic, almost overwhelming.

And then a supper break. Throats were dry after all their choral efforts. The sky was darkening, stars shone like silver cut-outs in the navy heavens, while the flames leaped red and golden. The sausages were demolished in ravenous bites and not by the dog. Gillian ate an apple and guzzled several glasses of wine between cigarettes. She barely left the arm of Dominic who remained confused, but just a little tickled by the young woman's constant attention.

After the meal, the second half of the programme was dedicated to Tom's compositions; one or two pieces Celia had already heard, but far from all. For an hour Tom held the audience in the palm of his hand. The music was original and yet familiar, intimate.

Dominic leaned towards his wife and shouted to be heard, 'He's not bad, is he?'

Celia nodded, smiled, as she swayed gently to and fro, lulled by the chords of Tom's guitar. She understood now what Gillian, the sorceress, was up to. This evening had been set up as an elaborate audition. Gillian had put it all together, choosing the ideal setting, the perfect opportunity, for Dominic to be presented with the composer the studio had been desperately seeking.

Madonna, smiled Celia, ruefully, wouldn't get a look in. Gillian had cunningly understood that Dominic must make this discovery himself. It needed to be his idea, his proposal, not a choice that was thrust upon him.

After the last note had melted away across the moonlit water, after the applause had died down, silence fell. A silence filled to the brim with wonder and satisfaction. As wondrous as listening to the beating heart of a new born baby.

With the approach of late night began the first steps towards packing up and hitting the road for home. Here and there folk were humming, smiling to themselves, replaying the notes, recalling the sensations the music had awakened within them. Sean, David, Adèle and several of the others were gathering the rubbish into bin bags, plates, knives and forks, leftovers not wolfed by the dog, to leave the beach as pristine as they had found it.

Dominic did not move from his picnic chair. His boat was waiting, rocking in the shallows that slapped against the makeshift jetty. He seemed unaware of it, of his daughter standing alongside Guillaume, in attendance. He glanced up, caught Celia's eye and beckoned her over. 'What do you think?'

'About what?' She was teasing him, amused.

He turned to his daughter, tugging at her trouser leg. 'Sit down. Listen to me, Sal.' Sally squatted at his side. Celia bent low. Their three heads together.

'We must ask him, don't you agree?'

'Tom?' enquired Sally.

Dominic nodded.

'Of course you must. It's a given. They'll love every note. Even the Italians can't top that.'

'He's damn good. "Like the sweet sound that breathes upon a bank of violets", eh? Who would have thought it? A composer in our midst while we've been tearing our hair out searching. Why didn't one of you alert me?'

And so it was that Tom was proposed to the producers. Of course, first there would be meetings among the higher echelons of the filmmaking team, the Studios, the voice of Hollywood, the leading lady would confer. Tom would be required to audition. His music had to be recorded under the best possible conditions and sent via internet links to the various parties. This would not happen overnight. But Dominic was confident. Gillian, it was agreed, was a little minx, but one to be congratulated. She could not have created a better setting for the springboard in her new friend's fortunes.

CHAPTER FORTY-ONE

A few mornings later, over breakfast, Celia learned that Frank would not be flying over because Sally was returning to London that afternoon. 'But why so soon?'

'Much work ahead. The network needs me at base to begin the planning, produce designs, create the sets, to find the look of the show, lock it in and get it on the road. I definitely want to offer Gill a role in all of this,' she was confiding to Celia, over hefty cups of early-morning coffee in the conservatory. 'I'll talk it through with Dad first obviously. She's certainly capable. She'll be a huge asset and she's a hoot to spend time with. It'll be an excellent opportunity for her, do you agree?'

Celia concurred wholeheartedly. 'Yes, I do, and I envy you the bond you've built with her, Sal. I haven't found it so easy.'

'Well, there's more at stake, isn't there? David's been her go-to, her dependable pal through all the shitty times. She's had it pretty rough. Sharing him is hard for her, and sharing him with someone she feared wasn't deserving of his love . . .

He's pretty fabulous, though, isn't he? I wouldn't mind a son like him.'

'You knew?'

'It shines out of him. His love for you. But you might have to fight Adèle for him.'

'Serious, you think?'

'Could be.'

Celia knew sadly that this would mean the departure of Gillian. Selfishly, silently, she resisted the prospect of the loss. If Gillian left, David would probably accompany her. Or would he? In her head, in a rather formless fashion, Celia had been intending to find him a role within the upcoming harvest, which was due to begin any day now. She was convinced he would be an asset to the teams. And he did seem rather taken with Adèle . . .

Claude was out in the vineyards with the estate's portable refractometer, checking acid levels and measuring sugar content in the grapes. Once they had reached the definitive sugar high, it was the moment to pick. Once that moment had been declared, it could not be delayed.

Usually all these decisions were Dominic's, essential steps that required precision and expertise. Dominic and Claude always made the rounds of the fields together, discussing, selecting which field, grape variety, to harvest when and in which order. There was a rhythm to it, a kind of poetry they both excelled at. This meant that without Dominic, today and in the upcoming weeks, the responsibility rested with Claude. And, ultimately, despite her lack of competence, with Celia. The storms had already cut deep into their potential profit. Any further losses could send their wine business spiralling into insolvency. It weighed heavily upon her already troubled shoulders.

Meanwhile, back at the pressing base, Tom was preparing the materials for the pickers to begin work, while Sean was sluicing the floors in the stainless-steel tank sheds at the winery. Henri was lending a hand too. David had taken over his tasks in the vegetable gardens. It seemed he was passionate about bees, had grown up with hives, which was yet another bonus.

Celia, nerves kicking, was praying that she was up to the task of leading such a crucial phase in the estate's winemaking. Their vintage this year depended on all these pivotal stages. Claude was, as always, a tower of strength. Between them, he assured her, they would bring in the harvest successfully.

The pickers awaited the call to arrive, to get their fingers on the fruits.

Magali was pre-cooking meals, dozens for the daily lunches. The count at the tables would be around fourteen for each sitting. Fourteen mouths to feed, mid-morning breakfasts and lunch, for approximately ten days.

Dominic and Sally were locked away in the winter drawing room, finalising script details before she sped off to the airport. These days Dominic could just about drag himself up and down the stairs, but why bother to disrupt everything at this point? His paperwork and the strongest WiFi signal were right where he was working. He could operate perfectly efficiently for the time being downstairs, as long, he insisted, as he was left alone.

Celia had found no opportunity for a quiet moment with her husband. It was later, on his way hobbling back from the bathroom, she fortuitously crossed his path. 'Dom . . .'

Speaking over her, he announced that he wanted Tom to travel to London with Sally.

'What? Today?' She swung on her heels, and strode after him into the drawing room, closing the door firmly behind her. She refused to be ejected. 'No, Dom! I need him for the harvest! It was one of the reasons we booked these chaps.'

'Yes, but circumstances have changed, Ceely. Dramatically, and all for the better. You need to let him go. In any case there will be less fruit to pick due to the devastations. What about that son of yours?'

That son of yours. Celia was upset. Upset on many levels. Her insides were churning.

She knew she couldn't hold Tom back and she didn't want to, but she had been, foolishly perhaps, counting on his extra pair of hands for a little longer. There was the harvest, all the chopped wood to shift and a million other chores to address. And, yes, she would remind *that son of hers* to request his employers to give him leave for a few more weeks.

'Where's Sal?'

'Packing.'

'Will you be joining her in London?' The prospect of Dominic alone in London filled Celia with dread.

No, he was intending to polish his final-draft scripts till they were flawless and then would fly to Rome, a mere hop from Nice.

'You're not worrying, are you?' Dominic took Celia by the arm and held tight on to her.

'About the harvest? Yes, I am.'

'I'm not talking about the blasted grapes.'

His vehemence took her aback. 'What, then?'

'She won't be there. You know that, don't you? Not until principal photography begins and that's two weeks away. I'll be home.' Celia tried to liberate herself from his clasp, stepping backwards. She hadn't been expecting *this* conversation. Not now, not at this moment. She was tense. Dominic held her fast, clutching her, his fingernails digging into her shoulder blades.

'And even if she were . . .' His eyes, dark and feverish, were boring into hers.

Sally was shouting from the stairs: 'Dad! Shall I call Gill now?'

Celia pulled herself free and stepped out of his range.

He shook his head impatiently. 'Give me five minutes, Sal . . . Ceely, I've never said this, we've never had this . . . a heart-to-heart.'

'Then, please, let's not do it now, Dom. Not all rushed with no time to think. There's so much to say and Sal's leaving and . . . Honestly, I don't think I can handle anything else. Let's have a glass of wine later, just the two of us . . .'

'It needs to be said,' he insisted.

She ignored him. 'Yes, it does but when our hearts are quiet, when . . . there's so much . . .' She bent to his wastepaper basket. It was spilling over with typed sheets of paper. She needed to be busy.

'I . . . I fucked up.'

'Please don't swear. It's so unlike you.'

'Don't nag me, and stop changing the subject. Let me speak.' He stamped his foot like a child and then doubled over in pain.

If the subject matter weren't so delicate, his behaviour would have been comical. It broke the tension a little bit. Celia giggled. 'Sit down, Dom.'

He used her kinder tone to draw her back towards him, flopping into a chair and dragging her into his lap. She was perched awkwardly on his good leg.

'Listen to me, Ceely. I've never managed to say this before, but I want you to hear me now . . .'

Sally pushed open the door, clocked her father with Celia on his knee. 'Look at you two, lovebirds. Production office is looking into a flight reservation for Tom. We need his passport details. And I need to find Gill. Catch you both in ten.'

The door closed.

Neither had moved.

'You are the woman I'm committed to, my wife and sweetheart. I made a mistake. Just the one. There have been no others.'

Celia twisted her face away from him, from the heat of his breath, his intensity. She didn't know if this was worse, to learn that Isabelle had a unique role in their marriage as Dominic's one and only mistress.

'When I look back, replay it in my mind's eye, I cannot imagine what drove me to risk all that we—'

The door opened. 'Sorry, guys, I meant to say that the production office want Tom to fly to Rome, not London.'

'Rome?'

'Test recordings.'

Celia lifted herself out of Dominic's arms and back on to her feet, relieved for the emotional space, fearing she might break down. Crumble. She was tamping down an emotional knock-back that had been bottled up inside her, eating at her, for more than a decade. 'I need to get on,' she mumbled.

She bent to the wastepaper basket and scooped it into her grasp. Dominic's hand rested on her back. She felt the tingle of his touch on her spine.

Outside in the courtyard, Celia was pacing back and forth when Gillian appeared, hurrying from the barn. She was splotched in a rainbow of colours, as was her style. As far as Celia was aware, Sally had not yet raised the subject of Gillian's departure, the offer of the job. Gillian was blithely oblivious to the imminent change in her fortunes. Her mind was occupied with her boat.

'Hi, Ceely, I've been thinking.'

'About your boat?'

The relationship between the two women was softening. Over these past few days, Gillian had been more inclusive with her, which brought joy to Celia's heart. David's presence close by and not in the hospital, plus the evident success of her beach party, had made Gillian less spiky. She was calmer, friendlier, more open to exchange.

'You need a horse, Ceely.'

'A wooden one, like your boat!'

'No, Ceely, a workhorse, perhaps two if you've got sufficient dosh to buy them. The animals could transport all that wood down the hillside from the forest to the stables where the logs will need to be cut and stacked. Animal traction is the way to go, Ceely. Mechanised farming? It's not what the world should be looking at right now. You know, climate change, petrol crises, a war with Russia, the Middle East. I had a really valuable chat with Claude about it yesterday and he agrees. He'll mention it to you, I'm sure.'

Celia stared at Gillian open-mouthed. The fathoming of her brain constantly astounded her. 'A horse?'

'A couple of drays, yeah. It would be financially much lighter on the estate's budget, and certainly kinder to the environment than trundling the tractor with a trailer up and down that hillside. Sean and I drove the tractor up to the forest several times to collect wood to build the jetty. It was insane. The tracks are poor, and it's so steep, the engine kept making a funny sound like it was grinding its teeth. Too many more trips like that will eventually ruin the mechanics. In any case you're going to need it to deliver the baskets of grapes to the crushing yards.'

'You've talked this through with Claude?' Celia wasn't sure if she should be impressed or cross. Should she tell the girl to

451

mind her own business, to stop meddling in affairs she knew nothing about? 'Which of us would have time to manage a horse? Animals require special skills, Gill, attention, care, and who could harness a dray? Henri might have done in his earlier years, but . . . It's a lovely romantic idea, but . . .'

'Don't be patronising. It's not a romantic idea. It's practical and it'd be a great opportunity for Dave. Give him a role here. He'd be in charge of the livestock. He grew up with horses on the farm where his parents were tenants. It will be the very best thing for him. He could stay here, live with you and Dom. Be your stable master. Then I can come back for holidays and spend time with you all. You know how we talked about families and Christmas? Well, not just Christmas. What do you say?'

Celia didn't know what to say. She was staggered, confounded. But a functional role for David was very tempting . . .

'Loads of farms are returning to animals for ploughing, sowing crops and heaps of other land chores. Think about it. I haven't mentioned it to Dave yet, didn't want to raise his hopes. I only said something to Claude, but I thought I should speak to you before taking it further.'

'So, is this about David's future?'

'Yes, but also what's best for the farm. It's the right decision. Dave should stay, work with you and Dom, build his family.'

At that moment Sally came haring out of the house. She was waving, calling, clearly in a tizzy with so much to organize before she left after lunch. 'Gill,' she yelled, 'can I have a quick word?'

Celia let out a sigh of relief. She was trying to keep up with the constant changes.

Gillian sprinted off. 'Think about it, Ceely,' she shouted, as she bounded into the house. 'Dave'll be over the moon.'

Celia watched Gillian's slender frame disappear through the door. She knew that within half an hour, if Gillian accepted Sally's offer – and why wouldn't she? – this odd, semi-stepgranddaughter of hers would be looking at a new future, throwing all her bits and pieces into her bags, vacating Sean's bedroom in the lodge, clearing out the chaotically untidy box room in the main house, her head in a spin at the prospect of all that lay ahead for her.

A job in the film industry.

Tom, Gillian and Sally, all of them off within the next few days, hours even. They would leave a mighty hole.

And what of her future with David? She hadn't touched upon the subject with Dominic. Barely with herself. There had been too much going on. It was as if a storm had blown through their lives and turned their worlds upside down. All of them. Of course, there had been the recent *actual* storm, but this one was different.

Invisible sparks.

People energy.

The unexpected arrival of a family. A wacky, unpredictable family at that.

Sally flew out that afternoon, disappearing down the driveway like a rolling cloud in her little blue Fiat. Gillian was not at her side. Over the moon at Sally's proposal, she had begged a day or two longer. Matters to wrap up before she returned to London. She needed to sort out her clutter. And time with David. It was difficult to leave, she admitted. And then there was her artwork, her boat, which Celia promised not to dismantle, but to leave where it was, undisturbed until Gillian's return. At Christmas. 'Promise.'

That night Dominic climbed the stairs to their bedroom for the first time since before his accident. Celia was already tucked up, lying on her side, reading. Dominic had worked late, beavering away. It was after one. She heard the creak of his footsteps. No one else was in the house. The room was mostly in darkness with just a halo of light shining from her bedside lamp. He shuffled in like a shadow, yawning, pulled off his clothes and dropped them untidily onto a chair. 'The pain in this bloody leg,' he muttered. She didn't respond, still clutched the book, felt his weight burrowing in beneath the duvet, wriggling up close to her. He slid an arm around her. His flesh was not warm like hers, less relaxed, still full of the day. She listened to his breath in her ear as they lay in silence, like a pair of dusty old spoons.

'Everyone's leaving,' she murmured. 'It's going to be lonely.'

'You've got me. I'm here.'

'You'll be off soon too.'

'Come with me, then.'

'And what about here? Claude is up to his eyes in it.'

'Can you forgive me, Ceely?'

She was stunned, and slowly, deliberately, placed the book on the console and switched out the light. He had never asked for her forgiveness before, had never until today admitted to the transgression.

'Can you accept me for who I am? Riddled with bad habits and faults.'

'I wish you didn't have to go.'

'I'll be back before you know it. But while I'm away I want you to be secure in the knowledge that you're the most precious gift life has given me. I love you, old girl.'

'Old?' she joked, tears welling.

'Old married people.'

She lay in the dark, remembering, trying not to, squeezing her eyes tight shut to ward off the memories that haunted her. Dominic's breathing was growing heavier, a prelude to his falling asleep. To snoring, oblivion. She envied him his ability to drift off so immediately while she lay awake, worrying, for hours on end. Had she forgiven him? Had she forgotten the humiliation? The bewilderment and loss? Not entirely, no.

'Did you love her, Dom?'

'What?'

'Did you love her?'

Silence. Outside, beyond the partially open window, an explosion of voices was followed by someone diving into the pool. A sequence of splashes. Dive-bombings. Squeals. Swimming by starlight. Giggling. Muffled cries. Her cottage folk. Or possibly David. With Adèle?

'I need to know what you felt, what she meant to you.'

'Yes.'

'Yes, you loved her?'

'For a moment back then, that autumn, yes, I thought I loved her. Maybe I did. It was a passion, Ceely. Burned itself out.'

She lay shivering, allowing this to sink in. The youngsters were still plunging in and out of the water. She toyed with the idea of getting out of bed, of heading down the stairs, of finding a spot where she could watch them, inhale their carefree laughter.

'Please don't feed on what I've said, especially while I'm away. Don't hold it tight and let it eat at you, Ceely. It was a long time ago. A difficult time for both of us. We were different people. And, as I said, I fucked up.'

'Did you consider leaving . . . leaving me, beginning again with her?'

'Please don't do this. Don't take us through the hoop.'

'Why didn't you?'

'Because I love you.'

Celia was thinking about it. Had he loved her while he thought he was in love with Isabelle? Had he and Isabelle discussed her, dug through their marriage, raking at its faults? What had Isabelle hoped to get out of the affair?

'There are so many questions.'

He lifted himself up and rested his body sideways, leaning on one arm. His eyes shone in the darkness but it was hard to discern his expression. 'Ask them, then. Let's get this behind us once and for all.'

She closed her eyes. 'Sometimes it frightens me how much I love you. The fear of losing you. Being without you.'

'Listen to me, Ceely. We're here. Still here. Together. Today. Thanks to you. Come closer.'

She opened her eyes, smiled up at him.

He took her tightly in his arms, negotiating her awkwardly towards his strength, then gently kissed her on the mouth.

CHAPTER FORTY-TWO

They were standing face to face in golden September sunshine alongside the open boot of the car. Celia had pulled in at one of the Kiss and Fly bays at Nice airport. It allowed them five free minutes of parking, sufficient time to unload and say their farewells. Gillian's hefty pieces of luggage were scattered about their feet.

Both hovered awkwardly.

'Thanks for the lift.' Gillian lifted her arms from her sides and let them flop again. 'It's weird,' she said. 'I was so determined to dislike you. And now, well, "you're the toppity tops, Ceely . . ."' She was singing, jiggling her feet. Passersby stared at her.

'Stop!' Celia laughed.

Gillian smiled. 'No, but really, the last thing I expected was to have such a blast here. It's been super cool – I mean, it's amazing for Dave that he's found you at last. I haven't seen him this happy ever.'

They fell silent, considering David and his well-being.

'Thank *you*,' Celia began, 'for accompanying David and, well, these last few weeks have been quite an experience. Special.'

Gillian nodded, kicking one of her bags. 'We're making speeches.'

They nodded.

'No more words. Come here.' Celia spread wide her arms and Gillian stepped into the embrace. They hugged tight, wrapping themselves around one another, rocking from side to side, with the strength of the love that had grown up between them in spite of all the apprehensions and misunderstandings.

Gillian suddenly pulled back. 'Ceely, I'm still worrying about my boat.'

'What about it?'

'You won't destroy it during my absence, will you?'

'Gill, I promised.'

'I know. It's just that I want to dismantle it myself.'

'Dismantle it, but . . .?'

'I want to reconstruct it somewhere where we can give it a real purpose. It's too tight against that wall in the barn. No fluidity. It needs a more flexible space. Like I said, that lawn would be ideal. You know, it's a bit like an amphitheatre down there with all those cypresses encircling the space.'

Check-in time was drawing closer. Cars were hooting, demanding the bay.

'I want to find a productive use for it. Theatre, children's interactive plays. Saturday-morning shows for kids from the village. Or I've got another idea I'm mulling over. I'll text you.'

Celia was incredulous. 'Gill, we'll do what we agreed. Leave your boat where it is. It won't get damaged, I promise. We can reconsider its future whenever you—'

'When I'm back for Christmas, yeah? Family and all that.'

Celia nodded. 'Family and all that.'

'Brilliant. At Christmas, I'll take the boat apart and rebuild it somewhere more suitable. If you don't want me to use the lawn, let's think of another spot.'

Celia smiled and rubbed a finger across her cheek. She was going to miss this crazy young woman. 'You're running late.'

'Gotta go, gotta go, Ceely. See you soon. A few months. Have a bumper harvest, make gallons of wine and look after Dave for me. '

'And you, make Sally proud.'

'You bet. Hollywood, here I come! Thanks for everything. Phew. What a trip, what a summer. And it's just the beginning, right?'

'Just the beginning. Now go before you miss your plane and I . . .'

Shed a tear.

They embraced once more, vigorously but hastily. Then Gillian heaved every piece of luggage about her person and staggered over the zebra crossing, waving her one unburdened arm skywards without looking back before she dived into the terminal.

CHAPTER FORTY-THREE

The mood and levels of activity were bordering on frenetic. Claude had called to say that it was Time to Get Picking. For peace of mind he was insisting that Dominic take a brief trip out to the property's principal Mourvèdre and Grenache vineyards. He wanted corroboration, the boss's say-so. It was not because Claude doubted his own science but because everything was at stake. He didn't want an error of judgement weighing on his shoulders.

When they returned from the fields, Dominic confirmed that the sugar levels were at fifteen per cent, some a little higher. Acid levels were where they needed to be, and going down.

'It's time to pick, Ceely. Call in the team.'

Time to pick!

After Claude's decision had been blessed, Dominic returned to his writing. 'No more interruptions,' he ordered. 'None.' And he closed tight the door, sealing out his wife and the farm's pursuits.

'It won't be the same without you,' sighed Celia, silently. Without Dominic's fiery energy at the helm, everything felt a little less stable. Claude led the teams admirably, but Dominic was the boss and everybody respected that. Without him, Celia felt less assured. She wanted no more mishaps, no bad surprises.

It was time for Tom to say his farewells, jetting off to Rome to record his music in one of the sound studios at Cinecittà. 'My first trip to the Eternal City,' he confided in Celia, when she drove him to the airport. He confessed that he was petrified.

'It's been a blast.' He grinned as he leaped from the vehicle and kissed her cheek. 'See you somewhere soon, Ceely. It's all thanks to you. You are my muse. I knew you would be.' He winked, as he hurried away with his guitar on his back. Celia stood watching him go, hurrying off to his new life.

David put himself to work without instructions from anyone. He slipped into the flow of things without fuss. At first, he worked alongside Henri. They were comfortable in one another's company, speaking little, not only because they had no shared language but because neither was a man of many words. They dug, pruned, fruit-picked in the walled garden, at peace with Nature and the earth. David was eager to be involved in the beekeeping, but there was need of him elsewhere once the harvest really got under way. He stepped in to replace Tom. And his mechanical skills proved to be priceless.

And a lifesaver when, towards the end of the first week of gathering, the mechanics on the tractor failed. One of the daily helpers was at the wheel when he lost control and panicked. Without warning the tractor, rigged up to a fully freighted trailer, still being loaded with the very last baskets of grapes to be transported to the winery, began to roll backwards. A few centimetres at first, but almost before any of the team grasped the danger, it was gaining speed. Hundreds of kilos of grapes already packed into the trailer started to spill over its sides, tossed to the earth. Clusters were being squashed beneath the spinning tyres. Pickers were shouting, screaming. As they jumped clear of the moving vehicle, they were aghast at the sight of their entire morning's work squelched under the wheels. The tractor was sliding faster and faster, down the incline.

David, spotting the potential accident before it happened, sprinted with the power of the wind. 'Handbrake!' he shouted to the terrified driver.

'Nothing's happening,' the young man yelled.

Henri, who had not heard the shouts or calls, was puffing up the incline, directly in line with and oblivious to the out-of-control machinery. David flung himself high and leaped into the cab, grabbing the wheel from the lad aboard. He slewed the tractor hard to the right and the vehicle skidded miraculously to a shuddering halt, causing the trailer to topple onto its side, disgorging the remainder of the collected fruits.

After a stunned silence while the reality of what might have happened to Henri, who was still approaching, sank in, everyone broke into applause and cheers, then cursed the loss of a morning's work.

Celia, meanwhile, was at the winery, awaiting the arrival of the grapes. Puzzled by the delay, she rang Claude who imparted the news. They had lost a couple of hundred kilos of fruit and the tractor was kaput.

'But we didn't lose Henri. Oh, Claude, it's not our year, is it?'

Remarkably, Henri and the other team members were unharmed. Celia telephoned Sébastien, their friendly olive-farming neighbour, and begged assistance. Séb towed the tractor back to their pressing yard, shaking his head. 'I fear this old girl's done for,' was his gloomy prognosis.

'There's fluid leaking from the master cylinder.' That was David's more upbeat diagnosis. 'I can fix that.'

He emptied the brake fluid, removed the cylinder, sealed the leakage and put the whole mechanical jigsaw back together. The precious machine was at work the following afternoon.

No more had been said on the subject of horse power. Celia had put the suggestion on the back-burner. Days later, when she and Claude were crossing to one of the vineyards to join the team for lunch after their penultimate morning in the fields, Celia brought up the subject. In spite of the recent near-miss accident, she was sure that Claude would propose good reasons why it was not a suitable alternative for their estate. Too steep, too rocky. Everything worked fine the way they ran the place now . . . But he didn't. And his response took her by surprise.

'You have stables aplenty, Celia. Most of them are doing nothing besides storing boxes. We'd need to clean up one or two, and refurbish them. David might be the man for the job.' Claude knew of several vineyards in the Var where they were transferring their activities to at least partially animal-powered enterprises. Friends of his owned a vineyard this side of the Camargue where they farmed with two horses. They had made the switch successfully. Few hiccups, producing terrific organic wine.

'Are these animals from one of the famous Camarguais ranches?'

'Not at all.' The farm Claude had been citing was a family business 'about the same size as ours, father, two brothers, one daughter and her husband, running their holding according to organic and biodynamic practices. No more synthetic chemicals.' Their stock were a breed originally from the north, Percheron.

'How many of our fields are organic? We only use a few chemicals, don't we? And none of us are experts in that sort of wine producing.'

'Sure, but what's fascinating and innovative is that these modern farms are using draught horses for some of the key jobs, ploughing, turning the soil between the vine rows, for example. We've never tried that. And they bring in sheep to keep the cover crops trimmed back. They use organic compost. Like us they're sited alongside the Med so maritime breezes help to give that unique component to the wines.'

'And could all this work for us?'

'It's a big switch. We can't do it overnight, but we have similar soil properties except that we're volcanic. Otherwise, sand, silt, gravel, pebbles. Clay and limestone. Pretty much the same blessings and the same curses as we juggle with.'

'And we could use horsepower to shift all that sawn wood?'

'That's a one-off, Celia. Once the fallen trees have been removed . . .'

'According to Henri, there are plenty of others in the forest that will need clearing.'

'Sure, but what we should be looking at is putting horses to work in the vineyards. It's a smart plan, commercially speaking. Quite apart from the ethics of the thing, organic is the way forward. Who knows? It could become a production obligation. We should be way ahead of any such legislation. Let's make ourselves trailblazers in the market. The prize-winning wines won't be coming from the pesticide-driven farms, I'll bet on that.'

Celia promised to talk it through with Dominic.

Dominic's response was, 'Let's wait until the last of the grapes are in, the fruits crushed and fermenting. There'll be ample time when I return from Rome.'

A few days after the harvest had been completed and the temporary team had been disbanded, Sean returned to Dublin to begin his last year at University College. Again Celia happily took on the role of chauffeur.

'When my thesis is delivered,' he said, 'I'm going to put myself forward for research work in the Mediterranean.'

She hugged him and made him promise to stay in touch, to come back and visit before too long. 'You're family now.' She grinned.

CHAPTER FORTY-FOUR

There had been a succession of farewells. Each had left Celia's heart a little lonelier, bluer. Now, the toughest of all on that autumnal morning was to be waved on his way.

'Ready?' Celia was jingling the car key in her hand, standing at the open door of the winter drawing room. A glance at her mother's clock on the mantel reassured her that they had plenty of time. Dominic was dawdling, still hobbling, walking with visible discomfort. 'I really think one of the walking sticks . . .'

'I've told you more than once, I'm not travelling with a stick! Don't hang about at the damn door. Come in, Ceely, and close it. You make me uncertain. I'm ready. Ready. I just need to slip the last of these papers into my briefcase and then I'm set.'

'Let me.' Celia strode across the room. She was feeling raw about Dominic's departure. The best way to counter it was to affect an air of efficiency. Dominic hovered in the centre of the room, indecisively, which usually meant that he was in turmoil. He was chewing a mint, biting it noisily.

They bumped into one another in their attempts at trying to shovel another batch of papers into a case that was already bulging. 'You need a bigger briefcase, Dom. This is impossible. Shall I run upstairs and grab one of my hand-luggage bags? We've time.'

With a gesture of impatience Dominic tossed the script onto the seat of the winged chair. A few of the pages slid to the floor.

'What did you do that for? We'll manage. We just need patience,' she chided.

'I sweated for those scenes,' he said, shaking his head at his own childishness. 'It'd be reckless to throw them away. Plenty of producers ready to do that.'

Celia was on her haunches gathering the sheets of paper back into some order.

'I hope this goddam show is going to come together.'

'Of course it will. The text is reading well.'

'You think so? She's a hard taskmaster that Isabelle Carter. Demanding.'

Celia rose, script in hand. 'Dom . . .'

'Perhaps I will need an extra bag. I can check everything through except my work.'

'You've got this, as Gillian would say. It's going to be a huge success.'

'I love you, old girl.'

'I love you too. Please, whatever happens . . . don't forget it'.

CHAPTER FORTY-FIVE

Autumn

The lodge stood empty, forlorn at its cliff's edge. The wind visited, whistling round its walls; the songs and whispers of Nature kept the old place company, but no one turned the handle on its unlocked door.

It was such a pity. A waste.

Dust was accruing; spiders were weaving the first of autumn's cobwebs. The seasons were shifting. The harvests at Les Roches du Soleil were in, the grape pressing completed, yeasted for this year. Claude and David were about to attack the mangled fence beneath the forest.

'This one last job, Celia,' David had announced, 'and then I must return to England.'

'You're leaving us? Oh, David, I was beginning to hope . . .'

Celia, alone, stepped inside the lodge. Its interior was forlorn; it smelled musty. She crossed to the kitchen and pulled open the windows above the sink. Leaning, listening to the sea, she thought of Gillian back in the United Kingdom, of Tom in

Rome and Sean in Dublin. Dominic was also still in Rome.

She glanced about, calibrating, considering the changes that might need to be made if she were to . . . It was then she noticed, pinned to the inside of the front door, a torn-off flap of a cardboard box painted in gold and orange. *PARADISE COTTAGE*, announced the lettering, in deep blue.

Gillian's work, without doubt. Left behind, forgotten, when the summer residents had packed up and flown away towards the next chapters in their young lives.

Everything felt a little flat. Celia was not unhappy, not even lonely even though Dominic was still absent, delayed once, then again, embroiled in script and director's meetings in the Eternal City.

Isabelle Carter would have arrived by now, though Dominic hadn't mentioned her during any of their daily Zooms. His silences usually said more.

The farm work was about maintenance now, replanting where they had lost stock. Celia's days lacked momentum. She hated not being busy, not having a project, a goal to keep her buzzing. Two were brewing in her head on this fine October morning. The first was the lodge. It was time to inject these four walls with new life and laughter. Transform it into a home for newly weds.

Paradise Cottage. Yes, this tiny corner of Heaven would make a comfy nest for a couple just starting out.

She'd rope in Béatrice. Béatrice had witnessed the love affair blossoming and would willingly lend Celia a hand with the refurbishments. Celia would jot down now all that was required for the betrothed pair.

On her return, dawdling along the paths in the red-leafed vine fields, Celia made a detour to the garage where the restoration of her father's Healey was almost complete. The door was open. She heard David's voice, followed by a peal of light laughter. He was inside. He rarely slept up at the main house these days. The last time she'd seen him was when he'd told her he would be leaving soon.

Oil splattered over his face, his bright-blue eyes were shining. He was kneeling on a pile of rags alongside the car, which had been dismantled but the individual parts, gleaming from their polish, were now being reassembled. Adèle was standing, pouring from a Thermos into a mug. Doubled over in laughter, she was trying not to spill David's coffee. Their happiness illuminated the dark old workspace.

'*Bonjour,*' trilled Celia. It was the first time she had visited the atelier in a while and she was impressed by the work David had achieved.

'You want some coffee?' Adèle offered, in heavily accented English. The two women spoke English together only when David was present. Celia shook her head, kissed both, the habitual French *bises*, and then after delivering her news, left them to it, proceeding back to the main house where she asked Béatrice if she would be kind enough to give the lodge a thorough cleaning, ready for a new occupant.

'Or two,' giggled Béatrice, hurrying away loaded with buckets and brooms.

Later she found David packing his travel bag in the bedroom he so rarely occupied these days. Daisy was sleeping at the foot of the chair by the window. David had expressed no desire, made no moves, to return to England until just a few days earlier. He'd decided to relocate, he'd told Celia, to make a new life here in the South of France. To achieve this he needed to return to Kent and close down the old one.

'Are you sure?'

'I couldn't be happier. I've found everything I could ever dream of here. And a whole lot more.' He grinned.

'When you return we must offer you a home of your own.'

'That's not necessary . . . We'll muddle along. Adèle's flat is quite comfy.'

'Of course we will. A home for you both here on the estate.'

She had not been there for her son the first time round. She hadn't had the financial resources or the emotional stability to rear him. It was possible he might never have developed into the loving human being he was if she had been responsible for his upbringing. She admitted it silently, only to herself. Now was different. This was her opportunity to redress the balance. Now she had the wherewithal to offer her son a present and a future. Plus, if he accepted her offer, she and he could spend plenty of time together, deepening the affection that was growing daily between them. Now, she and he had the possibility to live their lives close by one another, this soft-hearted adult who was her son, so unlike the short-lived wastrel who was his father. David cared for people, respected Nature, listened to the bees, watched their dance, was learning many new secrets from old Henri. Henri who had found his true successor in David and could, whenever he was ready, with peace in his heart, settle to his retirement in the house at Les Roches du Soleil where he had been born.

Of course, Henri warned, if it was fine by Celia, he would prefer not to relinquish his chores completely. To do what? Nothing? God forbid. In any case, his daily visits to the bees, his hens and goats were a part of the tapestry of what made his life go round, even if it was David who had offered, when he returned from Kent (promising to be back in time for Christmas), to take charge of the production of the honey.

How perfectly it was all knitting together. It was as though, for the first time, Celia's past had found its future.

Spring

The following spring, the estate of Les Roches du Soleil prepared for another party. This was a more modest affair than the banquet of the previous summer, and it was not for clients. It had nothing to do with business or sales. This was a family affair. A very Provençal love story. Everyone was gathering to celebrate the wedding of David Hawksmith and Adèle Bonneli.

They arrived for their service, to be celebrated in the garden, in Celia's father's Austin Healey, fully restored. David was proudly at the wheel, his bride in white at his side.

CHAPTER FORTY-SIX

Towards the end of that year, on a bright December day before Christmas, Ceely-Roxanne Hawksmith-Grey was born. A giggling gurgling bundle. Christmas was a merry get-together. Celia and Dominic were joined by Sally and Frank, and Gillian, who had returned to art school full time. Production on Dominic's film series had long since wrapped. It was already on air. Gillian announced that she was grateful for all that she had learned at Sally's side and the bit of money she had accrued, but she was champing at the bit to get her own credentials. Maybe later she would work again with Sally. Now she was studying art design for TV and theatre. 'I'm thinking we should shoot a show here at the vineyard.'

'Here?'

'You as the hostess, Ceely. You know, all things Provençal. We could convert one of the barns into a studio. Use my boat as background. I mentioned it to Sal a while back. She loves the idea.' Gillian was certainly in fine fettle, bubbling over with myriad plans and crazy visions. But that was not new. Celia did not take the girl's ideas too seriously, but she was delighted to see her again and noted that she was smoking less and eating more than mere pickings.

Soon into the New Year, Celia and Dominic jetted off to New York to the glitter and rivalry of the television award ceremonies. Tom was nominated for his musical score; the actress whose name Celia had dismissed from her mind was nominated for Best Actress in a Drama Series; Dominic for his 'profoundly moving screenplay'. Of these three nominees only Dominic carried home his much-deserved trophy. Tom, whom Celia hadn't seen since she'd hugged him farewell at Nice airport some eighteen months earlier, was residing in Malibu, 'a pad on the ocean' and a stone's throw from the buzz and madness of Hollywood. He was fully employed, 'busy as hell, Ceely', working on two film scores for major motion pictures. Tom whistled and hummed, chatted and flirted with Celia. He was brimming with excitement and confidence, with the ebullience of one who has been served the world on his plate. And, Celia admitted to herself, how bowl-you-over handsome he was in his tuxedo.

Later, after the ceremony, at the streaming network's post-awards party, where Dominic was flocked by admirers, Celia found herself face to face with Isabelle Carter, who was in New York with her two small children. Isabelle smiled and trilled, 'My, it's so good to see you again, Celia.'

Celia ignored this fiction and enquired politely of Isabelle, whether she had enjoyed playing the role at last.

'Different from the original, of course.'

After that their exchange petered out. Isabelle, eyes trained over Celia's shoulders, had spotted one of the executives of the streaming company who had produced Dominic's series and was hosting the lavish bash. With barely a word, she excused herself and hurried away to flutter in the light of more influential company.

Celia paced slowly to where Dominic, champagne flute in one hand, was holding court, in his element. Spotting her, he lifted an arm and drew her tight to his torso. 'My wife,' he announced, 'a formidable actress.'

She was so elated for him, so proud of his success, and she felt a certain satisfaction – dare she admit it even to herself? – that Isabelle Carter had not won in her category. Celia told herself that she was neither jealous (well, maybe a teeny bit) nor mean-spirited nor even a bitter ageing actress. She was just a woman who had been cheated on and deeply wounded. Fortunately, thank heavens, she and Dominic were finding their way through it.

Another year passed.

It was April, spring, a comfortable middle-of-the-day temperature. One of those days when it appears as though, suddenly, from one moment to the next, everything on the land has burst into colour and blossom. The grass was gilded with dandelions, the swallows were flying in. Summer would be following on the wing. Already the sun was brushing its warmth against her face. The day before, Celia had returned from a brief trip to England. Now, she was crouched at the edge of one of the vineyards on a patch of grass. At her side was a sandy-haired Labrador puppy, Speck, collected a few weeks earlier from a local refuge centre. Daisy had finally died at the grand old age of fifteen.

Celia was puffed out. She had carried two heavy picnic baskets all the way from the house. Dominic, at work on yet another recently commissioned screenplay, had promised to join her and the family for lunch. While Celia waited for him to arrive and the others to finish their morning's labours, she spread the goodies from the baskets on a tablecloth on the grass, taking care to avoid a large wasp hovering over the slices of ham that were not yet unwrapped from the cellophane, and to keep Speck from dribbling all over the rest of the food.

She was deep in thought, still reflecting on her visit to England while throwing glances towards little Ceely-Roxanne, amused by the child's antics. She waved at her two-year-old granddaughter. Yes, her granddaughter. A mischievous yet utterly adorable and spirited creature. The little girl was with her father, David, who was striding alongside their magnificent Percheron draught horse. They were turning over the alleys of soil between the rows of vines. The child was balanced on her father's shoulders. She was shrieking gleefully, bobbing and bouncing, attempting to run her stubby fingers through the mare's glorious off-white mane. Adèle was hurrying towards them, waving as though she were late. She always seemed to be running. Celia noticed the small bulge under her frock. Was she expecting? Early days, but was there soon to be a second grandchild for them all to dote on, to spoil and cherish? A boy, perhaps?

Such blessings. Blessings that had come late to Celia and for which she would be grateful until the end of her days.

She would never turn her back on this immense gift. No matter what might come to pass she would fight for the right to this family. A treacherous tear ran down her cheek. She wiped it away before anyone could spot it and quiz her about its cause.

None knew the details of her recent trip to England . . .

The West of England. Four days earlier

Celia was standing in an English country cemetery, knee-deep in dock weeds. It was approaching lunchtime. She peered about her. The site was wild, derelict. The grave she was looking for was nowhere to be found. No markers, no headstone, led her to it. It was buried in the depths of neglect, the passage of time and the adventitious circumstances of life. No one remembered its precise placement. Who was there left to recall such an insignificant detail besides her? Celia dropped to her knees and ruffled the tall grasses a mattress of weeds and wildflowers. Impenetrable.

Early that morning she had stepped off a train and exited the station situated in the middle of the small town. A modest nondescript municipality that once had been some distance from the outskirts of Bristol, but today was swallowed into the city's suburbs. She had made her way on foot from the station to the convent. She could have taken a taxi but she'd preferred to walk. The thirty minutes' exercise would offer her a brief trip down Memory Lane and time to adjust to her presence in the old homeland after many decades absent.

The convent address she had found in David's room on his adoption paper. During the week that he had been in hospital after his accident she had written to the convent but hadn't received a reply . . . until ten days previously.

Upon arrival, she saw that the religious house no longer existed in its original form, as the Mother Superior's letter had explained:

My sincere apologies, Mrs Millar, that this letter has taken so long. We lost our home, our beloved convent, and the period of relocation for those of us left has been drawn-out and traumatic. Not to mention all the mail that went astray or was overlooked . . .

The listed building which, once upon a time when Celia had been a desperate young woman, had provided a home for nuns and the children cared for in their orphanage, had been purchased by property developers and sold off to one of their subsidiaries.

The façade of the sixteenth-century mansion still stood intact in its sprawling elegant grounds while the interior had been gutted and converted into luxury flats. The few nuns who survived, most of them over seventy, had been rehoused in a discreet corner of the grounds, once the vegetable gardens, where a more modest residence had been constructed to give them shelter for the rest of their lives.

It was to this remote building that Celia made her path. The door was opened by an ancient woman, wrinkled and bent, clad in a black and white habit, a white coif and wimple. Celia gave her name and was ushered in. 'Reverend Mother mentioned she might be expecting a visitor. We've prepared a tray with some tea and biscuits. Please, follow me.'

Celia was led to a drawing room with a large picture window. It looked out across the tree-lined grounds that once had been the convent's playground. The interior space was simple in style and design, barely furnished, but pristinely clean. It smelled faintly of linseed oil and lavender polish. A nun, a little younger than she who had opened the door, was seated by a table where a plate of biscuits, two cups, a jug of milk and a teapot had been arranged. Celia saw instantly that the holy sister was not in good health. Her hands, little more than bones, trembled conspicuously in her lap. 'Sister Catherine?'

Catherine barely raised her head. 'Please sit. You'll need to pour the tea yourself,' she commanded, but her voice lacked authority. It was reedy, hoarse.

Celia obeyed, and waited. The silence was so drawn out that Celia worried the woman had fallen asleep or forgotten she had company. She coughed. 'Erm, I wrote to your abbess some time ago. I was enquiring about David Grey and his adoptive parents, Mr and Mrs Hawksmith. I've since learned they are both deceased . . .'

'Yes. Yes, I am aware of your letter. I was the one who replied. I am the Reverend Mother, the superior sister here now. And I was responsible for the . . . the error.'

'Error?'

'It seems fitting that you should turn up now, at this late stage in my earthly days. I have carried the burden of what happened all my life.'

'I don't understand.'

'David Grey was your son?'

Celia frowned. 'He is, yes.'

'David died before he was three months old.'

'Sorry?'

'He was never hardy.'

'But he's . . .'

'I found him. I was terrified. I couldn't detect a heartbeat. Bear in mind I was eighteen, a postulant lacking all experience. It was June, a clammy, rainy evening. I was doing the nightly rounds, checking the children were tucked up and sleeping. David Grey, as I said, not three months at the time, was the youngest in our care. I lifted him from his cot, held him in my arms. His body was limp but warm. I was petrified, in case I had somehow caused his passing. Of course that made no sense, but it was my fear at the time. I stood with him in my arms, squeezing him tightly . . .'

'Squeezing?'

'I was praying for an inhalation of breath, for some sign that he was still with us. When I was certain that the baby was no longer in this world, I carried his corpse through to the medical room and covered the lifeless boy with a sheet. I knew I must telephone the priest, ask him to anoint the child in preparation for the burial, but before I could make that call,' she continued, 'the father's housekeeper came knocking at the convent door. She was carrying a tiny infant. A boy. Left on the front step of the refectory not two hours earlier. No name, no papers accompanied the abandoned child.'

'No papers?' Celia repeated.

'The housekeeper dug about in her coat. "This," she said, "was delivered with the child." It was a hand-scribbled note on a scrap of damp paper. The writing was smudged. The downpour had been sufficient to distort the lettering. It read: "Please care for my boy." The next word – the baby's name, I supposed – was illegible. "I can't any more." I folded the paper into the pocket of my skirt. The bundle of damp clothes that contained the unidentified child was handed over to me. "I warmed him a bowl of milk," the housekeeper said. "I'll let Father know you've taken him. Let's hope he hasn't caught his death in this foul weather."'

Catherine, now cradling the boy, had nodded.

'The child smelled rank. He was in urgent need of changing. I hurried to close the door. Your son, Mrs Millar, at peace in the medical room, was no longer forefront in my mind. My thoughts had turned to the needs of the living. It was my duty to save this one. Once cleaned, and the poor mite took quite some cleaning, I laid him in the cot where David Grey had been sleeping.'

Celia placed her teacup on its saucer on the small wooden table. She was incredulous. 'And then?'

'I had a very restless sleep. It was a filthy blustery night. My novice's brain was turning in circles, exacerbated by the storm raging beyond the windows. I feared I would be severely berated for the mishandling of David. I feared that in some way his passing was my responsibility.'

Celia attempted to form a sentence. 'But why didn't you call someone? A superior?'

'Please, Mrs Millar, I know that what I did was unwise.'

'Unwise? It was wrong. On every level, wrong.'

'At the time it seemed the simplest, the most efficient solution for all involved, particularly the abandoned mite just arrived at our doors.'

'So, what happened to my David?'

'The following day, an unidentified baby boy was laid to rest in our cemetery. No autopsy was performed. The priest prayed over his tiny body and blessed him, urging God to take pity on his unknown soul. The other, now David Grey, survived and was eventually put up for adoption.'

'You switched the babies and told no one? Didn't anybody remark the difference?'

'If any of the sisters suspected, they didn't whisper a word.'

'They were complicit?'

'I don't know.'

Celia squeezed her eyes tight shut. She didn't know which David to mourn. Which son she was losing, had lost.

'Please, try to understand, there was a living boy . . . It was far better he had a name, an identity, a chance at a future, better that he was not obliged to deal with circumstances any more disadvantageous than those he had already suffered. There was nothing more to be done for your dead one, Mrs Millar. In my mind at the time, this resolution made sense. Over the years, I came to see that the decision I made had not been mine to make, but it was too late.'

Stunned, Celia stared in silence.

'Some twenty months later a farming couple of modest means, Harry and Jenny Hawksmith, bursting with pride, carried from the convent their newly adopted toddler, driving him home to their smallholding in Kent. The paperwork had been painstaking. The couple were in their late forties. Back then this was not in their favour for adoption, but our reverend mother at the time looked upon them with benevolence. Fate had done the infant, known to the nuns as David Grey, now adopted as Hawksmith, a fortunate turn.'

Her son buried as an unidentified orphan.

Celia's thoughts were spinning right, left and centre. They alighted on 'David' at home at the vineyard, on his newly created family. On Dominic who, although he had come to accept these unexpected relatives and was putty in the hands of little Ceely-Roxane whom he idolized, had remained sceptical. 'You could do a test,' he'd encouraged some while back, 'close the matter.' Celia had resisted the suggestion. Had she known, deep down?

'Might you be able to help me find my son's grave?' she asked eventually.

'It was such a long time ago.'

'I'd like . . . to pay my last respects.'

'I haven't been across to the cemetery for several years. We buried the dead child swaddled in the other's blanket in the pouring rain. Lashing it down. Miserable. That I do remember. I felt that misery in my bones for months and months after the events.'

Celia picked up her bag from the floor. 'No one would object if I walk over and take a look myself?'

'There's no sexton to object. No one remains. The graveyard has been left to Nature. The church has fared little better. Mass is said only once a month by a visiting priest. Like our convent, the presbytery has been sold off to developers.'

'Well, I'm grateful for your time.'

'I'll say a prayer for you. I have always prayed for your little boy, prayed that he is in Heaven.'

'Thank you, Reverend Mother.'

Celia stood alone in the cemetery, head bent, staring blindly at an insect clambering in the overgrown grass. What was she to do? Her flesh and blood was here somewhere, forgotten underfoot. For many a year, he'd been part of the process of dust to dust. It was heartbreaking to confront the fact that, after everything, David had not survived. She had no offspring; she was childless. What sort of man would her David of slender opportunities have grown into?

Possibly more prudent not to pose the question.

Instead, there was David Hawksmith whom Fate had smiled upon. There was Gillian West. There was Ceely-

Roxanne, precious, effervescent, loving. And statuesque Adèle.

They were her family now. They loved her, and she them.

Was she to deny them?

Would she share this story with them? If she did, would she destroy David Hawksmith's faith, his self-esteem? His identity? An identity that had already been rocked when Jenny Hawksmith had owned up to him that she was not his biological mother.

What would become of the loving ménage David and Adèle were creating at Les Roches du Soleil? Would they feel obliged to quit Celia's estate? They who would eventually inherit her farm.

How could she sabotage their happiness, their security? Never mind that it would break her heart to lose them.

Would she share this turn of events with Dominic? Possibly, yes, later, at some future date.

There was no one living who was party to this truth, other than one ailing nun.

If Celia said nothing, Catherine would carry the secret with her to her grave. No one would be the wiser. And the fact remained that the late Terry Strait's offspring had died quietly and, Celia prayed, peacefully in his cot. No action from her could reverse this actuality.

A splendid family was blossoming, with love at its core. It was little more than chance that Celia had uncovered the incidents that had brought her to this overgrown spot. Incidents best filed in a drawer in her mind or better still erased. She would always honour the memory of her long-departed son.

Now a present and a future were waiting for her, and for David, Adèle and their offspring.

She turned, exiting the cemetery to walk into town, to trace her steps down the long hill to the railway station and from there the journey back to France, to those she loved as dearly as her own life.

Today was surely the day to put this tragic affair to rest once and for all.

Back at the estate, Celia was cross-legged on the blanket. The picnic was spread out alongside her. She was plucking at a blade of grass, reflecting. Speck was biting at her wrist, growling playfully. She caressed his head to calm him and lifted her face to the healing warmth of the sun. A butterfly passed by, bright as a lemon. Dominic, in straw hat, was striding briskly, with the aid of a cane, along the baked earth path towards her, waving as he did so to their family, to the granddaughter he was besotted with.

'Penny for your thoughts.' Dominic smiled as he approached, bending low to kiss Celia's head, warmed by the April light, and to stroke the puppy at her side.

Second chances, was Celia's silent rumination. The miracle of second chances, and this one's mine. Loved ones arrive in many guises, gifted from unlikely places. Ours not to question, but to accept and celebrate with gladness.

'Mmm? Just musing on how lucky we are.' Celia smiled at her husband, slipped her hand into Dominic's, as he lowered himself onto the rug beside her.

'I'm getting too old for sitting on the grass.' He groaned.

'Oh, really? I was thinking . . . how nice to be old. Old married people.'

ACKNOWLEDGEMENTS:

This is the first novel Publishing Director, Sarah Hodgson, and I have worked on together and I really want to thank you, Sarah, for welcoming me to Corvus. It is the fifth novel copy-editor Hazel Orme and I have worked on together and, as before, Hazel, you have made the job easy and fun. Finding editors who are supportive and generous and get what one is trying to achieve is such a gift in publishing. Hugs to you both.

In advance of the publishing of this novel, I want to say hello to the team I will be working with at Corvus. I am hugely looking forward to a wonderful experience.

Sister scribe, Elizabeth Buchan, my special thanks to you.

To everyone at Curtis Brown, including my literary agent, Jonathan Lloyd, and his stalwart assistant Rachel Goldblatt, wonderful Mark Williams and the team in accounts, audio and foreign rights agents, thank you for keeping the boat afloat, I am grateful for your ongoing commitment to my work.

Booksellers everywhere, especially all you dear Indies, it's tough out there. I admire you and applaud you for your love of books.

To cherished friends, Pat Lancaster, Barbara Bannister and Rhona Wells, thank you for the wine and that comfy London bed.

To Michel Noll, my caring and supportive husband, your kindness and gentleness are my haven. You are the cherry on the cake. I love you deeply.

Readers, it is all about you. Thank you profoundly for all the emails, the support, the love, the purchase of the books and the feedback. I sincerely hope you enjoy this novel. There are always tough days at the desk, of course, but this story has brought me great joy in the writing of it. I hope you will find something in it too.

Don't miss Carol Drinkwater's
next heartwarming story

THE GIRL FROM MARSEILLE

Provence, 1938.

Seventeen-year-old Yvette Barbarin lives on a small
rural farm in the lavender-soaked hills behind the great
port-city of Marseille with her widowed father and
her five younger sisters.

When she learns that her father is planning to marry
her off to a local farmer, she runs away to the city where
she dreams of joining a troupe of travelling players.

In Marseille, Yvette is bowled over by the magic of
cinema, and the thrill of make-believe. She falls in love
with an actor, a rising star, but all is not as simple in real
life as it is in the world of movies, and war is coming...

Publishing 2026

Carol Drinkwater

multi-award-winning actress and writer,
best known for her portrayal of Helen Herriot in the
classic BBC television series *All Creatures Great and
Small*. She is the author of twenty-five books, both
fiction and non-fiction and including the
bestselling Olive Farm memoir series set in
the south of France. Carol lives with
her husband in France.

Join Carol's newsletter at
www.caroldrinkwater.com

 /olive.farm

 @Carol4OliveFarm